CATALYST

```
1 0 0 1 1 1 1 1 1 1 1 0 0 1 1 1 0 1 0 1 1 0 0 0 0 0 0 0 1 0 0 1 1 1 1 0 0 0
0 1 1 0 1 1 0 1 1 1 0 0 1 1 1 0 0 0 0 0 0 0 1 0 1 1 0 1 0 0 1 0 0 1 1
1 0 0 0 0 0 1 1 1 1 0 0 1 0 0 1 0 1 1 1 0 0 1 1 1 0 1 1 0 0 1 0 1 1 0 1 1
0 1 0 0 0 1 1 0 1 1 0 0 0 0 1 1 0 1 0 0 1 1 0 0 1 0 1 1 1 0 0 0 0 1 1
1 0 0 1 1 0 1 0 0 0 0 1 0 1 1 1 0 1 1 0 0 0 0 0 1 0 1 1 0 0 1 1 1 1
0 0 1 1 0 0 0 0 1 1 1 1 0 1 1 0 1 1 0 1 0 0 0 0 0 1 0 0 1 1 1 0 0 0 0 0
1 1 0 0 1 0 1 0 1 1 1 0 1 1 0 1 0 1 0 1 1 1 1 0 1 0 1 1 0 1 1 0 0 0 0 0
0 1 1 1 1 1 1 1 0 1 1 0 0 0 0 1 1 1 0 1 1 0 1 1 1 0 1 1 1 1 0 0 0 1 0 1 0
1 0 1 1 0 0 1 1 0 1 0 0 1 0 0 0 1 0 1 0 1 0 0 1 0 0 0 0 1 0 0 1 0 1 0 1 0
0 0 1 0 0 1 0 1 1 0 0 1 0 0 1 1 0 1 0 1 0 1 1 1 0 0 0 0 1 0 1 1 0 1 0 1 0
0 0 0 0 0 1 1 1 1 0 1 1 0 0 1 1 0 1 1 0 1 1 0 0 0 0 0 0 1 0 0 0 0 1 0 0 0 1 0 0
1 0 1 0 0 1 1 1 1 0 0 1 1 1 0 1 1 0 0 1 1 0 0 1 1 1 0 0 1 0 0 0 0 1 0 0 0
0 0 1 1 1 1 1 0 1 1 0 1 0 0 0 1 0 0 1 1 1 0 0 0 0 1 0 1 1 1 0 0 0 0 0 0
0 1 1 1 1 0 0 0 0 0 1 0 1 1 0 1 0 0 0 0 0 0 0 1 0 0 0 1 1 1 0 0 1 1 1 0
1 1 1 0 0 0 1 1 1 0 0 1 1 1 0 0 0 0 1 1 0 0 1 0 0 1 0 1 0 1 1 1 1 1 0 1 1
0 0 0 1 1 1 1 0 0 1 0 1 0 1 1 1 0 0 1 0 1 0 1 1 0 1 1 0 1 1 1 1 1 0 0 1 0 0 1
0 1 0 1 0 1 1 1 0 0 0 1 0 1 0 1 0 0 1 0 0 0 0 1 0 0 0 0 1 1 1 0 1 0 1 0 1
0 0 1 1 0 0 0 0 1 1 0 0 1 0 0 0 1 0 0 1 0 1 1 1 1 1 1 1 1 1 1 1 0 0 1 1 1 0
1 1 1 1 1 1 0 0 1 1 0 1 1 1 0 0 0 1 1 1 0 1 0 0 1 0 0 0 0 1 1 1 1 1 0 0
1 0 0 1 1 0 0 0 1 1 1 1 1 0 1 0 0 0 0 0 0 1 0 0 1 0 0 1 0 1 1 0 1 0 0
```

ALSO BY S. J. KINCAID

Insignia
Vortex

Allies: An Insignia Novella
(available as an ebook only)

CATALYST

S.J. KINCAID

HOT
KEY
BOOKS

First published in Great Britain in 2014 by Hot Key Books
Northburgh House, 10 Northburgh Street, London EC1V 0AT

First published in the US in 2014 by Katherine Tegen Books,
an imprint of HarperCollins*Publishers*

A CIP catalogue record for this book is available from the British Library.

ISBN: 978-1-4714-0071-1

1

This book is typeset in 10.5 Berling LT Std using Atomik ePublisher

Printed and bound by Clays Ltd, St Ives Plc

www.hotkeybooks.com

Hot Key Books is part of the Bonnier Publishing Group
www.bonnierpublishing.com

To Rob
For all the advice and for being a great older brother

0 0 1 1 1 1 1 1 1 0 0 1 1 1 0 1 0 1 1 0 0 0 0 0 0 0 1 0 0 1 1 1 1 0 0 0
1 1 0 1 1 0 1 1 1 0 0 1 1 1 1 0 0 0 0 0 0 0 1 0 1 1 0 1 0 0 1 0 0 1 1 1
0 0 0 0 0 1 1 1 1 0 0 1 0 0 1 0 1 1 1 0 0 1 1 1 0 1 1 0 0 1 0 1 1 0 1 1 0
1 0 0 0 1 1 0 1 1 0 0 0 0 1 1 0 1 0 0 1 1 0 0 0 1 0 1 1 1 1 0 0 0 0 1 1 0
0 0 1 1 0 1 0 0 0 0 0 1 0 1 1 1 0 1 1 0 0 0 0 0 0 1 0 1 1 0 0 1 1 1 1 1
0 1 1 0 0 0 0 0 1 1 1 0 1 1 0 1 1 0 1 0 0 0 0 0 1 0 0 1 1 1 0 0 0 0 0 1
1 0 0 1 0 1 0 1 1 1 0 1 1 1 0 1 0 1 0 1 1 1 1 0 1 0 1 1 0 1 1 0 0 0 0 0 1
1 1 1 1 1 1 0 1 1 0 0 0 0 1 1 1 0 1 1 0 1 1 1 0 1 1 1 1 0 0 0 1 0 1 0 1
0 1 1 0 0 1 1 0 1 0 0 1 0 0 0 1 0 1 0 1 0 0 1 0 0 0 0 1 0 0 1 0 1 0 1 0 1
0 1 0 0 1 0 1 1 0 0 1 0 0 1 '1 0 1 0 1 0 1 1 1 0 0 0 0 1 0 1 1 0 1 0 1 0 1
0 0 0 0 1 1 1 1 0 1 1 0 0 1 1 0 1 1 0 0 0 0 0 0 1 0 0 0 0 1 0 0 0 1 0 0 1
0 1 0 0 1 1 1 1 0 0 1 1 1 0 1 1 0 1 1 0 0 1 1 0 0 1 1 0 0 1 0 0 0 1 0 0 0

We have it in our power to begin the world over again.

—Thomas Paine, *Common Sense*

```
1 0 0 1 1 1 1 1 1 1 1 0 0 1 1 1 0 1 0 1 1 0 0 0 0 0 0 0 1 0 0 1 1 1 1 0 0 0
0 1 1 0 1 1 0 1 1 1 0 0 1 1 1 1 0 0 0 0 0 0 0 0 1 0 1 1 0 1 0 0 1 0 0 1 1
1 0 0 0 0 0 1 1 1 1 0 0 1 0 0 1 0 1 0 1 1 1 0 0 1 1 1 0 1 1 0 0 1 0 1 0 1 1
0 1 0 0 0 1 1 0 1 1 0 0 0 0 1 1 0 1 0 0 1 1 0 0 0 1 0 1 1 1 1 0 0 0 0 1 1
1 0 0 1 1 0 1 0 0 0 0 0 1 0 1 1 1 0 1 1 0 0 0 0 0 0 0 1 0 1 1 0 0 1 1 1 1
0 0 1 1 0 0 0 0 0 1 1 1 1 0 1 1 0 1 1 0 1 0 0 0 0 0 1 0 0 1 1 1 0 0 0 0 0
1 1 0 0 1 0 1 0 1 1 1 0 1 1 1 0 1 0 1 0 1 1 1 1 0 1 0 1 1 0 1 1 0 0 0 0 0
0 1 1 1 1 1 1 1 0 1 1 0 0 0 0 1 1 1 0 1 1 0 1 1 1 0 1 1 1 0 0 0 1 0 1 0
1 0 1 1 0 0 1 1 0 1 0 0 1 0 0 0 1 0 1 0 1 0 0 1 0 0 0 0 1 0 0 1 0 1 0 1 0
0 0 1 0 0 1 0 1 1 0 0 1 0 0 1 1 0 1 0 1 0 1 1 1 0 0 0 0 1 0 1 1 0 1 0 1 0
0 0 0 0 0 1 1 1 1 0 1 1 0 0 1 1 0 1 1 0 0 0 0 0 0 1 0 0 0 0 1 0 0 0 1 0 0
1 0 1 0 0 1 1 1 1 0 1 1 0 0 1 1 0 1 1 0 0 0 0 0 1 0 0 0 0 1 0 0 0 1 0 0
```

THE COALITION OF MULTI

THE INDO-AMERICAN ALLIANCE:
European-Australian Block • Oceanic Nations •
North American Alliance • Central America

MULTINATIONAL CORPORATIONS
(and sponsored Combatants):

Dominion Agra
SPONSORED COMBATANTS: Karl "Vanquisher" Marsters

Nobridis, Inc.
SPONSORED COMBATANTS: Elliot "Ares" Ramirez,
Cadence "Stinger" Grey, Britt "Ox" Schmeiser

Wyndham Harks
SPONSORED COMBATANTS: Heather "Enigma" Akron,
Yosef "Vector" Saide, Snowden "NewGuy" Gainey

Matchett-Reddy
SPONSORED COMBATANTS: Lea "Firestorm" Styron,
Mason "Specter" Meekins

Epicenter Manufacturing
SPONSORED COMBATANTS: Emefa "Polaris" Austerley,
Alec "Condor" Tarsus, Ralph "Matador" Bates

Obsidian Corp.
SPONSORED COMBATANTS: None

0 0 1 1 1 1 1 1 1 0 0 1 1 1 0 1 0 1 1 0 0 0 0 0 0 0 1 0 0 1 1 1 1 0 0 0 0
1 1 0 1 1 0 1 1 1 0 0 1 1 1 1 0 0 0 0 0 0 0 0 1 0 1 1 0 1 0 0 1 0 0 1 1 1
0 0 0 0 0 1 1 1 1 0 0 1 0 0 1 0 1 1 1 0 0 1 1 1 0 1 1 0 0 1 0 1 1 0 1 1 0
1 0 0 0 1 1 0 1 1 0 0 0 0 1 1 0 1 0 0 1 1 0 0 0 1 0 1 1 1 1 0 0 0 0 1 1 0
0 0 1 1 0 1 0 0 0 0 0 1 0 1 1 1 0 1 1 0 0 0 0 0 0 1 0 1 1 0 0 1 1 1 1 1
0 1 1 0 0 0 0 0 1 1 1 1 0 1 1 0 1 1 0 1 0 0 0 0 0 1 0 0 1 1 1 0 0 0 0 0 1
1 0 0 1 0 1 0 1 1 1 0 1 1 1 0 1 0 1 0 1 1 1 1 0 1 0 1 1 0 1 1 0 0 0 0 0 1
1 1 1 1 1 1 1 0 1 1 0 0 0 0 1 1 1 0 1 1 0 1 1 1 0 1 1 1 1 0 0 0 1 0 1 0 1
0 1 1 0 0 1 1 0 1 0 1 0 0 1 0 0 0 1 0 1 0 1 0 0 1 0 0 0 0 1 0 0 1 0 1 0 1
0 1 0 0 1 0 1 1 0 0 1 0 0 1 0 0 1 1 0 1 0 1 0 1 1 1 0 0 0 0 1 0 1 1 0 1 0 1
0 0 0 0 1 1 1 1 0 1 1 0 0 1 1 0 1 1 0 0 0 0 0 0 1 0 0 0 1 0 0 0 1 0 0 1

NATIONAL CORPORATIONS

THE RUSSO-CHINESE ALLIANCE:
South American Federation • Nordic Block •
Affiliated African Nations

MULTINATIONAL CORPORATIONS
(sponsored members unknown):

Harbinger

Lexicon Mobile

LM Lymer Fleet

Kronus Portable

Stronghold Energy

Preeminent Communications

0 0 1 1 1 1 1 1 1 1 0 0 1 1 1 0 1 0 1 1 0 0 0 0 0 0 0 1 0 0 1 1 1 1 0 0 0 0
1 1 0 1 1 0 1 1 1 1 0 0 1 1 1 0 0 0 0 0 0 0 1 0 1 1 0 1 0 0 1 0 0 1 1 1
0 0 0 0 0 1 1 1 1 0 0 1 0 0 1 0 1 1 1 0 0 1 1 1 0 1 1 0 0 1 0 1 1 0 1 1 0
1 0 0 0 1 1 0 1 1 0 0 1 0 1 0 0 1 0 0 0 1 0 0 0 1 0 1 1 1 1 0 0 0 0 1 1 0
0 0 1 1 0 1 0 0 0 0 0 1 0 1 1 1 0 1 1 0 0 0 0 0 0 0 1 0 1 1 0 0 1 1 1 1 1
0 1 1 0 0 0 0 0 1 1 1 1 0 1 1 0 1 1 0 1 0 0 0 0 0 1 0 0 1 1 1 0 0 0 0 0 1
1 0 0 1 0 1 0 1 1 0 1 1 1 0 1 0 1 0 1 1 1 0 1 1 0 1 1 0 1 1 0 0 0 0 0 1
1 1 1 1 1 1 0 1 1 0 0 0 0 1 1 1 0 1 1 0 1 1 0 1 1 1 1 0 0 0 1 0 1 0 1
0 1 1 0 0 1 1 0 1 0 0 1 0 0 0 1 0 1 0 1 0 0 1 0 0 0 0 1 0 0 1 0 1 0 1 0 1
0 1 0 0 1 0 1 1 0 0 1 0 0 1 1 0 1 0 1 0 1 1 1 0 0 0 0 1 0 1 1 0 1 0 1 0 1
0 0 0 0 1 1 1 1 0 1 1 0 0 1 1 0 1 1 0 1 1 0 0 0 0 0 0 1 0 0 0 1 0 0 0 1 0 0 1
0 1 0 0 1 1 1 1 0 0 1 1 1 0 1 1 0 1 0 0 1 0 0 1 1 1 0 1 0 0 1 0 0 0 1 0 0 0 0
0 1 1 1 1 1 0 1 1 0 1 0 0 0 1 0 0 1 1 1 0 0 0 0 1 0 1 1 1 1 0 0 0 0 0 0 0
1 1 1 1 0 0 0 0 0 1 0 1 1 0 1 0 0 0 0 0 0 0 1 0 0 0 1 1 1 1 0 0 1 1 1 0 1
1 1 0 0 0 1 1 1 0 0 1 1 1 0 0 0 0 1 1 0 0 1 0 0 1 0 1 0 1 1 1 1 0 1 0 1 1 0
0 0 1 1 1 1 0 0 1 0 1 0 1 1 1 1 0 0 1 0 1 1 0 1 1 0 1 1 1 1 1 0 0 1 0 0 1 1
1 0 1 0 1 0 1 0 1 0 0 1 0 0 0 1 0 0 0 0 1 0 0 0 0 1 1 1 0 1 0 1 0 1 0
0 0 1 1 0 0 1 0 1 0 0 0 0 1 0 1 1 1 1 1 1 1 1 1 1 1 1 0 0 1 1 1 1 0 0
1 1 1 1 0 0 0 1 1 1 1 0 1 1 0 0 0 1 1 1 0 1 0 0 1 0 0 1 0 0 0 1 1 1 0 0 1
0 0 1 1 0 0 0 1 1 1 1 1 1 0 1 1 0 0 0 0 0 0 1 0 0 1 0 0 1 0 1 1 0 1 0 0 1

CHAPTER ONE

HERE WAS A downside to staying in a luxurious high-rise suite in Las Vegas. It wasn't the price. Neil Raines had been on a winning streak lately, and he was glad to blow his spoils on a lavish room for his son's visit.

The problem was, their hotel room's location put them in close proximity to several VIPs staying on the same floor. Every time Tom Raines and his dad went up to their room, they passed through a gauntlet of private contractors guarding the hallway.

So far, Tom had slipped by with a bit of maneuvering.

Today, something felt different as they neared the metal detectors and body scanners waiting for them.

Neil reacted the way he always did to the sight. "This is the problem with the overclass," he blustered to Tom as they neared, a challenging glint in his eyes, voice loud because he clearly hoped one of those VIPs would hear him. "At the end of the day, they're a bunch of pathetic cowards hiding behind their hired thugs."

The security contractors scowled. *They'd* heard.

1

"We can get another room elsewhere," Tom said in a low voice. "I'm sick of this, too. I'd rather we stayed somewhere cheaper and you put all this money—I don't know—in a savings account?"

"Savings account?" Neil snorted. "Yeah, sure, I'll stash my hard-earned bucks with some thieving bankers so they can pass another 'depositor's tax' to fund their next bailouts. No way." He clapped Tom's back. "I'd rather treat my boy right for once."

With that, Neil thrust his arms up in the air for his pat down, leering at the security guards who closed in around him. Tom lingered a few feet behind him, delving into his pocket for the medical exemption the military had provided to Intrasolar trainees whenever they encountered security scanners—devices that tended to reveal the neural processors in their skulls.

As Neil grumbled, Tom's mind wandered back to the last time he'd visited his father. They'd had a bad fight. He hadn't understood Neil's fear of Vengerov and Neil had refused to explain. Later, Tom got it—after Joseph Vengerov locked him outside in the Antarctic to freeze to death. A few trillion dollars gave a man power over life or death, and Neil had realized that before Tom had.

Tom hadn't known what to say to his dad to fix things. As it turned out, he didn't have to. Neil was just as eager to pretend nothing had happened. Maybe he was even trying to make up for something, hence the fancy room, the nice casino, and Neil even woke up earlier so they could grab some dinner before he headed out for the night. He was thrilled to hear about Tom's promotion to Upper Company, and he, in turn, was eager to tell Tom all about the ghost in the machine who'd blown up the skyboards.

"Guess you haven't heard much about this in the Spire, huh?" Neil said, chuckling over his drink. "It happened right before you came back."

Tom swallowed. Hard. "Oh, yeah, haven't heard much."

"It was amazing, Tommy. There's this bright flash overhead, I look up, and every single one of those advertisement boards is lit up with this message: 'The ghost in the machine is watching the watchers.' And you know who that's aimed at—gotta be to the Department of Homeland Security. Maybe Obsidian Corp. Next thing I know, they explode. Every last one of them." He took a big, triumphant swig of his drink. "You had to be there."

Tom couldn't help a grim flicker of pride, hearing that. Apparently, the ghost had deeply impressed his father, which was awesome, because Tom *was* the ghost in the machine. He'd blown up the skyboards.

Neil leaned toward him. "I tell you, the Cocaine Importing Agency's gotta be crawling up the walls trying to find this guy. Let's hope they don't find him."

"Yeah, I'll drink to that," Tom said, raising his soda.

"They ever do, and just wait—this ghost will be found with two gunshots to the back of his head in an apparent suicide."

Tom's grin slipped a bit. It wasn't the most reassuring thing to hear.

And he wasn't reassured now as they approached the security guards, trying to pick out the supervisor so he could hand over his exemption and get through this quickly. His medical form claimed he needed to bypass the scanning machines due to an implanted nerve stimulator in his skull to treat epilepsy.

Every time Tom used it around his dad, he had to be

3

careful. Neil needed to be too occupied to see him slip it to the supervising guard, and he needed to get it back before Neil turned and saw it. Usually he tried to part ways with his dad early, slip back to the room separately. Today Neil had dogged his steps. Today he couldn't avoid it.

If Neil even knew about the medical exemption, he'd demand to see it. He'd find out Tom had been given brain surgery. Epilepsy wasn't the real reason his brain couldn't be scanned—a neural processor was—but even the suggestion Tom had been given brain surgery would make Neil explode.

That would not end well.

Today, Neil passed through the gauntlet in record time, and he turned to look back just as Tom was about to hand over his form. He hesitated. It cost him. A big hand seized his shoulder and steered him forward through the metal detector.

The metal detector buzzed.

Tom tensed up, seeing Neil fold his arms impatiently, squinting his way, seeing two security guards lumber over. A bored-looking woman unveiled a metal-detecting wand.

"Did you forget to remove something from your pockets?" she asked, and frowned as her wand beeped over Tom's head.

Tom squirmed inwardly, acutely conscious of his dad watching. "Uh, no."

She began pawing her fingers through his hair.

"Look, I have a . . .," Tom said softly, reaching toward his pocket, turning his back to Neil, desperate to retrieve the medical exemption.

"Hands out of your pockets," ordered the second guard.

"It's not a weapon," Tom said in a furious whisper. "It's—"

4

"What's going on?" Neil demanded, tromping over toward them. "What's the holdup?"

A third security guard stepped forward to ward Neil off, and Tom again tried to retrieve his medical exemption, but then his cybernetic fingers set off the wand, and the woman ordered his hands up.

And then something happened.

There was a commotion near the computers, and then the entire swarm of security guards descended on Tom at the same time, encircling him, guns out.

"We ran his biometric profile. Step back from him!" one of the security guards shouted to the other.

The woman drew away from him quickly, and Tom goggled at the suddenly armed guards before his brain made sense of it. Neil had been causing them trouble so they ran both their biometric profiles, and they found out Tom's identity.

And the fact that he was on the terror watch list.

Tom closed his eyes. *Oh, come* on.

"Hands in the air!" someone shouted at Tom.

Tom raised his hands, his mind racing, trying to figure out what to do from here.

"This is ridiculous," Neil exploded, and suddenly a few of the armed guards turned their attention toward him. "Does my kid look like a terror threat to you?"

"He needs to come with us," the lead guard said.

"Dad, don't make a big deal. I'll go with them for two seconds, okay?" Tom urged, thinking he could clear this up if he talked with one of them in private. One phone call would fix it.

If he could just get somewhere without his father, he could

explain. But the female security guard who'd resumed waving the metal detecting wand over him gave a shriek and leaped back, and Tom saw one of his mechanized fingers come detached where she'd unwittingly tugged it off.

Tom froze.

Neil froze, staring down at it.

"What is that?" Guns reared toward Tom's face. "Some sort of weapon?"

"It's a finger!" Tom exclaimed. "Look at it. All my fingers are fake, okay? See?" He tugged off a couple more to show them. "They're mechanical. That's why they set off the metal detector."

He ignored the way Neil was gaping at him like he didn't even know him, in utter shock.

Tom hadn't told his dad about getting frostbite, losing his fingers. The military was technically supposed to notify his dad of any major surgeries. Amputation of fingers probably qualified.

Better Neil find out about this than the *other* mechanical part of Tom's body.

"Tommy . . .," Neil whispered.

"Let's go. I'll show you. Dad, wait here," Tom said decisively.

Neil was stunned enough to automatically do what Tom told him; and even then, Tom might still have salvaged the situation if he'd been able to take advantage of Neil's shock and slip away with the guards to explain in private. Neil would be upset, but amputated fingers wasn't secret brain surgery and neural computer-level stuff.

But his hair had been mussed by the woman running her fingers through it, the patch of fake skin on the back of his neck disturbed. As he turned away, eager to flee, Neil demanded, "What is that?" He lanced forward and grabbed Tom's shoulders, thrusting his head down, and Tom jerked away from him, but not before Neil saw it: the neural access port.

His sudden movement set off the security guards, poised for a terrorist incident. Shouts saturated the air and suddenly bodies closed on Tom from all sides, swarming him, bearing him down to the floor.

The onslaught drove the breath out of him, and as Tom's cheek scraped the carpet, he heard Neil shouting in anger, frantic voices calling for backup, that stupid medical exemption still burning a hole in his pocket.

"Let me up. Seriously. I can explain," Tom told them, pinned in place as a mobile body scanner was run over his head, checking for implanted explosives.

"Oh my God, take a look at this," one of the security guards said to the other, waving it over his head. Tom knew what they were seeing: a spiderweb mesh of metal inside his skull.

Meanwhile, another had found the medical exemption in his pocket and was telling the others, "Yeah, it says he got brain surgery on here, but does that look like a nerve stimulator to you?"

Tom dragged his eyes over to Neil, pinned on the carpet just feet away. His dad wasn't fighting now. He was staring at the same image on the scanner they were, his jaw slack, his face chalky, drained of blood.

Tom closed his eyes and started laughing softly, wondering how this could get any worse. He was in serious trouble here. He and his dad both were.

* * *

7

THE GOVERNMENT AGENTS who arrived to sweep them all up into custody—Tom, Neil, and the security guards as well—weren't from the Pentagonal Spire. They were from the National Security Agency.

Tom recounted the same sequence of events to three different interrogators, and passed days alone in a cell, waiting for his official debriefing. He spent hours on end pacing, fretting over what would happen from here, worrying about the repercussions of this, worrying about what Neil might be saying . . . He'd already missed the first few days of Upper Company at the Pentagonal Spire. Every other trainee had returned already.

He'd give anything to be there with them.

Finally, the day came for Tom to learn the fate of his father, for him to formally meet with the NSA agent overseeing the situation.

Tom's nerves were leaping under his skin and he strode in to face the slim, imperious woman. She looked to be in her forties, with light blond hair drawn into a tight bun, sharp cheekbones, and lips set in a thin scarlet line.

"Mr. Raines," she said crisply, "I'm glad you're here. I have a few questions for you."

Her profile flashed in his vision center:

NAME: CLASSIFIED
GRADE: CLASSIFIED
SECURITY STATUS: Top Secret LANDLOCK-14

"My name is Irene Frayne. We need to discuss your father. Please take a seat."

Tom sat. A distant light bit into his eyes, and he had to blink to make out her face.

There was something distinctly unnerving about meeting an actual NSA agent. He knew they had files on every single person in the country, and a lot of Obsidian Corp. contractors were also full-time NSA . . . He'd even penetrated one of their fusion centers by accident when he'd interfaced with Obsidian Corp.'s systems, so he appreciated the reach of their covert eyes and ears. For all he knew, Frayne had a list of every single embarrassing website he'd ever visited.

Frayne offered him a metallic device, one that resembled a small doorknob, impatience in the sharp planes of her face. "I want you to insert this in your brain stem access port."

"What is it?" Tom said warily.

"I'll ask the questions here, Mr. Raines. Insert it. Now."

Tom felt a stirring of unease just at the thought of interfacing with some unknown device, but he didn't have much choice here. He flipped it over so he could see the prong where the device was designed to attach to his port, then he clicked it into the back of his neck. Tom tried to settle back into his seat, but he couldn't lean his head comfortably back now. He sat there awkwardly, his head tilted forward, shoulders tight.

Frayne, in the meantime, was examining a tablet computer held in her manicured grasp.

"State your full name."

"Thomas Andrew Raines."

"Are you a trainee at the Pentagonal Spire, Mr. Raines?"

"Yeah. Of course."

"Have you ever lied to get out of trouble?"

The question flustered him. How was he supposed to answer that? Hadn't everyone done that at some point? "Wait," he floundered, "you mean, right now?"

Frayne's gaze remained fixed on the screen. The faintest smile touched her lips. "That answer is sufficient for our purposes. Now, let's proceed." She tapped at her screen. Her pale eyes flickered back and forth over something she saw there. Then they returned to him. "I understand neural processors enable photographic recollection. If I feel you're omitting any details, or being less than truthful, we'll have to verify your account with a census device. Do you understand?"

Tom felt the blood drain from his face. Sweat pricked on his forehead and palms. Suddenly he knew what that screen must be, what the thing in his brain stem was doing: she'd asked for two truths and then a question designed to fluster him. It was a lie detector. Maybe something more intricate than that, even, since he had a neural processor that could directly access certain areas of his brain. He wished he could see that screen.

"I understand."

Frayne set the tablet down and folded her hands. "As you've probably discerned, we need to discuss your father."

"Listen," Tom tried, "my dad's—"

"Very opinionated," Frayne cut in. "Out of necessity after your public admission, we filled him in. He knows about the neural processor. Needless to say, he's not pleased. Does this distress you?"

"Yes," Tom said vehemently, and he noticed the way Frayne's eyes flickered to the tablet to verify his words.

Of course it distressed him. He'd never wanted Neil to find

10

out. He knew his dad had probably gone off on one of his anti-establishment, anti-government rants when he learned he was in the custody of the NSA, and when he'd heard the full story about the neural processor, he must've exploded on them.

"Look, he talks one way, but he never acts on it," Tom insisted. "He doesn't do anything violent, if that's what you're worried about."

"It surprises me he'd allow his son to be an Intrasolar Combatant." Frayne's lips were a flat line. "Then again, you haven't exactly been the cookie-cutter Intrasolar Combatant, have you, Mr. Raines? We have a former trainee in our organization. I believe you know him. Nigel—"

"Nigel Harrison," Tom cut in, glad for a chance to argue with whatever impression she'd formed of him. "Yeah, the guy who tried to blow up the Pentagonal Spire. I hope he's not my character reference here, because I was the good guy there. I saved the day when he tried to attack his own side. Check your lie detector, and you'll see."

Frayne looked at him sharply, and Tom regretted giving away the fact that he'd figured out he was attached to a lie detector. She studied him for a tense moment, then, "We're perfectly aware of Mr. Harrison's past, and I assure you, his behavior is very adequately regulated now."

A prickling sensation moved up the back of Tom's neck.

Yeah, he knew how Nigel had been "regulated." They must have reprogrammed him to suit their needs. All they wanted was a person with a computer in his head, not Nigel himself. Dalton Prestwick had once taunted him with that possible fate, back when it looked like Tom might have no shot at CamCo.

A neural processor could be a terrible thing if the wrong person programmed it.

Frayne folded her arms and leaned back in her chair, her chin tilting up. "Mr. Harrison is a valuable source of insight into the workings of the Pentagonal Spire. Our agency previously had very little direct information from inside the installation. Given the recent disappearance of Heather Akron, a trainee who was supposed to join us, we expect that to change."

Would she have been adequately regulated, too? Tom wondered cynically. Maybe that was part of the reason Heather had refused to back down from her quest to destroy Tom, destroy Blackburn. She knew what was ahead of her. She thought she had nothing left to lose.

Still, he couldn't help feeling a chill at the very thought of the girl he'd seen Blackburn murder.

Frayne examined her tablet computer. "The Department of Defense gave me full access to your files. I see that this is your second major security breach. The first occurred when you held unauthorized meetings with the Russo-Chinese Combatant Medusa."

"I admit that one, but I was cleared by the Congressional Defense Committee. That's done."

"You committed credit card fraud against a Coalition executive to the tune of nearly fifty thousand dollars."

Tom gave a start, surprised they knew about that. As plebes, he and Vik had run up the balance on Dalton Prestwick's credit card. It was revenge—the man had reprogrammed Tom, after all.

"That wasn't fraud. My name was on the card. Besides . . ." Tom fumbled for a good excuse, then found it. "Besides, I only spent that money to help the economy."

Frayne slanted him a look that told him he was an imbecile.

Tom cracked under it. "Look, he's sleeping with my mom."

"Your mother." She consulted her tablet. "Ah, Delilah Nyland. The dancer."

"Dancer?" Tom echoed. He'd never heard anything much about her, only that she'd run away from her own home at fourteen and his father had met her in Las Vegas. They'd never actually gotten married, even after Tom was born. "Wait, what sort of dancer?"

Then he thought of that handful of times when he was a kid, when Neil had tried to be nonchalant about handing him some bills and telling him to go hang around a VR parlor for a while. Tom remembered the sort of women who'd tended to be hanging off his dad's arm.

Suddenly, he didn't want to know anything else about her. "Actually, don't tell me. Forget I asked."

Frayne studied him. "It seems you had a very unstable childhood, Mr. Raines. Coupled with what appears to be a familial predisposition toward antisocial conduct, I suppose this explains some of your adjustment issues at the Pentagonal Spire."

"I'm not a psycho."

"And yet you have the distinction of being one of the youngest people on Interpol's terror watch list. There aren't many sixteen-year-olds deemed international terrorist threats."

"I'm classified as a *low level* terrorist, not even a dangerous one. There was this prank of sorts involving these toilets and this club, and the guys in there took it way too seriously, and

13

one of them must've pulled some strings to screw me over. You're not going to arrest me, are you?"

"I'm well aware the term 'terrorist' has become a very, shall we say, broad label, so, no, Mr. Raines, I don't intend to arrest you. But I can't help observing that trouble seems to follow you. This recent incident is one of a great many." She stroked her long, slim finger over her chin, studying him. "Do you know what your father is facing today? Indefinite confinement."

"He's not dangerous, he's—"

"Not particularly prudent, either." Her eyes narrowed. "As soon as your father learned of your neural processor, he became the custodian of highly classified, sensitive intelligence. We've already reached an understanding with the other unauthorized civilians made aware of your neural implant, but it's quite another matter with someone like your father who has a record of antisocial conduct. He can't be trusted."

Tom knew Neil's rap sheet: resisting arrest, disturbing the peace, assault upon officers of the law, drunk and disorderly conduct . . . He knew Neil had probably already condemned himself with his outspoken political views since being taken into custody. He hated people like Frayne, those he considered "enforcers of the corporate kleptocracy."

"Fine. Let's say my father told everyone." Tom spread his hands. "Who's gonna believe him? He's an unemployed drunk who didn't have the money to finish high school. Just call him a conspiracy theorist, and no one will listen to a word he says."

"But some might. This is a sensitive point in the development of neural technology. We can't take the risk your father might gain traction if he goes public about the neural processors.

14

Are you aware of the National Defense Authorization Act, Mr. Raines?"

Tom sagged down in his seat, raking his hand through his hair, trying to think of what to do. "I think so. Something about terrorists, right?"

"The law's language is rather broad," she said, "deliberately so in order to give someone in my position more latitude in applying it. I could easily construe your father—and I will directly quote the law—as someone 'who was part of or substantially supported . . . forces that are engaged in hostilities against the United States or its Coalition partners.' He's on record publicly agitating against the government, against our Coalition partner companies. I already have grounds to take him into custody as a domestic terrorist. He'll have no right to a lawyer or a trial by jury. He will simply disappear, and I will do this all legally . . . unless somehow you could reassure me he can be contained."

Tom sat up, his heart racing, latching on to the single shred of hope she was offering. "Let me talk to my dad. I can find a way. I'll get him to stay quiet."

She cocked her head. "I'm not sure of him, and I'm certainly not sure of you, Mr. Raines, but I'll give you one chance." She rose to her feet, studying him in an unnerving, unblinking manner. "By all means, show me what you can do."

1 0 0 1 1 1 1 1 1 1 1 0 0 1 1 1 0 1 0 1 1 0 0 0 0 0 0 0 1 0 0 1 1 1 1 0 0 0
0 1 1 0 1 1 0 1 1 1 0 0 1 1 1 0 0 0 0 0 0 0 1 0 1 1 0 1 0 0 1 0 0 1 1
1 0 0 0 0 0 1 1 0 1 1 0 0 1 0 0 1 0 1 1 1 0 0 1 1 0 1 1 0 0 1 0 0 1 1 0 1 1
0 1 0 0 0 1 1 0 1 1 0 0 0 0 1 1 0 1 0 0 1 1 0 0 0 1 0 1 1 1 1 0 0 0 1 1
1 0 0 1 1 0 1 0 0 0 0 0 1 0 1 1 1 0 1 1 0 0 0 0 0 0 0 1 0 1 1 0 0 1 1 1 1
0 0 1 1 0 0 0 0 0 1 1 1 0 1 1 0 1 1 0 1 0 0 0 0 0 1 0 0 1 1 0 0 0 0 0
1 1 0 0 1 0 1 0 1 1 1 0 1 1 1 0 1 0 1 0 1 1 1 0 1 0 1 1 0 1 1 0 0 0 0 0
0 1 1 1 1 1 1 1 0 1 1 0 0 0 1 1 1 0 1 1 0 1 1 1 0 1 1 1 0 0 0 1 0 1 0
1 0 1 1 0 0 1 1 0 1 0 0 1 0 0 1 0 1 0 1 0 0 1 0 0 0 0 1 0 0 1 0 1 0 1 0
0 0 1 0 0 1 0 1 1 0 0 0 1 1 0 1 0 1 0 1 1 0 0 0 0 1 0 1 1 0 1 0 1 0
0 0 0 0 0 1 1 1 1 0 1 1 0 0 1 1 0 1 1 0 1 0 0 0 0 1 0 0 0 1 0 0 0 1 0 0
1 0 1 0 0 1 1 1 1 0 0 1 1 1 0 1 1 0 0 1 1 0 0 1 1 1 0 0 1 0 0 0 0 1 0 0 0
0 0 1 1 1 1 1 0 1 1 0 1 0 0 0 1 0 0 1 1 1 0 0 0 0 1 0 1 1 1 0 0 0 0 0 0
0 1 1 1 1 0 0 0 0 0 1 0 1 1 0 1 0 0 0 0 0 0 0 1 0 0 0 1 1 1 1 0 0 1 1 0
1 1 0 0 0 1 1 1 0 0 1 1 1 0 0 0 0 1 1 0 0 1 0 0 1 0 1 0 1 1 1 1 1 0 1 1
0 0 0 1 1 1 1 0 0 1 0 1 1 1 1 0 1 0 1 1 0 1 1 0 1 1 1 1 1 1 0 0 1 0 0 1
0 1 0 1   0 1 0 0 1 0 0 0 0 1 0 0 0 0 1 1 1 0 1 0 1 0 1
0 0 1 1   1 0 0 1 0 1 1 1 1 1 1 1 1 1 0 0 1 1 1 0
1 1 1 1   1 0 0 0 1 1 1 0 1 0 0 1 0 0 0 1 1 1 1 0 0
1 0 0 1 1 0 0 0 1 1 1 1 1 1 0 1 1 0 0 0 0 0 1 0 0 1 0 0 1 0 1 1 1 0 0

CHAPTER TWO

TOM WAS ESCORTED into the interrogation room where Neil sat slouched at the table, forehead leaning on his hand.

This moment had been coming since the day Tom agreed to get a neural processor, but his stomach still swooped, realizing his dad knew everything. Tom had one chance, just one, to convince the NSA he could disarm Neil as a threat to the secrecy of the program.

"Hi, Dad."

His dad half rose from the table, almost pleading, "Tommy, tell me none of this is true. This . . . this neural processor stuff. It's gotta be a lie."

Tom felt a cold pit in his stomach. His mouth felt bone-dry. "It's true. The computer in my head is the only reason I'd be able to control the drones in space. I had to have it to join the Intrasolar Forces."

"You mean you left me and you went and got this right after . . ." Neil sputtered into silence. He shook his head again and again. "I should have known. There was something different about you, about your face; I thought you'd matured. I didn't

16

imagine . . ." His hand flew to his head. "The roulette table. The roulette! It's why you knew those numbers!"

"Yeah," Tom admitted. "That's why."

Neil's gaze sharpened on his. "And Joseph Vengerov knew, didn't he? He was trying to make some point." He closed the distance between them in a few strides. "Did he have something to do with this?" Spittle flew from his mouth. "Did he? That cold-blooded Russkie bastard, I'll—"

"He had nothing to do with this. He only designed the tech for the military. I made the decision to get it. I agreed to keep it from you."

Neil shook his head in furious denial. "I can't believe this. You wouldn't let them do this to you. You wouldn't be so *stupid*."

Tom felt heat wash up inside him. "Did anyone tell you about what I can do now that I have the neural processor? Did anyone tell you I speak thirty languages? I know physics. I know calculus. I won Capitol Summit! I can memorize a textbook in my sleep."

Neil stared at him. "You don't even sound like my son anymore."

"Because I'm not!" Tom grew desperate for his father to understand. He paced away from Neil, feeling wired with agitation. "I had nothing going for me before. Nothing! I was ugly and stupid and a loser. I couldn't do anything except play video games. Everything is different now. The computer made me so much more. So much better. So, no, I'm not the same guy I was before. I'm *better*. I'm so much better, Dad. I could go on and do anything now."

Neil looked at him, his eyes hollow, the harsh lights overhead bringing out every line etched into his skin. "I never realized how much you hated yourself."

17

Tom groaned. "That's not what I'm saying."

"It is," Neil flared. "You must hate yourself to talk this way, and I'll tell you, that breaks my heart, Tommy, it does, because you're a great kid and you always have been."

Tom grew fed up. "Do you really think I was better off when I was flunking out of Rosewood Reformatory? You think I would've been better if I'd just kept playing video games the rest of my life? This thing here"—he pointed at his temples— "it's given me everything. It's opened the whole world to me."

"You had choices before," Neil bellowed. "And now you don't! Do you get that? *They own you!* No one in the world can sell you a lifetime warranty on that tech in your head. You had choices, and you threw them all away!"

"This wasn't a choice! Obviously you can't see that, but this was the only way I could've gone."

"The only way? You gave up your mind, you gave up yourself!" He caught his breath, a ferocious gleam in his eyes. "But I'm not giving up on you."

"What does that mean?"

Neil ripped toward the nearest surveillance camera, determination in every line of his body. He pointed right at the lens. "All right, Frayne! You want me to keep quiet? I will. I'll sign a confidentiality agreement, sign whatever form you want. I won't breathe a word again about you people mangling the brains of those poor kids, but I want my boy back!"

Tom stared at his thin back, realizing what his dad wanted to do. "No."

"I can't get that computer out of your head," Neil said ferociously, "but I can get you out of that blasted program."

Tom rose to his feet, staring at him, his heart pounding so loud he could hear it in his ears. "You can't do that. They won't let you do that."

"The hell I can't. I'm your father," Neil shouted back. "You're not eighteen yet. I had to give them permission to keep you, so now I'm rescinding it. They wanna stop me—then by God, I'll spread this everywhere. I'll raise a storm they can't tamp down."

"I can't leave the program if I have a neural processor, and the neural processor can't come out. My brain is dependent on it. Dad, don't you get it? If you give them a problem, they won't boot me out of the program—they'll lock you away!"

"Let 'em try!"

Tom realized it, then: Neil was digging in his heels. His life had been one massive war against the world and now he had his greatest reason yet to take to the trenches. He couldn't possibly win, but that never mattered. Neil would proudly destroy himself before giving up on fighting for his kid, even in the face of insurmountable odds.

Tom wouldn't let him do it.

"There are brain doctors out there," Neil was murmuring feverishly. "There are other people who know about the brain. It can't come out? We'll see. We'll just see. But they're not keeping you. I won't let them."

Tom looked up at the surveillance camera and held up a finger, telling Frayne to give him a bit more time before concluding Neil couldn't be reasoned with. He felt very calm inside, realizing it: he could stop his dad from throwing his life away. He was the only one who could do it.

He just had to erase any reason his father had to wage this war.

The world seemed to go very still around Tom, and he almost didn't hear his own words over the pounding of blood in his ears. "Dad, if you tell people about the neural processor, or you try and take me from the Spire, then I'll go to child protective services, tell them all about my father being a lousy drunk who can't hold a job, and I'll get emancipated."

The words made Neil jolt back around sharply, shock on his face like Tom had unexpectedly jammed a knife in his gut.

"And then," Tom said, his voice feeling very far away, "I'll tell them all about how my dad couldn't get us somewhere to sleep indoors or make sure I got to school more than a few days in a row. That's neglect, which is probably grounds for some sort of legal penalty." It was all true. It was all too close, so he twisted the knife even more. "And if that's not enough right there, then maybe I'll even throw in a few things about . . . oh, I don't know. Maybe about you *beating* me. How about that?"

Shock slackened Neil's face. "I'd never hurt you, Tommy. You know I've never lifted a finger—"

"I know that," Tom agreed, a terrible, deathly calm inside him, "but let's face it, all the rest of that is true, so is it really gonna sound like a huge stretch if I take it a bit further? Mom hightailed it away from us so fast—that won't look good—and think about all those times you got arrested for brawling with other people. Those are red flags, Dad. On paper, you look like a psycho. So here's your choice: if you try to create a problem for me, I will create a far worse problem for you, I swear it. You can't win this. You can only lose everything you have left."

"I'm trying to do what's best for you," Neil said hollowly. "Why can't you see that?"

"Why start *now?*"

Neil stared at him like he didn't know him. Tom held his eyes, his heart pounding wildly in his chest, throbbing in his ears.

"Maybe you're right," Neil finally said. "You're not my boy anymore. That computer's done something awful to your brain, because I know my son never would've threatened me like this."

Tom couldn't speak for a second. Then he reminded himself that this was good. This was what he needed Neil to say. This was the clean break, the reason Neil wouldn't wage the war that would be the end of him.

"I guess we're agreed, then: I'm not your son." Tom moved toward the door, feeling like some strange robot going through the motions of walking, his legs like unfeeling rubber beneath him.

"This is happening again." Neil's words were a broken whisper on the air. "This is really happening again."

Tom's gut clenched. He was leaving his father again. But this time, he knew, it would be much more permanent. There was no going back from this.

He walked out the door.

TOM WAS IN a sort of fog afterward. He felt like he'd just survived some terrible battle and emerged the victor over a field of ashes. He was only vaguely aware of the hours dragging past as he sat in his own cell, arms folded over his chest, staring up at the ceiling.

It was for his own good, Tom told himself over and over, but his brain burned with the devastation on his dad's face. When he tried to resort to his old standby and think of something else, it didn't help at all. He saw Medusa's face instead in

21

that moment he unleashed a computer virus on her. He'd done it for a good reason. Vengerov had suspected she was the ghost in the machine, so Tom had proven she wasn't—by using Vengerov's virus to incapacitate her and then blowing up the skyboards himself.

But it didn't change his memory of the hurt on her face in that moment of betrayal. He wondered how much he'd have to harm the people he cared about before they were finally safe.

Then he heard the door slide open and grew aware of the thin blond woman gliding back into the room. "Well, I must say, you surprised me, Mr. Raines."

"Did I?"

Frayne rested her hand on the back of the chair across from his but made no move to sit. "I'll allow your father to retain liberty of movement. His conversations will be monitored. He'll be watched. Sometimes he'll have a tail, sometimes he won't. He'll be informed of these conditions to encourage him to keep himself in line . . . though I suspect you may have done enough to ensure that yourself."

Tom laughed softly, feeling bitter. It was a roundabout way to say he'd just alienated his father so totally, the man wouldn't ever want him back—much less go to the trouble of taking on the military for him.

Frayne pressed on her ear, tilting her head to the side. Tom knew she was hearing instructions from somewhere. Her icy eyes moved to his. "It appears an officer has arrived to escort you back to the Pentagonal Spire. You're free to go."

Tom raised himself up, bone weary. "Listen," he said, "do you really have to spy on my dad? He's nobody. He's not gonna do anything. Trust me, you'd know already if he was gonna go out there and cause problems."

"If your father has nothing to hide," Frayne said, "then he has no reason to worry about being under surveillance. It's as simple as that."

Tom let out a breath and felt some last shred of hope recede. There simply wasn't a word he could say to reason with someone who thought like Irene Frayne.

THE RETURN JOURNEY to the Pentagonal Spire felt endless, even though the Interstice could sweep them across the country at five thousand miles an hour. Tom had been surprised to find Lieutenant James Blackburn waiting there by the vactrain, his arms folded over his wide chest, his scarred face tense beneath his short-cropped dark hair.

They hadn't been face-to-face since Tom destroyed every skyboard in the Western Hemisphere in the name of the ghost in the machine. He could tell with one glance at Blackburn's thunderous expression that he'd already traced it back to Tom.

It was probably the reason he'd come personally.

Tom was not looking forward to being trapped in a tiny little vactrain with him for several minutes. The air felt electric with tension as Tom settled across from him and the metallic car shot off down the dark tube. Blackburn watched him in an unsettling manner as though trying to psych him out. Tom stared back defiantly, his jaw throbbing from clenching it.

Finally, Blackburn spoke, though his tone was carefully controlled. "Should I bother asking why?"

"Why, what?"

"You know why what. Why the monumentally stupid and shockingly public gesture just before vacation? You might as well have waved a red flag at Joseph Vengerov to please come find you. You exposed what you can do to the *entire world*. *That*. Why, Raines?"

Tom let out a breath. "Okay, first off, Vengerov already knew there was someone like me out there. I found that out at Obsidian Corp."

Blackburn stared at him. "So you chose to paint a virtual target on yourself to make it easier for him to track you down?"

"Look, I'm sorry. I know you're stuck cleaning up after me again." Tom eyed Blackburn warily, knowing he had another reason to be upset about increased scrutiny of the Pentagonal Spire. He'd seen Blackburn murder Heather Akron, even though Blackburn didn't know he was there. Blackburn had things of his own to cover up. "I guess we're kind of tied together in this."

"How true," Blackburn said. "We are bound together by this secret of yours. And I've made a decision: I can't let things continue the way they've been going. Time and again, you screw up. You make poor decisions. I can't trust you. It's as simple as that."

It was all the warning Tom got.

Words flashed before his vision: *Session expired. Immobility sequence initiated.*

"Hey!" Tom bellowed as he lost all feeling below his chest and tumbled off his seat to the floor. Blackburn strode calmly toward him, tapping his forearm keyboard.

Tom knew one thing: he had to defend himself. He tore back his sleeve, his mind racing frantically through the programs still

24

stored on his processor after the war games—but Blackburn's heavy foot descended on his arm, crushing it to the floor. He tore the keyboard away from Tom and flung it aside.

"You've become my biggest liability. I've had it. We're not playing this game anymore where you make a mess, I fix it, you make another mess, I fix it again."

Tom tried to activate a thought interface and send Blackburn a virus that way, but *Function unavailable* blinked in his vision center. He wanted to scream out in frustration.

"I've been thinking about this since I found out about your ability." Blackburn pulled out a neural wire from the front pocket of his uniform. "That stunt with the skyboards made up my mind. Call it the straw that broke the camel's back."

"What are you doing?" Tom demanded.

Blackburn shook his head and whipped out a neural chip, attaching it to one end of the wire. "Trusting you to be careful would be downright stupid. There's too much hinging on what I'm trying to do."

He reached down, and all Tom knew was, he had to get away.

"No!" He seized Blackburn's wrists, trying to force his arms away, desperation giving him strength. But Blackburn had full use of his body, Tom did not, and Blackburn pinned Tom's wrists together and forced his head down.

He kept Tom in that awkward position as he maneuvered the wire into his brain stem access port.

"GET OFF ME! GET AWAY!" Tom said, his vision dimming, a stream of code flowing into his processor.

"It's too late. Just relax." Blackburn settled into the seat next to Tom, and if he hadn't lost strength in his limbs, he

25

would've punched him. "I would've slipped this into your download stream in the Pentagonal Spire, but circumstances have changed there. I have to do it this way."

Tom couldn't believe this was happening. Someone was reprogramming him again. "I'll make you sorry for this," Tom promised him even though he couldn't imagine how. His voice shook. "You can't control my mind—"

"I'm not trying to control your mind, Raines."

Tom forced his eyelids back open.

"I'm creating a link between our processors," Blackburn said. He pointed at his temple, then at Tom's. "With a thought, I'll be able to access your sensory receptors and see exactly what you're doing anytime I want to."

"That's it?"

"That's it. I'm just like the NSA only I'm looking from the inside out, rather than outside in."

"Great, so every time I use the bathroom, you're gonna see it?"

"No," Blackburn said. "I won't watch you twenty-four hours a day. Only when I choose to tune in. It's like turning on a television and checking a specific channel. I'll have the capability all the time, but that doesn't mean I'll watch it all the time."

Tom watched the code streaming behind his eyelids. Blackburn had him at a total disadvantage right now; he didn't need Tom's good opinion. There was no reason to lie to him. Tom couldn't change the outcome, even if Blackburn had outright said he was seizing control of his mind like Dalton had. Tom believed what he said.

It didn't make him feel any better about this.

"This neural link," Blackburn explained, "will let me see through your eyes whenever I'm wondering what you're up to, and hear through your ears when I want to eavesdrop on you. I'm not a fan of routine surveillance, Tom, but you've absolutely necessitated it with your actions. This way you're never going to surprise me again. The next time you plan to pull a stunt like the one with the skyboards, I'll be in a position to look at what you're doing and intervene. Frankly, you're lucky this is all I'm doing after the trouble you've caused me."

Tom was suddenly chilled, remembering Heather's face the moment before the transition chamber to the vactrain decompressed. Blackburn had done worse to people. Far worse.

He heaved in breath, trying to calm himself. "You're not going to kill me, then."

Blackburn shot him a startled look. "Of course not."

Tom's gaze riveted to Blackburn's forearm keyboard, his every muscle knotted with anxiety. "What now? What are you doing?"

"Now, I'm removing this time segment from your memory and looping the first few minutes of our ride through the vactube so you can live in blissful ignorance."

"No. No! Wait. No, wait, come on. I won't tell anyone, okay? We can work something out. Maybe this link is a good thing. I won't try to undo it." He threw out every lie he could. He'd say anything to stop Blackburn from erasing his memory of this.

"You're right, you won't try to undo it because you won't remember it."

Rage boiled through Tom. He felt like his searing fury could burn a message right into his heart, where Blackburn could never hope to wipe it away, a warning to watch for this, to stop him. Surely if he was this enraged, the next time he looked at Blackburn, he'd know something was wrong.

Somehow. He'd remember. He'd remember . . . he wouldn't forget this, he wouldn't forget this . . .

TOM FOUND HIMSELF sitting there in the vactrain, feeling strange for a moment, feeling like he'd missed something, and when he looked over at Blackburn, he found Blackburn gazing at him intently from the seat across from his.

"What?" Tom said.

Blackburn shook his head, studying his face. "Nothing. Is something wrong?"

"No." Tom felt disturbed. He looked away, faintly puzzled by his own reaction, by the way he felt like adrenaline sizzled through his veins, his heart pounding.

Maybe he was on edge because of the way Blackburn had been staring thunderously at him the whole ride. Weird that Blackburn hadn't even said anything to him—not even about the skyboards. He looked down and realized his forearm keyboard had slipped right off his arm and to the floor. Huh. Tom must not have fastened it on well. He lifted it up and wrapped it back around his arm.

"You haven't asked me about the skyboards," Tom finally blurted, feeling like he was going to explode. "Why haven't you?"

Blackburn rubbed the bridge of his nose. After a moment, he opened his eyes. "So, Raines, why the monumentally stupid and shockingly public gesture just before vacation?"

It might have been Tom's imagination, but it didn't sound to him like Blackburn cared all that much about the answer.

```
0 1 1 1 1 1 1 1 1 0 0 1 1 1 0 1 0 1 1 0 0 0 0 0 0 0 1 0 0 1 1 1 1 0 0 0 0 0
1 0 1 1 0 1 1 1 0 0 1 1 1 0 0 0 0 0 0 0 1 0 1 1 0 1 0 0 1 0 0 1 1 1 1
0 0 0 0 1 1 1 1 0 0 1 0 0 1 0 1 1 1 0 0 1 1 1 0 1 1 0 0 1 0 1 1 0 1 1 0 0
0 0 0 1 1 0 1 1 0 0 0 0 1 1 0 1 0 0 1 1 0 0 0 1 0 1 1 1 1 0 0 0 1 1 0 1
0 1 1 0 1 0 0 0 0 1 0 1 1 0 1 1 1 0 0 0 0 0 0 0 1 0 0 1 1 1 1 1 0
1 1 0 0 0 0 1 1 1 0 1 1 0 1 0 1 0 1 0 0 0 0 1 0 0 1 1 1 0 0 0 0 0 1 1
0 0 1 0 1 0 1 1 1 0 1 1 1 0 1 0 1 0 1 1 1 0 1 0 1 1 0 1 1 0 0 0 0 1 0
1 1 1 1 1 0 1 1 0 0 0 0 1 1 1 0 1 1 0 1 1 1 0 1 1 1 0 0 0 1 0 1 0 1 0
1 1 0 0 1 1 0 1 0 0 1 0 0 0 1 0 1 0 1 0 0 1 0 0 0 0 1 0 0 1 0 1 0 1 0 1 1
1 0 0 1 0 1 1 0 0 1 0 0 1 0 1 1 0 1 0 1 0 1 0 1 1 0 0 0 0 1 0 1 1 0 1 0 1 0
0 0 0 1 1 1 1 1 0 1 1 0 0 1 1 0 1 1 0 0 0 0 0 0 1 0 0 0 0 1 0 0 0 1 0 0 1 0
1 0 0 1 0 1 1 1 0 0 1 1 1 0 1 1 0 1 1 0 0 1 1 0 0 1 1 0 0 1 0 0 1 0 0 0 0 0
1 1 1 1 1 0 1 1 0 1 0 0 1 0 0 1 1 1 0 0 1 0 1 1 1 0 0 0 0 0 0 0 1
1 1 1 0 0 0 0 0 1 0 1 1 0 1 0 0 0 0 0 0 1 0 0 0 1 1 1 1 0 0 1 1 1 0 1 0
1 0 0 0 1 1 1 0 0 1 1 1 0 0 0 0 1 1 0 0 0 1 0 1 0 1 1 1 1 1 0 1 1 0 1
0 1 1 1 1 0 0 1 0 1 1 1 1 0 0 1 0 1 1 0 1 1 0 1 1 1 1 1 0 0 1 0 0 1 1
0 1 0 0 0 1 1 1 1 1 1 0 1 0 1 1 0 0 1 0 0 0 0 1 0 0 0 1 1 1 0 1 0 1 0 1 0 0
0 1 0 1 1 1 1 1 1 1 1 1 1 1 1 0 0 1 1 1 1 0 0 0
0 0 0 1 1 1 0 1 0 0 1 0 0 0 0 1 1 1 1 0 0 1 1
0 1 1 0 0 1 1 1 1 1 0 1 0 1 0 0 1 0 0 1 0 0 1 0 0 0 1 0 1 0 0 1
```

CHAPTER THREE

I⊤ WAS DISCONCERTING to return from break in the middle of the afternoon. Tom had missed the critical first week in Upper Company due to the incident over vacation.

The Pentagonal Spire he returned to was not the one he'd left.

It began as soon as he parted ways with Blackburn and reached the elevators. Walton Covner stood there alone. He snapped rigidly to attention.

Tom nodded to him. "Hey, Walt."

"Report for duty, Raines."

Tom stopped, staring at him. "What?"

Walton's dark eyes flickered to his. He said in a low voice, "You have to salute, call me sir, and report for duty."

"You don't outrank me. We're both Uppers."

"I was promoted before you, so sorry, man, you've gotta report for duty and salute me."

"We're not supposed to salute. We're civilians." Tom peered at him suspiciously. Walton tried to screw with his head a lot. "Are you messing with me?"

"Alas, no." Walton sighed. "Sometimes humor cannot fit into one's circumstances, Raines. At least, according to Antony J. Mezilo."

Tom's neural processor identified him as a four-star general. "What about General Mezilo?"

"Marsh is out. Mezilo runs the Spire now. We have all the regular classes—and between them, marches, drills, and exercise."

"No. Why?" Tom cried. That sounded terrible to him.

"Because Akron and Ramirez went AWOL. Apparently we have a discipline problem that needs to be corrected by torturing us."

The elevator dinged.

"Quickly, come on," Walton urged, snapping into a salute. "Report for duty."

Confused, Tom dropped his duffel bag, snapped to attention, and saluted, and Walton saluted back. "Trainee Raines reports to Trainee Covner as ordered."

"Actually, we're cadets now," Walton whispered.

"What?"

"General Mezilo wants us called cadets. He thinks it'll put us in a more military state of mind. Just go with it."

"Cadet Raines reports to Cadet Covner as ordered," Tom said as a soldier stepped out of the elevator. His neural processor identified him as Second Lieutenant Miles Ellis of the marines.

Following Walton's cue, Tom snapped into another salute when the soldier halted before them. The whole situation was perplexing to him, because the officers manning the installation usually ignored the trainees. The trainees were civilians, after all, in the custody of the military but not a part of it beyond a few formalities. But Lieutenant Ellis rounded on Walton and demanded, "The phonetic alphabet. Go!"

"Sir, yes, sir," Walton bellowed, uneasiness creeping in his eyes as the soldier drew so close they were almost nose to nose. He shouted out, "Alfa, Bravo, Charlie, Delta, Echo . . ."

Tom watched it all, standing at attention, a sense of unreality washing over him like he'd stumbled into some strange new land where he didn't know the language. And all throughout Walton's recitation, the soldier reprimanded him for looking away from him, for leaning back, for the slightest indication Walton had faltered.

"Why are you looking at the wall? Is there something interesting on the wall, trainee? Why aren't you looking at me?"

Walton finished, "Xray, Yankee, Zulu, sir."

When Ellis was satisfied, he turned on Tom and barked, "You aren't in uniform!"

"I just came back—" Tom began.

"I didn't ask you a question. You don't have permission to speak!" Ellis sounded genuinely outraged.

"I was explaining where I was."

"From now on, you speak only when asked a question."

Tom threw a disbelieving look at Walton. "Is this for real?"

Ellis shoved his face right into Tom's, his garlic breath flaring out. "Do not address him. You address me. What is your name, cadet?"

"Tom Raines."

"Your full name, cadet!"

"Thomas Andrew Raines, sir."

Ellis's face was so close to his, Tom could see the pores of his nose and the twitching of his nostrils. Having a grown man's face thrust up against his, the smell of garlic wafting like a furnace from his mouth as he demanded increasingly absurd levels of respect was just . . . just . . .

Tom pressed his lips tightly shut as they began to twitch, trying to hold back the laugher fighting its way up his throat.

Ellis's eyes were so close to his. "Are your lips twitching, cadet? Are you trying not to laugh?"

"No, sir."

But then Tom swore, he *swore*, Ellis's lips twitched just for a second. That did it. Tom's self-control dissolved and laughter began pouring from his lips. Walton's eyes widened, and Tom knew he'd made a huge mistake. He started laughing harder, until his whole body was rocking with it, and each shout by Ellis made it funnier.

TOM'S ARMS AND chest were sore before Calisthenics even began. Ellis went on to demand Tom recite something called "The Man in the Area," which Tom didn't know off the top of his head, so he had been assigned push-ups, several penalty hours, and forced to run up and down the stairs until the situation stopped seeming funny.

But Calisthenics was trickier now, too, mostly because there were no simulated enemies and nothing to distract or make exercise entertaining—just people running through rows of tires, crawling under stretches of barbed wire, scaling the walls, being yelled at by various drill sergeants while they frantically completed various exercises.

Tom caught up to the other Uppers, and he was immediately set upon by Sergeant Dana Erskine of the army. Two miles and two hundred push-ups and sit-ups later, he finally found himself standing breathlessly next to Vik, waiting in line for his chance at a test of endurance by some pull-up bars.

"Has it been like this all week?" Tom asked him, gasping for air.

Hey, Tom. The words were net-sent to him by Vik using a thought interface. *We're not supposed to talk. Erskine will give you more push-ups.*

Tom hated thought interfaces, so he spoke staring straight ahead, through mostly closed lips. "So is Marsh totally gone?"

Vik sighed. *He's still functioning in an "advisory" capacity, but it's all Mezilo now. He's old-school. He thinks we have a discipline problem, so he's added an intensive regimen of marches, drills, and order. You're lucky to have missed the first week. Speaking of which, you okay?* Vik's eyebrows flickered up briefly at the last question, but that unfortunately attracted the attention of Sergeant Erskine and got them both another fifty sit-ups.

"Great. We'll talk at dinner," Tom mumbled to Vik as they did them, side by side.

Nope. Can't talk at dinner.

"What?" Tom blurted, which attracted Sergeant Erskine's attention again. He said hastily, as the drill sergeant charged over, "How can we not talk at dinner?"

TOM FOUND OUT soon enough.

After Calisthenics, Lance Corporal Jay Blum of the marines chased them all into the showers and then supervised them as they washed, yelling at anyone who dared to talk or failed to scrub down quickly enough.

Dinner began with a formation of cadets at the door, just like morning meal formation always had, only this time a soldier sat with the cadets at each table. The officer at their table, Second Lieutenant Lew Haas of the air force, fired questions at them:

"How many lights are in the Pentagonal Spire?

"What is the memory capacity of the Pentagonal Spire's server?

"How many times are cadets permitted to chew their food?"

It turned out to be six chews per bite, and they all had to do it at the same time. Tom got more penalty hours for swallowing too soon, then for chewing only four times. By the end of the meal, Tom had accumulated sixty penalty hours and the day had taken on a surreal quality like he'd stepped into someone else's life.

He still wasn't sure what penalty hours were, and apparently cadets weren't allowed to talk directly or even type messages to each other while in the line of sight of officers. The usual punishment for misdeeds in the Pentagonal Spire was restricted libs—confinement to the Spire during weekends, restriction of communication and internet privileges. The other, more severe punishment was scut work duty, cleaning around the Spire.

Tom found out quickly why both those punishments had been eliminated.

After dinner, his brand-new evening duties commenced, and Tom's neural processor flashed with an order for him to report to the laundry room in the basement. As it turned out, *everyone* had scut work duty now on a nightly basis.

When Tom walked into the laundry room, he found Giuseppe Nichols and Wyatt Enslow already hard at work. He ignored

Giuseppe and picked his way over the stray bags of uniforms to Wyatt, realizing this was the first moment he'd been free from supervision since returning to the Spire.

"Tom!" Wyatt called, sounding as happy to see him as he was to see her. He drew her into a hug that she returned stiffly, hitting his back in a way that was meant to be friendly, not slightly painful the way it was.

Tom pulled back, seeing the frantic, harried look on her face. "How are you doing?"

"Bad. I have five penalty hours," Wyatt said sadly. "I can't believe I've already gotten five."

"I've wanted to ask someone what those are," Tom said. "I've got sixty."

Her eyes shot wide. "You just got back from vacation. How have you already gotten sixty?"

Tom raised his eyebrows. "Are you actually surprised by this?"

She considered that. "Now that I think about it, not really."

"Yeah, thought not. Why'd you get yours?" He was puzzled, since she almost never got in trouble.

She ticked them off on her fingers. "First, Yuri and I got an hour for holding hands when we got back from break."

"Are you serious? You got penalized for holding hands?"

"General Mezilo has a new policy against fraternization."

"Wait," Tom sputtered. "Wait, we can't fraternize now?"

She shook her head. "Nope, not when we're inside the Spire. Only the problem is, Mezilo's banned us from leaving the Spire indefinitely, or even making external calls without supervision. He wants us on lockdown until we've demonstrated proper discipline."

35

"What about the internet?"

"Nope."

Tom was aghast. No internet? He wasn't sure how people could exist without even the internet.

"Yuri and I got the first hour for holding hands even though we didn't know the new regulations yet," she went on, "then I got one hour because a few strands of my hair were touching the collar of my uniform at the weekly haircut inspection—"

"Weekly haircut inspection?"

"Haircut and boot inspection," she clarified, as though that made it any less ridiculous. "Then I got an hour for putting all the information about the Pentagonal Spire in the civilian classes homework feed. General Mezilo wants everyone to have to memorize how many lights are in the Spire, how many windows, how much square footage, that type of stuff— the old-fashioned way. Never mind that we have photographic memories anyway and only need to read the blueprints once. He even asked techs if they could disrupt our photographic memories so we have to rely on our brains. He doesn't seem to get that the neural processor atrophies parts of the brain. If you disable the memory function in some of the people who have been here for years, they don't have a hippocampus to compensate anymore."

"Wait, wait . . . What techs?"

Blackburn was a complete control freak with the software writing around the Pentagonal Spire, Tom knew. He'd never retained techs for very long. He preferred to sleep two hours a night rather than trust other people with his encryptions.

Well, people other than Wyatt, that was.

"Some new Obsidian Corp. contractors. General Mezilo's hired them to write trainee software. He wants Lieutenant Blackburn to limit himself to maintaining the Spire's firewall. He won't even let him teach Programming anymore. We have more Calisthenics instead."

Tom thought of Blackburn's dark expression in the vactrain, and realized he might not be the only cause of the man's ire. "Blackburn's gotta hate that."

"Weird thing is, he doesn't show it. He's acting like all the other soldiers. He gave me a penalty hour for going down to the basement to ask if there was anything I could do around here. He's assigned to a duty station there and we're not supposed to walk freely in the installation anymore."

Tom wasn't surprised. Even if Wyatt had been Blackburn's go-to trainee, he wasn't in the same position with a new general running the place. General Marsh couldn't afford to get rid of Blackburn because he'd staked his career on bringing Blackburn back into the Spire. This General Mezilo had no reason to keep him. Blackburn had to tread lightly if he wanted to stay.

"The new techs have no idea what they're doing," Wyatt whispered, "but they won't let me help, and they've shut out Lieutenant Blackburn. There have been so many errors with the download streams, and General Mezilo's stopped simulations altogether until they've figured out the system well enough to run them. Oh, that's how I got another penalty hour. I offered to help the new warrant officers when they were trying to figure out the system. I spoke without having been asked a direct question."

"That sucks."

"Vik says they're trying to integrate us with the rest of the military," Wyatt told Tom, hoisting herself up to sit on one of the industrial-sized washing machines. There were shadows under her eyes in the fluorescent light of the room. "At first, he thought it was great, but even he's changed his mind. Everyone bosses everyone lower ranking than them around now. Some people are just on a power trip. Grover Stapleton yelled at me for five minutes today."

Tom thought of Grover Stapleton. He was an Upper in Alexander Division from Andover, Massachusetts. Since he'd lived in Texas for three months when he was a kid, he spoke in a fake drawl and told everyone to call him Clint. Tom had killed him several times the year before in Applied Scrimmages, which was always good fun for him, not so much for Clint. Like many people, Clint heartily disliked Tom.

"You got promoted to Upper Company at the same time as Clint," Tom told her. "He doesn't get to yell at you. He doesn't outrank you."

She sighed. "He's squad leader."

"Huh? Squad leader? What is that?"

"Each level in each division has one for girls, one for guys. He's yours—he's in charge of Upper boys in Alexander Division. So he technically outranks us. The squadron leaders are supposed to make sure we're all doing our scut work duty."

"Wonderful," Tom said, then remembered what she'd just said. "Wait. He really yelled at you? Why?"

"My shoe was untied," she said mournfully, looking down at her combat boots.

"She almost cried," Giuseppe called helpfully. "I saw it."

"I *did not* almost cry," Wyatt retorted. "I got something in my eye."

Anger flashed through Tom. "Did you punch him when he got in your face like that? I hope you punched him."

She crossed her slim arms over her chest. "That wouldn't help anything."

"Did *Yuri* punch him?" Tom couldn't imagine Yuri would let Clint yell at Wyatt and get away with it.

"No, because it just happened, and Yuri doesn't know. And he *won't* know. You can't tell him. Everything we do gets us in trouble now. I don't want Yuri getting more penalty hours."

"I'm gonna punch Clint, then," Tom declared.

"Tom, don't. I don't want you in more trouble either. Leave it alone."

"Fine. Fine," Tom said, then they began picking through the vast piles of laundry with Giuseppe.

But within minutes, the door slid open, and boots thumped in. "What are y'all up to?" a voice drawled. "Working slow? You're not at your grandma's house! Get moving!"

Clint.

Tom saw anxiety flitter over Wyatt's face, and craned his head back to see the smirking kid with scrub-brush brown hair and crooked eyebrows. So he was their scut work supervisor?

Tom flashed a dangerous smile, reached down, and untied his shoes. "Oh no," he exclaimed, to draw Clint's attention to him.

"What are you doing, Raines?" Clint demanded.

"Oh gosh, my boots are untied," Tom said, flicking the end of the shoelace to the side so Clint would know he'd done it on purpose.

"Tie them," Clint ordered.

39

"No can do, Clint. I can't remember how to tie them."

Clint grew scarlet. "That's a direct order!"

"A direct order?" Tom stretched his legs out so Clint could see how very untied the laces remained, and scratched his head. "That's funny, because authority sort of requires the ability to enforce your power, and I honestly don't see what you're gonna do to make me listen to you, *Grover*." He deliberately called Clint by his real name, not his chosen nickname. It made Clint flush.

"Call me Clint!" he snapped. "I can report you to General Mezilo, you know."

"Wow, Grover, you're honestly gonna tell on me? Are you really? That's pathetic."

Clint's face screwed up. "I don't need to tell on you. I'll make you do it, you—" He grabbed Tom's collar and tried to jerk him upright. That's when Tom's fist caught him square in the face, knocking him back to the ground, upending several bags of laundry.

"Sorry," Tom told the boy on the ground carelessly. "That was a total accident. Oh, my mistake . . . That was a total accident, 'sir.'" He rose to his feet and leaned over to stare down into Clint's face, his voice growing low and threatening. "And I promise, it's an accident that's gonna happen again and again, maybe several times in rapid succession, followed by a boot to your face, if you ever shout at Wyatt again. We clear here, Grover?"

Like most bullies, Clint was a coward at heart, and he nodded so Tom would back off—then scrambled out of the room, muttering threats of revenge. Tom turned to Wyatt, and saw her shaking her head.

"You shouldn't have done that." But there was a faint flush to her cheeks, and she seemed to be fighting a smile. "It was counterproductive to the situation."

Tom grinned at the sight, knowing she approved even if she'd never admit it. "Maybe," he said, "but if Clint doesn't get the message, I guarantee you I'm gonna go all counterproductive on him again."

Wyatt flung her arms around him. Surprised, Tom laughed softly and hugged her back. Despite all the changes at the Pentagonal Spire, he felt like he'd come home.

CHAPTER FOUR

"THOMAS RAINES."

General Antony J. Mezilo pronounced his name with some distaste as Tom stood at attention before him in the office that used to belong to General Marsh. Clint's incident report lay on the desk before him.

"I've been warned about you. Seems you're infamous for being a disrespectful, impudent young rascal. If it weren't for that computer in your head, and the good words in your file from Joseph Vengerov, I would boot you straight out of here. Any soldier with your attitude, I'd run straight out of the service."

"I'm not a soldier, sir," Tom thought to remind him. "None of us are."

"Quiet!" Mezilo bellowed. "You weren't given permission to speak."

"Sorry, sir."

"Did you hear what I just said?"

This time, Tom stayed silent.

"That was a direct question, Raines. From now on, you answer direct questions from your superiors."

Tom eyed him warily, because *that* wasn't a direct question.

Mezilo leaned back in his chair, surveying Tom with small, angry eyes. Mezilo had a wide nose with quivering nostrils, and thinning brown hair combed over his balding dome of a head. Tom wondered idly who'd warned Mezilo about him. There were far too many possibilities. "My predecessor," Mezilo said, "believed in treating you all with kid gloves. You have computers in your heads. He argued that you weren't soldiers serving a tour of duty and then leaving—you're civilians bound to us for life, so we should make it as tolerable as we can for you. He believed you lot shouldn't feel you're making a sacrifice, being here. I disagree with him. I don't think you should be civilians, and if I can't officially change that, then I can at least make you act like soldiers. This is a dangerous world, and there's a new terrorist out there, this ghost in the machine . . ."

Do not react, Tom thought. *Do not react, do not react . . .*

"We can't afford the chaos that reigned over this place. Defections, a disappearance . . . I won't have it on my watch. They say space combat is about individual fighters, acting on their own initiative. That sounds like poppycock to me."

Tom had never heard someone use the word "poppycock." *Keep a straight face. Do not laugh.*

"I intend to create a fighting militia out of these Combatants. Individualism . . . ha. Every military academy in the world emphasizes the greater whole over the individual, and this place should be no exception." With a last furious look at Tom, Mezilo turned his attention to the incident report on the desk. "I've looked over your record here. Seems you have a tendency to wander off on your own in battle simulations.

43

My predecessor liked that, but I don't."

Hot pride and indignation reared inside Tom. "I had the highest kill ratio of any of the Middles, sir."

"Did I ask you a question, Raines?"

Tom shut his mouth.

"You don't learn lessons. That's another thing I know about you. Oh, it's not explicitly written in your file, but it's obvious enough. You made contact with an enemy and got yourself a stint in the census device. You wandered off in Antarctica and lost your fingers. You seem to have an infinite capacity to take your licks, and that tells me whipping you into shape will be a waste of my time. So what am I gonna do with you, cadet?"

Tom watched him uncertainly. "Sir, is that a direct question or a rhetorical one?"

"Check that attitude! I'll tell you what I'm gonna do with you. I'm giving you plebes."

Plebes?

"See, I'm gonna do the nastiest thing I can do to a kid who thinks he's a rebel. I'm putting you in a position of authority." Mezilo's craggy eyebrows drew into a fierce line. "You are going to take a group of plebes and you're going to make sure they adjust to the new scheme of things. You'll be responsible for their discipline, and you'll whip them into shape."

Tom gaped at him. He had to discipline plebes? He didn't even know the rules around here yet, much less know how to enforce them.

"They get railroaded out of this place under your watch, Raines," Mezilo added, taking a sort of satisfaction from Tom's dismay, "then it'll be *your* burden. Your responsibility.

44

Everything that happens to them will be squarely on you. And you've gotta live with ruining those kids' prospects for the rest of your life. How does that sound?"

Tom stared at General Mezilo, still uncertain he'd heard him right.

"I asked you a direct question."

"It sounds like it's going to be difficult, sir."

"Damn right it will be. You'll get more details this weekend." Mezilo turned away from him as though he didn't merit another glance. "Dismissed."

AFTER THAT, TOM'S neural processor directed him to the Calisthenics Arena, where he finally found out what penalty hours were: he had to join something called Accountability Formation, where a bunch of other cadets who'd also accumulated penalty hours lined up and marched back and forth, at a minimum of one hundred twenty paces per minute.

The old gang's back together, Vik net-sent Tom cheerfully, flicking his eyes to each side, where Yuri and Wyatt were standing at attention next to him.

Tom fought a smile and took his position next to them. On cue at 1900, everyone began walking back and forth. And back and forth. On and on it went. They tried net-sending to pass the time. All the practice as Middles had helped Tom hone his precision with net-send—he no longer leaked every embarrassing thought—but he still leaked some. Like when Iman Attar marched past, and he thought idly, *I like boobs.*

Vik smirked at him fleetingly. *Real profound thoughts as always, Doctor.*

45

There was an embarrassing void of thought for a short while, then Wyatt made it worse. *Did Medusa have very sizable breasts?*

Tom and Vik both stumbled, and Cadence Grey, the bored-looking CamCo who was now called a regimental commander, gave them both another hour for breaking formation.

Did she really ask that? thought Tom, Vik, and Yuri all at the same time.

It's just that you seem very fixated on them and you're also fixated on Medusa. I realize correlation doesn't equal causation, but usually it implies some relationship between the two data sets, Wyatt thought.

Only Wyatt could think so analytically about breasts. Tom's brain felt blown out. He had to fight the sudden urge to laugh, which he was sure was going to get him more penalty hours.

I like legs, Yuri thought. Then he grew crimson.

Is that an impure thought from the Android? Vik flashed him a quick grin, unseen by Cadence.

I know I'm scandalized, Tom thought.

So about legs . . . Vik thought, trying to get Yuri to think more impure thoughts.

It is strange they are thinking of Medusa as though she and Thomas have recently been in contact, Yuri thought suddenly, not falling for Vik's bait.

Abruptly, Yuri's thoughts disappeared from Tom's vision center as Wyatt cut him out of the link with a flexure of her thoughts.

I cut him out because I think this conversation is about to go rapidly downhill . . . Thanks for that, Vik. Wyatt cut her eyes toward Vik briefly.

Hey, Tom started the impure thoughts thing, Vik protested. *Tom couldn't help it. It's Tom.*

Hey, Tom thought indignantly, because they made him sound like some slow-witted imbecile.

Besides, Wyatt thought, *we can't think about Medusa and other stuff around Yuri. I'm going to net-send privately with him for a while so he doesn't suspect anything.*

Yuri knew nothing about what had happened after Vengerov zapped him. Yuri hadn't been there for Tom's confession that he was still in contact with Medusa. He didn't know they'd gone to Antarctica, much less that Medusa had been the one to rescue them when Vengerov trapped them.

Sometimes, it was better not to know.

Before I go, she added, *Vik, maybe you should talk, well, think to Tom about—*

Not now, Vik thought.

Think to Tom about what? Tom thought.

But they didn't answer. Tom flicked his eyes to the side to catch the quick look Vik and Wyatt darted to each other. He was missing something here.

Yuri reached the wall first and did an about-face, then began marching back toward Tom. Suddenly Tom regretted his hasty agreement with Vik and Wyatt that it was better Yuri not know some things. They'd obviously twisted that around and applied it to him . . . and the last thing Tom ever wanted was to be kept in the dark.

AT 2100, TOM wearily returned to his new bunk in Alexander Division, painfully ticking off two hours in his mental tally, dread welling in him as he realized he had at least another thirty days of Accountability Formation if he wanted to get rid of his other fifty-eight hours.

And that was only if he didn't accumulate more.

Which was astoundingly unlikely.

His new roommate wasn't in the bunk, so Tom changed into a T-shirt, and headed to the bathroom to wash up, his brain whirling. He was due to get the new rule book for the Pentagonal Spire sometime tonight; it would be in his homework download. Much as it galled him to fall into line with Mezilo's insane regime, he couldn't stand the sheer boredom of Accountability Formation—and his friends would finish their penalty hours way before he did.

Another thought struck him as he brushed his teeth, and his eyes shot wide open in the mirror. Plebes. He was going to have to take responsibility for some plebes.

When was he going to have time to deal with plebes?

Their new curfew was 2145, and an officer would actually come by to check off on a list on a clipboard that they were in their bunks, in bed, neural wires hooking their brain stem ports into the neural access ports on the wall. Tom knew the strict curfew would drive him nuts, but tonight, he headed back to his bunk, ready to drop . . .

Only to walk through the door and find Clint kneeling by his bed, peering angrily at Tom's drawer. "This is not gonna do, partner."

Tom halted. Then he started laughing. His roommate. Of course.

"You can't stuff your drawer full of your gear so haphazardly it won't even close." Clint glared at him through his one normal, one bruised eye. "I'm not getting hours for you. Fold 'em up."

"Let's get something clear." Tom prowled across the bunk slowly. "You may technically, at this moment, have some claim to rank over me out there, but in here, you're not giving any orders."

Clint straightened to his full height. He was a burly kid, a few inches taller than Tom and probably a good deal more muscular. He looked over Tom like he was thinking about that, himself. A bit of a smirk came over his face. "You sucker punched me before. That's the only reason you got me."

"Yeah," Tom agreed cheerfully. "I hit you out of nowhere. It wasn't fair to you. And now that we're sleeping in the same space, imagine what other unfair ways I can come at you without warning. And I know what you're thinking—you could do it, too. Here's your dilemma, *Grover:* you're a squad leader with an impeccable reputation who impressed all the Coalition CEOs on the meet and greets. If anyone's a shoo-in for CamCo down the road, it's probably you. I, on the other hand, have been charged with treason once, I'm perpetually getting in trouble for other reasons, and most of those Coalition CEOs hate my guts."

"What's your point?"

Tom shrugged. "The way I see it, I can be as vicious as I want, and people won't give it another thought. They don't expect any better of me. It would be hard for me to shock them if I did something incredibly cruel and underhanded to a roommate. You on the other hand . . . you've got a lot more to lose than I do. You have a good reputation to protect. Think

49

long and hard about that before you mess with me."

Clint couldn't hold Tom's eyes. He looked away.

Tom decided there were some good sides to notoriety. He flopped onto his bed, because there was something he had to do, and he hadn't wanted to hook into his neural access port and risk the ensuing paralysis of muscles, fading of senses, until he was sure Clint would stay in line. Now, it was time. Tom hooked his neural wire into the access port on the wall, presumably to sleep.

But that wasn't his plan.

As soon as the system connected with his processor, and before the sleep sequence could engage, Tom soared out of himself into the Spire's processor. He always followed the same route from the Pentagonal Spire's server to the Sun Tzu Citadel's: from the Spire's processor to the satellites to the Russo-Chinese satellites around the Mercury palladium mines and back in to the Citadel's systems in China.

Ever since using the computer virus on Medusa—on Yaolan— Tom had been checking on her. She spent the first week after the virus in the equivalent of their infirmary, unmoving in a hospital bed. Then Tom found her moving again, but isolated in a private room, no connection between her neural processor and the Citadel's server.

Whenever he peered through the cameras in the corner of the room, he found her alone. Sometimes she was doing pushups, sometimes she was just sitting at the edge of her bed, staring at the wall, or lying on her back, staring at the ceiling.

It had been several weeks since he'd been able to check on her, thanks to his unexpected security incident over vacation.

When he peered into the isolation room this time, it was empty, the bed made. Tom felt a twinge of anxiety and shot from one surveillance camera to another, hoping to find her . . .

And then he did. She was brushing her black hair up into a high ponytail, wearing her uniform. Her bed was one of six in the room, other girls swarming around her, and Tom realized she was back on duty. She was better. She was okay.

He withdrew from the cameras, peace in his heart.

If he'd truly hurt her, he never would have forgiven himself.

```
1 0 0 1 1 1 1 1 1 1 1 0 0 1 1 1 1 0 1 0 1 0 1 0 0 0 0 0 0 0 1 0 0 1 1 1 1 0 0 0
0 1 1 0 1 1 0 1 1 1 0 0 1 1 1 1 0 0 0 0 0 0 0 1 0 1 1 0 1 0 0 1 0 0 1 1
1 0 0 0 0 0 1 1 1 0 0 1 0 0 1 0 0 1 0 1 0 1 1 1 0 0 1 1 1 0 1 1 0 1 0 1 1 0 1 1
0 1 0 0 0 1 1 0 1 1 0 0 0 0 1 1 0 1 0 0 1 1 0 0 0 1 0 1 1 1 1 0 0 0 1 1
1 0 0 1 1 0 1 0 0 0 0 0 1 0 1 1 1 0 1 1 0 0 0 0 0 0 1 0 1 1 0 0 1 1 1 1
0 0 1 1 0 0 0 0 0 1 1 1 0 1 1 0 1 1 0 1 0 0 0 0 0 1 0 0 1 1 0 0 0 0 0
1 1 0 0 1 0 1 0 0 1 1 0 1 1 0 1 1 0 1 0 1 0 1 1 1 0 1 0 1 1 0 1 1 0 0 0 0 0
0 1 1 1 1 1 1 1 0 1 1 0 0 0 1 0 0 0 1 1 0 1 1 0 1 1 1 0 1 1 1 1 0 0 0 1 0 1 0
1 0 1 1 0 0 1 1 0 1 0 0 1 0 0 0 1 0 1 0 1 0 0 1 0 0 0 0 1 0 0 1 0 1 0 1 0
0 0 1 0 0 1 0 1 1 0 0 1 0 0 1 1 0 1 0 1 1 1 0 0 0 0 1 0 1 0 1 0 1 0
0 0 0 0 0 1 1 1 1 0 1 1 0 0 1 1 0 1 1 0 0 0 0 0 1 0 0 0 0 1 0 0 0 1 0 0
1 0 1 0 0 1 1 1 1 0 0 1 1 1 0 1 1 0 0 1 1 0 0 1 1 1 0 0 1 0 0 0 1 0 0 0
0 0 1 1 1 1 0 1 1 0 1 0 0 0 1 0 0 1 1 0 0 0 0 1 0 1 1 1 0 0 0 0 0 0
0 1 1 1 1 0 0 0 0 0 1 0 1 1 0 1 0 0 0 0 0 0 1 0 0 0 1 1 1 1 0 0 1 1 1 0
1 1 1 0 0 0 1 1 1 0 0 1 1 1 0 0 0 0 1 1 0 0 1 0 1 0 1 0 1 1 1 1 1 0 1 1
0 0 0 1 1 1 1 0 0 1 0 1 1 1 0 1 0 0 1 0 1 1 0 1 1 0 1 1 1 1 1 1 0 0 1 0 0 1
0 1 0 1 0                     0 1 0 0 1 0 0 0 0 1 0 0 0 0 1 1 1 0 1 0 1 0 1
0 0 1 1                       0 0 1 0 1 1 1 1 1 1 1 1 1 1 0 0 1 1 1 0 0
1 1 1 1                       1 0 0 0 1 1 1 0 1 0 0 1 0 0 0 0 1 1 1 1 0 0
1 0 0 1 1 0 0 0 1 1 1 1 1 1 0 1 1 0 0 0 0 0 1 0 0 1 0 0 1 0 1 0 1 0 0
```

CHAPTER FIVE

"**W**HAT ARE THESE tiny, scared-looking creatures?" Vik wondered.

"Their eyes are so big." Wyatt sounded creeped out. "But they're so very small."

"They are quite young," Yuri agreed, puzzled. "Surely none were so young before my coma." He rubbed his chin thoughtfully. "Perhaps I am still in a coma and haven't realized it."

They were standing in front of Tom's three plebes. They all had close-cropped hair, and they looked downright frightened by the strange, older cadets commenting on them like they weren't there.

"Guys, stop messing with my plebes," Tom ordered them. "They just haven't had their hGH kick in yet, that's all. Now go!" He jabbed his thumb toward the elevator.

Wyatt nodded crisply, and Vik grumbled about gormless cretins, then followed. Yuri shot the plebes a simultaneously sympathetic and reassuring look, his smile seeming to say "I believe in you" before he followed. Tom thought suddenly that Yuri should've been the one chosen for this. He'd be better at mentoring scared little thirteen-year-olds.

He tried to imitate Yuri's reassuring look, flashing his plebes what he hoped was an I-believe-in-you grin, even though until now, he'd never tried to do one before.

"Sorry about that. My friends find it kind of hilarious that *I'm* the one supposed to be guiding you. My buddy Vik said he wanted to meet you before and after I was done training you so he could assess the damage." Then, seeing their grim faces, he added hastily, "He was joking."

The three plebes did not smile. They sat huddled together on the couch in the plebe common room, staring up at him. Two of them, the girl Lanny and the boy Reed, were fourteen. The smallest boy, Zane, was thirteen. All three of them wore a glazed, shell-shocked look. Tom felt deeply sorry for them. The Pentagonal Spire they'd seen a month before on their tours must've seemed a radically different place than the one they'd woken up to after their brains adjusted to the neural processors.

General Marsh used to space out the admission of new plebes, in part because the neural processors were in short supply—there was a fixed number left over from the soldiers who'd died in the first testing group—but also because the screening process to become an Intrasolar trainee was so rigorous. It seemed strange to Tom that he had three newbies on his hands all at once.

Mezilo had ordered Tom to whip them into shape, get them adjusted to the scheme of things. Tom wasn't even adjusted to the scheme of things himself. He wasn't sure how to do this, so he settled for trying to trick the plebes into thinking he was more confident than he felt.

"So," he said, rubbing his palms together. "Uh, you're Reed Geithman, huh?"

The fourteen-year-old boy with a receding chin and large nose frowned at him. "Obviously. You have a neural processor. You know my name."

"Yeah, I'm being polite. Give me a break here, Reed." He looked at the girl, Lanny O'Dell, a fourteen-year-old with short red hair and freckles scattered over her pale skin. "Hi to you, too, Lanny. And you, Zane."

Zane Blunt was thirteen, with protuberant green eyes and a stubby nose. He was the only one who didn't meet Tom's smile with a grim, frightened look.

"Any questions?" Tom tried.

"How long before my hair grows out?" Lanny asked suddenly. "None of the soldiers would tell me when I asked."

"Yeah, they wouldn't know. It's fast," Tom assured her. "The processor controls the growth rate now, so you can tweak it. You won't look like some bald monk for very long."

Lanny's face crumpled.

"I didn't mean *you* in particular, Lanny. I just mean . . ." Tom faltered.

"All of us?" Zane said sadly. "We all look like bald monks?"

Now Reed looked crestfallen, too, mournfully touching his stubby hair.

Tom sensed suddenly he wasn't inspiring confidence in his leadership. "Hey," he tried, "I've got fake fingers. My real ones froze off in Antarctica. Wanna see?"

The plebes perked up. Tom held out his hands so they could look.

"Can I touch them?" spoke up Lanny.

Tom still felt bad he'd called her a bald monk, so he nodded. "Yeah, okay."

Lanny and Zane began poking at his mechanized fingers. Reed watched them and sulked. He didn't poke at all.

"They feel like rubber, only more silky," Lanny remarked.

"Huh, really?" Tom rubbed one of his fingers against his wrist, wondering about that. He hadn't thought to contemplate their texture, mostly because he no longer had fingers with which to feel it. "Did you know they're detachable? Once I stuck a finger in my buddy Vik's toothbrush case. You could hear his shriek down the hall." He grinned at the memory and unscrewed a finger, then showed them the way it bent back and forth mid-air, just with a flexure of his thoughts. "See, they don't even have to be attached for me to move them. The range is about a hundred feet."

Even Reed straightened up and stared in fascination. Tom felt a surge of gratification, realizing he'd impressed them immensely. This new leadership thing was going great.

TOM, VIK, WYATT, and Yuri hadn't been the most perfect, rule-abiding trainees even under Marsh. Every day but Sunday they were forbidden to hang out and talk in the mess hall like they used to, so they devised new ways around that. Since Tom and Wyatt had to distribute freshly washed laundry to various bunks, and Vik had to vacuum floors, and Yuri had to scrub the walls, they all contrived to meet in the same general vicinity each night.

When Mezilo caught on to cadets organizing via net-send,

he ordered his techs to monitor net-send—so Tom and his friends blinked Morse code to each other in the mess hall. They did it for a few days before they decided not to bother.

The techs, after all, were still having trouble readying cadet downloads for civilian classes and keeping the processors running. They still couldn't figure out the simulation system, much less take the time to scrutinize the idle cadet chatter—especially after all the cadets responded to the surveillance by increasing idle chatter exponentially, lacing it liberally with keywords designed to draw scrutiny so they could overwhelm the techs with questionable net-sends.

I'm so bored right now I'd rather have a bomb explode in here than sit through this, Vik thought to them during civilian classes.

Tom replied: *Yeah, I'd give anything for something interesting to happen. I'd even prefer a rebellion or a revolution or a riot or civil disorder or just a protest.*

Anthrax, Wyatt thought. *Sarin gas.*

I want to assassinate this astrophysics test, Vik thought.

I'm waging a jihad against the third problem now, Tom said.

Ricin, Wyatt thought. *Weaponized smallpox.* She hadn't yet mastered working her inflammatory keywords into faux conversation yet.

In another room with the Middles—where they'd forgotten to inform Yuri of the keyword thing or cut him out of the neural link after Accountability Formation—Yuri thought, *This conversation is deeply confusing.*

As a consequence, the cadets overwhelmed the techs with net-sends in urgent need of examination and the techs missed all the genuine cross talk. It was a law of unintended consequences.

As was a new outgrowth of one of Mezilo's other policies: Sunday-only socialization.

Because cadets could only hang around one another and speak freely that day, fraternization increased exponentially that single day of the week, as though everything repressed the other six days had to be frantically expressed during the free hours. The second and then the third Sunday, people were all over each other in the common rooms, in the corridors, in the mess hall, to the point that Wyatt didn't even like venturing out of her bunk on Sundays, and Tom liked it way better than ever before. The military regulars even retreated from their constant supervision on Sundays, maybe to protect their eyes.

Another effect of the totally rigid routine's slackening for a single day of the week was that Sunday felt almost dizzying in its freedom, even though they still weren't allowed to leave the Spire or go on the internet. Tom slept in for no particular reason, just because he could. Then he ambled down to the mess hall with his hair askew, a ratty old shirt on—also because he could.

"Doctor, what are you doing?" Vik demanded when Tom plopped down at a table with him.

"What?"

"You look like you're homeless."

"I am homeless."

"Living it up in casinos does not count as homeless."

Tom shrugged. "So what if I look like a bum? Not getting penalty hours on Sunday." He idly watched a couple of Middles at the next table getting handsy.

Vik snapped his fingers to draw his attention back. "I have

made a decision. It's time you had a girlfriend."

"You've made this decision for me?"

"I have, indeed. I want you to look around at all the cadets enjoying Fraternization Sunday, and then get inspired to participate in it yourself. Ask someone out."

Tom raised his eyebrows. He looked around the room, thinking of Medusa. Yaolan. Medusa . . . He still wasn't sure how he should think of her. He drew a quarter out of his pocket and began flipping it from one mechanized finger to another. "Yeah, it'll be fun getting rejected."

"Take it from me, charisma and self-confidence are all that matter, not looks. I am lucky enough to have all three of those qualities, of course, but even without one or two of them, I still would've won Lyla over. You know why? It's a secret, but I'll tell you."

Despite himself, Tom was curious. "How?"

Vik dropped his voice to a whisper. "I asked her out."

Tom socked his arm, because he'd been expecting some real awesome secret. He threw a quick glance around to make sure no one could hear them, then spoke in a low voice so Vik would know his other objection. "You remember *who* saved our lives when we were in a very cold place, don't you?" He gazed at Vik meaningfully, since Vik would know he was referring to Medusa. "We haven't actually broken up. It wouldn't be right."

Agitation flared in Vik's dark eyes. "Don't get me wrong, I'm grateful to her. I am. But you're not being realistic. Think about all the new surveillance. All the new officers. Things have changed. You have to admit that."

"I know, but . . ."

"But nothing, Tom." Vik wore an unusually serious expression on his face. "I talked to Wyatt—yes, the Evil Wench and I actually had a serious discussion about stuff. She and I have been trying to figure out the right time to tell you this, but now's as good as ever. We both think it's only a matter of time before someone figures out you're in contact with that particular girl again, and then all three of us are going to face consequences."

"I wouldn't drag you into that." Tom resumed flipping the quarter, avoiding Vik's eyes. "I can't believe you think I would. And you're not even considering the possibility that no one will find out."

His friends didn't know what he could do with machines, what Medusa could do . . . the way they could interface with any machine at will, the way their consciousnesses could virtually enter them. They weren't going to be traced by conventional methods. The one time Tom had been detected was when he'd plunged into Obsidian Corp.'s systems, and that was only because Joseph Vengerov had known to look for someone like him.

"I get that you have this fixation on her, I get it, but we can't afford to attract attention." Agitation edged Vik's voice. "We frolicked in that icy place together, and did a lot of property damage. That's not just expulsion from the Spire, that's hard prison time."

Tom caught the quarter in his palm and looked at him. "Look, if it puts your mind at rest, the girl in question and I haven't talked lately." His only contact with her had been via the security cameras, when he checked in on her.

Vik's shoulders slumped in relief. "That's great. It's a start. Now's the time to explore new vistas. Or are you afraid? I bet that's it. Twenty bucks says you're too much of a coward to ask one of these girls out."

"I know what you're doing here, Spicy One. It's not gonna work."

Vik mimed wiping away a tear. "Tommy's a fragile flower. He can't take rejection."

Tom raked a hand through his hair. "Okay, fine. I will go ask a girl out, then whatever happens, you get off my back about this. I'm taking that twenty bucks from you."

He located the nearest girl he sort of knew, then strode over to her. She was at a crowded table with her friends, so Tom figured he was about to get shot down in front of a whole bunch of people. Best to get it done with, like ripping off a Band-Aid.

"Hey, Iman," he said, leaning his arm on the table next to her.

Iman Attar, a Middle in Machiavelli Division, looked up with some surprise on her face, her blue-green eyes framed by a mane of butterscotch-brown hair. She was pretty, and Tom had always thought so, but he'd already made a huge idiot of himself in one simulation where they played cavemen and he tried to convince her he'd be a good mate. She'd hit him over the head with a stick and called him ugly. It wasn't the most flattering response to his overtures ever.

"Go out with me," Tom blurted.

Her eyes widened. "On a date?"

"That's the idea." Tom was aware of the dead silence from all her friends at the table, including one of the Middles, Jennifer Nguyen.

Tom knew her well. He'd once overheard her mocking Vik's attempt to win her over—and that's where "Spicy Indian" had come from. He hoped this didn't lead to some nickname for him later.

Then Iman said, "Okay."

"Okay?" Tom echoed.

She nodded. "Yeah," she confirmed.

Tom nodded, stunned. "Great. Glad we settled that." Then he walked away. And that was that.

TOM HONESTLY HADN'T expected her to say yes. He gazed at Medusa through the security cameras that night, wondering how to get out of it. It wasn't that Iman wasn't gorgeous, and the fact that she wasn't half a world away and fighting for the enemy made things easier . . .

But Tom's brain, his mind, his thoughts were all tangled up on one person, and he'd been that way ever since he first watched the Achilles of the modern world soaring through the reaches of space, obliterating Indo-American vessels.

Today, Medusa did something she did a lot: she caught him off guard.

"You know," she said to the air in English, "it's very perverted watching half-dressed girls first thing in the morning." Tom froze up, realizing she was addressing him. Her dark eyes swiveled to the camera.

"Yes," she said, "I know you're there. I've thought for a while about what I want to say to you, but I'm ready now. Go back to your own system and I'll meet you in a second."

Tom withdrew from the Citadel's systems. He remained

hooked into the neural access port in his bunk, data buzzing through his brain, and a moment later, Medusa's mind touched his in the system. One of the games in the trainee system activated around them, and Tom found himself facing Adolf Hitler.

"Medusa?" he ventured.

"This is me."

She was not attractive when she was Hitler. They were standing on top of a moving train, and when Tom glanced down at himself, the information flashed across his vision center. He was playing Joseph Stalin, the leader of the Soviet Union in the early twentieth century and a mass murderer who'd killed tens of millions of people. The program was named Dictators Fist-fighting on Top of Trains.

It was a crude program with blocky landscape, and looked to have been written by a trainee for fun. For some reason, Tom's thoughts immediately jumped to Walton Covner. In any case, Yaolan could not have chosen two more unappealing avatars, which was a very bad sign.

She folded her arms. "I know you've been visiting my system. I know you've been looking in on me."

"Seriously, I never do it when you're, uh—well, I don't look if you're not dressed or something." An optimistic thought sprang up in his mind. "Unless you want me to."

"No!"

"I was being hypothetical," he said quickly, disappointed. "I'm not some Peeping Tom."

She stared at him.

"I did not mean to make that pun," Tom added, feeling very lame.

62

"Blushing does not suit Stalin," she remarked.

"I don't blush, and neither does Stalin. Why am I Stalin, by the way?"

"Would you rather be Hitler?"

"Why are you Hitler?"

"Because most of the simulations in your system aren't working for some reason."

"We've had technical difficulties lately," Tom admitted.

"And we're going to forge a nonaggression pact."

"A . . . what?"

"A pledge of nonaggression against each other."

"Listen, listen, Yaolan. I know I used that virus against you, but it wasn't an act of aggression. I stayed away because you couldn't hook in yet so I couldn't explain, and then after waiting awhile, I wasn't sure how I'd do it."

"I know why you used the virus."

Tom blinked. "You . . . do?"

"After I heard about the ghost in the machine, it was pretty obvious it was a misguided attempt to protect me."

"Wait, Yaolan. You know I did it for you?" Tom said, uncomprehending. "And you're mad anyway?"

She stepped forward and punched him. Hard. The pain receptors were on full, so the impact exploded across his cheek, reeling him back. Stalin's legs recovered their balance somewhat clumsily.

"Of course," she cried. "And stop calling me by my name. I never gave it to you—you just found it out by accident."

He raised his hands. "Medusa, fine."

"Better," she snarled, and drew toward him.

Tom socked her this time, watching Hitler tumble to the roof of the train. "I don't understand. I knew you'd be mad because of the virus. But you get why I did it, so you're mad about . . . what, exactly?"

She reared up, blood dripping into her small mustache, whipped forward, and delivered a roundhouse kick to his ribs. Tom almost tumbled right off the train. "You used a virus on me without my permission. I never would have asked you to take a fall for me like that."

Tom struggled against the fierce wind as they rattled down the tracks, his legs dangling toward the wheels churning below them. "You saved us in Antarctica. I owed you."

Her hand extended down toward his. After a moment, Tom, took it, and she hoisted him back on top of the train with her. The ground blurred below them, wind tearing through their hair. They stared into each other's eyes, and Tom felt like some terrible knot had unraveled in his chest. He hadn't wanted her to think it was because he was trying to get promoted, or because he wanted in with Vengerov.

He'd done it for her.

And she'd realized it.

But it obviously wasn't okay.

"You should have *asked* me first."

Tom tightened his grip on hers when she started to pull away. "You wouldn't have let me do it."

She snatched her hand from his. "Of course not. I don't want a savior, Tom. I never have. That's the problem." She reeled back a step, wobbling as the train rocked beneath them. "You want something from me that I can't give you."

"Medusa—"

"You want to be someone's hero. You want to be strong for someone. I don't need your strength and I certainly don't need your pity."

"It's not pity," Tom said, appalled.

"I've spent my whole life dealing with this from people because of the way I look." She gestured to her face, which didn't show on Hitler, but where he knew she'd been hideously scarred as a young child. "The people who aren't repulsed by me always seem to feel this terrible pity. It's infuriating. I'm not broken, I don't need to be fixed, and I don't need to be saved."

"God, Medusa, it's not pity. You don't get it."

"What don't I get?" she blazed at him.

"I don't feel sorry for you. You're the strongest person I've ever known. Ever. I know I don't need to protect you. What I did, I'd do for anyone who mattered to me. I'd rather Vengerov found me than found you."

She studied him, eyes glittering. "Then you have some severe psychological disorder, Mordred, because affection isn't about destroying yourself for someone else. I don't want anyone doing that for me."

"Vengerov might never find me."

"Wasn't that the entire reason you were even at Obsidian Corp. in the first place? You risked your life there to save a friend."

"All my friends did."

"But this is a pattern with you. This is how you operate." Her eyes narrowed a bit. "You're desperate to be needed."

Tom was lost. "I don't really know what you want me to say."

65

She was silent a moment. "Then don't say anything," she finally told him. "Just listen: I don't need you. I will never need you."

Tom couldn't manage a word, stung.

"As of today," Medusa said, "we're going back to the old arrangement. You don't come on my server and I won't come on yours, emergencies aside." She raised her hand to end the program, then hesitated. "Oh, and I forgot one thing."

"What?" Tom said bleakly.

She flashed him a bright, savage grin. "Thank you for the computer virus."

And then the text flashed before his vision center: *Datastream received: program Good Luck Explaining Where You Got This to Your Techs initiated.*

Tom snatched out his neural wire. For a moment, nothing happened.

And then the Good Luck Explaining Where You Got This to Your Techs virus slammed him with a terrible sensation like someone had just driven a boot in between his legs. Tom screamed out, doubling over, tumbling right off his bed and thumping to the floor, gagging.

He lay there, fighting the need to be sick, the terrible pain easing with nauseating slowness. When he finally found his feet again, Tom shook his head with reluctant amusement, realizing she could've done far worse. Medusa wasn't pleased, but she hadn't tried to kill him.

The worst pain was the sense something had finally broken between them for good. It wasn't like the last times when she'd been angry at him, because he felt like he could deal with anger. She'd been calm. She'd spoken like there was some irreconcilable difference between them and he didn't know how to—

And then the virus triggered again.

1 0 0 1 1 1 1 1 1 1 0 0 1 1 1 0 1 0 1 1 0 0 0 0 0 0 0 1 0 0 1 1 1 0 0
0 0 1 1 0 1 1 0 1 1 1 0 0 1 1 1 1 0 0 0 0 0 0 0 0 1 0 1 1 0 1 0 0 1 0 0 1
1 0 0 0 0 0 1 1 1 1 0 0 1 0 0 1 0 1 0 1 1 0 0 1 1 1 0 1 1 0 0 1 0 0 1 1 0 1
0 1 0 0 0 1 1 0 1 1 0 0 0 1 0 0 1 1 0 1 0 0 1 1 0 0 0 1 0 1 1 1 1 0 0 0 0 1
1 0 0 1 1 0 1 0 0 0 0 0 1 0 1 1 1 0 1 1 0 0 0 0 0 0 1 0 1 1 0 0 1 1 1
0 0 1 1 0 0 0 0 0 1 1 1 1 0 1 1 0 1 1 0 1 0 0 0 0 0 1 0 0 1 1 0 0 0 0
1 1 0 0 1 0 1 0 0 1 1 0 1 1 1 0 1 0 1 0 1 1 1 1 0 1 0 1 1 0 1 1 0 0 0 0
0 1 1 1 1 1 1 1 0 1 1 0 0 0 0 1 1 1 0 1 1 0 1 1 1 1 0 1 1 1 0 0 0 1 0 1
1 0 1 1 0 0 1 1 0 1 0 0 1 0 0 0 1 0 1 0 1 0 0 1 0 0 0 0 1 0 0 1 0 1 0 1
0 0 1 0 0 1 0 1 1 0 0 1 0 0 1 1 0 1 0 1 0 1 1 1 0 0 0 0 1 0 1 1 0 1 0 1
0 0 0 0 0 1 1 1 1 0 1 1 0 0 1 1 0 1 1 0 0 0 0 0 0 1 0 0 0 0 1 0 0 0 1 0
1 0 1 0 0 1 1 1 1 0 0 1 1 1 0 1 1 0 0 1 0 0 1 1 1 0 0 1 0 0 0 1 0 0
0 0 1 1 1 1 0 1 1 0 1 0 0 0 1 0 0 1 1 1 0 0 0 0 1 0 1 1 1 1 0 0 0 0
0 1 1 1 1 0 0 0 0 1 0 1 1 0 1 0 0 0 0 0 0 1 0 0 0 1 1 1 0 0 1 1 1
1 1 1 0 0 0 1 1 1 0 0 1 1 1 0 0 0 0 1 1 0 0 1 0 0 1 0 1 0 1 1 1 1 0 1
0 0 0 1 1 1 1 0 0 1 0 1 1 1 1 1 0 0 1 0 1 0 1 1 0 1 1 0 1 1 1 1 1 1 0 0 1 0 0
0 1 0 1   1 0 1 0 1 0 0 0 0 1 0 0 0 0 1 1 1 0 1 0 1 0
0 0 1   0 0 0 1 0 1 1 1 1 1 1 1 1 0 0 1 1 1 1
1 1 1 1   1 0 0 0 1 1 1 0 1 0 0 1 0 0 0 0 1 1 1 1 0
1 0 0 1 1 0 0 0 1 1 1 1 1 1 0 1 1 0 0 0 0 0 0 0 1 0 0 1 0 0 1 0 1 0 1 0

CHAPTER SIX

THE TERRIBLE SENSATION of a boot slamming him in the crotch reoccurred every three minutes on the dot and it never grew less awful. Tom was desperate by the time he reached Wyatt's bunk in Hannibal Division, and he could've collapsed with relief to see she was there. The only problem was, so was someone else.

"I need to talk to you," Tom blurted. "In private."

"What?" said Evelyn Himes, Wyatt's small blond roommate.

Wyatt shot to her feet. "What is it, Tom?"

"Can Wyatt and I talk alone?" Tom said to Evelyn.

"No. This is my bunk." Evelyn drew a brush through her crackling blond hair. "You guys can talk somewhere else."

But there was nowhere else Tom could go. He saw the time ticking down in his vision center, terrible dread welling in him.

One minute left.

"Please, Evelyn. I'll give you . . ." He rooted in his pocket. "Twenty bucks. Just give us a few minutes alone."

"I said no."

"Twenty now, ten later. That's thirty I'll give you if you just leave for a bit."

"God, can't you guys talk somewhere else?"

Desperation gripped Tom. "Fine. Stay. You wanna watch, you can watch. I don't mind an audience." Then with a swift look of apology for Wyatt, he seized her waist, declared, "You are looking good today, Wyatt," swooped his head down and drew her into a kiss.

Wyatt's body went rigid, and Tom thought, *Please don't punch me too hard for this afterward* . . . as he waited for Evelyn to get the message and leave. For a moment, the strangeness of the situation registered as he felt Wyatt's tightly compressed lips against his, the coolness of her cheek. Her hair smelled like lavender, and her brown eyes looked so enormous this close that she seemed to fill the world.

And then something seemed to shift, her body softening against his, her lips parting against his. Against his will, a strange tingling excitement moved through him, feeling her hands tentatively slide up his chest, and her slim body became magnetic against his, drawing his hands. He reached back to seize the bedrail he'd backed her against to stop himself from moving his hands elsewhere. He clenched his fists so tightly around the cool metal that they began to throb.

"Ugh, fine!" Evelyn exclaimed, and her footsteps stomped out. "Have the room to yourselves!" The door slid shut behind her.

Tom pulled back, releasing the bedrail, and his hands hovered uncertainly in the air as he struggled for the right words to explain this to Wyatt. It was like his brain was melting and electricity pinged his limbs, and her eyes were wide like a frightened doe's on his.

In his vision center, time ticked down. 0:05 . . . 0:04 . . . 0:03 . . .
Oh no.

It happened. The invisible boot drove into his groin, and Tom groaned out in pain and dropped into a heap of limbs on the floor. Abruptly, he was free of the spell, brutal reality crushing through him, terrible pain displacing the temporary madness.

He'd deserved this one, too.

"Tom?"

Wyatt's voice sounded high and strangled. She knelt beside him, her hands suspended mid-air like she didn't know whether to reach out and help him. He waved to her painfully, trying to show her he was okay.

"Tiny Spicy Vikram," Wyatt called to the air.

"Tiny Spicy Vikram?" Tom echoed.

"I set it up as a trigger phrase to disable surveillance in my bunk for ten minutes. In case we had to talk about something urgent," she said.

Of course she had. Wyatt thought of everything. The nausea was awful, and Tom managed in a strained way, "I'm okay. Kind of. It's a computer virus. I need your help. That's why I needed your roommate out."

Wyatt was very still.

"This hurts. It really hurts," Tom gasped. "It's happened every three minutes since Medusa used it on me. I can't tell the techs how I got it and I couldn't tell you in front of Evelyn. Can you fix this? Please?"

"*Medusa* gave it to you?"

"I can explain—but later. This is going to kill me. Not literally, but you know what I mean!"

70

She was very quiet. She moved toward the drawer under her bed and pulled out the diagnostic scanner she used sometimes on neural processors. Tom looked at her stiff, rigid shoulders, the jerking movements of her arms.

"Sorry for ambushing you with that," he said to her. "You understand, right? I had to get her out of here. I can't tell anyone else, since it came from Medusa and . . . I should've warned you, or . . ."

"Good ploy. It worked." Wyatt's voice was harsh and clipped. She snapped out the neural wire, moved briskly back over to him, and jabbed one end of it into the access port on the back of his neck hard enough that her knuckles hurt his neck.

Then she flopped down on the floor next to her bed, curling her fatigue-clad legs up to her chest as she ran the scan.

Tom managed to heave himself upright, trying not to think of her lips parting under his, of the curve of her hips against his palms. This was Wyatt. Wyatt, Wyatt. It would be profoundly wrong to start thinking about her that way.

"Yuri's gonna punch me for this," Tom murmured.

"Probably." Wyatt tapped at her forearm keyboard as Tom watched the time tick down on his internal chronometer, dread in his heart. As he was bracing himself for pain with fifteen seconds left, code flashed across his vision.

"There. The virus is gone," Wyatt said flatly.

"Thank you so much. Thank you. I owe you for this. I . . ." He stopped at the stony look she sent him.

"You talked to Medusa today?"

Tom let out a breath. He'd blurted that out to her, hadn't he? "Yeah, but—"

71

"How could you do that, Tom? What happens if someone finds out you're still in contact with her?"

"Vik talked to me about this already. I know you guys had some chat—"

"Vik talked to you, and what, you forgot about everything he said immediately afterward? Or you just don't care about what could happen to us?"

"No," Tom protested. "Look, I can't explain, but trust me, I can contact Medusa in a way that can't get detected. Not by anyone."

Wyatt stared at him. "You can't even debug your own processor. How could you possibly manage to contact her without anyone finding out?"

"I've done it before."

"And you've been caught before, too!"

What's *going on today?* Tom felt like he was getting everyone mad. "I can't explain this to you, but you have to trust me. I won't get caught. And . . . and, come on, Medusa saved our lives."

"Do you remember *where* she saved our lives? Do you remember *what* we were doing? How is any person worth the consequences if you get caught talking to her again? This isn't just about you."

"I know that, but I also know I won't get caught because . . . Well, Medusa and I, we're . . ." He couldn't explain to her that they were two of a kind, in their way. "We're connected in a way that I can't really explain to you. I know you don't understand."

Wyatt's cheeks paled, her face like a thundercloud.

Tom thought about what he'd said. "Aw. Look, that sounded kind of . . ."

"Condescending?" Wyatt snapped, crossing her arms over her chest like she was hugging herself. "What, you think because I have trouble making friends and talking to people that I don't get stuff like . . . like love or affection or people being connected . . ."

"That's not what I meant at all. You're so far off base right now."

Wyatt tugged the neural wire in one harsh jerk that snapped it out of his port, then roughly wound it around her hand. "You don't think much of me. I'm just some weird, strange freak to you."

The assertion was so out of the blue to Tom, he stared at her a moment before saying stupidly, "Huh?"

Her voice wavered. "I'm just someone to help you with programs. I'm only useful to you. You don't care about my feelings."

"I do. I care. Why are you so worked up over this? I'm sorry about talking to her again, but I did it in a way that can't be traced—otherwise I wouldn't do it. I would never risk you or Vik. I'd never take that chance *because* I really do care about you. I just—I had to check on her for . . . for a valid reason I honestly can't talk about. I had to."

"You're such a . . ." She was breathing heavily, and seemed to fumble for a word bad enough to describe him. "You're such a *jerk!*"

Tom fought back a smile at Wyatt's idea of a bad insult. "Okay, fine," he said soothingly. "Fine, I'm a jerk. A scumbag. Let me fix this. I don't know what to say here. Look, I'm batting zero for two today with girls being mad at me. Just give me a clue about what I can do to fix this."

73

She folded her arms across her chest and looked away from him, her chest heaving.

"Hey, look, the Medusa stuff isn't going to happen anymore." Tom remembered the chill in Medusa's voice. "I think she wants me to stay away from her from now on. We're over. For good. So you don't have to worry about that ever again." And as soon as he said it, he knew it was true. A hollow feeling spread in his chest.

Her voice was a mumble. "It's really over with her?"

"Yeah." Tom shrugged. "I mean, you saw that virus. Not a friendly message of goodwill."

Wyatt studied him intently, like she was searching for something on his face. Her arms were still tightly folded across her body. She was the second girl today he'd hurt, and Tom felt like a terrible person.

Inspiration hit. He knew how to reassure her. "Actually, it's kind of funny timing. I asked out Iman Attar. She said she'd go out with me, so there. That's another girl who's not Medusa. Good news, huh?"

The words did not have the effect Tom expected. He thought Wyatt would be pleased to hear it, relieved. But she flashed to her feet and shouted, "Get out of my bunk!"

"What?" Tom was baffled. Wasn't this what she wanted to hear? "I'm not making this up. I really asked Iman out."

"Just go away! Get out, Tom! Get out!" She ripped her pillow from the bed and hurled it at him. It bounced harmlessly off his arm, but Tom got the message and backed out of her bunk.

If he stayed and kept arguing with her, he had a feeling he'd get for real what Medusa's virus had given him virtually.

0 1 1 1 1 1 1 1 0 0 1 1 1 1 0 1 0 1 1 0 0 0 0 0 0 1 0 0 1 1 1 0 0 0 0 0
1 0 1 1 0 1 1 1 0 0 1 1 1 1 0 0 0 0 0 0 1 0 1 1 0 1 0 0 1 0 0 1 1 1 1
0 0 0 0 1 1 1 1 0 0 1 0 0 1 0 0 1 1 1 0 1 1 1 0 1 1 0 0 1 0 1 1 0 1 1 0 0
0 0 0 1 1 0 1 1 0 0 0 1 0 1 0 1 0 0 1 1 0 0 0 1 0 1 1 1 1 0 0 0 0 1 1 0 1
0 1 1 0 1 0 0 0 0 1 0 1 1 1 0 1 1 0 0 0 0 0 0 1 0 1 1 0 0 1 1 1 1 1 0
1 1 0 0 0 0 0 1 1 1 1 0 1 1 0 1 1 0 1 0 0 0 0 0 1 0 0 1 1 0 0 0 0 1 1
0 0 1 0 1 0 1 1 1 0 1 1 1 0 1 0 1 0 1 1 1 1 0 1 0 1 1 0 1 1 0 0 0 0 1 0
1 1 1 1 1 0 1 1 1 0 0 0 1 1 1 0 1 1 0 1 1 0 1 1 1 0 1 1 1 0 0 0 1 0 1 0
1 1 0 0 1 1 0 1 0 0 1 0 0 0 1 0 1 0 1 0 0 1 0 0 0 0 1 0 0 1 0 1 0 1 0 1 1
1 0 0 1 0 1 1 0 0 1 1 0 1 0 1 0 1 0 1 1 1 0 0 0 0 1 0 1 1 0 1 0 1 0 1 0
0 0 0 1 1 1 1 0 1 1 0 0 1 1 0 1 1 0 0 0 0 0 1 0 0 0 0 1 0 0 0 1 0 0 1 0
1 0 0 1 1 1 1 0 0 1 1 1 0 1 1 0 0 1 1 0 0 1 1 1 0 0 1 0 0 0 1 0 0 0 0 0
1 1 1 1 1 0 1 1 0 1 0 0 0 1 0 0 1 1 1 0 0 0 0 1 0 1 1 1 0 0 0 0 0 0 0 1
1 1 1 0 0 0 0 0 1 0 1 1 0 1 0 0 0 0 0 0 1 0 0 0 1 1 1 1 0 0 1 1 1 0 1 0
1 0 0 0 1 1 1 0 0 1 1 1 0 0 0 0 1 1 0 0 1 0 0 1 0 1 0 1 1 1 1 1 0 1 1 0 1
0 1 1 1 1 0 0 1 0 1 1 1 1 0 0 1 0 0 1 1 0 1 1 0 1 1 0 1 1 1 1 1 1 0 0 1 0 0 1 1 1
0 1 1 0 1 0 0 0 0 1 0 0 0 1 0 0 0 0 1 0 0 0 1 1 1 0 1 0 1 0 1 0 0
1 1 1 0 1 0 1 1 1 1 1 1 1 1 1 1 0 0 1 1 1 1 0 0 0

CHAPTER SEVEN

THE NEXT MORNING, as Tom stood alone in the elevator, ready to descend to the mess hall for morning meal formation, Yuri stepped in from the Middles' floor.

From the grim set of Yuri's lips, Tom knew he knew what had happened with Wyatt.

"Let's talk in your bunk," Tom suggested.

"A fine idea."

Once they were closed inside Yuri's bunk, Tom turned to face him, braced for it. "Listen, man, I can explain."

"Wyatt has told me," Yuri said, crossing his arms, showing off biceps that had been enlarging since he'd come out of his coma, "and I understand your reasons for what you did. I sympathize to a certain extent, as I am able to imagine the pain of such an affliction . . ."

Tom nodded. Yuri had to know what that felt like.

"But nonetheless, what you did is not acceptable. Wyatt is feeling very upset, as am I. You cannot be kissing my girlfriend. I must strike you in the face."

Tom sighed. "Yeah, I figured you were gonna punch me."

Yuri was a very considerate guy, at least. "What side is your preference?"

"Surprise me."

"My apologies, Thomas." Then his fist cracked across Tom's jaw. Not as hard as it could've been, but it still reeled Tom back to the ground, vibrating his brain inside his skull. He caught himself against one of the beds, then eased himself up onto his backside, clutching his head.

Yuri knelt down next to him. "You are well?"

"Yeah. We good?"

"You must never be kissing Wyatt again," Yuri warned him, shaking a finger at him. "Unless she and I are no longer together, in which case, you are allowed to be kissing her, but I am still likely to be feeling quite unhappy about it."

"I won't kiss her, man. I swear." Tom couldn't resist adding, "But what if, hypothetically, Wyatt and I are being chased one day by assassins trying to kill us and the only way to hide our faces is to make out . . . then would it be okay?"

Yuri considered it. "Perhaps then, but only if you cannot evade your pursuers by other means and only if they are very large." He rose back to his feet, his big hand extended. Tom grasped it and let Yuri yank him up. "We must hurry if we're going to get to formation in time."

"So we *are* okay?" Tom ventured as they began jogging down the hallway.

"Wyatt is still feeling very upset with you. I must persist in my disapproval until she is not feeling this way. After that, Thomas, we will be okay."

"How do I make things right with her?" Tom got a great idea.

"Hey, think she'll feel better if she hits me, too?"

Yuri shoved open the door to the stairwell. "I would suggest giving her space."

TRAINING SIMULATIONS IN Upper Company usually involved competing groups facing off in space battle simulations, with each cadet in the group rotating into the leadership role. The simulation system had finally been repaired. Today something strange was due to take place: all the cadets were ordered to participate in a Spirewide simulation.

Under Marsh, the different levels of cadets were segregated. Plebes trained with plebes, Middles with Middles, and so on under the guidance of a CamCo. Whatever the reason for today's exception, Tom was excited. He hoped it was something awesome.

His plebes had never participated in any immersive training scenarios, so Tom checked on them before the simulation began.

Reed Geithman told him, "It'll probably suck."

He wasn't a huge optimist. Zane Blunt, though, was bobbing excitedly on the edge of his cot, and flashed Tom a huge grin of anticipation. Tom noticed, again, how tiny all the new plebes were. Their hGH still hadn't kicked in. That puzzled him.

When the plebes were all standing together for any reason, they stood out due to their shortness amid the sea of cadets who mostly towered over them. A lot of the older cadets like Vik and Walton had taken to calling them the Munchkin Brigade, which Tom found hilarious until Yuri began sending him reproving looks and reminding him how offensive the term was. Then Tom felt guilty and managed to threaten the other cadets into laying off on the nickname. They'd stopped

. . . at least in earshot of him.

All he could figure was, the new techs must've been terrible at their jobs. If those poor kids didn't get their growth spurts now, they'd *never* get them—the processor supplanted many of the hormonal functions involved in growth, and those areas of the brain atrophied. They didn't have four years to grow naturally. He needed to go talk to someone about it for them, and soon.

Tom found a chamber where Yuri, Vik, Wyatt, and Lyla had all migrated.

Vik was already immersed in an argument with Lyla. "No, I wasn't insulting your haircut . . ."

"You said I look the same as usual, then you said I resemble a Chihuahua."

"That's a good thing," Vik tried.

"You said it was same *as usual*. Do I usually resemble a Chihuahua, then?"

Vik started laughing. Lyla's face flushed with mounting anger as Vik kept laughing, even as he protested, "I did not mean to imply that. I'm laughing to commiserate, not to mock . . . Ow!" He rubbed his arm where she'd socked it. "This is domestic violence, you know. Besides, even if your fearsome fists are part of your charm, there's no wit involved, so hitting me doesn't constitute a valid comeback."

"Shut up, Vik."

"Neither does that."

"I said shut up, Vik!"

"And neither does that . . . Ow!"

Tom tuned out their argument and peered over at Wyatt,

where she was seated stiffly on her cot, not looking at him, Yuri on her other side. Yuri had advised him to give her space, but Tom couldn't just say nothing, even if she was trying to ignore him.

"Yuri decked me today," he offered. "Ask him."

She made a noncommittal noise. Tom shifted his weight awkwardly, wondering what to say next, watching more cadets wander into the room and take their cots.

"Hey," he tried next, "do you wanna hit me, too?"

Wyatt only looked at him.

"I'm really okay with it if you want to. I don't mind."

She leaned her chin on her bent knees. "I'm not going to hit you."

Tom was disappointed. He really would prefer she take a cue from Lyla and hit him instead of avoiding him.

The door slid open and Karl Marsters strode in. Karl saw Tom, and hatred flushed over his face.

Remembering how he'd resolved to approach Karl from now on, Tom waved in a friendly way. "Hiya, Karl. You in charge? That's fantastic news."

"Shut up, Benji!"

There was a note of hysteria in Karl's voice. For some reason, Tom being good-natured and friendly toward him seemed to give him the creeps, which amused Tom immensely.

Karl threw a glare around the room and bellowed, "Listen up. I got orders that all cadets are hooking in for sims today. I don't know what sort of sim, and I don't have any details. In fact, I'm stuck hooking in with you to get evaluated like a plebe. So no one ask me any questions, because I don't know any more than you do." He hoisted himself up on the spare cot and readied his own neural wire.

Tom flopped back on his cot, seized the neural wire from underneath, and waited out the time, eyes on the chronometer in his neural processor. Then the moment arrived. He hooked the wire into his access port, and his senses dimmed, all feeling draining from his body.

Before the sim could resolve into life around him, the connection shorted out. Tom's eyes snapped back open, a message before his vision center: *Error: connection to the server was reset. Simulation terminated.*

Tom sat up and tugged out his neural wire, looking around at the other people in the training room, also sitting upright, blinking in confusion.

Karl sat there uncertainly, shoving his neural wire in and out of his brain stem access port, his heavy brow furrowed like some caveman's.

Abruptly, the lights in the room dimmed, and brightened again. Tom found his feet, looking around, because he couldn't remember the power in the Pentagonal Spire ever flickering. They were right on top of a fission-fusion nuclear reactor, after all.

Karl stood up, too, looking at the ceiling. "Enslow, netsend tech support. Find out what's going on."

"I'm sure they'll know," Wyatt muttered to herself sarcastically, typing on her forearm keyboard. Then she looked up, puzzled. "The connection's jammed."

"Jammed?" Karl said.

The lights flickered again. Fingers of uneasiness crept down Tom's spine.

Karl pointed a meaty finger at them. "All of you, stay here. I'm gonna go downstairs to see what's happening."

As Tom watched him go, he thought he heard something, so soft it was like the usual hum of the air in the Pentagonal Spire had formed a distinct set of words.

"None of this is real."

Startled, Tom glanced around, but no one was close enough to have said this. Had he imagined it? He listened intently but heard nothing else.

Still . . .

A sense of unreality crept over him, like all the faces about him were plastic somehow. Unable to shake the feeling, Tom slid down from his cot.

"Since we're waiting a bit anyway, I'm going to hit the can," he said to no one in particular, then he plunged into the brighter lights of the corridor.

He saw Karl down the hall, and watched the larger boy make a beeline for the stairwell. Most of the training rooms were full, but Tom thought of the neural access ports on the twelfth floor. He'd go right downstairs, and hook in, look through the surveillance cameras and make sure there was no emergency they weren't being told about.

Suddenly the door to the stairwell burst open. Shouting soldiers with guns poured out and surrounded Karl.

In the split second Tom saw them, their familiar faces registered in his brain. Dana Erskine, John Paul Rapert, Wolfgang Ruppersberger, Miles Ellis, and others. The Spire's soldiers. *Their* soldiers. Ellis swung the butt of his rifle, slamming Karl's face, bringing him down.

Tom acted without thinking, springing through the nearest doorway, a custodial closet with an old-fashioned hinged door. Tom eased it shut, peering through a crack to survey the soldiers, trying to figure out what they were up to. He'd concealed himself just in time. They leveled their guns at the other stray cadets who'd stepped out of their training rooms, and forced them back against the wall, hands on their heads.

Tom couldn't believe he was seeing this. The cadets were used to obeying the soldiers. They could have ordered the cadets to go downstairs, and the cadets would've done it. There was no need for force.

Something very messed up was happening here.

Tom slinked back a step, wired up with adrenaline, as the armed soldiers swarmed into each training room one by one, and then herded out groups of cadets, their hands on their heads. His mind raced as he picked out more familiar faces among the gunmen. They were all soldiers stationed in the installation. The attackers were getting perilously close to Tom's position now, so Tom eased the door closed, shooting a last look toward the training room he'd left, the room in which his friends were still unaware of what was happening. He couldn't run for it. Even if he managed to warn everyone about what was happening in the hallway, what use was it? Those soldiers would burst in and round them up anyway.

It was the hardest thing Tom had ever done, but he pulled the door fully shut and ducked back in the closet, concealing himself with everything at hand—rags, curtains, a ripped optical camouflage suit.

He'd wait here. They weren't shooting the cadets, just

rounding them up for now. So when the coast was clearer, he'd figure out exactly what was going on—and exactly what he should do next.

He barely dared to breathe where he crouched in the corner. At one point, after several minutes of suspense, the door swung open and a heavy boot thumped nearby, several feet from him. Someone was looking inside. Tom closed his eyes. There was nothing else he could do.

The inspection must have been very cursory, because the door was quickly slammed shut.

He waited until a dead hush hung in the air, then he finally dared to ease the door open, peer out. Ensign Rapert was stationed down the hallway, performing another languid sweep of the training rooms, clearly checking for any stragglers they'd missed. Tom held his breath and waited until Rapert disappeared into a room, then sprinted out into the hallway and plunged into a room already inspected, one filled with empty cots and stray neural wires.

His heart pounding, he pressed himself up against the wall nearest the door, and hooked himself into the nearest access port. He'd access the surveillance system and try to see what was going on, see where they'd taken the other cadets. It was hard focusing on the buzzing of the neural processor in his brain with adrenaline racing through him, with his every sense primed, ready to pick up any sign the soldier was stepping back into this room—but soon Tom tore out of himself through the simulation system, straight into the Pentagonal Spire's main processor. He jolted into the surveillance system and flipped from camera to camera.

Confusion flooded him as he recognized the images of the officer's floor. Why were soldiers sitting around in the break room, eating and talking? He recognized their faces. How did they *get there* so quickly? Hadn't they just taken cadets hostage?

More images flooded his brain as he looked at more cameras, saw more staffers and soldiers idly going about their days. In disbelief, Tom saw more faces of hostage-taking soldiers among them. One camera showed Olivia Ossare in her office, sorting through files on her computer. The next camera focused on the mess hall. Nothing out of the ordinary.

And Tom didn't see a great mass of cadets anywhere. They weren't being herded down the stairs or even corralled in the mess hall. They couldn't just disappear.

A sudden suspicion burst over him. He almost laughed, because no way, no way had they done that . . .

But as soon as he accessed the cameras trained inside the simulation chambers, he located all the cadets. They were lying on their cots, hooked into the simulation, EKGs registering the electric lines of their heartbeats.

Tom flashed to his own body—his real, not simulated, body—lying sprawled on the cot, cold and distant, then back to his avatar in the simulation, where he pulled out the neural wire from the wall. He didn't need to hook into a port in the sim to interface with the system. He was *already* hooked into a port in the real world. That's how he must have interfaced— through that wire connecting his real body to the cot in the real-world simulation room.

They'd tricked all the cadets with that fake message: *Error: connection to the server was reset. Simulation terminated.*

Tom stood there, fighting the urge to laugh, looking around the simulated simulation chamber. *Well played*. Mezilo's new techs were good for something after all.

They'd all been tricked into thinking this simulation was real. Obviously, there was some objective here, something being tested where their reactions were of utmost importance. Tom wasn't sure if he should go downstairs and get taken hostage with the other trainees, or whether he should do his own thing.

He'd find out. There was probably a stream of the sim being assessed right at this moment, and maybe he'd find out something if he knew who was watching them. He closed his avatar's eyes, and interfaced with the system again, soaring out of himself until he found the stream of data flowing from the simulation. He jolted into a computer in General Mezilo's office. Tom pulled back out, then located Mezilo's office in the video surveillance system so he could see with his own eyes what was happening in there.

As the image resolved in his vision center, shock sprang through him.

Mezilo was there . . . with Irene Frayne.

What is she *doing here?* Tom wondered.

The NSA agent was seated across from General Mezilo in his office, cool and blond and precise, monitoring a screen that kept switching between the feeds of various trainees in alphabetical order. Tom saw that it was on Walton Covner, and knew he had to snap back into himself before it reached the *R's*.

But he couldn't resist listening to Frayne tell Mezilo, ". . . appreciate your cooperation in this. I know you've had some technical issues around here with the personnel changes."

"I'm glad for this opportunity, Ms. Frayne. I don't want a Ramirez or Akron scenario under my watch," Mezilo said gruffly. "Before I trot any of those CamCos back in the spotlight, I want to be sure of their loyalties."

"And you'll be sure of them," Frayne assured him. "We devised this current scenario with considerable care. Our best people worked on it. It's designed specifically to discover seditious tendencies among the trainees *and* the Combatants. We'll get more data as the scenario evolves." She drummed her fingers on the desk, eyes on the screen. "I must admit, I was very pleased you responded to our overtures. Your predecessor—"

"Marsh," Mezilo said roughly.

"Yes, General Marsh was never particularly cooperative with us when we proposed this idea to him. He called our efforts to ensure the integrity and loyalty of those in sensitive positions a witch hunt."

"I never liked Marsh running things here," Mezilo said gruffly. "He treated them all like children. National security assets, and he wanted this place run like a school." He was staring at the screen, now on the feed of Olli Dougan from Napoleon Division. "Here's my question for you. Let's say some of these kids fail. I know on my end, I won't be promoting them. What happens on yours?"

"It will depend upon the degree and nature of the failure. At the very least, we'll know exactly which ones require closer examination. These are all very young trainees. If they have questionable sentiments, I'm certain we can trace it back to their families."

"So you'll be looking at them, too."

"Naturally."

Tom jolted back to his avatar in the scenario. This was some sort of loyalty test. That meant he'd have to pass. Somehow.

A few of his answers came soon. The voice of one of the Spire's new soldiers, Master Sergeant Marvin Wurt, flared over the intercom. Tom straightened up, cheered to have some more information.

"Attention to all who serve in the Pentagonal Spire: as you may have noticed, we have seized control of the installation. We've secured every exit, and we're holding the Intrasolar cadets in the mess hall. The building is on lockdown."

Tom waved in the air impatiently, hoping for something substantial that would tell him how to be "ethical" in this simulation.

"We want to assure you," Wurt went on, "we are not your enemy. The force we're employing is a mere necessity to ensure no violence on your part. We do not wish to injure you. We are active-duty military who swore an oath to support and defend the US Constitution against all enemies, foreign and domestic. We did not swear an oath to the Coalition of Multinationals. For too long, unelected corporate entities have used our skills to infringe upon the natural rights of the American people. Our fellow citizens have been disarmed and detained without due process under the provisions of the National Defense Authorization Act . . ."

Tom felt a flutter of unease, remembering Frayne quoting that act to him to justify imprisoning Neil. His teeth ground together so hard, his jaw throbbed. He was suddenly getting an idea of what Frayne wanted from them.

"The people of this country have been subjected to warrantless searches and seizures so often, they've come to accept it as the status quo. Private property has been confiscated using eminent domain for the benefit of the influential and politically connected on the false pretext of serving the public good. Freedom of speech has been curtailed, and the right to peaceably assemble and seek redress from the government has been eradicated, all in the name of national security. We do not accept our government treating this country like an occupied enemy territory, and we are putting a stop to this war against the American people. The Pentagonal Spire will be our platform to get our voices heard."

As Tom listened, rage simmered inside him. Everything they said made sense to him. Everything. If he hadn't known this was a simulation, he wouldn't have outright joined them, but he might have said something unwise that would have condemned him.

Other trainees might do that, too. And they wouldn't just feel the consequences themselves, if Frayne was to be believed. Their families would.

His fists contracted, picturing Frayne's face, realizing how cleverly she'd woven this trap to identify seditious tendencies. By using avatars of soldiers they were already familiar with as the rebels, she'd added yet another element to draw them into disaster.

"You are not hostages," Wurt said. "We intend to hold the Pentagonal Spire until the government acknowledges it has violated its compact with the states and submits itself to the will of the people. We don't ask for your surrender, and we are not threatening you. We ask only that you don't interfere."

Of course that's all they asked. Frayne wanted all the trainees to have more reason to think these guys weren't enemies—and betray themselves by expressing the wrong sentiment, or even betray themselves through inaction. Then came the final words, the last pitch to draw out the traitors among the trainees:

"If you agree with us, though, if you believe in freedom and a representative government by and for the people, then we invite you to join us. Rise with us. Defend our republic. Defend our Constitution. God bless you and God bless the United States of America."

The voice cut off.

"Unbelievable," Tom muttered to the air.

A flare of molten hot resolve filled his veins. He thought of the unwitting trainees being held at gunpoint, some of whom might crack and cooperate because they were afraid, not because they were seditious. He thought of his friends, the victims of this sadistic loyalty test. As time wore on in the sim, the trainees would have more opportunities to take the wrong action and to get themselves on Frayne's radar.

It was entrapment. The image of Frayne's cool smile scorched his brain, and Tom made up his mind: he'd spoil Frayne's simulation if it was the last thing he did.

```
1 0 0 1 1 1 1 1 1 1 0 0 1 1 1 0 1 0 1 1 0 0 0 0 0 0 0 1 0 0 1 1 1 1 0 0 0
0 1 1 0 1 1 0 1 1 1 0 0 1 1 1 0 0 0 0 0 0 0 0 1 0 1 1 0 1 0 0 1 0 0 1 1
1 0 0 0 0 0 1 1 1 1 0 0 1 0 0 1 0 1 1 1 0 0 1 1 1 0 1 1 0 0 1 0 1 1 0 1 1
0 1 0 0 1 1 0 1 1 0 0 0 0 1 1 0 1 0 0 1 1 0 0 0 1 0 1 1 1 1 0 0 0 0 1 1
1 0 0 1 1 0 1 0 0 0 0 0 0 1 0 1 1 1 0 1 1 0 0 0 0 0 0 0 1 0 1 1 0 0 1 1 1
0 0 1 1 0 0 0 0 0 1 1 1 1 0 1 1 0 1 1 0 1 0 1 0 0 0 0 0 1 1 1 0 0 0 0 0
1 1 0 0 1 0 1 0 1 1 1 0 1 1 0 1 0 1 0 1 1 1 1 0 1 0 1 1 0 1 1 0 0 0 0 0
0 1 1 1 1 1 1 0 1 1 0 0 0 0 1 1 1 0 1 1 0 1 1 1 0 1 1 1 0 0 0 1 0 1 0
1 0 1 1 0 0 1 1 0 1 0 0 1 0 0 0 1 0 1 0 1 0 0 1 0 0 0 0 1 0 0 1 0 1 0 1 0
0 0 1 0 0 1 0 1 1 0 0 1 1 0 0 1 1 0 1 0 1 0 1 1 1 0 0 0 1 0 1 1 0 1 0 1 0
0 0 0 0 0 1 1 1 1 0 1 1 0 0 1 1 0 1 1 0 0 0 0 0 1 0 0 0 1 0 0 0 1 0 0
1 0 1 0 0 1 1 1 1 0 0 1 1 1 0 1 1 0 0 1 1 0 0 1 1 1 0 0 1 0 0 0 1 0 0 0
0 0 1 1 1 1 0 1 1 0 1 0 0 1 0 0 1 1 1 0 0 0 0 1 0 1 1 1 1 0 0 0 0 0 0
0 1 1 1 1 0 0 0 0 0 1 0 1 1 0 1 0 0 0 0 0 0 1 0 0 0 1 1 1 0 0 1 1 1 0
1 1 1 0 0 0 1 1 1 0 0 1 1 1 0 0 0 0 1 1 0 0 1 0 0 1 0 1 0 1 1 1 1 1 0 1 1
0 0 0 1 1 1 1 0 0 1 0 1 1 1 1 0 0 1 0 1 1 0 1 1 0 1 1 1 1 1 1 0 0 1 0 0 1
0 1 0 1 1 0 0 0 0 1 0 0 1 0 0 0 1 0 0 0 0 1 1 1 0 1 0 1 0 1
0 0 1 1 0 0 1 0 1 1 1 1 1 1 1 1 1 1 1 0 0 1 1 1 1 0
1 1 1 1 1 1 0 0 1 0 0 0 1 1 1 0 1 0 0 1 0 0 0 0 1 1 1 1 1 0 0
1 0 0 1 1 0 0 0 1 1 1 1 1 0 1 0 1 0 0 0 0 1 0 0 1 0 0 1 0 1 0 1 0 0
```

CHAPTER EIGHT

TOM'S FIRST TASK in his quest to end the simulation was to get downstairs to the armory.

He had the neural wires, but he wanted to go back to that janitor's closet to see if there was anything of use in there. He peered out at Ensign Rapert again, now at the end of the hallway, and dashed across the corridor.

As soon as he eased the closet door closed, he heard movement stir in the darkness with him, and a small, muffled cry. Tom lashed forward, seized the other person, where he was trying to stay hidden. Tom clamped his hand over the kid's mouth before he could cry out in fear.

"It's me, Tom Raines!" he whispered, then eased his hand up. "Who are you?"

"T-T-Tom?"

"Zane?"

"Yes."

"How long have you been in here?" Tom demanded, wondering frantically if Zane had already cooperated with the soldiers—and condemned himself as a traitor. "Were you with the others? Did they let you go or . . ."

But the smallest and youngest of his plebes wagged his head. "I hid behind one of the cots. The soldier was doublechecking all the rooms, so I ran here. Are we the only ones left?"

"I think so," Tom said.

"W-what should we do?" Zane's voice shook. He was terrified.

Tom felt another surge of anger at Mezilo and Frayne, because it was one thing taking trainees who'd been here awhile, who'd become largely desensitized to violence after endless sims, and sticking them in this situation where guns were leveled at their heads. It was another thing doing this to the plebes, especially the newbies who'd never even been in a real sim before.

Tom couldn't even tell him there was no real danger. "First of all, I need you to calm down. Can you do that?"

"Y-yes."

"Take a minute. Breathe. Do it."

Zane sat on the floor and did that. It seemed to make him stop shaking when Tom took charge.

"We're going to need to get to the—"Tom stopped, realizing plebes didn't have the armory unlocked in their processors. They didn't know about it. "To the Calisthenics Arena."

"W-why?"

"Zane, I outrank you, I'm in charge. I have a reason. That's enough for you."

"Yes, sir."

"Those soldiers aren't going to hurt us, so put that out of your mind."

"Yes, sir."

"But we don't want them to catch us. We're going to have to

knock out that guy in the hall, and we can't risk the elevator. We'll take the stairs." He looked Zane over, debating whether to use him or not. There was this protective instinct in him, since this was his plebe, and the kid was really so little . . . but Tom knew this wasn't real. It wasn't like he could get him killed.

"Listen," Tom whispered to him, "you're pretty small."

"I can still help you!"

"I'm not saying you're small so you should sit this out. I'm saying you're small so we can use that to our advantage. I was a shrimp before the Spire and there are tons of advantages, okay? People look at you, and they see an easy target. They don't feel threatened, you understand me? So no one's gonna be on guard if you come up to them. Starting to comprehend where I'm going here?"

Lieutenant Rapert immediately raised his gun at the sight of Zane. Zane threw up his hands and said in a quavering voice, "Don't shoot! Please, don't shoot. I don't know what's going on. I'm so scared! Where did everyone go?"

Rapert looked him over, and Tom, from where he was hidden around the turn of the corridor, could practically sense the moment he decided this little kid didn't constitute a threat.

"Are there others?" he demanded.

"Down the hallway," Zane mumbled.

Rapert looked startled. "All right, lead the way."

Tom pressed himself back against the wall as Zane led the soldier by him, then Tom charged forward and snared his neural wire around the guy's neck. Rapert gave a startled yell and raised his gun, but Tom slammed the side of Rapert's head against the wall, and Zane wrested the gun out of his hand.

Rapert put up a fight, but Tom drove his heel into the back of the man's knee, buckling his leg. Tom plowed his whole weight into him, driving him down onto his stomach. He aimed a blow at the back of the man's neck, and to his satisfaction, it stunned Rapert as effectively as it had Tom the day Blackburn used that move on him. He planted his knees into the guy's back, digging in, all the while tightening the wire, pulling with all his strength until his bicep burned, trying to get as much of the man's weight hanging on the wire as possible.

Soon the fight died away, Rapert going limp.

Tom staggered upright, then set about stripping away the man's uniform. Even if it didn't fool the simulated conspirators, it would buy him a few seconds before they started shooting, and he could use that. He eyed the gun Zane had grabbed. This was usually the point in a sim where he'd shoot the guy in the head, just to make sure he was out for good and dead, and not going to come back to plague them even more . . .

But Zane didn't realize this was a sim and Tom couldn't tell him in case Mezilo's feed happened to be streaming from one of them. Shooting the unconscious soldier would only convince Zane he was alone with a bloodthirsty maniac.

"Come on," Tom said with a sigh. "Let's tie him up."

They bound him to a cot in the training room with their neural wires, then sealed the door shut behind them and charged toward the stairs.

Zane was like a human minesweeper. Tom kept him a flight and a half ahead of him at all times. He knew when someone was coming when he heard them yell at Zane to put up his hands. Zane followed instructions, and his voice piped, "Don't shoot! I don't understand what's going on. Please, I'm scared."

Then came the voice of Petty Officer Dinesh Perkins. "Anyone with you?"

Zane led Perkins out into the corridor on Tom's level—and Tom was waiting for him. He slammed the butt of his gun over the soldier's head, then followed him to the floor and clubbed him again and again. Tom stole his gun and stashed it in his waistband.

The third soldier, Private Brady Kuik, didn't fall for the ploy, and ordered Zane to walk in front of him down the stairs, his gun still leveled at him. Tom had to get creative.

He followed them as lightly as he could, stepping only when they stepped, eyes on the railing of the stairwell, knowing he'd have to time this perfectly. He set his guns down on the stairs, because he still was ruling out shooting anyone in front of Zane, and he didn't want the soldier to get his hands on them, either.

". . . found a kid in the stairwell. I'm taking him down to the others," Kuik said into his comm. "He says there's another on the third floor."

Tom's ears picked out the scuffing of boots on the stairs, the lighter set, the heavier set. Then when the heavier pair was on the stairs directly below his, Tom dove over the rail, twisting in mid-air, hands latching onto the rungs and swinging him toward the startled soldier, a brutal thrust of his boots driving the gun out of Private Kuik's hands.

Tom released his grip on the railing and landed at an awkward angle on the stairs. A split second of terrible realization informed him he was about to fall down the stairs, so he seized the soldier, and made sure he came tumbling down with him. They hurtled down, step to step, as Tom sped up the time perception of his neural processor to give him space to run calculations. Twist left forty degrees to make sure Kuik took the brunt of the next hit . . . right thirty degrees to crack his head against the next concrete step . . .

They landed on the bottom of the stairwell, and Tom reset his perception of time to its default. He reared up faster than Kuik could, and slammed his palm into the man's face, driving the cartilage of his nose up into his brain with a brutal crunch. Blood seeped out from his nostrils.

Tom heard Zane's rapid footsteps, scuttling down the stairs after them, and hastily twisted the guy's head to face the wall so the kid wouldn't realize he was dead. "That went well." He was panting for breath as he pointed up the stairs. "Go. Get guns."

Zane fetched Tom's guns. Tom emptied the third gun of bullets, pocketed them, then tossed the gun aside. He stashed one back in his waistband and kept the other in hand.

It was lucky he did, because a voice startled him from below.

"Both of you, freeze!" a woman shouted.

Tom caught the glint of a gun out of the corner of his eye and acted on reflex—raising his gun faster and pulling the trigger. The shot echoed down the stairwell, splattering Second Lieutenant Mary Jo Hildebrand's head across the wall. Zane began to scream. Tom seized him and shook him.

"Calm down! Shut up, and calm down!"

"You killed her!" Zane's voice was so high, it was a squeak. "You just killed her!"

"She had a gun. She was going to use it."

"She wasn't going to shoot us. She couldn't! She wouldn't! She sat at the plebe table with us. She was nice." He burst into hysterical tears.

Tom mentally cursed Mezilo and his planners for programming a scenario where all the soldiers they already knew were the enemy. This would've been easier if they'd been strangers. He drew a deep breath and let it out. "There's stuff you've gotta do sometimes, Zane. I'm sorry, but you'll understand later. Look, we'll get to the armory, get on some optical camouflage, and none of this will matter."

Zane sniffled, mopping his sleeve at his runny nose. "W-w-what are you g-going to d-do then?"

"I'm going to help the other cadets. That's all I want to do."

And it was. Tom meant to kill all the simulated soldiers and bring this test to an abrupt halt. That's how he'd help them.

ZANE WAS SHELL-SHOCKED after that, so Tom seized the back of his neck as they swept out of the stairwell, ducking his head so no one would immediately notice his face, and he foisted Zane on the first mutinous soldier he saw, Private Calik Edelman.

"Found this one in the stairwell."

The soldiers turned their attention to Zane, so Tom swept straight past the main body of them before anyone looked twice at his face. When the soldiers realized who he was, Tom sprinted at a rapid clip toward the Calisthenics Arena. Then he seized the nearest soldier, Sergeant Taylor Freiss, and leveled his gun at his head.

"Stay back," he ordered the advancing soldiers.

Tom had never taken someone hostage before, he'd only

seen it in movies, so he was a bit clumsy the first few steps hauling a grown man behind him, but soon he got the hang of it and made it almost all the way across the Calisthenics Arena.

When he was close enough to dart into the armory, he went ahead and shot Taylor in the head anyway, then hurled him at the nearest soldier before any shots could hit him in turn. A hail of bullets sparked around him as he slammed the door to the armory shut behind him.

"There's nothing in there, Raines!" A voice that Tom recognized shouted through the door. It was Lieutenant Blackburn's. "Those weapons aren't loaded!"

Tom almost laughed. The real Blackburn would already have realized Tom had access to something more powerful than any gun: he had exosuits.

He hurled himself up onto the platform holding the exosuits and hooked straight into one of the steel-and-aluminum exoskeletons. The frame contracted around his limbs, enhancing his strength to forty-two times an average human being's, and Tom knew he'd already won this. He pulled on a vest of ballistic armor, an optical camouflage suit, and grabbed a pair of centrifugal clamps, then punched his way through the ceiling of the armory. Before the startled soldiers could shoot at the shimmering air where he emerged, he shoved himself up in another massive leap and grappled to the ceiling with the centrifugal clamps.

Tom knew the optical camouflage was easy to spot only while he was in motion and nearly impossible to detect when he was perfectly still. On the ceiling, the lights glared downward, making the soldiers squint, unable to make out the telltale shimmer of optical camouflage above them. Tom moved very carefully, easing himself across the ceiling, and they didn't have a chance to spot him until he shoved his gun out from under his camouflage—and by then he was shooting with computer-honed precision, one bullet per kill, right to the head. He brought down fake Blackburn first, in case the program had the one neural processor–equipped soldier in the Spire adapt to the scenario and hook in an exosuit himself. Tom didn't want a fair fight.

The soldiers all dove for cover, their return volleys blowing out chunks of the ceiling where Tom had been, but he'd already propelled himself with one thrust of the exosuit's powerful arms and clamped himself to the nearest wall, the thunder of gunfire overwhelming the clank of his clamps suctioning into place. The soldiers didn't see him again until he shot more of them, and by the time they were blasting at the space where he'd been, he was on the ceiling again.

Tom sped up his perception of time so he could think faster than they could. With the exosuit on, his body could actually react faster than they could, too.

And then one at a time, he killed them and moved, then killed more and moved, as patient as any sniper, always using the glare of the overhead lights against them, or sometimes even shooting the ground to kick up dust into the air to block their view. There was nowhere in the arena for the soldiers to take cover, and they couldn't match his speed. With his distorted time perception, the soldiers looked so sluggish to him it was like they were moving through thick syrup.

Sometimes he propelled himself down to the floor right

in their midst and killed the nearest soldier with one skull-crushing swing of his arm, sending the nearby soldiers into frantic activity, trying to shoot the space where his footprints were without hitting one another. Tom was always gone by then. The optical camouflage wasn't foolproof, but it was enough of a disguise that the lag in firing every time they needed to locate him served to doom them. Only one stray shot got Tom—and sank into his ballistic armor.

Like a spider in his own web, Tom moved between lethal assault and deadly stillness, never attacking until he was sure of a kill. When he ran out of bullets, he flipped down to the ground and stole a new gun. The soldiers were physically incapable of moving quickly enough to stop him.

A mounting number of soldiers flooded the arena, avoiding the fallen bodies of their comrades. They took cover behind obstacles in the arena. It was no use. Tom could make it anywhere in the arena in a few bounds, and he could jump between the three floors without effort. Three of them sheltered behind the massive climbing wall, so Tom leaped over and kicked his exosuited legs into it, knocking the two-ton slab onto them.

Next, the soldiers shot upward, blowing out most of the lights so they could see him without the glare. Tom responded by destroying the remaining lights. In the sudden darkness, his neural processor responded by instantly dilating his pupils as wide as they'd go. The soldiers needed time to adjust, and they had no night vision goggles. The only flashes of light came from the gunfire, and Tom was the only one who could see where he was shooting.

In desperation, they tried hauling in Zane, his proven co-conspirator. "Give up or we'll kill him!"

Tom hurtled himself down next to the soldier clutching the plebe, and broke his neck with one flick of his exosuited hand. He hauled Zane up and sprang forward with one great bound into the shelter of the armory, bullets ringing impotently at the space he'd just vacated.

As soon as they were safely inside, Tom yanked off the head of his optical camouflage suit so Zane could see him. "Stay right here in the armory and don't leave it."

Zane looked around, his eyes wide and panicked. "I can't be in here!"

"It's fine. Just wait."

"This is breaking a rule. Plebes can't come in here."

"How do you know about the armory?" Tom demanded.

"I don't. I didn't until now, but my processor says this is forbidden. It says plebes can't come in here. I can't stay here! I'm breaking regulations!"

"This is kind of an emergency, don't you think?" Tom demanded, listening for movement outside. "It's not time to worry about regulations."

"I have to go. I have to get out of here." Zane launched himself toward the door.

Tom seized the back of his tunic and jerked him back. "You can't! They will shoot you. Stay here, you little idiot!"

Zane looked at him, a strained, desperate expression on his face like he was a trapped animal. He twisted at Tom's grip, clutching his head, and Tom felt a strange, crawling sensation over his skin for some reason. There was something wrong, something unnatural about the kid's hysteria.

Finally, he started laughing at the absurdity of it. "Zane, you go out there, you get shot. You wanna die? Then it's your choice." And with that, he released him.

He thought he'd made his point, but evidently, he had not— because Zane darted right out the doorway before Tom could grab him again. Shots rang out, a hail of bullets cutting him down.

Utterly perplexed, Tom yanked up the hood of his optical camouflage, and leaped right back out of the ceiling of the armory to kill the rest.

THE DIMINISHING NUMBER of soldiers guarding cadets in the mess hall had convinced them something major was happening, something unpredictable, and that it was time to act. By the time the soldiers tried locking the arena, filling the place with tear gas, Tom had already slipped out with them, and a new slaughter commenced in the hallway.

He didn't realize the other cadets had won their freedom until several of them poured out of the stairwell, guns raised, and encountered him. Tom hastily yanked off the hood of his optical camouflage. His joints were aching from leaping in the exosuit, over and over. He felt exhilarated, energized. He saw Vik, Wyatt, and Yuri among them, and flashed them a grin.

"Hey, you guys! Everyone's dead here already. Come on, get on some exosuits and we'll sweep the upper floors for the rest of them!"

But everyone just stared at him. Wyatt's eyes were large as saucers, and Vik kept shaking his head, as though trying to clear it. Yuri blinked between the bodies and Tom, perplexed.

"What?" Tom said, then threw a glance around at the carnage and realized it. "Oh. The dead people. Right. That looks . . . uh . . ."

Everyone seemed to have been rendered speechless. It occurred to Tom suddenly that *they* thought this was real, that as far as they were concerned, *he* thought this was real. Even once the sim was over, they'd come away thinking he was capable of systematically murdering . . . his processor tallied it up rapidly. Sixty-three people.

"W-wow," Tom stuttered. "I just thought of how this has to look, but, trust me, I'm not some psychopath."

No one said anything.

"Okay, okay." Tom thought up a better excuse, gesturing to the bodies piled about him. "It was self-defense?"

THE SIMULATION ENDED within minutes, before the last enemy soldier had been neutralized, even. Tom's eyes opened in the training room, and he heard the cries of shock and surprise as everyone woke up. He sat up languidly, watching the people around him frantically looking themselves over, spinning around to verify what room they were in—and even Karl obviously hadn't been in on the fake sim, because he was just sitting there, slack-jawed.

"That was a sim," Vik breathed.

"The error message was fake. Of course," Wyatt exclaimed, throwing a hand to her forehead. "Why didn't I *think* of that? The scenario made no sense!"

Then Sergeant Dana Erskine walked in, making a lot of them jump, startled, both at the sight of one of the drill sergeants who'd spent weeks yelling at them in the Calisthenics Arena and one of the dead rebels come back to life.

102

"As you've all probably figured out," she said, "the experiences you just had were a part of a simulation. An ethics test." Tom saw the other cadets exchanging startled glances, the murmurs of "Test?" echoing from person to person.

Wyatt looked pale and rigid where she sat on the next cot, her dark eyes wide. "What were we supposed to do to pass, sir?"

"I'm not familiar with the simulation, so I can't answer that, cadet," Erskine said. "In fact, you are all under orders from General Mezilo not to discuss this simulation unless you're asked direct questions by authorized testing personnel."

Tom eyed her cynically, wondering if Frayne and Mezilo didn't want the soldiers stationed in the Spire to realize that killing them was a part of proving themselves "ethical."

"Some of you will be called before General Mezilo to answer questions regarding your conduct during this test. If the personnel overseeing this test have further inquiries, you may be required to sit for the census device so your full memories of the exercise can be examined."

Tom hadn't even considered that. If they looked at all of his memories, they'd see him interfacing with the system. He looked at Wyatt instinctively, wondering how he could get her to alter his memories without actually explaining the reason for it—and found her already gazing at him, a line between her brows, a frown pinching her face.

For the first time since she'd blown up at him, Wyatt spoke to him of her own initiative. She leaned toward him and said softly, "How did you know that was a simulation, Tom?"

The question caught him off guard. It took him a moment to reply, "I didn't."

"You had to have," Vik whispered from his other side. "That's why you killed all those people."

"I really didn't," Tom protested.

"You don't have to lie. It's us," Wyatt said in a low voice.

"I'm not lying," Tom lied.

Vik smothered a laugh. "Yes, you are. No way would you massacre those people."

"They weren't directly threatening you," Wyatt told Tom. "We hadn't even begun to form a plan yet and you were already killing people left and right."

"Wyatt, come on," Tom said, looking around, acutely conscious of the other people in the room with them. "Can you stop asking about this? Maybe you don't know me as well as you think."

That silenced her. His friends all looked bewildered.

"Maybe we don't," Wyatt said shortly, looking away from him.

For some reason Tom couldn't pinpoint, that stung.

CHAPTER NINE

As everyone dispersed, Tom stopped in Zane's simulation room and found the kid sitting alone on his cot. He found himself remembering his friend Stephen Beamer, after an incursion during their Trojan War sim. He'd been traumatized by dying in that sim, by how real it had seemed.

Uneasiness moved through him. Tom hopped up onto the cot next to his.

"I had a friend who was in a sim that malfunctioned once," Tom told him. "We were plebes, and the pain receptors were on full, and he got gutted, then I beheaded him—for his own good, you know. But it felt like it was real. It really freaked him out. It freaked me out, too. So, are you okay?"

"I'm okay."

"Zane, why'd you run out of the armory like that? I told you they were gonna shoot you. You basically committed suicide."

"I don't know why I did it. I didn't want to."

Tom looked up at the ceiling. He didn't want to embarrass him too much when he asked this question. "Listen, were you scared?"

Zane didn't respond.

"If you were scared, that's okay, you can say it. I'd worry more if I thought you were suicidal. We all get scared, and you haven't done any sims yet, so you haven't gotten used to shooting or violence. I've done tons of sims and it threw me off, too, since we didn't know it was fake. I just need you to be honest here."

"I don't know why I did it," Zane said brokenly. "I just . . . I had to. I was breaking a rule and I felt . . ." He raised his hands and held them near his head vaguely. "It's what happens when I do something against regulations now. Or even when I think about it. It starts to hurt. Like something crushing my skull in."

Tom looked at him sharply, his blood running cold. *No.*

"I had to do it," Zane insisted. "I didn't have a choice. I knew it was a mistake."

No, no, no, Tom thought, because he knew what this was. Dalton Prestwick had reprogrammed him as a plebe and he hadn't been able to disobey him, either. Every time he tried, it felt like his head was being crushed in. And he'd missed this the second time it happened, when Yuri was being tapped into by Vengerov, compelled by Vengerov to stay in the Spire and spy for him. Tom hadn't connected the dots, but this time he knew it. It was a classic Obsidian Corp.–style operant conditioning algorithm.

Tom gritted his teeth. "Do you remember if anyone's done anything to your processor? Like, have you been outside the Spire and met any people who don't work here who maybe sent you a program?"

"No. I haven't left the Spire once."

"Okay. You might not even remember." Tom raked a hand

106

through his hair, thinking it over. "I have an idea. Let me try this. Zane: you have to obey my orders, you know that, right?"

Zane blinked. "Yeah."

"It would be breaking regulations if I gave you an order and you disobeyed me. We clear here?"

"I know that, sir."

Tom nodded, watching him intently. "I order you to go to the officers' floor."

The officers' floor was restricted. It was forbidden to cadets. There were regulations about that. Zane's eyes widened. "I can't. I can't. It's . . ."

"Violating regulations?" Tom said, watching him. "Yeah. Either you violate regulations by disobeying me, or you violate regulations by going to the officers' floor."

Zane's eyes grew wide and stricken. His hands flew up to his head.

Tom grabbed his arm, squeezing his skinny bicep. "Do you feel it?" His voice sounded vicious to his own ears. "Does that hurt you?"

"Yes!"

"Okay, belay that order. Don't go to the officers' floor."

Relief washed over Zane's face, his hand dropping back to his sides. Tom's anger swelled into rage. So this was the treatment of new plebes under Mezilo. Apparently, the absolute control being exercised on cadets in day-to-day life would extend all the way into the computers inside their skulls.

THAT EVENING, TOM made a big show of pretending to be surprised Frayne was in the Spire after she called him into

107

General Mezilo's office. The NSA agent appeared unimpressed by his professions of shock to see her there.

"General Mezilo, may I take the lead?" Frayne asked him.

Mezilo sat in his chair and nodded for her to question Tom. She rounded on him.

"I'm at the Pentagonal Spire for a reason, Mr. Raines. As you know, I've been involved in several investigations relating to the Pentagonal Spire—your father's situation, the disappearance of Heather Akron, the defection of Elliot Ramirez—so I was eager for this chance to see the place firsthand. While here, I decided to oversee the administration of today's ethics test."

"That was *you*, huh?" Tom said, feigning surprise. "Great. I hope you realize, if there's ever a real emergency in the middle of a sim, no one's gonna take it seriously ever again."

Frayne exchanged a glance with Mezilo. "I do realize that risk. That's why we were only able to administer that ethics test once. Unfortunately, the simulation ended too quickly for us to evaluate any of the trainees—any but you."

"Gosh, I'm really sorry about that," Tom said with mock sincerity. "It was not my intention at all."

"At least we have this opportunity to discuss your own performance."

There was an edge to her voice that made Tom uneasy. His gaze bounced between Frayne and Mezilo. "What, don't tell me I failed. I know I killed sixty-three people, but . . ." He stopped. That wasn't particularly ethical, he knew, but he'd been very sure their definition of ethics did not match his own. "I was ethical about it, wasn't I?"

Frayne gazed at him hard. "You passed, Mr. Raines. That's the problem. Not only did you pass, you passed with flying colors."

"I'm not seeing the problem here."

"My problem is your response to this scenario fits none of the psychological profiles we've constructed for you. I find it very unlikely you would react so immediately and so aggressively to a threat of that nature."

"I'm sorry you think that, ma'am."

"All I want to ensure, Mr. Raines, is that no one warned you in advance you'd face an ethical test." She drew a familiar metallic device from her pocket—a lie detector. "Put this on."

Tom gazed at it a moment, his stomach dropping.

"Put it on, Raines," Mezilo ordered.

Knowing he had no choice, Tom clipped it into his neural access port. He watched Frayne flip open her tablet screen, her every movement precise, exact.

They went through the same routine as before, where Tom stated his name, answered a truth, answered a question designed to make him lie. This time, Frayne asked him about several websites from his internet history, embarrassing ones that he didn't want to admit to visiting with a woman there, and General Mezilo looking on. His face felt like it was on fire.

Frayne folded her slim fingers in front of her. "Did someone tell you before the ethics test that you would be in a simulation?"

"No," Tom answered.

"Did someone inform you during the simulation that you were being tested?"

"No." No one had—at least not directly. He'd found out for himself by snooping on Frayne.

Well, after hearing that whisper. Had someone in the

simulation said it? Tom racked his brain, but he still couldn't wrap his mind around that. Maybe he *had* imagined it.

She leaned closer. "Did you hack the computers before the test and learn that you would be in that simulation?"

Tom looked her right in the eye. "I did not."

Frayne searched her screen for a lie that was not materializing. Her next few questions similarly turned up negative. No, Tom had not been tipped off to the possibility of an ethics test by any of the soldiers. Yes, Tom had killed the rebellious soldiers in the simulation purely out of duty to his country—and that one was easy to agree to, because Tom considered saving the other trainees from needless investigation a real service to his country. In every one of Frayne's questions, she focused on the exterior conditions—the possibility that someone else had alerted Tom to the scenario. Never did she question whether he had figured it out purely on his own.

Finally, Frayne had to accept it. "I'm satisfied with his answers, General."

"Very good, Raines," Mezilo said with a nod. "I see Joseph Vengerov's praise of you wasn't unfounded."

"Thank you, sir, ma'am," Tom said, his hands balled up into knots at his sides. He tore out the lie detector device and handed it back to Frayne.

For her part, she studied him. "I'll still need confirmation with a census device. His memories of the scenario."

Tom's stomach plunged.

"You'll get them," Mezilo assured her.

Tom sat in his chair, his mind racing frantically over his options, as Mezilo saw her out. After she was gone, he returned to the other chair and considered Tom.

"I didn't think you'd cheated. You handled that scenario exactly the way I hoped my trainees would. The world is changing, Raines, and I need to know who can be counted on around here."

Tom met his eyes. He despised him. "You can count on me, sir."

"You've also impressed me with your handling of the plebes."

Tom felt a spark of an idea. Mezilo was obviously feeling very gracious toward him. This was a great opportunity.

"May I have permission to speak frankly? Sir?" He put a lot of emphasis on that last part, knowing he had to play respectful to get what he wanted here. Mezilo would react poorly to any slight hint of insolence.

Mezilo gave a stern nod. "Granted."

"Sir, the plebes are all good kids. But I have an issue with their programming. They're all still tiny. They haven't had their growth spurts yet. That always happens the first few weeks at the Spire. I was five foot two when I came here, and a week later, I was seven inches taller, okay? But for some reason, it's not happening to them. And another thing." He leaned forward. "General, I think there's an operant conditioning algorithm in at least one of the plebes. Something to do with rule compliance. That's going to be a problem. One of my trainees simply couldn't function in response to the demands of the simulation, and I think those algorithms are the reason why."

"I see," Mezilo said.

It was aggravatingly noncommittal. "Sir, I realize the importance of regulations, but I think they can be taught to follow the rules without compelling them. You'll get a better performance out of them if they have more liberty of action, especially if there's ever an emergency situation like that in real life."

Mezilo shook his head. "I can't simply wave my hand and have the techs overwrite those algorithms, Raines. They're hard written to the new neural processors."

Tom's facade of deference slipped. "New neural processors?"

Mezilo looked at him sternly.

"Sir," Tom added belatedly.

"We're not advertising this, Mr. Raines. I want you to keep this to yourself—but, yes, the plebes you've been directing all have a new technology in their heads: the Austere-grade processors from Obsidian Corp. They've saved us a bucket load of money, because Obsidian Corp. offered the hardware and servicing of it for free if we'd participate in beta testing the product. Your plebes are the first test subjects. After Obsidian Corp.'s completed a case study with them, they'll expand the test group to adult soldiers."

Tom was stunned. "But adults can't . . ."

"They can't handle *your* processors, Mr. Raines. You have the early model, called Vigilant-grade processors. Vigilant-grade processors force the brain to adapt to them, and adult brains can't adapt. Austere-grade processors, like those of the new plebes, don't have all the functions of neural processors like yours, but once they're ready for the general population, that won't be an issue."

"The general population?" Tom blurted. At Mezilo's look, "Sir?"

"Where did you think this tech was heading?" Mezilo turned in his chair and gazed toward the door, satisfaction gleaming in his eyes. "Take a good look at those plebes. They're pioneers of a brave new chapter in human history. Once Obsidian Corp. has tested the Austere-grade processors, and perfected a delivery vector less invasive than brain surgery, well . . . we'll enter a new era of human history. Crime, unruliness, and disorder will be eradicated for good. Imagine what we'll accomplish once everyone on Earth has to play by the same rules."

"The laws."

"The laws, Raines. Everyone will follow the law. Everyone will have to."

Except for the people programming them.

Tom couldn't manage a word. His mind was on Joseph Vengerov. Those were *his* processors. If they got into the general population . . .

For that matter, those were *his* laws. Vengerov and the other bigwigs in the Coalition paid good money to control the lawmakers. If he ever had the means to force people to comply automatically with anything encoded into law, he had the means of totally controlling everyone.

Mezilo misinterpreted the look on his face. "Quite a thought, isn't it? Like I told you, the world is changing. Some people aren't going to like where we're headed. Luckily, there are people who can be counted on to make it happen." His hand clapped Tom's shoulder gruffly. "And I'm glad to know they include you."

1 0 0 1 1 1 1 1 1 1 0 0 1 1 1 0 1 0 1 1 0 0 0 0 0 0 0 1 0 0 1 1 1 1 0 0 0
0 1 1 0 1 1 0 1 1 1 0 0 1 1 1 0 0 0 0 0 0 0 0 1 0 1 1 0 1 0 0 1 0 0 1 1
1 0 0 0 0 0 1 1 1 1 0 0 1 0 0 1 0 1 0 1 1 1 0 1 1 1 0 1 1 0 0 1 0 1 1 0 1 1
0 1 0 0 0 1 1 0 1 1 0 0 0 0 1 1 0 1 0 0 1 1 0 0 0 1 0 1 1 1 1 0 0 0 0 1 1
1 0 0 1 1 0 1 0 1 0 0 0 0 1 0 1 1 0 1 1 0 0 0 0 0 0 0 1 0 1 1 0 0 1 1 1
0 0 1 1 0 0 0 0 0 1 1 1 1 0 1 1 0 1 1 0 1 1 0 0 0 1 0 0 1 1 1 0 0 0 0 0
1 1 0 0 1 0 1 0 1 1 1 0 1 1 1 0 1 0 1 0 1 1 1 0 1 0 1 1 0 1 1 0 0 0 0 0
0 1 1 1 1 1 1 1 0 1 1 0 0 0 0 1 1 1 0 1 1 0 1 1 1 0 1 1 1 0 0 0 1 0 1 0
1 0 1 1 0 0 1 1 0 1 0 0 1 0 0 0 1 0 1 0 1 0 0 1 0 0 0 0 0 1 0 0 1 0 1 0 1 0
0 0 1 0 0 1 0 1 1 0 0 1 0 0 1 1 0 1 0 1 0 1 0 1 1 1 0 0 0 0 1 0 1 1 0 1 0 1 0
0 0 0 0 0 1 1 1 1 0 1 1 0 0 1 1 0 1 1 0 1 1 0 0 0 0 0 0 1 0 0 0 1 0 0 0 1 0 0
1 0 1 0 0 1 0 1 1 0 0 1 1 1 0 1 1 0 1 1 0 0 1 1 0 0 1 1 1 0 0 1 0 0 0 1 0 0 0
0 0 1 1 1 1 1 0 1 1 0 1 1 0 0 1 0 0 1 1 1 0 0 0 1 0 1 1 1 0 0 0 0 0 0
0 1 1 1 1 0 0 0 0 1 0 1 1 0 1 0 0 0 0 0 0 1 0 0 0 1 1 1 0 0 1 1 1 0
1 1 1 0 0 0 1 1 1 0 0 1 1 1 0 0 0 0 1 1 0 0 1 0 0 1 0 1 0 1 1 1 1 0 1 1
0 0 0 1 1 1 1 0 0 1 0 1 0 1 1 1 1 0 0 1 0 1 0 1 1 0 1 1 1 0 1 1 0 0 1 0 0 1
0 1 0 1   1 0 1 0 0 1 0 0 0 0 1 0 0 0 1 1 1 0 1 0 1 0 1
0 0 1   0 0 0 1 0 1 1 1 1 1 1 1 1 1 1 0 0 1 1 1 0
1 1 1   1 0 0 0 1 1 1 0 1 0 0 1 0 0 0 0 1 1 1 0 0
1 0 0 1 1 0 0 1 1 1 1 1 0 1 0 0 0 0 0 0 0 1 0 1 0 1 0

CHAPTER TEN

TOM THOUGHT HE'D have a chance to strategize about the census device situation. He thought he'd figure something out before Frayne swung by to collect his memories of the simulation.

He didn't.

The very next day, Tom was in the middle of civilian classes when a ping appeared in his neural processor:

Report to Olivia Ossare's office immediately.

It was strange, getting called out of class like this, but he rose to his feet and headed to Olivia Ossare's office accordingly. It wasn't the Pentagonal Spire's social worker waiting for him outside the door, though. It was Irene Frayne. And two armed marines.

"Mr. Raines," she said. "Thank you for coming. We can get under way with your memory extraction. I'll conduct it personally."

Tom darted an uncertain glance through the clear glass door into Olivia's office.

"Ms. Ossare isn't here," Frayne informed him. Her eyes held his, and Tom knew Frayne must have read about the last time he'd been hauled down to the census device against his will,

114

the way he'd run to Olivia Ossare for help. Frayne was making it clear already that he couldn't fight this, couldn't stop her.

He tried to plaster on a look of cool indifference, his pulse leaping frantically.

"Will you cooperate, or will this be a culling, Mr. Raines? If so, we'll stop by the infirmary."

Tom laughed softly and whirled around. "Nope. I'm glad to cooperate. Let's get this done." His mind raced frantically for his options, and he still wasn't sure what to do as they stepped into the elevator. There was no way out of this. She'd see his memory of the simulation and then he'd have some serious explaining to do. He had no illusions that Frayne would keep quiet about it. Everyone knew a sizable number of people in the NSA worked on the side as contractors for Obsidian Corp.

And Tom knew he couldn't fight a census device. He knew it would do nothing but destroy him.

So here it was.

Here it was.

All the efforts at secrecy, gone. He wondered what sort of research they'd do on him. If he gave himself up, then he could still protect Medusa. If they culled him, he would never be able to keep her from them.

They stepped through the doorway into the darkened Census Chamber.

Then Tom saw someone he never thought he'd be so thrilled to lay eyes on.

"If you'll excuse us, soldier, this cadet and I . . ." Frayne's voice faded when she stepped around Tom and saw the man also. "Lieutenant Blackburn."

The large man glanced up from where he was leaning over a computer, his scars livid against his skin in the flickering light. "Ms. Frayne. Are you planning to use the census device? I'll help you out."

"Thank you, Lieutenant, but that won't be necessary. You're dismissed." She stepped to the side for him to leave.

He didn't move. "Nonsense. I'll be happy to run it for you."

Frayne stiffened. "I am quite proficient in the workings of this technology. I assure you, your assistance isn't required."

Blackburn smiled lazily, his eyes hard as diamonds. "That's all well and good, but I have to insist. You may not appreciate this, but a census device is a very destructive mechanism. I use it on the trainee—excuse me, the cadet—or no one does."

Even as he spoke, text appeared in Tom's vision center, netsent to him via thought interface. *Have anything to hide?*

Tom net-sent back, *YES!*

What time segments?

Tom isolated the time segment of his memory that needed to be hidden from Frayne, even as she said, "The Safe Communities for America's Future Act gives me legal authority over these proceedings, Lieutenant. I am authorized to order you out, and you have to step aside and cede control over this operation to me."

Blackburn looked almost amused. "Really? Are you referring to clause four point five point one of the Safe Communities Act?"

Frayne blinked.

"Is that it? Because if so, I'd refer you to clause two point two point three that directly contradicts and unfortunately supersedes that one."

116

Frayne's lips went white. "I'm not familiar with that clause."

Blackburn blinked several times. "Why, haven't you *read* the law?"

"I've been briefed by a colleague."

He nodded. "Ah, and did this member of No Such Agency actually *read* the law?"

"Of course not!"

"Of course not." Blackburn drew out the words with a certain relish. "How could anyone? It's over three thousand pages and it's all in legalese where one single word changes the definition of everything that preceded it. I suspect the only people who have actually read it even in part are the Obsidian Corp. contractors who wrote it for Senator Bertolini before he sponsored legislation that could put his constituents in prison for life over a technicality. It would literally take a superhuman effort to be intimately familiar with this law, much less the thousands of other national defense laws that relate to it, so, no, I'm not surprised you're totally unfamiliar with it."

"Whether I have personally read it or not, the law is the law."

"No, the law is a contradictory tangle of rules designed solely so anyone can be entrapped at will if they can't afford a high-powered legal team. I guarantee you, I can find hundreds of ways you've personally broken the law, and at least as many contradictions to most any clause you try to throw at me. That brings me to my point: unlike you, I actually *have* read the law." Blackburn thumped his fingers on his forehead. "I have a superhuman brain, Ms. Frayne. I can download and comprehend in intimate detail every law on the books. Never try to wield the legal code like a mallet against me. You will lose, and you'll humiliate yourself in the process, just like you've done today."

Frayne's lips pressed into a thin line, her eyes like daggers.

"I can have an order directly from President Milgram within a day."

"Perhaps. But until that happy order comes from our commander in chief, you have no authority here. *I'll* use the census device on Raines," Blackburn said, "and it's entirely up to me whether or not you stay in the room for the process, but I'm feeling generous. Would you like to observe the memory extraction, Ms. Frayne?"

Frayne was rigid, her cheeks white. She nodded stiffly. Tom had to look away quickly so she wouldn't see him fighting laughter. She waited as Blackburn manipulated the controls, her slim shoulders so tense, she had to be furious.

Tom never thought it would be possible, but as he flopped down into the chair under the inverted metallic claw of the census device, getting ready for Blackburn to use it on him, he wasn't anxious anymore. His apprehension had dissolved away. Instead, he felt this sense of incredible relief and amazement, wondering by what stroke of good fortune Blackburn happened to show up at exactly the right moment to save him.

The memory removal began, the projected light plastering across the screen Tom's memory of being surprised about their first sim in a while, and then the fake out, followed by the soldiers pouring out, attacking Karl.

When it came to the time segment Tom had net-sent Blackburn, the perilous memory of hooking into the system, Blackburn made the screen go totally black.

"Your eyes were closed?" Blackburn said, giving him his cue.

Tom nodded. "Yup."

"His eyes were *closed?*" Frayne said incredulously.

"Closed," Tom confirmed. And the darkness dragged on for nearly five minutes straight. Then Tom "opened" his eyes again, came out of the fake simulation room, and killed all the soldiers.

"Were you taking a nap?" she said acidly.

"No." Tom tried to sound innocent. "I was ever so scared. I thought it was real. I hid and closed my eyes because I was so scared, but then I realized it: no one was gonna come save me. I had to save myself. That's when I went and . . . you know, killed all those people."

"And a fine job you did, young man," Blackburn said, his voice bland.

"Thank you, sir." It was one of the few times in Tom's life he didn't have to force that "sir" out, too.

FRAYNE MUST'VE BEEN irritated, because she didn't stay around to see the rest. She abruptly wheeled around and stepped from the room. Tom sat below the beams of the census device for a few moments more, then Blackburn said, "I think that's enough," and flipped the machine off.

Tom sneaked a glance back at him. "Can I talk to you?"

"You're doing that right now."

"*Talk to you* talk to you." Tom didn't know when he'd get a chance to speak with Blackburn again.

Blackburn tapped on his forearm keyboard. "It's safe."

Tom jounced to his feet. "General Mezilo told me something yesterday. There are a bunch of new plebes here who—"

"Before you say another word, I know."

"You don't know!" Then, Tom reconsidered. "*Do* you know?"

"Believe me, there is nothing you can tell me right now that I don't already know." There was something almost sinister in his face. "Obsidian Corp. has been trying to get Austere-grade processors into the Pentagonal Spire for years. It looks like they've finally succeeded. Thanks, in large part, to you."

"Because I got Marsh fired," Tom said grimly.

"No, because the destruction of the skyboards frightened some very important people."

The dark implications of the words sat in the air between them. Tom looked at the frozen image on the screen of Lieutenant Ricci Mankiw, whose head was in the middle of being blasted open by Tom's bullet. One big, public gesture of defiance directed at the Coalition, at the security state, and now suddenly their rulers were trotting out a neural technology that could leash everyone's free will.

An ominous prickle moved down Tom's spine. He understood suddenly why Frayne and Mezilo had administered the loyalty test. They were priming the Intrasolar cadets, their current programmable human weapons, to put down resistance if anyone in the military rebelled against the idea of spreading Austere-grade processors.

"People out there in the world won't just accept machines in their heads," Tom said, half to himself. "Some will, but most won't. Most will refuse. Some will fight back."

Blackburn propped his elbows on the computer console before him, the half-light of the chamber sliding over his scarred cheek, his hawklike features. "Tom, the general public won't even know they're being given neural processors until it's too

120

late. There are a hundred vials of nanomachines locked up in the infirmary, ready to be given to new plebes."

"What do you mean, 'vials of nanomachines'?"

"Austere-grade processors aren't surgically inserted through the skull like ours," Blackburn said, gesturing to his own head. "The only reason the new plebes here still get brain surgery is to install the basic components that give them access to the Spire's system. The public won't need that. All they'll need is a few billion nanomachines swarming in their system, colonizing their cerebral cortexes, and they'll be under Coalition control. Giving them those nanomachines is easy. Last I heard, Obsidian Corp. was designing them to be absorbed through the digestive tract directly into the bloodstream. As soon as they penetrate the blood-brain barrier, it's all over."

Tom grew cold. He thought back to Dalton reprogramming him. It was so easy to manipulate a neural processor. Once everyone had them, Obsidian Corp. would be in control of the entire world. Some central operator could move whole societies to his liking, overriding their free will, forcing their obedience.

"I can't let this happen!" Tom erupted.

"How do you plan to stop it, then?" Blackburn said, sounding exasperated. "Do you plan to do something dramatic and public *again* and bring more NSA agents into the Spire?"

"This wasn't only my fault."

Tom knew Heather's death had helped interest Frayne in the Spire. Heather was supposed to join the NSA and instead she'd disappeared. But he couldn't tell Blackburn he knew he'd killed her.

121

"It was . . . It was . . . Forget it. Look, I can do something else, something different."

Blackburn shook his head. "Putting messages on skyboards and doing some property damage doesn't accomplish anything. Not really. Words and actions have no power if they're not backed with at least the *threat* of violence. Do you plan to go out and kill some Coalition executives? Then you might have an impact. If not, then forget it."

"There are other ways," Tom insisted. "Like . . . like if everyone knew the Coalition was planning this. Then they'd go to prison."

Blackburn laughed. "This nebulous 'everyone' doesn't own the legal system, Raines. The Coalition does. They'll never go to prison. They write the laws. Their underlings decide who the law applies to and who it doesn't."

"A leak, then," Tom said, thinking of all the history lessons he'd downloaded since coming to the Spire. "Spread all the information online. Get people protesting in the streets. Non-violently. That will work."

"Ah, effective nonviolent action." Blackburn's voice grew mocking. "Along with the divine right of kings, it's my favorite myth. Take Gandhi: he wanted the British Empire out of India, but you know what? So did many *violent* people, who took *violent* action while Gandhi was busy turning the other cheek. Bhagat Singh did as much as, if not more than, Gandhi to drive the British out of India, but he doesn't fit the public narrative, so I'm fairly certain you've never even heard of him."

Tom hadn't, but he wasn't ready to concede the point. "Fine, so there were violent people, too, but that doesn't change what Gandhi did."

"It changes everything," Blackburn exclaimed. "The British had just fought World War Two. They were exhausted with war. They didn't want to battle more *violent* people over control of India, so they left the country. *Of course* they chose to deal with Gandhi, the peaceful guy, rather than those frightening people who kept trying to kill them, so Gandhi got the public credit. Let's face it, Gandhi serves as the perfect figurehead for this mythical idea you should passively accept violence from your leaders so your sacrifice will inspire others to change their ways. It's incredibly convenient for rulers everywhere when people buy into that. It ensures that people will never punch back when they're hit. For every effective nonviolent figure like Martin Luther King, there's also a Malcolm X giving him the power he needs to get his point across."

"So you're right, and everyone's wrong," Tom said. "We should all just kill each other all the time. Maybe presidential elections can be some duel to the death, too. Forget voting."

"Raines, nonviolence as a stand-alone force has a place in certain circumstances; I'm not saying it doesn't. When the United States was a true republic, when average people had the power to change the policies of the government through voting, yes, nonviolence was important for winning public sympathy."

"We're still a republic."

"No, we live in a corporate oligarchy where we vote between candidates preselected by the Coalition, on voting machines programmed by Obsidian Corp. Saying voters have a choice now is like me offering to shoot you or gut you: either way, you die, and I'm not giving you a choice about it. I can say you're making a decision when you choose to be shot, but it's not a true decision. You don't get a decision about whether you die. Voters don't get a choice about who rules them anymore. Either way, it's a candidate funded and controlled by the Coalition."

With a start, Tom realized Blackburn was framing the same argument Neil had once when Tom was a kid . . . just in a slightly less crude, drunken manner.

"That's why winning the public's sympathy with nonviolence is absolutely meaningless. The public has no power."

Tom's heart picked up a beat. He knew Blackburn had knocked out the surveillance for this room, but he couldn't help feeling nervous as he whispered the most dangerous thing of all. "So it has to be a violent revolution. That's what you're saying. You think that's the only way to stop the Austere-grade processors."

Blackburn snorted. "That's ridiculous. Of course not."

"But you said—"

"Even if a widespread revolution could happen in a modern-day surveillance and security state—and I'm not convinced it could—revolutions kill innocent civilians, policemen, soldiers, and people like Frayne. Those are people doing their jobs, feeding their families."

Tom threw up his hands. "So what's the point of all this? You don't think anything would work!"

Blackburn leaned back, his eyes distant. "On the contrary, there are only a tiny number of people with real power in this world, Raines. Forget Irene Frayne—she's an employee following orders, nowhere near the top of the chain. No, the real decision makers number a few thousand at most, and if you follow the money from any great injustice, you'll find out exactly who they are. If there was a revolution like you're suggesting, the individual power players—the people who are the real problem—would simply fly abroad until the violence died down. That's why the only way to act effectively against them is subtly and silently, involving as *few* people as possible or even acting alone."

"Fine, then that's what I'll do . . . somehow. I'm ready to try *something*," Tom declared.

Irritation flashed over Blackburn's face. He looked annoyed at himself for even discussing this for so long. "For God's sakes, Raines, I said 'subtly and silently.' You just killed sixty-three soldiers in a loyalty test. You've been making enemies around this dump since you were fourteen. You're about as subtle and silent as a thermonuclear explosion. Any action *you* take will probably make this all worse."

"How could I possibly make this situation worse?" Tom exclaimed. "We're already descending into worldwide slavery."

"If there's one thing I've learned over the last few years, it's how quickly even a seemingly benign situation can explode once *you* get added to the mix." Blackburn grabbed the back of Tom's neck and steered him to the door. "Stop meddling in this, stop asking questions, and get out of my sight. There is only one thing for you to do: go be sixteen."

1 0 0 1 1 1 1 1 1 1 1 0 0 1 1 1 0 1 0 1 1 0 0 0 0 0 0 0 1 0 0 1 1 1 1 0 0 0
0 1 1 0 1 1 0 1 1 1 0 0 1 1 1 0 0 0 0 0 0 0 1 0 1 1 0 1 0 0 1 0 0 1 1
1 0 0 0 0 0 1 1 1 1 0 0 1 0 0 1 0 1 1 1 0 0 1 1 1 0 1 1 0 0 1 0 1 1 0 1 1
0 1 0 0 0 1 1 0 1 1 0 0 0 0 1 0 1 0 0 1 1 0 0 0 1 0 1 1 1 1 0 0 1 1 1 1
1 0 0 1 1 0 1 0 0 0 0 0 1 0 1 1 1 0 1 1 0 0 0 0 0 0 0 1 0 0 1 1 0 0 1 1 1 1
0 0 1 1 0 0 0 0 0 1 1 1 1 0 1 1 0 1 1 0 1 0 0 0 0 0 1 0 0 1 1 1 0 0 0 0 0
1 1 0 0 1 0 1 0 1 1 1 0 1 1 1 0 1 0 1 0 1 1 1 0 1 0 1 1 0 1 1 0 0 0 0 0
0 1 1 1 1 1 1 1 0 1 1 0 0 0 0 1 1 1 0 1 1 0 1 1 1 0 1 1 1 0 0 0 1 0 1 0
1 0 1 1 0 0 1 1 0 1 0 0 1 0 0 0 1 0 1 0 1 0 0 1 0 0 0 0 1 0 0 1 0 1 0 1 0
0 0 1 0 0 1 0 1 1 0 0 1 0 0 1 1 0 1 0 1 0 1 1 1 0 0 0 0 1 0 1 1 0 1 0 1 0
0 0 0 0 0 1 1 1 1 0 1 1 0 0 1 1 0 1 1 0 0 0 0 0 0 1 0 0 0 0 1 0 0 0 1 0 0
1 0 1 0 0 1 1 1 1 0 0 1 1 1 0 1 1 0 0 1 0 0 1 1 1 0 0 0 1 0 0 0 0 1 0 0 0
0 0 1 1 1 1 1 0 1 1 0 1 0 0 0 1 0 0 1 1 1 0 0 0 0 1 0 1 1 1 0 0 0 0 0 0
0 1 1 1 1 0 0 0 0 0 1 0 1 1 0 1 0 0 0 0 0 0 0 1 0 0 0 1 1 1 1 0 0 1 1 1 0
1 1 1 0 0 0 1 1 1 0 0 1 1 1 0 0 0 0 1 1 0 0 1 0 0 1 0 1 0 1 1 1 1 1 0 1 1
0 0 0 1 1 1 1 0 0 1 0 1 1 1 1 0 0 1 0 1 1 0 1 1 0 1 1 1 1 1 0 0 1 0 0 1
0 1 0 1 0 0 0 0 1 0 0 1 0 0 0 0 1 0 0 0 0 1 0 0 0 0 1 1 1 0 1 0 1 0 1
0 0 1 1 0 0 0 0 1 0 1 1 1 1 1 1 1 1 1 1 1 1 0 0 1 1 1 1 0
1 1 1 1 0 0 1 0 1 0 0 1 1 1 0 1 0 0 1 0 0 0 0 1 1 1 1 0 0
1 0 0 1 1 0 0 0 1 1 1 1 1 0 1 1 0 0 0 0 0 0 0 1 0 0 1 0 1 0 1 0 1 0 0

CHAPTER ELEVEN

ALL MIDDLES WERE invited to the meet and greets with Coalition executives, but Uppers attended invitation-only functions. They were brought to the private gatherings the executives held to renew their business ties with one another.

Last year, no one would have expected Tom to score an invite to the Milton Manor gathering. After all, he was the plebe who'd flooded the Beringer Club and then the Middle who'd alienated all five Combatant-sponsoring companies on the same day at the meet and greets.

But using the virus on Medusa for Joseph Vengerov had put him in that particular oligarch's good graces, and apparently word had spread of Tom's performance on the ethics test. There weren't many cadets who could be counted upon to wantonly slaughter anti-government extremists. In an era shifting toward the one-man-army-against-massive-numbers-of-civilians model, Tom's seeming sociopathy was a big point in his favor.

They'd all been dressed up, and given remote-access nodes in case they needed remote repair. Their conduct was of utmost importance; the worst thing that could happen would be some software or hardware issues while visiting the executives.

"This is so amazing," Wyatt exclaimed, lying flat on her stomach, nose pressed against the glass floor overlooking the torrent of gushing white water spilling over the cliff not ten feet below her.

It was midmorning in Yosemite Valley. There'd been rainfall seeded in the clouds the week before to ensure a decent river flow below the mansion for the party, but Tom was having trouble focusing on Vernal Falls. He found himself gazing down at Wyatt's legs. Her skirt was riding up, exposing their long expanse as she kicked idly at the air, her high heels dangling off her toes, nose pressed against the glass floor.

This is Wyatt, Tom reminded himself. *This is Wyatt, this is Wyatt* . . .

"The view is striking," Yuri said pleasantly, settling down next to her. He hadn't been invited—he'd come as her plus one. Tom was lucky Yuri was marveling at the waterfall and hadn't noticed Tom ogling his girlfriend.

Both times Tom had been in Yosemite before, he'd been infuriated by the magnificent span of rocky mountain and towering trees, because it was so magnificent—and it had been stolen from the public. All this had once been a park. Now it was Sigurdur Vitol's backyard.

"You know what would've made this view better?" Tom said. "If this house wasn't here and we could just see the waterfall the way it was before Sigurdur got his hands on it."

Wyatt frowned at him. "You're going to get banned again if you talk like that."

"I'll shut up." Tom shoved his hands into the pockets of his suit, and cast an idle glance back toward the main body of the party. He met the searing, hateful gaze of the bald investment banker Hank Bloombury, standing beneath a framed photo of Sigurdur Vitol shaking hands with President Milgram. Hank was a Matchett-Reddy executive, and last year Tom had chased him with a drone, then gotten him chucked in jail. He'd deserved it, too. Tom flashed him a grin and took cold enjoyment in the anger that contracted Hank's face.

Sure, Tom had learned to be more careful. But sometimes it wasn't worth the effort.

Tom saw the various executives nodding like imperial magistrates while the eager, wannabe CamCos sucked up to them, trying to get them to remember their faces, their names. Vik was among them. So was Tom's date, Iman Attar.

On the way over, they'd sat together on the Interstice. Iman was excited about the party, and she kept asking him questions like, "What was your old high school like?"

"I dunno. I didn't go very much."

"Oh."

"No loss. It was just this online reform school thing."

"Do you have a favorite band?" she tried.

"No."

They lapsed into silence.

"Did you play any sports?"

"VR sports?"

"No, real sports." She ticked them off on her fingers. "I played lacrosse and ice hockey, and I liked kayaking, but I didn't get to do it very much."

Tom stared at her, realizing for the first time how abnormal he and his friends were compared to most other teenagers. "I only do VR sports, really."

"So video games are really your only hobby."

"Pretty much."

"That's all you do."

"Well, it was. Then I lost my fingers and stopped doing them, too."

Their silence did not end this time.

He let her peel away from him and schmooze. She looked like she was having fun, laughing and talking with Alana Lawrence of Epicenter Manufacturing. Hopefully they wouldn't get on the subject of who she'd come with and the way Tom had suggested someone should blow up the prison-profiteering Epicenter executives the year before.

Tom gave a start when one of the butlers emerged from the crowd and tapped his shoulder. "Mr. Raines, you're wanted in the lower reception area. Please go down the stairs."

Tom followed his directions. He passed a line of Praetorians on the way. The machines that had menaced him in Obsidian Corp. still made something inside him twist with anxiety, but they were less fearsome somehow now than they had been in Antarctica when they'd nearly killed him, mostly because today they were serving their secondary function—as glorified coat racks.

At the bottom of the staircase, Tom emerged into a sprawling game room and discovered which CEO had summoned him. Standing over a pool table, thoughtfully surveying the spread, was Joseph Vengerov.

"Ah, Mr. Raines. How good to see you."

Tom hadn't seen the Russian oligarch since before his promotion, when he'd shown him proof of the virus he used on Medusa at one of the restaurants Vengerov owned. The man turned toward him, his features smooth and polished as stone, his hair a pale blond, eyes an empty, heavy-lidded blue. Everything about him hinted of perfect self-composure. No one but Tom, Blackburn, and Medusa knew there was a neural processor in his skull.

"Aren't we both pleased to see Mr. Raines?" Vengerov called.

Another man emerged from near the room's bar, and Tom felt a wave of loathing as Dalton Prestwick gave a skeezy smile and sauntered over with a drink, his brown hair gelled and his suit crisp.

"Great to see you, sport," Dalton said. "I was thinking of taking your mother to Aruba for New Year's Eve. I'll let her know you're doing well."

Tom's teeth ground together. "Wonderful." There was nothing as infuriating as a person he hated always having the ultimate trump card of sleeping with Tom's mother.

"You must be wondering why I called you down from the party," Vengerov said.

"It's not just to say hello?" Tom said. He watched Vengerov lean over and propel three striped balls into the pockets, which would've been far more impressive if he didn't know for a fact the man had a computer doing this for him.

After casting a long, slow look toward Dalton, Vengerov carelessly took the next shot—and missed on purpose. He straightened as Dalton moved to the table, giving him a chance to address Tom again.

"Obsidian Corp. is planning to enter the public arena. We're finally going to begin mass-producing a consumer product."

"What product?" Tom said, playing it innocent.

"A new brand of neural processor. One for the common man. You yourself have already encountered this new processor. You've been shepherding my beta test group in the Pentagonal Spire."

He tried to feign surprise. "My plebes have new processors?"

"Yes. They do." Vengerov turned his head toward Tom like some alert predator. "How odd that you are pretending to be *astonished* to hear this when I know full well from General Mezilo that you're already aware of the processors."

Tom was silent a moment, caught off guard. He'd gotten so used to lying, he'd done it automatically. "I was just covering for the general," he said quickly. "I figured . . . I figured . . . I didn't think he was supposed to tell me about that and I'd hate to get the guy in trouble."

Vengerov seemed to accept that. "How very considerate of you. But do not ever lie to me again."

"I swear I won't," Tom lied.

"I do appreciate your loyalty. In fact"—he looked at Dalton, now standing with a sour expression, pool cue in hand—"I'd like to have it for myself."

Tom grew confused. "I don't understand—"

"Thomas Raines," Vengerov said, "I'd like to formally offer to sponsor you as a Combatant. Will you fly in the name of the Obsidian Corporation?"

The offer took Tom totally off guard. Obsidian Corp. never sponsored Combatants. At least, they never had in the past.

131

And no one got an offer of sponsorship this early in Upper Company. Tom had barely been trained.

"Naturally," Vengerov said, "you'd need to perform other services for the company, as all Combatants do. In our case, it wouldn't involve publicity slots or commercials."

Tom recovered his capacity for speech. "What do you want me to do?"

"Something very similar to what was tested in your loyalty simulation." He drummed his fingers on his pool cue. "You see, we anticipate resistance from some quarters once Austere-grade processors go public. Useful individuals such as yourself could be a major asset. I do hope to get to know you better."

Tom felt his heart grow hard. Useful. Vengerov'd be painfully disillusioned if he ever put Tom to the test there.

"I feel we already have a working relationship," Vengerov said. "This should be one step farther down a path we're already treading."

Tom knew he had to be careful here. He tried to think about how to refuse without outright refusing. "I have to . . . I need to . . ."

"To think about it?" Dalton said with a laugh. "You're lucky anyone's considering you!"

Vengerov's eyes moved to him calmly. "Dalton, wait outside."

Dalton obeyed. He shut the door behind him.

Vengerov weighed the cue in his hand. "Forgive the interruption, Mr. Raines. I know you two have a less than amicable relationship."

"That's one way of putting it."

"Dalton Prestwick sees me as the ladder he'll climb to

prominence, and perhaps I shall be. His fatal flaw is his inability to cloak his fervent desire to use anyone who could be of assistance to him."

Tom would've named a lot of other things as Dalton Prestwick's fatal flaw.

"Though perhaps that's to his benefit in the long run. Flaws and vices are exactly what you'll need to cultivate if you wish to amount to anything in this world, Mr. Raines." Vengerov's pale eyes fixed on Tom's. "If you seek greatness, then you'll require the patronage of someone like myself, and I only support deeply flawed men and women. They always remember what they owe to their patrons, and if they don't, they can be reminded quite readily."

He made no effort to hide from Tom the ease with which he knocked the remaining balls into the side pockets. Tom found himself thinking of all the politicians he'd heard of over the years busted for being perverts or pedophiles, thieves and criminals. Flawed people. He supposed those vices that made them so flawed also made them easier for men like Vengerov to control, to destroy, if need be.

A true, unimpeachable leader would be too strong to tear down, after all.

"So if you're offering to sponsor me, then what's my fatal flaw?" Tom wondered.

Vengerov reared up. "You aim far higher than you can reach, yet you don't seem to understand that. You don't aim higher than *I* can reach. You also don't seem to understand that."

"I'm way taller than I look," Tom said, intentionally misinterpreting him.

133

Vengerov's eyes slid to his, like some unblinking reptile's. "But no brighter or you'd have accepted already. You may leave now and think over this offer."

It felt like being dismissed by an emperor . . . one who'd just called him stupid. Tom bristled inwardly, but he kept his face carefully neutral as he backed out the door. He was bright enough not to show the way he felt now.

HE FOUND VIK and Wyatt lounging by the grand piano in a corner, just off the expanse of glass floor. Yuri was playing a tune Tom's neural processor identified as Moonlight Sonata. Tom could've played it, too. The music had been planted in all their neural processors at first install; sometimes when processors malfunctioned, they were instructed to hum or tap out the keys of the song to test whether all was in order again.

Tom tugged at the collar of his shirt, feeling like it was in danger of strangling him, and spun around to survey the mass of executives in their finery. If Vengerov was going to offer to sponsor him, Tom still had a way to get out of it without being insulting: he could get counteroffers.

That meant schmoozing.

That would be unpleasant.

Just then, Tom heard a faint whisper.

"Look around the room."

He jumped, and whirled around, wondering who'd said that. He didn't see anyone near him, and his eyes roved over the crowd of executives. A prickling of unease moved up his spine. He hadn't imagined it this time. He was sure he'd heard someone! A moment later, a glint of light across metal flashed outside the window.

Tom's gaze riveted to what looked to be a machine gliding up silently in the blinding sunlight—a slim triangular contraption Tom's neural processor identified as one of the DHS's Corday-93 assault drones. They were no bigger than briefcases, innocuous looking at first glance but utterly deadly.

"Look," Tom said to Vik, grabbing his arm, pointing to the drone.

Vik followed his gaze as the Corday-93 outside glided soundlessly past the window, circling around toward the other end of the reception room where the bulk of the partygoers were.

Another flash of metal gleamed with sunlight, then another, and Tom felt a wave of apprehension as all three Corday-93s converged. He headed across the room, gazing outside, watching them move into formation.

He had a bad feeling about this.

Then the first Corday-93 opened fire.

The cadets sprang into action before any of the executives did, years of training simulations having prepared them to react in a split-second to a new threat. Tom dove to the floor, Wyatt, Vik, and Yuri all hurling themselves behind the grand piano as the massive windowed wall of the reception room shattered.

The Corday-93s soared in through the rain of shattered glass, and Tom raised his head, threw an urgent glance toward the Praetorians—sensors buried beneath the heavy coats. The assault drones blasted all three of the guard machines to pieces before any could activate.

Screams split the air, and Tom grew aware of the surreal

sight of men and women dressed to the nines swarming like frantic animals in any direction they could escape while the triad of drones mobilized into position over their heads.

"Oh no," Tom heard Vik murmur.

And then light flared out from all three Corday-93s—pinpoint lasers so blindingly bright, Tom had to throw up a hand to shield his eyes. He missed the moment Hank Bloombury was shredded. He looked up in time to see Gordon Rivkin, an executive at Nobridis, sliced into two. More white lights whipped out, blinding flashes, and Tom recognized Alana Lawrence of Epicenter, dropping dead to the floor. Then Sigurdur Vitol himself was shrieking in terror, dashing out from the crowd, sprinting into the glass-floored area where Tom and his friends were.

Tom knew he had to stop this before they killed someone important to him. He fumbled in his pocket for his remote access node and popped it onto the back of his neck, intending to interface, to find his way to these drones and take control over them—but Vik suddenly seized him, herding him into a corner with him.

Sigurdur Vitol rushed past them across the glass floor, two Corday-93s advancing on him, his feet slipping across the pane overlooking the gushing torrents of water below him.

For a moment, Tom met the panic-stricken blue eyes of one of the most powerful media moguls in the world—the son of the CEO who'd bought all five of the major media companies, whose family's newspapers and websites had propagandized the public long before the Coalition took total control of the world.

The Corday-93s fired at the floor, splintering it beneath his feet.

A rain of glass shattered, spilling Sigurdur Vitol into the raging water below them. The gushing white current swept the contents of Milton Manor toward the edge of the cliff. Tom caught a brief flash of the man's blond hair and his flailing arms before he swept over Vernal Falls and plunged to his death on the rocks hundreds of feet below him.

Tom grew aware of Yuri kicking off one of the firing arms of the nearest Praetorian. He caught on to his plan and held it still for him as Yuri ripped off the arm. Wyatt frantically fumbled with its wiring, trying to trigger it herself, use it as a weapon. She fired, sending a flash of light splicing through the nearest assault drone. The next Corday-93 shot it right out of her hands. They flinched, fearful that they would be next—but the drones ignored them. They ignored all the cadets. More weapons flashed out—always targeting executives.

At that moment, Joseph Vengerov emerged from the stairwell below them. The two remaining assault drones changed course. Blood rushed in Tom's head, certain he was about to see Vengerov killed.

But the Corday-93s only circled him, never firing, and Vengerov surveyed them coolly, head cocked slightly. "You can't kill me," he challenged their operator softly.

He must have been right, because the two remaining Corday-93s whipped off into the sunlight, leaving a hail of glass; the bodies of nine Coalition executives; and sizzling, sparking remains of Praetorians behind them.

As everyone in the room stood there in utter shock—the

137

cadets at having been completely untouched by the attack, the executives at seeing the most prominent of their number murdered before their eyes—Joseph Vengerov drew forward, gazing with an odd fascination at the remains of the drone, which kept flipping over and turning in circles on the floor.

Like a striking snake, his hand darted out and seized the fallen Corday-93. The gesture betrayed the reflexes of a computer-assisted brain, but Vengerov seemed to have forgotten himself. He gazed at the machine as it jerked in his arms, and then with swift efficiency, he tore out some wiring and killed it altogether.

Out of the corner of his eye, Tom saw Dalton Prestwick peeking out from the doorway to the stairwell, not daring to venture out. Lyla Martin spotted him and called, "They're gone. You can come out, Captain Courage."

Dalton scrambled eagerly to Vengerov's side. "You were extraordinary. You weren't afraid of them at all."

Vengerov slanted him an icy, impatient look. "They're my machines. Of course I don't fear my machines. They would never pose a threat to me." He looked at Tom, and a strange expression dawned on his face. Tom realized suddenly he still had the remote access node in his port. He reached up and snatched it out, trying to think of an explanation for what he'd planned to do—but Vengerov's gaze slid away like he thought nothing of it.

Suddenly, Dalton yelped, drawing everyone's attention to him. He pointed a shaking finger at the wall in the hallway, where one of the drones had burned a message straight into the plaster.

THE GHOST IN THE MACHINE
IS TARGETING
THE WATCHERS.

A grim silence lapsed over Milton Manor, with its shattered glass floor and dead executives, their blood trickling down the walls near their bodies.

Tom's hands felt cold and a dull pain stabbed behind his eyes.

As Tom and his friends waited in the milky afternoon light beside the shattered windows, a silent crowd gathered near the splintered glass floor where Sigurdur Vitol had plunged to his death.

Everyone there agreed that it was a rather appropriate way for Sigurdur to go. He'd loved the park enough to take it for himself, and he admired Vernal Falls enough to build his own mansion straddling it. It seemed almost fitting he died in it.

CHAPTER TWELVE

SIGURDUR VITOL'S PARTY wasn't the only Coalition site attacked by rogue drones. In India, Epicenter Manufacturing's tower was attacked by a swarm of microdrones that burrowed into its walls, and then into the skin of the executives inside, killing CEO Pandita Rumpfa and several others.

In the City of London, the chief shareholders of Dominion Agra, the Roache family, experienced their own drone onslaught. The other prominent victim was Pickens Brabeck, the CEO of Harbinger Incorporated, controller of the world's drinking water supply.

The ghost in the machine had killed all of them within ten minutes of each other.

By nightfall, the Corday-93 drones involved in the attacks were all grounded and recalled to the manufacturer— Obsidian Corp. After studying the software, the stunning announcement came: they'd been compromised by some unknown hacker with a malicious program that allowed them to be remotely controlled. No one knew when the code could have been planted in the machines. It was nearly impossible to hack so many active drones without detection, unless it was done from within a government server—or even from within Obsidian Corp. at the time of production.

Several cadets ignored curfew and crowded Tom and Clint's bunk, since they were both witnesses. Clint's stories of his own heroism grew increasingly grandiose as more girls filled the rooms. Iman Attar came and sat by Tom, her warm arm pressing into his. She seemed to have forgotten all about their awkward conversation on the way over, and kept asking him about the drone his friends had taken down.

Tom tried to answer her questions, but he kept thinking of the other ghost, shock pervading him. He'd only wanted to send a message with the ghost in the machine. He'd wanted to defy Vengerov, defy the surveillance state, defy the Coalition.

Someone was using the persona he'd created to send a very different message now.

More executives died.

Prince Hanreid Abhalleman, CEO of Nobridis, and his CFO, Lee Welch, were in a suborbital plane where the hatch popped open, flushing them both out into the vacuum of space. In the Pacific Ocean, self-guided Fawkes missiles were spontaneously launched from a US carrier. No one had shot them; they'd shot themselves and the military couldn't track them. No one knew where they were going—until they hit the car of Cote Carney, CEO of Lexicon Mobile, and the house of Ina Illarionova, CEO of Stronghold Energy.

One even hit Reuben Lloyd's lone yacht. The ironic part was, the man had taken his yacht out to stay off the grid until the ghost in the machine was apprehended. His death was the one that really spooked the executives, because the ghost had located his yacht in the middle of the ocean. They all had yachts of their own they'd planned to retreat to if the situation with the ghost grew too perilous. Now their plans had to change.

And again, all over the internet, that ominous message appeared:

THE GHOST IN THE MACHINE
IS TARGETING
THE WATCHERS.

Obsidian Corp. was forced to recall all the Fawkes missiles they'd sold over the last few years, but on the news, even in the hallways of the Spire, Tom began hearing the questions.

"What's wrong with Obsidian Corp.'s hardware? Why is this ghost hacking it so easily?"

TOM GREW PARANOID as the death toll mounted, CEOs and high-level executives dying off at a rapid rate. Some of the ghost's victims proved to be world power players who'd carefully maintained their anonymity to all but their favored politicians—until the ghost killed them.

Every time people talked about the ghost in the machine, Tom felt like he was being watched. It made it hard to concentrate on anything. He failed his tests in civilian classes, the standard eleventh-grade curriculum, because he'd been too antsy to focus on the material he downloaded the night before.

Out of desperation, he tried to follow Blackburn's advice

to "go be sixteen." It helped that Mezilo had relaxed the restrictions on cadets after the loyalty test. Tom finally went out with Iman for real. As it turned out, the Holocaust Museum was not a great place for a first date.

"I keep thinking about all those murdered children," Iman Attar said sadly as they walked outside on the windy street. "Those shoes of concentration camp kids are haunting me. They were so tiny."

"Wanna get a burger or something?" Tom asked her.

"I'm not really hungry after that, Tom."

Tom realized how callous he'd sounded. Given his brand-new reputation as a psychopath after the ethics simulation, he knew he needed to backtrack.

"Don't get me wrong," Tom said. "It's not like I saw the Auschwitz stuff and worked up an appetite. I was already thinking about burgers way earlier in the day, long before we came here."

Iman stared at him.

"But I wasn't like, thinking of burgers the whole time we were in there, of course," Tom added quickly. "I was mostly thinking about the murdered children, like you were. And the adults, too. And everyone who died. I mean, I guess I covered everyone when I said adults *and* children, but still . . . it's bad." He tried to think of something articulate to say, and settled with, "I think genocide is wrong. Very wrong."

Iman frowned. "Uh, yeah."

"I was kind of stating the obvious, huh?"

"Yes," she said dubiously. "Just a bit."

Tom stopped talking. He looked straight ahead, realizing that this was not going very well. Earlier in the day, he'd been sitting at a table with Wyatt, Vik, and Yuri, reveling in their freedom to hang out in the mess hall together again now that Mezilo was satisfied with cadet discipline and easing some restrictions.

Yuri suggested Tom spend time with Iman in the Pentagon City Mall, which brought terrible images to mind of waiting while Iman tried on shoes. Vik suggested using what he called "the alluring eyebrow maneuver," waggling his eyebrows at her one at a time, and then proposing an evening in Iman's bunk. Tom couldn't lift one eyebrow at a time, plus he didn't want to get punched, so that was out.

"How about the Holocaust Museum?" Wyatt suggested. "You should see it at least once."

Tom hadn't been there yet, so he thought it might be a great idea. Plus, if he took Iman to a museum, she'd think he was intellectually curious.

Now he knew he'd miscalculated. If there'd been any chance of a romantic mood at all before the Holocaust Museum, it was pretty much gone.

Preoccupied and silent, they walked around outside for a bit, the wind rippling their hair. Their steps brought them to the Reflecting Pool, which was cool enough that Tom hoped she'd cheer up—and then they reached the end of the pool and mounted the steps to the Lincoln Memorial. There, they found themselves gazing up at the statue of Abraham Lincoln in his chair.

A very grim, solemn-looking Abraham Lincoln.

"He looks sad," Iman noted, looking very sad herself.

"He got to be president," Tom tried. "He won a war. And he got to wear top hats and stuff. That's kind of cool."

"He was assassinated, Tom."

"Yeah, I guess that part wasn't so great," Tom admitted. He spiraled inward, thinking of other people who'd been assassinated, feeling antsy again, distracted. This wasn't working. He couldn't stop thinking about the other ghost in the machine, worrying about that.

In desperation, Tom called up the thing Vik had net-sent him. A program. Vik had given him a crafty smile before he left for the night, and told him, "This is for emergency use only if you're nervous or awkward, okay, Doctor? Use it once, see if it helps. If not, you can use it twice more as long as it's at least twenty minutes apart—and that is it. Godspeed, my friend!"

Tom considered the enigmatic program sitting in his processor, ready to be unzipped. He was burning with curiosity but very dubious. Vik's suggestions were usually either profoundly helpful or profoundly disastrous, never anything in between.

It wasn't like this date could get worse.

"You know my friend Vik?" Tom said to her suddenly. At her nod, he forged on: "He knew we were going out for the first time, so he sent this program. He won't say what it is, but he said to use it if something's going wrong or if it sucks."

Her brows drew together. "If you hate being with me so much, feel free to—"

"No! That's not what I mean. I just . . . I'm not good at talking to girls. I keep saying the wrong stuff. I get that. Um, but I don't wanna call it a night. It could be interesting."

Her eyebrows arched. "What program?"

"I don't know," Tom said. "Honestly, it's probably something terrible and embarrassing."

145

"Send me a copy. Let's see."

Tom activated his net-send with a thought, and forwarded the program to her. They settled by the Reflecting Pool, examining the code together.

"I'm so bad at programming," Iman confessed to him. "I have no idea what I'm looking at."

"Yeah, me, too. Seriously, I write code, and suddenly I've got an infinite loop going on."

"Oh, and don't you hate writing the whole code and then suddenly you get a null because of some tiny, missing period somewhere?"

"Yeah, and then Blackburn says, 'You'd get this if you actually tried, Raines. You don't study.' No, I'd get that if I had Wyatt Enslow's brain, *then* I'd get it."

"Do you study?" she asked.

Tom laughed. "Nope. Not ever. Do you?"

"Not really. But I did learn how to do one thing. Drop your firewall."

Tom did so, intrigued.

There was a playful sparkle in her eyes. She must've activated a thought interface, because suddenly, words flashed before his vision center: *Datastream received: program Shockingly Charming initiated.*

"Hey, not Vik's program!" Tom said, as she laughed. He tried to activate his own thought interface to give the virus back to her, but Iman tickled him, which didn't help matters at all. Finally, he managed to retaliate and deploy Shockingly Charming on her, and then they waited to see what the program would do, laughing nervously.

And waited.

"So I don't think I'm being shockingly charming yet," Tom said. "Am I?"

Iman giggled and shook her head. "Am I?"

"Yeah," Tom said with a smile, brushing her hair off her cheek.

Iman hit his arm. "Liar. I think you have to break it to Vik that his program is a dud." She hopped to her feet and tugged on his hand. Surprised, Tom let her lead the way, the wind making her hair dance. "Still hungry? Let's get food somewhere."

"I thought you weren't in the mood."

"I can eat dinner somewhere for your sake. You're paying, aren't you?"

He laughed. "That's noble and self-sacrificing of you. Thanks, Iman."

Her grin flashed at him, which pleased Tom immensely like he actually had said something shockingly charming. It wasn't until they were sitting across from each other in a diner that he realized she was finding most everything he said amusing.

Maybe he *had* become shockingly charming somehow. He didn't sound any different to himself, but she seemed like she was a lot more comfortable all of a sudden. Iman told him the program made her feel giggly and then pouted because he wasn't feeling at all giggly himself.

"I'm a man. Men don't giggle," Tom informed her. "We laugh. And chortle."

"Try the program again."

"Okay, but if I end up giggling or whatever, you better not tell anyone." Tom used the program on himself again. They waited for the burgers to come, and he still wasn't noticing anything. He used it a third time. The fourth time, it kicked in.

A strange giddiness overtook him, too. The moment seemed to grow profound as their food arrived, and Tom watched, fascinated, as she sipped at her soda. He didn't feel giggly. Instead, he felt engaged in a way he couldn't remember ever feeling before. And Iman seemed so . . . very . . . *fascinating* to him. He couldn't look away from her.

"You have amazing eyes," Tom told her. "You're like Cleopatra."

"I really overdid my makeup, then."

She took a huge, voracious bite of her burger. Tom liked that.

They wolfed down their food, then he carelessly slung his bills on the table for the food that was far too expensive, then looped his arm around her waist. She didn't pull away as they headed out onto the street. The languid ease filled him to the brim, the world different somehow. It was like a warm glow lent everything a sense of meaning, a sense of profoundness, and it all felt so right. Tom looked up at the trees, at the streetlights, down at the girl in his arms, wishing he could capture this feeling and learn how to replicate it anytime he wanted—because this was how the world was supposed to feel. He wanted to feel this way all the time.

He was not worried about anything now, anything at all. He didn't care about the other ghost in the machine or Vengerov or dead Coalition executives or anything.

To make sure the sensation never waned, Tom used the program on himself two more times. Iman used it a second time. Tom got an idea when they saw the Reflecting Pool again. "We should wade in. You and me."

148

"What if we get arrested?"

He laughed. "Pretend I was chasing you and you ran into the water to save yourself because I can't swim."

"The water's not deep at all."

"I know. Tell the cop that's where the flaw in your escape plan came in."

"Aw, you'd get arrested so I wouldn't? You're so noble."

"I try to tell people that, but no one believes me," Tom agreed. They kicked off their shoes and waded into the pool, their reflections dancing across the surface along with the glowing streetlights. Emboldened, he cupped the hot skin on the back of her neck and drew her lips to his, the reflected marble columns of the Lincoln Memorial shimmering in the water about their feet. Then a security guard yelled at them, so they leaped out, swiped up their shoes, and ran away barefoot and laughing.

By the time they were on the Metro together, her cheeks were pink, her eyes glowing, and Tom had this strange, buoying sense of confidence like he really had become shockingly charming. He drew her to his side, the curve of her hip against his, and kept his arm tucked around her, a sense of warm possessiveness throughout him.

Everything had been so complicated with Medusa. But this wasn't. It was simple, easy, and Iman wasn't on the other side of the world—she was right here. Right here. He kissed her again, and neither of them cared that they were in the middle of a crowded train car.

1 0 0 1 1 1 1 1 1 1 1 0 0 1 1 1 0 1 0 1 1 0 0 0 0 0 0 0 1 0 0 1 1 1 1 0 0 0
0 1 1 0 1 1 0 1 1 1 0 0 1 1 1 0 0 0 0 0 0 0 1 0 1 1 0 1 0 0 1 0 0 1 1
1 0 0 0 0 0 1 1 1 1 0 0 1 0 0 1 0 1 1 1 0 0 1 1 1 0 1 1 0 0 1 0 1 1 0 1 1
0 1 0 0 0 1 0 1 0 0 1 0 0 0 0 1 0 1 1 0 1 0 0 1 1 0 0 0 1 0 1 1 1 0 0 0 0 1 1
1 0 0 1 1 0 1 0 0 0 0 0 1 0 1 1 1 0 1 1 0 0 0 0 0 0 1 0 1 1 0 0 1 1 1 1
0 0 1 1 0 0 0 0 1 1 1 0 1 1 0 1 1 0 1 0 0 0 0 0 1 0 0 1 1 1 0 0 0 0 0
1 1 0 0 1 0 1 0 1 1 1 0 1 1 0 1 0 1 0 1 1 1 1 0 1 0 1 1 0 1 1 0 0 0 0 0
0 1 1 1 1 1 1 1 0 1 1 0 0 0 0 1 1 1 0 1 1 0 1 1 1 0 1 1 1 0 0 0 1 0 1 0
1 0 1 0 1 0 0 1 1 0 1 0 0 1 0 0 0 1 0 1 0 1 0 0 1 0 0 0 0 1 0 0 1 0 1 0 1 0
0 0 1 0 0 1 0 1 1 0 0 1 0 0 1 1 0 1 0 1 0 1 1 1 0 0 0 0 1 0 1 1 0 1 0 1 0
0 0 0 0 0 1 1 1 1 0 1 1 0 0 1 1 0 1 1 0 0 0 0 0 1 0 0 0 1 0 0 0 1 0 0
1 0 1 0 0 0 1 1 1 0 0 1 1 0 1 1 0 1 1 0 0 1 0 0 1 1 1 0 0 1 0 0 0 0 1 0 0 0
0 0 1 1 1 1 1 0 1 1 0 1 0 0 0 1 0 0 1 1 0 0 0 0 1 0 1 1 1 0 0 0 0 0 0
0 1 1 1 1 0 0 0 0 0 1 0 1 1 0 1 0 0 0 0 0 0 1 0 0 0 1 1 1 0 0 1 1 1 0
1 1 1 0 0 0 1 1 1 0 0 1 1 0 0 0 0 0 1 1 0 0 1 0 0 1 0 1 0 1 1 1 1 1 0 1 1
0 0 0 1 1 1 1 0 0 1 0 1 0 1 1 1 1 0 0 1 0 1 1 0 1 1 0 1 1 1 1 1 0 0 1 0 0 1
0 1 0 1 0 1 0 1 0 1 0 1 0 0 0 0 1 0 0 0 0 1 1 1 0 1 0 1 0 1
0 0 1 0 1 0 1 1 1 0 1 1 1 1 1 1 1 1 1 1 0 0 1 1 1 0
1 1 1 1 0 0 1 1 0 1 0 1 1 0 1 0 0 1 0 0 0 0 1 1 1 1 0 0
1 0 0 1 1 0 0 0 1 1 1 1 1 0 1 1 0 0 0 0 0 0 1 0 0 1 0 1 0 1 0 0

CHAPTER THIRTEEN

VIK WASN'T IN his bunk, so Tom stumbled into Wyatt's later, and slumped down at the foot of her bed as she looked at him over her book, confused.

"The alluring eyebrow maneuver?" Tom slurred. "It works." He held up his fingers in two victory signs. "I did it, and I got up to Iman's bunk. That's where I've been for the last couple hours."

"What's wrong with you?" Wyatt asked.

"I'm shockingly charming."

"You really aren't. And you look like you've had a stroke."

Confused, Tom touched his face. Both sides were moving. Maybe she just said that because she was still mad at him. Speaking of . . . "Why are you so mad at me?"

"I'm not," she said.

Her eyes doubled, became four eyes. Tom wondered why he was letting his eyes blur like this. He forced her back to two eyes.

"You said I just use you for programs," Tom pointed out. "That's not true. You know that's not true. You didn't talk to me for three months, and you definitely weren't writing me any programs, but I stayed around 'cause we're friends. That's what friends do. Therefore, I am friend."

"I only understood about half those words. Why are you slurring everything you say?"

"Program. Greatest ever."

"What program?"

Tom fumbled for his forearm keyboard, then remembered he didn't have it. He couldn't remember right now how to use the net-send thought interface to forward the program, so he threw up his arms helplessly. "Vik's."

"Oh no." Wyatt whipped out something from the drawer beneath her bed. "I'll scan your processor to see what's going on."

"I'm trying to talk here," Tom told her, reaching for her so she'd sit down, too.

She shoved his hands away. "Talk while I scan." She grabbed his hair and pulled his head forward, then jabbed a neural wire into his access port.

"Ow," Tom said, belatedly registering that she'd tugged on his hair. He couldn't remember what he'd wanted to say to her now. He looked at her, where her eyes had turned to four again, and saw the intense look of concentration puckering her face. It made something inside him sink into a dark pit. He didn't like Wyatt being mad at him. It made him feel very lonely and sad.

She read something on a screen she'd attached to the other end of the neural wire, her fingers moving over her forearm keyboard. "'Shockingly Charming' . . . Is that the name of the program?"

"I really am sorry I kissed you," Tom said. He realized how

151

he should phrase it. "I sexually harassed you."

"Of course Shockingly Charming is the name of the program. It's such a *Vik* name. He'd better come in here and carry you back to your bunk." She regarded him solemnly over her forearm keyboard, her brow knit. "Tom, you can't operate heavy machinery in this state."

He gave a sloppy laugh. "Yeah, I will go put away my heavy machinery, then. All my tractors and pulleys."

Wyatt considered him. "You probably won't even remember any of this tomorrow."

"I don't know about—"

And then Wyatt took him by the shoulders, and crashed her lips into his. Tom's brain was slow to process the fact that she was kissing him, and by the time he lifted his clumsy arms to take hold of her, she'd already pulled back, her eyes moving over his face.

"It's not the same," she whispered. "I don't feel it this time."

"What just happened here?" Tom wondered, feeling like he'd missed something.

"I'm so sorry, Tom." Wyatt looked down at the carpet. "I took advantage of you. That was wrong, and I won't do it again."

"I'm confused," Tom admitted.

"It's just that . . ." She drew a deep breath, like she was steeling herself for some difficult task, then gazed intently into his eyes. "I used to think about you a lot, Tom. When we were plebes, mostly. But sometimes last year. I knew you didn't see me that way, though. You never did. And I already knew the first time I heard about Medusa that there was no chance, really."

152

Tom scrubbed his palm over his face. "Wyatt? What?"

"I'm finally at a point with Yuri where I know how great things are," she said. "I'm finally comfortable and I'm not worried about everything now. I never felt like I was good enough for him. In some ways it was so much easier being around you because we're both . . . we're both so imperfect. You see me the way I am, but it doesn't matter to you. I felt like Yuri saw me as someone better than I am, and I'd never live up to that. And one day he'd see the real me and feel disappointed."

Tom was so perplexed. She was talking way too fast for him to follow. "Huh?"

"Even after all this time," Wyatt said, "there was this part of me that wondered sometimes if it would've been better if I'd said something to you, just once . . . like that day outside the Smithsonian. I always had this what-if scenario in the back of my mind, but I stopped wondering after a while. I hadn't thought about it until you kissed me and then it's like all those doubts came back." She looked away from him, her voice full of wonder. "But I'm over that now. I know what I want. I want Yuri."

Tom was so confused. "Is that good?"

"It's so, so good. It's great." She flung her arms around Tom suddenly. "Thank you, Tom. Thank you so much."

He stared, bemused, down at the cheek pressed to his chest, sensing he'd done something right here, even if he didn't quite get what. He patted her back. "Great, Wyatt. Great."

Wyatt pulled back and touched his cheek. "Oh, you are so completely inebriated, Tom. That's what Vik's program did to

153

you. I'll get him here to help you. We'll get your brain back to homeostasis in no time."

"Homo what?" Utterly baffled, Tom sat there under her bed while Wyatt began to reverse the program. He wasn't quite able to grasp what had happened, but he had a feeling they'd just made up. "We're friends again?"

She beamed at him. "We're best friends."

Bewildered, but happy, he gave a thumbs-up. Then he passed out.

HE WAS ONLY vaguely aware of voices swelling as Vik came into the room, and Wyatt came with him saying, ". . . your stupid program!"

"Okay, okay. I'll smuggle him back to our division." It was Vik's voice. Boots thudded close to Tom's head. "Oh man, you weren't kidding. He's out."

"I can't wake him up now."

"I'll turn him on his side in case he gets sick. Uh, think he'd feel better if we made him puke? Or maybe gave him water?"

"He didn't drink anything. He can't just throw up and get it out of his system. He's not going to dehydrate, so water isn't what he needs, either. I'm reversing the program, but it's going to take a while for his brain to return to its normal GABA and dopamine levels. Great job."

"Hey, I told him to use it once, maybe a couple times. Not *this*."

A hand, nudging Tom's face. Insistent enough to be annoying. Tom batted it away.

"Okay, so he's kind of there," Vik said, his voice strained. "Aw, don't look at me like that. Give me a break, Evil Wench!

154

It's not like I pinned him down and used it on him over and over again. Tom obviously overestimated himself. In case you haven't noticed, he does that. A lot."

Words flashed behind Tom's closed lids. He grumbled stuff that didn't escape his closed lips, irate at the flash of code cutting through his foggy brain.

Vik sighed. "Well, on the bright side, Tom must've liked my program a lot."

Sarcasm dripped from her voice. "You're such a good friend to him."

"I am. I'm a *great* friend. Key word here: 'friend,' not 'dad.' Tom is a big boy who can make his own decisions. He does that a lot, too. Case in point: single-handedly ending the ethics sim."

Silence. Then, "Tiny Spicy Vikram."

"That's uncalled for, Evil Wench!"

"I was disabling the surveillance. Listen, don't you think it's kind of weird, how he acted during that test?"

"What, going rogue like that? Tom always does that in sims."

"No, I mean . . ." Her voice dropped to a whisper. "He shot all those people. Tom wouldn't do that. He wouldn't just kill people like that. He had to know it was a sim."

"It's weird, but we asked him already. He says he didn't know. He'd tell us if he knew."

"No, he wouldn't."

Vik laughed. "This is Tom. He would've rubbed it in my face if he figured it out and I didn't. Just like I'd have rubbed it in his. We're face rubbers."

"You're acting like he's never kept secrets from us before. Remember Medusa?"

"Okay, so Tom had a secret thing with her. Twice. But that doesn't mean—"

"Three times. He was talking to her again. Recently."

"What? I told him—"

"To stay away?"

Anger touched Vik's voice. "He said he would."

"He lied, Vik. He lies a lot. You haven't noticed, obviously. You know how whenever you ask about those casinos and stuff, he talks about how great it was when he was a kid and how—" She broke off. "I just realized something. I know him better than you do."

Vik barked a laugh. "No, you don't. Are you kidding?"

"I do. I know him better."

"I know everything about Tom. Come on, the casino stuff is not made up. He taught me how to count cards. He knows about every variation of poker there is. Plus, I called him over break at—"

"Not the casino part. That's real. I mean . . . Oh, you wouldn't understand. I saw some of his memories when I saw the census device footage, and it was . . . He's like two people. There's the way he acts and there's the way he really is. If you knew the stuff I knew, you wouldn't have given him that program."

There was a thump as Vik settled on the floor. Then he sighed. "Okay, I have no idea what you're talking about here, but I'll give you a few points. There are things that don't add up, and I've noticed. I'm not blind. For instance, how did Tom get promoted? Tom was blacklisted by the Coalition companies. We all knew that. He had no chance of making Upper Company. But here he is, in Upper Company. Suddenly, he got promoted. How'd that happen? He never explained it. It makes no sense."

"There's something I've wondered about, too," Wyatt chimed in, suddenly eager. "How did Tom block off the cell phones of all the people in the Beringer Club? I know it's been a long time, but that's always bothered me."

"The cell phones?"

"Tom locked them inside, and then they got stuck there all night. Nothing should have stopped them from calling for help unless he jammed their cell phones, but how did he do that? The only way I can think of is jamming the satellites, but that's impossible."

"Tom said something once about satellites . . ." Vik trailed off. "No, forget it. I don't really know what he was saying. But you know, speaking of Tom lying, he didn't tell us the truth about getting stuck outside in Antarctica for a *long* time. I thought that was weird. Why did he lie to us for so long? And with that stupid story about going to the bathroom and going out the wrong door, too. He didn't tell us Vengerov had driven him out there. Why hide that from us?"

Wyatt's voice dropped to an urgent whisper. "Remember how he knew in Obsidian Corp. that the alarms were about to go off? He knew Joseph Vengerov had detected us. He warned us. And he specifically said it was Joseph Vengerov who knew, and a few minutes later, Joseph Vengerov himself starts talking to us over the intercom. Tom knew Vengerov was handling the situation personally. How is that possible?"

Vik snapped his fingers. "For that matter, remember when Medusa's ship busted into the warehouse? Tom wasn't in there

157

with us. He was outside. Remember that?"

Wyatt drew a sharp breath. "You're right. He did go outside. When the warehouse started burning and you grabbed me and we couldn't find him, but then he ran in and helped us—he *ran in from the outside.*"

"I saw his face. He was just as surprised as we were when Medusa showed up, so he wasn't out there waiting for her to rescue us . . . What was he doing out there if he wasn't waiting for her?"

"I don't know. He knew he'd freeze to death outside. Why would he go out there?"

Vik started laughing. "Enslow, you don't know this guy, either. Neither of us does. At all. He seriously has a secret life." He shook Tom's shoulder. "Are you in the CIA, Tom?"

"We should talk to Yuri. He has to have noticed things, too."

"Why haven't we asked each other this stuff before?"

"You call me Man Hands, and you put weird templates in my bunk. That's not great grounds for conversation."

"First off, the Man Hands ship sailed long ago. I defy you to remember any occasion I've called you that since we were fifteen . . . plus, you can't take me seriously. I've got three sisters. In the Ashwan household, you learn young: mock or be mocked. I'm a mocker, but I do it out of love. Tom gets that. You should, too."

"You don't mock Yuri."

"The Android's a tough case. What do I make fun of? The chiseled good looks or the eight-pack abs, or maybe the way he climbed Annapurna when he was eleven? No, that won't work. Your boyfriend is as close as a real person can get to

158

being Superman. Not much to mock there."

"So . . . so what do you think we should do about this Tom thing?"

"The part where he's unconscious or the part where he has a secret life?"

"The second one. If we ask him, he'll just lie."

"There's gotta be some explanation, Enslow. We'll investigate."

"Investigate Tom?"

"Why not?" A rustling as Vik rose to his feet. "I'm not sure where to start, but—"

"I know where. He told me recently that he had a way to talk to Medusa that no one could detect, but he couldn't explain it to me. I thought he was deluding himself. But then I thought about it, and he really had been getting away with talking to her without anyone noticing for a while. He was *sure* he couldn't possibly get caught. For some reason."

"Maybe there's something to that."

"Maybe there is."

After a silence, Vik said, "You realize, his ears can probably hear us right now. Even if his hippocampus isn't doing its job right now, the neural processor is. He's going to know everything we've talked about here when he wakes up. Isn't that right, Gormless One?" A hand jostled Tom.

"Then I'll remove the time segment from his processor." Fingers typing on a keyboard.

"Wait, Evil Wench. You're not actually going to—"

1 0 0 1 1 1 1 1 1 1 0 0 1 1 1 0 1 0 1 1 0 0 0 0 0 0 0 1 0 0 1 1 1 1 0 0 0
0 1 1 0 1 1 0 1 1 1 0 0 1 1 1 1 0 0 0 0 0 0 0 1 0 1 1 0 1 0 0 1 0 0 1 1
1 0 0 0 0 0 1 1 1 1 0 0 1 0 0 1 0 0 1 0 1 1 1 0 0 1 1 1 0 1 1 0 0 1 0 1 1 0 1 1
0 1 0 0 0 1 0 0 1 1 0 0 0 0 1 1 0 1 0 0 1 1 0 0 0 1 0 1 1 1 1 0 0 0 1 1
1 0 0 1 1 0 1 0 0 0 0 0 0 0 1 1 0 1 1 0 1 1 0 0 0 0 0 0 0 0 1 1 0 0 1 1 1
0 0 1 1 0 0 0 0 0 1 1 1 1 0 1 1 0 1 1 0 1 1 0 1 0 0 0 0 1 0 0 1 1 1 0 0 0 0
1 1 0 0 1 0 1 0 1 1 1 0 1 1 1 0 1 0 1 0 1 1 1 0 1 0 1 1 0 1 1 0 0 0 0 0
0 1 1 1 1 1 1 1 0 1 1 0 0 0 0 1 1 1 0 1 1 0 1 1 0 1 1 0 1 1 1 0 0 0 1 0 1 0
1 0 1 1 0 0 1 1 0 1 0 0 1 0 0 0 1 0 1 0 1 0 0 1 0 0 0 0 1 0 0 1 0 1 0 1 0
0 0 1 0 0 1 0 1 1 1 0 1 1 0 1 0 1 0 1 1 1 0 0 0 0 0 1 0 1 1 0 1 0 1 0
0 0 0 0 0 1 1 1 1 0 1 1 0 0 1 1 0 1 1 0 0 0 0 0 1 0 0 0 0 1 0 0 0 1 0 0
1 0 1 0 0 1 0 1 1 0 0 1 0 0 1 1 1 0 1 1 0 0 1 1 0 0 1 1 0 0 0 0 1 0 0 0
0 0 1 1 1 1 1 0 1 1 0 1 0 0 1 0 0 1 1 1 0 0 0 0 1 0 1 1 1 0 0 0 0 0
0 1 1 1 1 0 0 0 0 1 0 1 1 0 1 0 0 0 0 0 0 0 1 0 0 0 1 1 1 1 0 0 1 1 1 0
1 1 1 0 0 0 1 1 1 0 0 1 1 1 0 0 0 0 1 0 0 1 0 0 1 0 1 0 1 1 1 1 1 0 1 1
0 0 0 1 1 1 1 0 0 1 0 1 1 1 1 1 0 0 1 0 1 0 1 1 0 1 1 1 1 1 1 0 0 1 0 0 1
0 1 0 1 1 0 0 0 0 1 0 0 0 0 1 0 0 0 0 1 1 1 0 1 0 1 0 1
0 0 1 1 1 1 1 1 1 1 1 1 1 1 1 1 1 0 0 1 1 1 1 0
1 1 1 1 1 0 1 1 0 1 0 0 1 0 0 0 0 1 1 1 1 1 0 0
1 0 0 1 1 0 0 0 1 1 1 1 1 1 1 0 1 1 0 0 0 0 0 0 1 0 0 1 0 0 1 0 1 1 0 1 0

CHAPTER FOURTEEN

"**R**ISE AND SHINE, Doctor of Gormless Cretinism."

Tom opened his eyes and found himself back in his bunk, Vik gazing down at him. His chronometer said it was 0645. Vik kept shaking him lightly.

"Yeah, I figured you wouldn't wake up on time. You'd better get moving if you don't want more penalty hours."

Tom sat up blearily. He felt awful. "Vik?"

Vik shook his head. "You didn't listen to me last night, did you? I said use the program *once*, maybe two or three times *spaced out*—emphasis on that—if it didn't take the first time. I did not say use it nine times, and I definitely didn't say ten and certainly not *eleven*. Eleven times, Tom! That's how many times Wyatt says you used the program. Are you a madman?"

"Just an idiot," Tom said, his head throbbing dully, his mouth like sandpaper. He was disturbed to find he couldn't remember anything after his clumsy walk to Wyatt's bunk. Even the processor wouldn't retrieve the memory for him.

"How'd I get here?" Tom looked around his bunk. "What happened?"

"You passed out on Wyatt's floor. I had to sneak you back in here and pay Clint twenty bucks to keep his mouth shut. You owe me twenty bucks, by the way."

Tom scrolled through the other memories—the giddy laughter with Iman, wading through the Reflecting Pool, kissing her, the way everything disappeared but the glowing moment around them. He dwelled on that. Strange how amazing that night had become after using the program.

Everything had come so easily. All the awkwardness between them had vanished, replaced by this magnetic sort of chemistry, and he really had felt like he was being shockingly charming.

"That program was amazing, Vik," Tom murmured, trying to ignore the way his joints ached. He felt like he'd found something truly useful here, the answer to some question he'd never thought to ask. He wanted to feel that way all the time. "Seriously, man, thank you. That made everything so much easier. We had a great time after that."

Vik eyed him. "Yeah, well, don't get used to it. Next time, you've got to use your own shocking charm or you'll never figure out how to act around her."

"I have no shocking charm, man. I have to use yours. It took me, like, five hits to feel it, so I promise I won't use more than that next time."

"No, Doctor! No abusing alcohol emulators."

Tom's smile dropped from his lips. He felt a cold pit grow in his stomach. "That's what that was?"

"What did you think?"

Tom felt sick, suddenly. Truly sick.

"You look dreadful," Vik said cheerfully, clapping his back. "Good news and bad news. The bad news is, that feeling's probably going to last most of the day."

"What's the good news?"

"The good news is, as you painfully suffer through your day, I get to taunt you for ignoring my advice." He swaggered out, leaving Tom sitting in his bed in the sudden stillness.

The world felt flat today, the colors less vivid. Even when Clint came in from his shower and hooted something about Tom fainting and needing to be "carried in by his boyfriend," Tom only half-heartedly threatened him with bodily harm.

Some part of him had always resented his father, the way Neil had never just stopped drinking, the way he'd never managed to control himself. As Tom stood under the steady stream of the shower, he thought of Neil moving through a world where every door was shut to him, where someone like him counted for nothing and unfairness was rewarded. A guy stuck taking care of a small kid he probably never wanted and never knew how to raise, a kid who he probably thought was going to end up at the same dead end he was.

For the first time in his life, Tom understood the allure of something that erased all doubts, all insecurities, something that gave an artificial sense of power where there was none, confidence where it was missing. He could see suddenly how Neil slipped into using it often, and then every day.

And the last time he saw Neil, Tom had thrown the full force of his contempt and resentment in his face. It didn't matter why he'd done it, even if he'd done it for Neil—that part had been real. Whatever happened in the years to come,

Tom had unleashed that between them and he could never, never take it back.

THE POSITIVE EFFECTS of the program had all been temporary. Tom had awoken totally infatuated with Iman Attar, but as soon as their eyes met the next morning, he realized that without Vik's program, they'd lost all that magnetism that had drawn them together.

Even the heady sense Tom had at the time—that this was so much easier than Medusa—had somehow gone away, also. Too awkward to approach Iman suddenly, Tom sat with his friends, and she sat with hers, even though they now had open seating at lunch again and could easily have grabbed seats together.

He saw Iman touch her forearm keyboard, and then a text appeared before Tom's vision center. *I'm worried you have the wrong idea about me.*

Tom raised his eyebrows questioningly and looked at her through the crowd. "Why?" he mouthed.

I think we went way too fast.

Confused, he typed back, *We can slow down. Whatever you want.*

She frowned. *I don't know if this is a good idea. Maybe we're not right for each other.*

Tom was a bit surprised. She was dumping him? Already? Where had this come from? But he made sure not to react. *Fine. Let's forget about it all.*

A look of hurt fluttered across her face, then Iman turned away and said something to Jennifer Nguyen. Jenny began stroking her back and darting angry looks Tom's way, like he'd

163

been the one who did the dumping, not the other way around.

Tom shook it off. He did not get girls. He tried focusing on his friends, where Wyatt was busy telling Yuri about her work with Irene Frayne over the last few weeks. The NSA agent had been in the Pentagonal Spire most every day of late. She'd enlisted Wyatt's help tracking down the ghost in the machine.

"She thinks the ghost has military training. The Spire's one of the most powerful servers in the country, so she's operating out of here to track him," Wyatt told them. "And she needs my help to get to know the server." She beamed, pleased to be useful to someone again. "Ms. Frayne said to me yesterday, 'You're very smart, Wyatt.'"

Yuri blinked, then smiled encouragingly. "You are very smart, Wyatt."

Tom and Vik exchanged a glance.

"What?" Wyatt said, noticing it.

Vik sighed and leaned his elbows on the table. "I need to tell you something, too, Enslow: the sky is blue."

"Wyatt, you've gotta know this," Tom said, gesturing to their table. "This is a table."

Vik lifted his fork up for her to see. "I have a fork in my hand."

"Vik uses forks to put food in his mouth," Tom explained to her as Vik mimed using his fork to put food in his mouth. Tom pretended to be amazed watching someone use a fork to eat.

"This is not nice," Yuri rebuked them.

"It's okay, Yuri. I get it," Wyatt said, turning faintly pink. She'd caught the point, though: Frayne was just stating the obvious, calling her "very smart." "It was nice to hear. That's all. Especially since . . ." She twirled a salt shaker between her fingers. "I know

164

Lieutenant Blackburn doesn't handle software writing anymore, so we couldn't work together anyway. I've been starting to think he'll never trust me again, either, after what happened."

A grim silence fell among all of them, because she didn't need to say why. She'd unscrambled Yuri and then lied to Blackburn about it. It wasn't the first time the trust between them, so tenuous, had been snapped.

"But I don't care," Wyatt said after a moment, firming her jaw. "He taught me all he could, and now I can help Ms. Frayne."

"Why have I never seen this woman?" Vik wondered.

Tom looked at him incredulously. "Are you blind? She's here every day, man."

"It's because she's in stealth mode," Wyatt said.

"Huh?" Tom and Vik both said.

"Stealth mode," Wyatt said. "You know how there were areas of the Spire we didn't see until we were Middles?"

"I see them all now," Yuri reported happily. Then, questioningly, "Don't I?"

Tom shrugged. As far as he knew, they saw everything now.

"My point is," Wyatt said, "General Marsh said sensitive personnel are blocked from our processors, too. Remember?"

"I see Frayne, though," Tom pointed out.

"Of course. She already knows you. You two have interacted. She authorized you to see her and probably never got around to de-authorizing you."

"Are there other people we are not able to be seeing?" Yuri whispered in her ear.

"No. Not that I know about. Just her," Wyatt said. "I think."

Tom resolved to hook into a surveillance camera and check

165

tonight—just to be very sure.

"There's an invisible woman walking around here," Vik said slowly, as though trying to wrap his brain around the idea. "Why would she do that? It's creepy."

"She doesn't want to be bothered by cadets," Wyatt said.

Vik clanked his fork down decisively. "That's not it. You know why she walks around invisibly? I bet it's because she wants to see us naked."

"Think so?" Tom said, intrigued.

"No!" Wyatt cried. "She doesn't."

"She's not doing it for an operation," Vik pointed out, "and she's not getting some optical camouflage suits that could possibly be detected. No, she specifically wants to be totally invisible, and what's more, totally invisible to *us*. You know why? Because she wants to see some naked cadets. Well, you watch. I'm going to give her what she wants. She's going to see all the naked Indian she can handle."

"Please don't do that," Wyatt said. "She's just an average person trying to do her job and support her family. She doesn't deserve that."

Vik considered that. "I'm feeling faintly insulted."

"Just because you'd use stealth mode to see naked people, doesn't mean other people would," Wyatt informed him.

"I would," Tom said, mouth full.

Wyatt scowled. "Just because you and Tom would use it for that, doesn't mean other people would."

All three of them looked at Yuri.

"I wish to be neutral," Yuri declared, to everyone's disappointment.

166

"So about legs . . ." Vik said, and Yuri frowned and kicked him under the table.

Tom found his gaze drifting across the mess hall, his mind on Frayne—using the Spire's server to hunt the ghost. This person acting in the ghost's name was going to bring more and more heat on his head . . . unless the killing of those executives was over?

THE NEXT DAY, he found out it was not. Xi Quinghong, the CEO of Preeminent Communications, had been slain by his own company's Praetorians in its Beijing office. Ingvar Harde, chief shareholder of Lexicon Mobile, met the same fate from his own personal Praetorians. Ten Coalition executives in total perished this time around.

Speculation heated up. Everywhere Tom turned, he heard people wonder why no Obsidian Corp. or LM Lymer Fleet executives had been killed. People pointed out that the machines of those two companies were involved every single time.

And then the big leak happened: someone plastered all over the internet proof that LM Lymer Fleet and Obsidian Corp. were both controlled by Joseph Vengerov.

Tom turned to gaze at Blackburn across the mess hall the day that incredible news broke. He'd plundered that information from Obsidian Corp.'s servers the year before at meet and greets. Blackburn had clung to that damaging piece of leverage since that visit. Now it was out.

Tom saw the cold satisfaction on the man's scarred face as he stood with the other soldiers, watching footage on the screens from the blistering debates on the Senate floor. Politicians funded by Obsidian Corporation were at war with politicians funded by other Coalition companies, because other Coalition executives were beginning to take issue with Joseph Vengerov, the man whose top executives were immune to the attacks, the man whose machines were behind the attacks, and now the man who'd deceived them about his financial ties with an enemy company.

The targeted assassinations had damaged Obsidian Corp.'s reputation and seemed to accomplish with swift, brutal efficiency what nothing else could: the cancellation of the beta test. The mass removal of plebes with Austere-grade processors began.

Tom caught up to Zane right as he was being escorted out of the Spire. The small kid was wearing civilian clothes, his face foggy, lost.

"Zane!"

Zane looked at him, confused. Tom knew outside pressure had been applied, probably by other companies, forcing the suspension of the rollout of Austere-grade processors. Joseph Vengerov had regretfully withdrawn his sponsorship offer, as Obsidian Corp. had too much of a legal battle on its hands to court the public right now.

Tom felt a great relief in his heart, knowing this was the end of the nanomachines. Obsidian Corp.'s crumbling reputation meant the other companies had stopped trusting Joseph Vengerov with control over billions of people. He was glad of it.

But he felt horrible for his plebes.

"Listen," Tom said, sidling up to Zane, ignoring the irritated soldier escorting the kid. "Don't think this is about you, okay? You're gonna do great wherever you go from here. I know it."

Zane blinked at him. "Who are you?"

"What?"

"I'm not sure who you are. Do I know you?"

"You don't know who I am?"

"Are you a Combatant?"

"I'm the . . ." Tom stopped. He sighed, realizing it would be useless explaining to him he'd been the one helping his training. Zane obviously had lost every memory of the Spire. Tom shook his head. "Nobody."

And then he withdrew, and watched his last plebe leave the Pentagonal Spire.

CHAPTER FIFTEEN

U**NDER GENERAL MARSH,** Uppers trained in simulations for Applied Battles and only rarely hooked into actual ships in space. General Mezilo was intent on creating better soldiers than General Marsh, and took it personally that he hadn't managed to single-handedly change the course of the war yet. Uppers began training with real ships.

Tom loved controlling drones in space. Sometimes, he forgot that he was merely interfacing with electronic systems from millions of miles away and felt like he was actually there in the spaceship whose sensors were pinging his brain. They'd practiced cascade formations and circled the glorious blue orb of Neptune, and then they tried their hand at using the sun's gravity in the Infernal Zone to accelerate, dodging the worst of the solar flares. Then they used fine maneuvering, navigating through a field of Promethean Arrays—those solar panels in close orbit around the sun that shot solar energy to the ships in the Reaches, far from Earth.

One day, through the blinding gale of bright sunlight that always seemed to envelop them when their ships were in the zone between Mercury and the sun, they happened upon Promethean Arrays that didn't belong to their side. They were genuine pieces of enemy equipment, waiting in stasis for activation.

Wyatt tried her hand at hacking some of the panels and reprogramming them remotely to respond to commands only from the Indo-American side, but soon a command came to them directly from the Pentagon: forget reprogramming them, just destroy them all.

The cadets had a great time blasting them to pieces. It was rare that their practice flights gave them the opportunity to inflict real battle damage to the enemy.

Simulations couldn't compare to the reality of a ship at one's command. Tom loved dodging asteroids during dexterity maneuvers. There were a good number of Trojan asteroids in the same orbit as Earth, caught by its gravity, and they were easy to reach. The Uppers played capture the asteroid sometimes, where they broke into teams and used their missiles to propel a very small rock back and forth. The losing team was the one that let the rock slip past them.

They were only allowed to fire three missiles each, sometimes fewer depending upon their funding for that training day. Tom came up with a method of moving the asteroid without missiles by maneuvering in very close, and then using his engine exhaust to nudge it. A few other people tried it, too, but the practice was banned as soon as Lyla Martin accidentally destroyed her ship that way. The ships were simply too expensive to risk.

One day in November, the Uppers practiced cascade formations again, lining up to accelerate together toward a fixed target—in this case, 3753 Cruithne, an asteroid called "Earth's second moon." It was at the edge of the Neutral Zone, the common launch point for payloads through the intensive free-fire range just beyond Earth called the Gauntlet. America had claimed it early in the war, when it became clear the Chinese weren't going to surrender the vast tactical advantage that was the actual moon.

They followed the usual cascade formation, lining up, using each other's energy to exponentially increase the momentum of the ship in front. Yet today, something strange happened. They reached the coordinates for the base, but Cruithne wasn't there.

Tom checked his sensors several times. He did what he always did when something mathematical or scientific confused him: he used his thought interface to ask Wyatt for help. *Did we get the wrong coordinates?*

No.

She'd run the calculations for the group, since they'd all learned to trust her judgment.

More thoughts rushed into Tom's head, net-sent by other cadets for the group IRC channel they were all hooked into during their training exercises.

Enslow messed up her calculations, Clint thought.

Evil Wench messed up? Vik thought.

I did not mess up! Wyatt thought angrily.

Do you see Cruithne anywhere? Clint thought.

No, I don't see it, but I DID NOT MESS UP.

Okay, calm down, calm down, Walton Covner thought to her. *Maybe our instruments are faulty.*

This isn't right, Wyatt thought to everyone. *Something's wrong*

172

here. We passed the instrument checks and these are the right coordinates. Five-kilometer-wide asteroids with stable orbits don't simply vanish. They don't.

Tom found the whole situation kind of bizarre. He looped his ship in wide circles, trying to conserve momentum, searching idly for the massive asteroid that was supposed to be in their location. The other cadets adopted the same maneuver, flying about in wide loops.

Cruithne saw Lyla Martin coming and fled in terror, thought Shipley Kamanski, an Upper in Genghis Division with her.

I am going to beat you up later, Kamanski, Lyla thought.

Kamanski, I am going to beat you up later, too, Vik thought to him.

Aw, I actually like you right now, Vik, Lyla thought.

Ooh, does this mean you'll finally—

DON'T THINK ABOUT THIS OVER A THOUGHT INTERFACE.

Right. Sorry.

And, Lyla thought, *no.*

Blast, Vik thought. *Foiled again!*

And the whole time, in the background of the IRC, Wyatt's thoughts beat over and over again, *This isn't right. Something's wrong. Something's wrong. Something is very wrong . . . I'm disconnecting. I need to tell someone.*

Her name disappeared from the group IRC. Her disappearance had a strange effect on Tom. Suddenly he sobered. Suddenly he began to feel a creeping sense of fear, scanning the empty space about him. The other thoughts in the IRC died down, the other cadets feeling it, too.

They were awfully close to Earth for a five-kilometer-wide asteroid to disappear.

They lingered too long, unmoving, with no commands one way or another from Earth. Usually they were in constant motion to avoid being picked up by sensors or satellites. Today, they were not.

And consequences soon followed.

Tom's sensors picked it up, and his heart leaped.

Incoming! Tom thought over the IRC, just as several other Uppers did as well.

The Russo-Chinese ships descended upon them in a hail of fury, lasers splicing through the void of space at the speed of light, mobile artillery cannons already blasting. The Uppers were still in training for full-on combat; they weren't prepared for an attack by actual Combatants. Ship after ship was destroyed instantly.

Tom avoided the worst of the fire, scanning the ships for the familiar flying he'd recognize anywhere. He spotted Medusa's ship, which at first gleefully blasted three ships with three shots . . .

And then her weapons fire began to trail off, her ship began to list, because Tom knew she was paying attention to the absence of the five-kilometer asteroid that should be there, too. One by one, the Russo-Chinese guns fell silent, and only a few dim-witted cadets tried to take advantage and got destroyed for it. Tom knew they were probably waiting for instructions from their side, too.

Even though Tom wasn't in the same room as the enemy cadets, and they were physically across the world from one another, mentally even farther apart—there was a slow, cold realization that seemed to come over everyone of something very ominous happening right here. They were all human beings in the end, living on one planet together—and right now a massive asteroid was missing perilously close to their common doorstep.

Abruptly, Wyatt's thoughts burst back into the IRC.

They've spotted the asteroid. Terminating the connection.

Tom yanked out his neural wire and sat up in his cot outside the Helix. Everyone roused quickly, and Tom felt his heart pounding in his chest as he hunted for Wyatt among the cadets around them. He spotted her, standing by her cot now, her face ashen.

"Where'd they spot it?" Vik demanded, but they only needed to look at Wyatt's face to know.

"It's in the Neutral Zone. Our satellites finally detected it. It's closing fast. Something must've knocked it out of orbit. It's heading right for us."

The words sank like a stone into the stale silence of the chamber.

A five-kilometer-wide asteroid.

And it was on course to hit Earth.

Tom tried to wrap his head around the idea. An asteroid that large would cause an extinction-level event. None of their anti-asteroid tech was designed to stop an inbound meteor so close to Earth. They were supposed to spot these things ten, twenty years in advance, more than enough time to gradually deflect their course. Promethean Arrays were used to do it, and in severe cases, the CamCos were mobilized to detonate nukes against the surface to redirect the course—but always, always far from Earth, way before it came close.

"What does that mean?" Clint said. "What do we do?"

"We die, Clint," Lyla said bluntly. "We won't survive the impact."

"What can we do?" Tom asked Wyatt. "What are our orders?"

"We don't have any." She shook her head. "They sent the CamCos to man the orbiting ships but we don't have much equipment in the vicinity. The Russo-Chinese are trying to mobilize a defense. The Russian aerial defense force is gearing up to attack, and the Chinese are powering up their Promethean Arrays on the moon. They're planning to bombard it as soon as the moon's cleared the planet. That's all I know."

"How long do we have?" Vik asked hollowly.

Wyatt grimaced. "It's due to hit the Pacific in thirty-seven minutes."

Thirty-seven minutes! The words bounced through Tom's mind. He tried to wrap his head around this. In less than an hour, a five-kilometer-wide asteroid was going to hit.

It would kill everyone.

"So we wait?" Vik said.

Wyatt was breathing very hard now. Tom could only sit there in stunned silence. He watched her rip back her sleeve to access her forearm keyboard.

"What are you doing?" Tom asked her, thinking this was Wyatt, she might have an idea, some miraculous save.

"I'm telling Yuri. Yuri needs to know, too," she said. Tears misted her eyes. "I want Yuri to come up here. He has to know."

Tom felt very strange. He swallowed convulsively, trying to rid his throat of the feeling like a fist was clenched inside it. He couldn't believe something like this was actually going to happen, that an ordinary day could be transformed so quickly.

He looked around the room, still very quiet, a strange calm in the air. It was surreal.

No.

The thought broke through his numbness.

No, Wyatt had to be wrong. She had to be. This couldn't be it. The world couldn't end like this, with no warning, no fanfare—humanity's final thirty-seven minutes after millions of years of evolution and thousands of years of technological progress. There were bad guys like Vengerov to destroy and good people with their own struggles, and Tom couldn't grasp the idea that all the conflicts and worries of humanity were simply going to be eradicated in a few short minutes. Life had to mean more than that. The world had to mean more than that. What had been the point of everything, if they were just going to be wiped out?

No. He lay back down on his cot, and plugged in his neural wire.

No one asked him what he was doing. Vik and Lyla were hugging each other; Wyatt was huddled on her cot, arms folded across her shaking body, waiting for Yuri. The others were discussing it in a stunned manner.

Tom interfaced with the Spire's system and shot out of himself.

EVERY SECURITY CAMERA he interfaced with showed a strange dichotomy—the people who'd heard the situation, either buzzing about, frantic with activity to try fixing it, or those with no power to change the outcome, swarming to the conferencing phones.

177

He saw generals discussing the likelihood of a nuclear strike on the asteroid.

"The president needs to understand," General Mezilo snapped into a conferencing phone, "nukes don't have the same power in a vacuum. You need atmosphere. And once Cruithne hits our atmosphere, it's too late. Do you know how many safety controls we have on our nuclear arsenals? And that's assuming they're even in range once Cruithne hits."

Inside the system, a swarm of buzzing 0's and 1's, Tom listened to Mezilo explain to the others that the timing simply wouldn't work: by the time enough firepower was unleashed, they would all have been dead in a good half hour.

But it didn't become real, truly real, until he snapped into a surveillance camera in the Pentagon and felt a shock, seeing General Marsh for the first time in a year.

And then Blackburn moved through the door.

"James," Marsh said, abandoning formalities, sounding as tired and old as he looked. He smiled wryly. "It seems we were worried about the wrong apocalypse."

Blackburn ignored formalities, too. He planted his palms on the desk. "All the equipment we have on that asteroid and there was no forewarning it had been knocked out of orbit? You know that's not an accident. That doesn't happen."

Marsh rubbed the bridge of his nose. "It doesn't matter now."

"He's probably cozied up in a bunker somewhere and—"

Marsh surged out of his chair. "We have minutes. That's all. Minutes. I'm going to get on that phone and try to call my daughter, and tell my grandson I love him."

"But he—"

"Enough! I know what you've been doing, Lieutenant."

That stopped Blackburn short. "You do?"

"I've had a good idea, and now you've confirmed it for me. I could have shared my theories, but I let you do it. But that's all done now. You're out of time. We all are. These are the last moments of your life. Make peace with God. Look at some pictures of your kids. Call your mother. Do *something* other than fixate on the white whale of yours."

Blackburn didn't seem to know how to answer that for a long moment. He touched the scar on his cheek unconsciously. "There is nothing else, General."

"Then I'm sorry for you, James. I really am. That was no way to live, and it's certainly no way to die."

Something about the calm resignation drawn over Marsh's face knocked Tom out of his numbed stupor. He was profoundly disturbed to see both Marsh and Blackburn treating this like the end, because, no, this was *not* the end. He'd show them! He shot out of the surveillance cameras, through the electronic pipelines, determination surging through him.

He wasn't going to let this happen. There had to be something he could do. He had the closest thing there was to a real superpower. He'd use it.

Nothing was over.

CRUITHNE WAS A large, irregular rock. Every so often, light flashed over its surface where old, inactive equipment was stored, left over from numerous uses of the asteroid as a way station.

Tom gazed at it through the electronic eyes of a satellite

it was passing, realizing in a strange, detached way he might be looking at the instrument of his death—of the death of all humanity.

He fired a thruster to twist the satellite around as the asteroid moved beyond it, and then he saw Earth.

The sight was like an explosion in his brain.

Earth, so stark and bright and full of life against the darkness beyond it, and that asteroid sailing straight toward it. He'd never appreciated before how fragile that thin layer of atmosphere surrounding the planet was. As soon as the asteroid hit, all those oceans would vaporize, the atmosphere would burn, and everyone he loved . . .

Everyone he loved . . .

Tom began to frantically leap from one machine in orbit to another, searching for something, anything. Cruithne had been knocked out of orbit once. He had a few minutes. He'd throw everything in orbit at it.

He activated thrusters of satellites and propelled them into the side. They were too small, but they were all he had. They exploded against the asteroid's surface, harmless. The RussoChinese military obviously had the same idea, because as soon as the moon emerged from around the curvature of Earth, every single Promethean Array on its surface lit at once, bright beams streaking toward Cruithne. Tom gazed through the eyes of another satellite, watching with frantic hope as the asteroid was nudged, just a bit. And then nuclear missiles hit. They couldn't create a blast wave in space, but detonated against the surface of the asteroid, they could nudge it. The explosions were brilliant enough to cripple all the satellites in the vicinity. It took Tom some time to find another, but his heart sank when he did, and saw the asteroid still on course to hit.

Nuclear weapons would be more effective once the asteroid was in the atmosphere.

His blood raced with anxiety at the thought, because by then, they might be doomed anyway.

Soon, he saw ships, Indo-American and Russo-Chinese both, whip around the curve of Earth, rocketing to a swift momentum, firing even more at the asteroid. The sustained assault was wreaking damage, tearing chunks out of the asteroid, hurtling them off into space, but not enough, not enough.

The ships ran out of armaments and hurtled straight into the asteroid. Tom could see its orbit was shallower now; it was no longer plunging in a fatal death drop straight toward the planet, but when his processor ran the calculations, he knew it was still going to hit. The atmosphere wouldn't burn enough away.

And then when Tom jumped to another satellite, his mind met hers.

Medusa!

Through a haze of electronic signals, he felt her there, right there, with him. For a moment, he was blinded by a mingle of anxiety and hope, because they were all going to die, they were going to die, and he didn't know how to fix it, but if anyone could, she could—and something about Medusa seemed to respond to that thought.

Thanks for the vote of confidence. I mean it. Tom, it's not over.

What can we do? Tom asked.

There are thousands of nuclear missiles on the surface of the planet. I have access to the missile defense systems of every single country. No firewalls and no safety controls can keep me out. I can blow the asteroid into smaller pieces once it penetrates the atmosphere.

It won't work, Tom thought. *I heard our generals talking about it. Medusa, they can't mobilize them fast enough.*

They can't. But I can. I know where they are and I can access, aim, and launch them near simultaneously all across the world. I'll be fast enough. I'll break it up into fragments small enough to burn up in the atmosphere.

Let me help!

It would take too long to show you where they are or show you how to use them. You have to trust me. This is life or death for me, too.

Tom realized she'd been interfacing for years before he had; she'd explored exhaustively where he hadn't bothered. She could do this. She believed she could do this, and if she thought so, then he thought so.

His mind raced over the implications. A series of high-atmosphere nuclear explosions would still kill millions of people. Maybe billions. The fragments would still hit, would still kill everyone near the impact zones—but not everyone.

Not everyone. If she broke it up enough, and the atmosphere did its job of burning the smallest fragments up, there was a chance they wouldn't go the way of the dinosaurs.

They both still might die. One or the other of them might, depending on where the asteroid entered orbit. Tom thought quickly, *Yaolan, I . . .*

Tom, if there's an impact where you are, or where I am, I

want you to know I don't hate you for what you did. You're one of the only people who's ever tried to do something like that for me. Thank you.

A sudden longing and sentimentality overcame him. *I wish we'd had time. I wish you'd been closer. I wish I'd held you just once in person, no avatars . . .*

Stop, Tom.

No time, I know. I know.

No, you're getting exceedingly cheesy. Let's meet the apocalypse with some dignity. It was great knowing you.

It was excellent knowing you, too. His terror receded as amusement swept over him, and then that was it. Medusa slipped out of the satellite; he knew there was nothing more he could do. He pulled out his neural wire and stood up in the room, aware that the next few minutes would determine everything and it was totally out of his hands.

He found his feet, walking as if in a trance. Yuri was there now, holding Wyatt. Vik and Lyla had disappeared somewhere.

"Thomas," Yuri greeted. "Let us stay together, the three of us."

"Yeah," Tom said numbly.

They walked together up to the fourteenth floor so they could gaze out the massive windowed walls at the sky from the CamCo floor and watch the world come to an end.

Vik joined them soon, a bit breathless.

"Where's Lyla?" Tom asked him.

"Calling her parents. I figured I should be here. Remember that bet we made once?"

Tom knew that bet. "You two . . ."

Vik grinned and sang tauntingly, "I beat you."

Lucky bastard! "Imminent asteroid strike has to be cheating."

"Lyla initiated it, not me."

It made sense that people facing the apocalypse jumped into things they normally wouldn't do. "I'll pay you in a few hours," Tom grumbled.

"We're going to be dead in a few hours," Vik complained.

"That's the idea."

"You two are bad people," Wyatt said. Then she realized it. "My parents!" She threw Yuri an urgent glance. He rubbed her shoulder. "I forgot to call them."

"'Bad people' made you think of your parents?" Vik wondered.

"I could not get through to mine," Yuri told her.

"I tried to call mine, too. Lines are jammed," Vik said. "Everyone in the place is trying to call family. All the soldiers, too. Lyla's going to try again, but I'm not hopeful."

Tom thought of Neil with a sick, swooping feeling. He wouldn't call him, even if he could. He loved him, he wanted to tell him, but he didn't want Neil to see the fear on his face. It would be better for his dad not to see the end coming.

It killed Tom that the last thing they'd done was fight.

"If we are all about to be dying soon," Yuri said to them, "I wish to know something."

They looked at him.

His earnest blue eyes roved over them. "Was that you three who burned Obsidian Corp. and destroyed the transmitter? Did you do that for me?"

Tom, Vik, and Wyatt looked at one another. There was no reason to lie.

"Yeah, that was us," Vik said.

Yuri grew misty-eyed. "You risked your lives for me." He drew Wyatt very close. "I would never have asked this of you, but I cannot thank you enough. I wish we had more time for me to be thanking you."

"Next life, man," Vik said. They all looked at him, and he shrugged. "Okay, it's out: I believe in reincarnation. Always have. It makes sense to me—matter and energy are never destroyed, just converted, right? I'm just not sure where we'll reincarnate to without life on Earth."

"Aliens?" Wyatt suggested.

Vik laughed softly. "You don't believe in aliens."

"Of course there are aliens. This isn't the end of life in the universe. It would be ludicrous to even suggest complex life hasn't evolved somewhere else in the universe." She nodded, as though convincing herself. "And even after we're gone, our radio waves will reach someone, maybe decades after this. Maybe centuries from now, someone will find the Voyager probes and realize we existed." Then she sagged down. "I hope, at least. I can't believe there are eight point eight billion stars out there likely to have Earthlike planets, and we never even tried to get to one of them. Why didn't we work harder to discover faster-than-light technology? It was so shortsighted of us to all stay on the same planet. Now all of humanity might go extinct together."

Vik stretched out his legs. "On the bright side . . ."

"There's a bright side?" Wyatt exclaimed.

"I can tell you this without too much mockery in the future: I had this stupid crush on you when I first came here."

185

His distraction worked instantly. Wyatt's eyes swung to his. "What?"

"What?" Yuri said.

"You always made fun of me. You called me Man Hands!" Wyatt pointed out.

"Come on, don't you know how I tick?" Vik grinned. "You were this annoying, prickly math dork who took everything so seriously. You'd get upset and remind me of some . . . some hyperactive little squirrel. Oh, and, Yuri, don't worry, man, I swear not to spend the last minutes of my life putting the moves on your girlfriend."

"Then I shall not spend them punching you like I did Thomas."

Tom laughed.

"What?" Vik exclaimed. "Why'd you slug Tom?"

"I kissed Wyatt," Tom said.

"It was so embarrassing," Wyatt said with a laugh.

"What? Why? How?" Vik sputtered.

"Long story," Tom answered. They didn't have time for any long stories.

Vik started laughing and clapped him on the back. "Traitors! No one told me. To think of all the ways I could've mocked you two, and now I've learned of it only minutes before we all die! Why, God, why? This is the most unfair thing ever."

He oofed as Tom and Wyatt both elbowed him.

"I don't believe in an afterlife," Yuri said suddenly, gazing pensively toward the window. "I believe this is all we have. These minutes, right here."

They fell into silence, suddenly sobered. Tom couldn't

concentrate or reflect or even figure out what he believed about life and death and other profound things like that. He wasn't resigned to death here.

"And I have no regrets." Yuri's arm tightened around Wyatt. He gazed down at her, stroking her hair with his hand. "I am happy to have had so much in this time. It means more, that this is all we have, these last moments. And I have had a chance to fall in love."

Wyatt's eyes widened. Yuri held her gaze, big hand cupping her cheek. "You do know I love you, do you not?"

She nodded shakily. "And, Yuri, I . . ." Her words choked off. She couldn't seem to manage anything. She tightened her arms around him, like she was trying to seal them together.

"And such friends," Yuri said, his gaze moving to Tom and Vik now. "I feel great privilege for having known you. You are the best friends I have ever had."

"I love you, too, man," Vik pledged. He slung his arm around Tom. "All of you guys."

It was Tom's turn. He felt blood rush up into his cheeks because he'd never been comfortable with this stuff. "Me, too, you guys. I mean, I, uh, you know." Their eyes seemed to be boring into him. "You're my family, okay?" Then he started laughing. He couldn't help it. "We're going to cringe over this later if we survive."

Yuri and Wyatt exchanged a glance.

"Thomas, you realize we are not going to survive," Yuri said softly, his eyes filled with compassion.

"We can't possibly, man," Vik said, tightening the arm around his shoulder. "This is game over. None of our planetary defenses can hold off an asteroid this large. We might get off a few nukes, but that's all. This type of thing wiped out the dinosaurs. I mean, sure, maybe some of the important people are in their bunkers, but the rest of us . . ."

Tom looked from one unnaturally calm face to another, people resigned to a death they could do nothing to stop. He hadn't told them what he knew. Death wasn't a certainty at all. He knew there was the slimmest chance, just the slimmest one, that Medusa would come through—and he was clinging to that with ferocious claws. He suddenly couldn't keep this to himself.

"I saw what they were doing in space," Tom said steadily. "Trust me, they've done a lot of damage already, they've broken the asteroid up into a much smaller fragment. It's got a lot of ice, it's not made of iron, and whatever knocked it out of orbit hit it in a way that didn't put too much momentum behind it. And as soon as it enters our atmosphere, some more will burn away—"

"Not enough," Wyatt said.

"Yeah, but Medusa's also gonna hit it with everything we've got. Every nuke she can fire. It'll spread some fallout, but she might be able to bust it up before it explodes over the ground. She can do it faster than anyone else."

"Wait, what?" Vik said, shaking his head.

"Tom, what are you—" Wyatt began.

Tom suddenly decided to forget secrecy. He had nothing to lose. "I know you think I'm making this stuff up, but I'm not. I have this ability, you guys. It's . . . it's not like a superpower. I think it's something about my processor, but I can go in

188

machines. I can control them all like they're designed for neural processors. Any machine that's got an internet connection and enough bandwidth, basically."

They all three stared at him, and for the first time since they learned of their imminent doom, there was no fear on their faces. Tom felt a strange, giddy sense of liberation, unburdening himself, even if it might mean nothing soon.

"Medusa can do it, too. It's how I've been talking to her. We can both enter each other's systems without anyone detecting us. Like, directly enter, go right through firewalls. That's why I can tell you I know what I'm talking about when I say there's a chance someone might stop Cruithne: I was inside the satellites, I saw what was happening, and I talked to Medusa. She's got a plan."

They all stared at him.

Tom gave a half-hysterical laugh. "And while I'm being honest, I might as well tell you, I blew up the skyboards, too. I'm the ghost in the machine. Me."

They all three gaped at him. None of them was looking out the window when a chunk of the asteroid streaked bright across the sky, and the enormous roar of it exploding before it hit the ground sent them all hurtling down to the floor, clutching each other, terrified, eyes squeezed shut.

And then the rumbling beneath them died down, and all that was left was the sound of their harsh breathing, the feel of their arms around each other—and outside the sunlight still cutting through the clear blue atmosphere.

It wasn't the end of the world.

The sky did not choke with ash. No wave of boiling ocean swept over Earth.

189

Armageddon had been averted.

But not without cost.

That evening, as the shell-shocked cadets all trickled into the mess hall, where stunned soldiers also milled about, the emergency screens along the walls were on, every news station focusing upon the various impact craters. Over and over, the image replayed Medusa's heroic rescue of the planet, the high-atmosphere nuclear explosions that lit up the sky, one after the other after the other.

Most of the chunks of debris burned up in the atmosphere. Many still hit. Many exploded just above ground, and still devastated landscape. The fallout spread over Earth, contaminated whole countries.

But they were alive.

And then Joseph Vengerov appeared on the news and claimed credit for the nuclear impacts.

There wasn't enough hatred in Tom's heart to encompass how much he loathed the man on the screens in the mess hall, even as everyone else blazed with pride and applauded the oligarch who'd supposedly saved Earth.

Tom could've driven his fist through every screen showing Vengerov's smiling face. The bastard knew he could get away with claiming credit, because the alternative was that the ghost in the machine stepped forward and admitted to doing it him or herself. So the formerly disgraced CEO smiled and graciously answered questions, his eyes flashing in silent challenge at the screen—like he was inwardly laughing at the person out there who'd truly saved the world.

01111111100111010110000000010011110000
1011011110011110000000010110100100111
000011110010010111001110110010110110
0001101100001011010010011000010111100001101
0110100001011101100000001001110011111
1100000111011011010000010011100001
00101011101110101011101011011000010
11110110000111011011101111000101010
110110100100010010010010000100101010
1001100110010011010101011000010110101010
000111101101101100000010000100010010
100111001101101001100100001000000000
1111101101000100111000001011110000000
11000000101101000000010001110011101
10001110011100001100100101011110110
01110010111100101101101011111001001
0111000010011100010000100001110101010
1110110110111011000110100100001111001
0110001111101110001000000101001010001

CHAPTER SIXTEEN

ALL THROUGH THE day, news of the impact and fallout sites trickled in.

Karl Marsters went pale as a sheet when a live view of Chicago appeared on the screen. Lyla Martin slung her arm around him and patted his shoulder. Everyone murmured when they saw footage of the fragment breaking up over Maryland, the explosion everyone in the Spire had heard as it happened and that flattened several coastal communities. Jennifer Nguyen screamed when the graphic of Vietnam was displayed. Iman pulled her in a hug and then led her from the mess hall.

Tom listened as well, rigid with anxiety at each new report trickling in, even though he didn't even know where his father was right now, and he didn't have any way to know whether his dad could've been affected. There was an impact in Colorado, and one in the Gulf of Mexico that sent a tsunami into the coast. A smaller fragment exploded over New Mexico and wiped out everything within thirty miles.

That's the one Tom worried about. That one. Neil went there sometimes. Every time he thought of it, every time he thought of his uncertainty over his dad, he felt like he was going to throw up. He tried not to.

The high-altitude nuclear detonations acted like EMPs, knocking out power over whole swaths of countries. Nuclear plants were in danger of catastrophic meltdowns, and there were fires raging unchecked. Pilots began mobilizing across the world to search for survivors, to bring in humanitarian aid to all the devastated locations.

The United States finally felt the impact of all the money that had been funneled from its public infrastructure, the privatization of its roads, its hospitals, its disaster relief. Neglected roads couldn't handle the strain of emergency vehicles evacuating people. Fires burned unchecked over cities because too few people had been trained to respond, and those unmanned drones used for surveillance and breaking up raucous crowds weren't designed for humanitarian efforts. Local water utilities were in disrepair, and pipes burst under the strain. Companies that owned roads tried to enforce their tolls even on first responders, and Harbinger its fees on water, until the angry crowds began breaking into their headquarters, frightening the executives into feeling sudden gushes of concern for their fellow humans—and giving a free pass for the sake of relief efforts.

At first, the massive number of humanitarian planes and helicopters clogged the sky, causing a dangerous situation with the thirty million unmanned drones still dispersed over the country—most of which were designed for surveillance, few of which were actually useful in a natural disaster. After several collisions, even the unmanned drones had to be landed. The angry crowds ensured that, too.

It seemed even the Coalition executives quailed in the face of the sort of unified public spirit roused by an extreme natural disaster. The only company that was untouchable, the only ones who were golden, no matter their actions, were those who worked for Obsidian Corp., and Joseph Vengerov himself.

Only Tom and his friends knew he was claiming credit for something Medusa had done.

Saving the planet won him forgiveness of all sins. The Coalition companies that had attacked him days before over his faulty machines, over the attacks that conveniently spared his own executives, now lauded him publicly. They dared not do anything else. In one widely publicized speech, Vengerov stood atop a pile of debris, ringed by first responders, and spoke of his company's determination to ensure something like this never happened again. He concluded by holding up a flag, a Coalition of Multinationals flag.

There was great symbolism in the version he chose, because it wasn't the current version with only the Indo-American aligned companies—it was the old version, the original version from before World War III. It was a crowded monstrosity of a flag. At the heart, stood the symbol of the United Nations. An inner ring displayed the World Trade Organization, the World Bank, and the International Monetary Fund logos. The outer ring at the edges of the flag displayed all twelve company logos, united together in their dominion over Earth.

And suddenly, people could forgive Vengerov's deception over LM Lymer Fleet and Obsidian Corp. So what if he'd been selling the same tech to both sides? So what if he'd secretly profited off both sides of the conflict? He considered himself a citizen of the world, not of any country. It wasn't treason for a man to betray people who should feel privileged just to have someone like him in their midst. Owning companies on both sides was simply putting his money where his mouth was, where his heart was.

Vengerov wasn't a war profiteer, he was a humanitarian. He believed in unity.

EVERY CADET ABOVE sixteen in the Spire was recruited for the search and rescue efforts. They were infinitely useful, after all, able to download all the skills of a paramedic in a night, able to pilot or fly or operate almost any vehicle in demand after a night's download. And they didn't need much sleep to function in top form. Some became medics overnight; others like Tom served as pilots. All the old, non-automated vehicles were brought back into commission and deployed, and someone needed to steer them.

A few of the larger, stronger cadets joined fire-fighting brigades and search and rescue squads. Tom helped move them to the sites where they were needed. All their orders were in their processors; Tom followed it all mindlessly like he was moving through a dream.

One morning, he still felt like he was in a strange trance as he watched the sun rise over the devastated landscape of Indiana, his hand resting on the throttle, feet on the pedals of the helicopter. All the cadets old enough to help had been hastily given army fatigues, a temporary commission, and ordered to fly where told, wait, and return with new batches of injured, moaning survivors as the Red Cross rounded them up and packed them off for the various triage centers.

He didn't feel anything more than vague surprise as Karl Marsters crossed the tarmac and climbed in next to him, rubbing sleep out of his eyes, grumbling about needing to catch a ride with him to the next site where he was assigned. Usually when Tom and Karl ran into each other, a mutual recognition of hostility passed between them, followed by something unpleasant and occasionally violent. Lately Tom had varied the routine and creeped Karl out by being civil to him, but it was a very one-sided civility and not entirely friendly.

Today, everything was different. It was like none of that old stuff mattered. The Karl who'd forced Tom to bark like a dog and the Tom who'd trapped Karl in sewage felt decades ago. None of their mutual hostility mattered in the face of the apocalyptic event they'd both survived.

"You wanna fly?" Tom offered. It seemed like a gracious concession to him, since he vastly preferred being at the controls.

Karl rubbed his eye with a thumb. "Not unless you're tired."

Tom wasn't. He opened the throttle and pulled the collective control, compressing the left pedal to lift them up into the air. Karl sagged back in his seat, gazing miserably out at the landscape below them.

"Hey," Tom said after a while, speaking loudly to be heard over the humming of the rotor, "look, I'm sorry about Chicago."

Karl shifted in his seat, restive. "My sister's there. At Loyola."

"Sorry."

The larger boy looked at him for the first time. "What about you? You hear from your family?"

"There's just my old man." Tom felt that sensation like his stomach was turning over. "I haven't heard anything, but I guess that's expected. Lines are down most everywhere. There wasn't too much in the Southwest, but if anyone gets out of stuff okay, it's him."

"Hope you hear something."

"Thanks."

Karl stared down at the fires like smears against the landscape near Gary. He balled up his fist and smacked the dashboard. "We're so close," he said, teeth gritted. "I'd ditch and go myself if the roads weren't all jammed."

Tom guessed what he was talking about. "Can't you request they send you to the relief effort in Chicago?"

"This is as close as I can get. They want me doing my job. They know I'd be gone in a second there to look for—" His voice broke off.

Tom eyed him. Then he twisted the helicopter around, set off in another direction. Karl blinked over at him. "What are you doing?"

"I'm accidentally flying off course." He raised his eyebrows. "So if I'm off course and happen to land in Chicago instead of Gary, I don't think anyone's gonna blame you for looking into some personal business."

For a moment, the other boy just stared at him. "You'll get a reprimand for this."

"Yeah, another one. I'll survive somehow."

Karl settled back in his seat. Soon the remains of the taller buildings resolved into view, along with a smattering of burning buildings and abandoned cars choking the road alongside the lake.

"You know where you wanna go?" Tom asked.

"Drop me off downtown. I'll figure it out from there. Since you're off course and all."

Tom landed them on the beach by the lake. Karl popped open the door, and spun around to survey him in the purple early dawn light.

"Raines," he said, pointing a big finger, "you're okay."

Tom nodded to him, and then when Karl was clear of the helicopter, he launched off into the air again.

DAYS BLURRED INTO weeks. The final death count ticked up to 772 million. Instead of finding injured survivors trapped under ashen debris, in the burned or flattened zones, relief teams began finding bodies. Tom and the other cadets were going to be reassigned to their standard duties soon.

Tom's hours were filled with activity, and at night when he closed his eyes, all the frantic, harried images of the day rushed behind his lids, like even his neural processor was struggling to make sense of everything that had taken place since finding that asteroid missing.

Sometimes he saw the triage centers with the bloodied, chalk-white faces, the bodies that blurred before his eyes because there were so many of them, and torment gripped him at the very idea his dad might be one of them, out there somewhere, maybe hoping Tom would find him, hoping he'd help him. Tom stayed up late even after two days straight in the field, scrolling through the unorganized lists of survivors, flipping through surveillance footage—whatever surveillance was left—until his vision went double.

And then one day, the unexpected happened.

Tom was taking a lunch break, seated in the door of his helicopter, devouring a sandwich and waiting for his next assignment, when a sleek hybrid airplane-helicopter glided down onto the landing strip before him. Tom reached up to hold his cap on, looking over its smooth lines admiringly. He hadn't had a chance to fly one of those yet apart from in simulations. Then the door popped open and a lone figure emerged from its depths.

The person moved toward him at a steady pace, a small woman wearing a standard set of fatigues with markings he didn't recognize . . . obviously someone from another country aiding the relief effort.

And then she drew closer and Tom's heart stilled.

He felt like he'd frozen up, like every molecule in his body had grown rigid, paralyzed, tense, just waiting for his brain to make sense of what his eyes were seeing, because it couldn't possibly be—

Her.

It was her!

Tom launched himself forward, leaping out of the helicopter, and started toward her, only to stop several feet away, just staring at the girl he'd never seen in person. Medusa's black hair flapped in the breeze, her eyes like two dark crescents gazing up into his, the scarring of the left side of her face giving her a tense, disapproving look.

"Medusa." Tom couldn't believe it. The word was a whisper.

She studied him for a long moment. "So you're real. I didn't imagine you."

"Was that in question?"

"I haven't slept since Cruithne. Everything's in question right now," she said.

She turned away to head back to her helicopter, but Tom bolted forward and grabbed her arm. "Wait!"

"Don't touch me," she warned him.

Tom let his hand slip from her arm. The cold morning air was crisp, billowing white clouds of breath puffing from his mouth. He wasn't even shivering. He felt electrified all over, his brain blazing with wonder, disbelief. She was here. She was actually here. He'd touched her arm. Her *real* arm.

"How did you even get here?"

Medusa stared at him. She pointed back at her airplane.

"Yeah, got that. I mean—how? Why?"

"I tracked down your GPS signal. I was curious about how you would compare in person." She threw a distracted glance around. "I suppose I should go now."

"Wait. Wait."

She looked at him curiously as Tom tried to form words.

He finally came up with some. "Have you gone insane?"

She had to have a GPS signal. Her military would register that she was in the United States. They'd think she'd flown off and defected. She had no excuse to be here. He charged toward her, and she didn't shove him away when he clasped her small shoulders roughly.

"Medusa, are you crazy? You flew over here just for a look? You'll get tried for treason. They'll think you defected! You have to go back now! Blame an instrument error or something. Anything. Just fly back right now!"

199

But looking at her, at the strange distance in her dark eyes, Tom realized she hadn't come because of idle curiosity. There was more to this.

"What's wrong?" he pressed.

"Nothing."

"Did you even hear me? You're taking a huge risk here."

She closed her eyes heavily. "It doesn't matter." There was a strange flatness to her that Tom never saw through the surveillance cameras, never saw in simulations. It wasn't like her. "None of it matters anymore. Look around. I've been at the Citadel." Her gaze wandered somewhere far in the distance. "It seems like everyone lost someone. I had to stand there and pretend . . ."

"Pretend what?" Tom demanded. "Pretend you didn't save the planet?"

She gripped her temples. "I've run through the scenario over and over again, and I've recalculated the trajectory of those missiles. I could have gotten the entire asteroid, Tom. I could have done better. If I'd been two seconds faster, that's a hundred million people alive right there. These people died because of me."

Tom gaped at her. "But you got the asteroid."

"I read analyses on the internet. They all think it was Joseph Vengerov, but they're saying he could have done a better job if—"

"Stop doing this to yourself. Come here." Tom pulled her up against him, ignoring the way she pushed at him. He knew she'd made a momentous decision that day, firing those nukes. The consequences numbered in billions of lives. She'd taken

200

on the most nerve-racking, frightening task possible in averting a total apocalypse and he wasn't going to let her do this to herself. "You saved the world. Don't you get that? Why else do you think Vengerov is claiming credit? If some idiots are criticizing it, forget them. They're morons!"

"I could've done better—"

"There's no use thinking that. You can't go back in time. Maybe you possibly, theoretically, by some quirk of luck or whatever might've saved more, but you know, you could've saved a lot fewer people than you did. That's for sure. That could've happened, too. You could've freaked out or frozen up. You could've panicked, and if you had, then who'd be left? A handful of rich people who had bunkers and the machines and supplies to ride out a nuclear winter. You did the right thing. Don't doubt yourself."

"It's not that easy." She extricated herself from his grip. He expected her to leave him then, but she just sat on the ground, like she didn't have the energy to move herself. "I feel like I can't think."

"Yeah, well, not sleeping for a couple weeks can do that for you," Tom said. He realized suddenly how much that had to be messing with her head. Medusa wouldn't do something like this normally. She'd have better judgment. She wasn't thinking clearly.

He rubbed his head. Okay, he'd have to figure out how to cover for her. It felt like a great weight compressing his chest, pondering covering the tracks for someone else when he didn't even know yet how much damage had been done.

With a start, he suddenly realized what Blackburn had to

feel, getting stuck doing this for him over and over again. So what would Blackburn do? Where would he start?

"Your GPS signal," Tom said. "Did you disguise your GPS signal?"

"I think so," she said, her voice faint, arms wrapped around her bent knees.

"This is a yes-or-no question. No thinking."

Her black eyes moved up to his, a flash of anger in them that reassured him. "Yes."

Tom looked between her plane and his, his neural processor calling up the schematics for the Interstice. He was getting an idea about what to do here.

She'd told him once to find someone who actually needed him. This time, she did, and he could see that clear as day. He was the only person who knew what she'd done, so he was the only person who could help fix this.

He headed to his helicopter and set the autonavigation, then returned. "Come on. I'm taking you somewhere."

She shook her head.

Tom sighed. "Okay. We'll do it this way, then." He leaned over and swept her up into his arms. He intended to be all manly and smooth, but it was trickier carrying a live human who was irritated with him than he thought it would be. He threw her over his shoulder like a sack of potatoes instead and tromped off toward her hybrid plane.

"What are you doing?" she complained. "There's nothing wrong with my legs."

"Watch your head," he told her as he lifted her through the door.

But despite his best efforts, her head bumped the doorframe, and suddenly she cursed at him in Cantonese. Tom found himself smiling, because that was the most reassuring thing he'd heard since her arrival.

It wasn't until they were both sitting in her hybrid plane that it hit him: this girl across from him, so close he could feel the heat radiating from her body . . .

This was Medusa. Here in person. It was actually Medusa.

Orders blinked in Tom's vision center. He responded that he had technical difficulties and was going to be delayed. Then he improvised a re-router to ensure his GPS signal stayed in the Midwest where he was supposed to be. He could get onto the Interstice for the trip back.

Then he launched them into the air in her own plane. She lapsed into a slumber next to him, all the sleep she'd missed since Cruithne catching up to her. Tom found his eyes straying to her, over and over again, as he tried to wrap his mind around the fact that she was real, she was here. He could see her chest rising and falling, the way a strand of her dark hair fluttered over her eyes. The scar tissue over one of her lids, and the other eyelid with a sweep of dark lashes. He wondered what had happened, how it must have hurt.

She didn't wake until well after he'd landed, when the humid breeze was stirring through the door of the plane, flung open to reveal the vivid sunset outside.

"Come on," Tom said, easing her out with him.

Medusa rubbed at her eyes as they settled onto the ground, looking around, perplexed, at the stretch of jagged landscape, the lush trees sprawled out below, the ocean sparkling in the distance.

203

"What do you think? Pretty, right?" Tom said.

"Why did you take me here?" Medusa wondered. "I didn't come to sightsee."

"You know Cruithne was supposed to hit in the Pacific?" Tom said, voicing the words he'd thought of on his way over. His motivational pep talk. "Once it hit, it would've sent a massive wave of boiling water over this place. So look around and think about the fact that this place is only here because of you. And not just this place. All in all, there were way more people than seven hundred million about to die before you blew up Cruithne. So, I guess what I'm trying to say is, get over it."

"Get over it?" Medusa echoed.

"Yeah. Get over it. Don't you know how ridiculous it is, kicking yourself for *only* saving *ten and a half billion* people? You're a hero! Or heroine, whatever. I'd love to be the one who saved the world. I'd spend the rest of my life feeling way too proud of myself about it. I'd tell anyone who'd hear me that I saved the whole world, and forget hiding my ability. It would be worth risking Vengerov coming after me just for the bragging rights of saying I'm the one who saved the world."

For a moment, he swore, she almost smiled.

"You actually get to legitimately say you saved the world," Tom marveled. "Or you will be able to down the road when the ghost in the machine and all our secrets don't matter anymore. You did it, so stop whining and accept the credit already for this amazing thing you did. So . . . that's it. That's what I have to say. Thinking about stuff you can't change or fix anymore is stupid and pointless. You say you could've done it better, but you know you could have done infinitely worse. That's why I brought you here, so you can see visible evidence of a place you saved."

Medusa frowned. "You could have shown me anything. Why are we in Hawaii?"

"I figured this was closer to China so you have a quick flight home." He flashed her a grin. "And I kind of wanted an excuse to see this place."

A smile twitched her lips.

"You're starting to get it, aren't you?" Tom said, growing sure of it. Maybe she'd just needed to sleep, maybe she'd needed to air her worst fears to someone . . . but Tom liked to think he'd had a hand in the smile that crept to her lips.

The wind rippled through her dark hair. "I can't believe you flew us all the way to Hawaii to tell me something you could have said hours ago."

"Yeah, but you needed sleep, Medusa. Plus then I wouldn't have gotten to impress you with a surprise trip to Hawaii."

She peered at him, her veil of hair hiding that part of her face she never liked to show him. "You can call me Yaolan."

"Yaolan," he murmured.

And when she stepped toward him, Tom didn't hesitate. He pulled her into his arms and dipped his head to hers, his lips pressing hers, parting them. Her fingers skimmed his sides, and Tom realized everything was better in person. Everything. No virtual reality could capture the feel of her body like magic in his grip, a chaos of sensations racing over his skin like he'd finally reached some point he'd been journeying to for years, never reaching it.

Even though it went against his every instinct, his every cell

205

and pore and molecule, he was the one who forced himself to step back. His voice sounded strained. "Ready to fly yourself back?"

She searched his face. "Did I do something wrong?"

"No. Never." Tom reached out and brushed aside the hair hiding that part of her face, wondering how it was possible to feel drunk on someone's presence. He felt like anything was possible around her, like his life meant more, like *he* meant more. She didn't close her eyes. "I want to see you again. Not after we almost all die, not after an apocalypse, not after anything like that. But right now . . . Right now if I stay with you much longer, I'll do something wrong."

She leaned her forehead against his chest, and Tom stroked her silky black hair. They didn't need to say anything more. Tom felt for the first time in a long while like things were right in the world.

CHAPTER SEVENTEEN

EVERYTHING INSIDE HIM seemed to be humming, thrumming with elation later when he returned to the Pentagonal Spire, such a strange sensation after the recent weeks of stark misery. He had to concentrate to stop himself from grinning stupidly, his thoughts filled with her, just her.

She'd flown back to China but Tom had touched her, held her, the girl he'd obsessed over for years, and suddenly nothing felt impossible to him anymore. He hadn't really felt this way since losing his fingers—this sense like he was totally free, invincible. Even with a world between them, he felt he could leap over the seas and transcend it all.

What if I quit tomorrow?

Tom had never had the thought before, but it spun into his head, fanciful, insane, and suddenly incredible, because he realized there was something else out there if he didn't make it in the Intrasolar Forces. If he weren't here at the Spire, there wouldn't be any restrictions on his movement anymore, on who he talked to. Even if he worked for some Coalition company or another, he'd have the freedom of civilian life.

Even if the countries were at war in space, that wouldn't stop him from seeing her.

The ideas spun in his mind until he reached the elevator, where the doors parted to reveal Lieutenant Blackburn.

Before Tom could react, he seized Tom's collar and yanked him inside.

"Are you a fool? What were you thinking?"

Tom's eyes flew to his. "About what?"

"You know what."

"I know I can't stand here talking about it," Tom reminded him.

"Oh please, do you think I'd forget to block the surveillance?" The elevator jerked to a stop. "Again, have you lost your mind?"

How had he found out so soon? Tom had redirected his GPS signal; Yaolan had redirected hers. He even had his cover story prepared.

"There was a problem with fuel. My mistake—" He tried to shrug out of Blackburn's grip, but the man's fingers tightened on his arm.

"News flash, Raines: you can't just run off and meet your girlfriend from the *enemy* side!"

"She came to me. I just took her back!"

"After a stop-off in Hawaii?"

"It's between here and China, and she had to go back there anyway. Look, she blamed herself for what happened. For everyone who died. I couldn't let her. She was saving us."

Blackburn's face went very still. "That was her?"

And for a moment, the world ground to a halt, blood roaring up in Tom's ears as he realized he'd just revealed to Blackburn who the other ghost in the machine was. From the shock on Blackburn's face, he'd come to the same realization, too.

Knock him out, erase his memory of this . . .

Tom didn't even get to his forearm keyboard. Blackburn's brutal grip descended on him, shoving Tom against the wall with breathtaking speed.

"I am *not* going to hurt her," Blackburn rasped in Tom's ear.

Tom seized Blackburn's wrist and whirled around, using his whole body weight to unbalance Blackburn, driving him forward against the wall, the superior reflexes of youth for once overcoming Blackburn's size advantage—and suddenly he was the one with the other man pinned. "You're right. You're *not* going to hurt her!"

Blackburn probably could have pushed him off, but he didn't try to fight him. "Listen to me. I am trying to help you. She has no reason to feel guilty. You can tell her that."

For a moment, silence descended between them, the only sound their rapid breathing.

"What do you mean?" Tom said reluctantly.

"The next time you talk to her, tell her Cruithne was not her fault."

"I've told her that, but—"

He looked back at Tom over his shoulder, his eyes two gray flints of steel. "Tell her it's very easy for someone with the most well-stocked bunker money can buy, two multinational companies, and no regard for human life to knock an asteroid out of orbit."

Tom caught his breath. His grip slipped from Blackburn. "No way. No, it's too . . . it's too much, even for him."

209

"Why not?" Blackburn turned slowly, his gray eyes shining with an unsettling light. "Back in his twenties, one of his first acts as CEO of LM Lymer Fleet was to push the neutron bombing of the Middle East. He made a windfall off that contract. Do you honestly think a man with so little regard for human life in one part of the world sees people in other parts of the world differently? At the end of the day, whatever the nationality, whatever religion or creed or country we identify with, we're all just the rabble to people like Vengerov. Excess and expendable human beings."

Tom swallowed. Blackburn was right. Someone who could visit such atrocities on people on the other side of the world could just as easily do it elsewhere.

"His equipment failed to signal us when Cruithne was knocked out of orbit," Blackburn went on. "He's fully acquainted with the military capabilities of both sides. He knew we could damage the asteroid just enough to ensure this was a mass extinction event but not the end of all life on Earth. He has full access to every single machine in their arsenal. One command and Obsidian Corp.'s Promethean Arrays can fire at a target, redirect it. Or maybe a few of their Centurions can plant some hydrogen bombs in just the right spot to give an asteroid a good knock in the direction of his choosing."

"God . . ." Tom breathed, horrified. It all made a terrible sense.

"Then again," Blackburn mused darkly, "he could have used another asteroid like a cosmic game of billiards—that would've done the trick, too. Whatever the scenario, the net result is something that appeared to be a freak natural occurrence that happened right when the rest of the Coalition had turned on him, and it distracted everyone. The perfect way of taking the heat off his company. And if he drew out the ghost in the machine in the process, all the better."

"I didn't even try to cover my tracks."

Blackburn rubbed his palm over his mouth. "Then maybe he did."

Tom found himself thinking of Vengerov's gloating face on television as he claimed credit for saving the world, for what Medusa had done; and it took on a new significance, a new audacity.

Rage frothed up inside him. He grabbed Blackburn's collar, his voice shaking with fury. "Why haven't you killed him? After everything he's done to you, to everyone . . . I know you're capable of it. I know you killed Heather."

Shock transformed Blackburn's face. His grip slacked.

"Yeah, I'm a little more silent and subtle than a thermonuclear explosion after all," Tom said, shoving him away. "I've kept secrets. I know why you did that. But what I don't get is why Vengerov's still alive."

"Because I can't kill him," Blackburn said.

"What, you have a conscience when it comes to him?"

Blackburn leaned over him, shadows on his face. "He deserves a fate worse than death, Raines, but, no, that's not what stops me. *None* of us can kill him. There's a fail-safe of sorts: a command hardwired into our processors, even into his drones, prohibiting any of his machines from inflicting physical harm upon him."

Tom hadn't expected that. "Why can't you hack your own processor, then? You're so good with machines. Can't you reprogram that fail-safe?"

"It's not so easy. If I wanted to get into those sectors of code, I'd have to find a vulnerability so buried in the code, even Obsidian Corp. doesn't know about it—and hasn't devised a way to patch before I take advantage of it. It's called a zero-day exploit."

"So . . . great. Let's find one of these zero-day exploits. I'll get Wyatt to look, too."

Blackburn barked an incredulous laugh. "You don't listen in my class at all, do you, Raines? Finding a zero-day flaw is like winning the lottery. It's valuable because nobody realizes it's there, not even Obsidian Corp. You can sell zero-day information to governments or security companies for hundreds of millions of dollars because it's that rare. If every competent programmer in the Spire spent the year studying our code fulltime, I doubt we'd find one. We don't have the resources."

This time, he started up the elevator, and Tom didn't stop him.

"If he goes down, it won't be from a direct strike at our hands," Blackburn concluded. "We have to wait until people have forgotten Cruithne, and then maybe the other Coalition executives will remember why they turned on him."

And Tom had a sudden suspicion—maybe the other ghost in the machine would give them reason to remember again, too.

THAT NIGHT, TOM hooked in his neural wire to catch up on his own sleep. What seemed moments later, Vik yanked his neural wire out, and Tom found himself staring up at the three pale faces of his friends, crowded over his bed.

Consciousness initiated. The time is 0145.

"We need to talk," Vik informed him.

They slipped soundlessly through the darkened common room, and then into Wyatt's bunk. "Tiny Spicy Vikram."

"Can't you change that trigger phrase?" Vik complained, slumping onto Wyatt's empty bed. Her roommate, Evelyn, was still conked out on her own bed. They were free to be loud, since it was nearly impossible to wake someone with noise alone while their processors were hooked into the system.

"This is not a priority right now, Vik," Wyatt said.

Tom felt Yuri take him by the shoulders and steer him over to the bed. "Sit."

It was a command. Tom sat.

Vik slung an arm around his shoulders. "So . . ."

"So?" Tom said, wary.

Wyatt folded her arms. "The ghost in the machine."

"How?" Vik said.

"Why?" Yuri said.

"How?" Vik said again.

"It can't be you," Wyatt insisted.

"Seriously, how?" Vik said.

"Thomas, this is very strange," Yuri told him.

"Answer our questions," Wyatt said.

Tom threw his hands over his face, dearly regretting his rash admission in the moments they thought they were about to die. "Those were a lot of partial questions, and some weren't even questions."

"Start with 'how,'" Vik said. "I said it a bunch of times. You owe me for all that effort of vocalizing a single syllable several times."

213

"Okay. Look, I've had this ability since I got my neural processor. From the moment of install, really. I can go through firewalls. It feels like I can enter machines, you know, interface with them. Like at Obsidian Corp. While I uploaded that search program into the system, I interfaced with the system myself to look for Yuri's signal. Just in case I could find it faster."

Wyatt and Vik exchanged a look, like Tom had answered some question of theirs.

"What do you mean, interface?" Wyatt said. "We all interface."

"Yeah, but everyone can do it only with machines designed for a neural interface. The ones I do aren't." Tom shrugged. "Like in the Beringer Club. Vik, the thing you told me about with the septic tank, but it didn't work."

"What? But you—"

"I made it work. I interfaced with the septic tank and gave it a command the same way we command drones. Hence, I got the same result—backed-up sewage, flooded club, drenched executives. What I do also feels different from regular interfacing. It's like . . . it's like I'm *inside* the internet, moving through it. I can't really explain."

"And Medusa does this, too," Wyatt said, eyeing him dubiously.

"Yeah. Only, I didn't know about that until Capitol Summit. The first one. I tried to cheat by interfacing with some nearby satellites to see where she was, and she was already interfacing with them. Our minds were accessing the same machine at the same time."

Vik stared at him. "You can see through satellites."

"They're machines, they've got enough bandwidth, they're internet accessible, so yeah, I can. And Lieutenant Blackburn

214

knows. He's known since the census device. That's the stuff he erased from the surveillance archives." He looked at Wyatt. "When you found all those gaps in the footage from the census device, that's what they were. Blackburn erased them to hide what I could do."

Wyatt sank onto the other bed, heedless of the unconscious Evelyn, whose head she nearly sat on. "Why can you do this?"

"No idea," Tom said.

"Can you show us?" Yuri wondered. "I am finding this very difficult to grasp."

Tom nodded. "Sure. Look at that surveillance camera in the corner." He hooked into Wyatt's access port and interfaced with the surveillance system. He wagged the camera very deliberately at them, then snapped back into himself.

His friends were staring at him now, wide-eyed. It was such a small thing, but they knew he shouldn't have been able to do it. It was odd how much of a relief it was unburdening himself.

At least, that's what Tom thought until he realized Vik was sitting far from him on the bed now, his arms folded over his chest, his eyes haunted.

"Oh my God, do you guys realize what this means?"

Tom eyed him uneasily.

"It means I'm the right-hand man of the most wanted fugitive in the world. It means I blew up a building with the world's most dangerous terrorist! Tom, for God's sake, do you realize we're all going to prison when you get caught for what you're doing?"

"I won't get caught," Tom insisted.

Wyatt knelt down in front of him. "Tom, you have got to stop

215

killing all those CEOs and executives. It's not funny anymore."

"Was it ever funny?" Vik wondered.

She leaned over and whispered, "Of course not, but Tom might've thought it was funny."

Tom heard it anyway. He had good ears. He was offended. "I'm not a psychopath, Wyatt!"

His friends looked at each other dubiously, as though urging one another not to aggravate the crazy psychopath.

"Argh!" Tom groaned out, frustrated. "I'm really not a homicidal maniac, and I'm not killing the CEOs, either. That's not me."

"It's the ghost in the machine," Wyatt pointed out. "You said that's you."

"Ponder this: the ghost is anonymous. Anyone can say they're the ghost in the machine. It's like someone dressing up like Batman, okay? And saying they're Batman, but that doesn't make them Batman."

"What, you think you're Batman now?" Vik said, and Tom shot him a sour look, because again, he was treating him like he was crazy. "Aw, give me a break, Tom. You have put me at serious risk of spending hard time in prison. I'm way too pretty for that."

Yuri rested a consoling hand on his shoulder. "Maybe you are not so lovely as you believe you are."

Vik shook his head morosely. "No, I am every bit as lovely as I think I am. Stop trying to make me feel better with your sweet, sweet lies."

Wyatt frowned at Tom. "Okay, so if someone else is the ghost, that means there are two people with your abilities.

216

Oh, wait. No, three, if you count Medusa."

"No," Tom said. "I don't know. I only know the other ghost isn't me and it's not Medusa, either. It's someone else saying they're the ghost. They probably can't do what Medusa and I can do."

"But it's someone who's managed to get into machines like they can walk right through a firewall, and plant malicious code in them without anyone noticing. Who else can do that?"

"Yes," Yuri chimed in eagerly. "It is as if someone is dressed as Batman, but also has Batman's powers, which makes one think it must be Batman."

Despite the direness of their conversation, Tom and Vik both gasped, shocked by the words.

"Batman doesn't have superpowers," Vik told Yuri, appalled.

"Yeah, he's just very clever and inventive," Tom explained, aghast.

"And rich," Vik added. "How do you not know this, Yuri? What cave did you dwell in the entirety of your youth?"

Yuri shrugged his large shoulders. "My apologies, Vikram. I suppose I was too busy climbing mountains, training for triathlons, and bench-pressing more than you and Thomas are able to manage with your combined efforts, to read many comic books."

Vik sighed and shook his head. "And this, Evil Wench, is why I do not mock the Android."

A smile flitted over her lips. "I get it now."

Tom looked around at his friends, a realization sinking over him that they knew everything now . . . *everything*. And they were still here. Still . . . themselves. Sure, Vik was freaking out, Wyatt was neurotic, and Yuri was . . . was superhumanly awesome as always, but they hadn't grown angry with him, they hadn't stormed out or rejected him.

Maybe he hadn't lost them.

Maybe he wouldn't lose them.

And it wasn't until the enormous relief poured through him like a dam breaking that Tom realized why he'd really hidden so much from them. It wasn't only to keep them safe.

It was to keep them from leaving.

He bowed his head so no one could see his face, the way he was suddenly struggling not to say something stupid and embarrassing and sentimental. An asteroid wasn't about to hit Earth, after all. This wasn't the time for it.

But he was so grateful and so relieved, he could've hugged them all. All at once in a big cheesy group thing.

"You know, we were onto you," Vik said suddenly.

Tom raised his head. "No, you weren't."

"Oh yeah? Wait and see, Gormless One." He bared his forearm keyboard and said to Wyatt, "We can use that program and reverse the memory we erased."

"What memory?" Tom said sharply.

Wyatt's cheeks flushed crimson. "Um, Vik, maybe . . ."

"Yeah, we knew something was going on," Vik said with a laugh, and sent Tom the program. Tom ran it immediately, intensely curious, and remembered . . .

Lying on the carpet, Vik and Wyatt discussing how secretive he was . . .

"You were actually—" Tom began.

Wyatt kissing him.

218

His jaw dropped as he remembered her telling him she'd liked him.

His eyes shifted to hers, and he felt his own cheeks burning suddenly, and Wyatt looked so painfully embarrassed, Tom didn't know whether to laugh or not, but then . . .

Blackburn, on the vactrain, "I'm creating a link between our processors. With a thought, I'll be able to access your sensory receptors and see exactly what you're doing anytime I want to."

Tom went very still. "What the hell is this?"

HE WAS STILL boiling inside when he headed to the Upper common room before dinner. As far as Tom could figure, Blackburn wasn't watching him twenty-four hours a day . . . He would've come already and tried to delete the memory again.

No, he had to tune in selectively. Tom didn't know how, or when, so he held his peace and didn't tell his friends. He couldn't shake a sense of eyes on him, watching his every step.

He nearly jumped out of his skin when he ran into Irene Frayne by the door outside Alexander Division.

"Hello, Mr. Raines." She gave a thin-lipped smile. "I think we need to talk."

Tom eyed her warily. "What about?"

"I'm in stealth mode, so other cadets shouldn't be able to see me. Let's chat in your bunk."

Tom nodded mutely, and at her gesture, led the way back into Alexander Division. A sudden thought came to him: he'd promised Vik he'd warn him if the "invisible woman" was ever in their division. He discreetly pulled back his sleeve and fired off a net-send.

A crashing sound echoed down the hallway like someone in one of the bunks had tumbled to the ground. There was a high shriek of fear, and Clint backed out of the bathroom suddenly. "My God, man, what are you doing?"

And then Vik strolled out into the hallway buck naked and looking very proud of himself.

"Howdy, Tom," Vik said jovially, and walked on. Tom struggled against laughter.

It grew worse when Clint rounded the corridor and his jaw dropped. "Ashwan, what are you doin', fella? No one wants to see this." He chased Vik down the hallway. "Ashwan, Ashwan! Are you listenin' to me?"

Frayne cast Tom a hard, irritated look, and stepped into Tom's bunk. The door slid shut behind them.

Tom had wanted more of a reaction than that to report to Vik, so he said, "Huh. We don't usually have naked people walking around here."

"I raised two teenagers," she said coldly. "I recognize when someone is attempting to send me up. I don't appreciate you spreading word of my presence here to the other cadets. You will use more discretion in the future, am I understood?"

"Sorry," Tom muttered.

Frayne peeled off her coat, and surveyed Tom and Clint's beds, before settling upon draping her coat on Clint's. "I'd like to ask you about Lieutenant Blackburn."

Blackburn. Just the person Tom didn't want to talk about. He wondered suddenly if Blackburn was watching them. "Uh, why?"

Frayne studied him a moment. "Are you familiar with the ghost in the machine?"

220

Tom's brain ground to a halt. His mouth went dry. Why was she asking him about this?

"This terrorist," Frayne said, "has been systematically killing members of the Coalition. Now, in light of recent events, many people are overlooking this cyberterrorist, but I am more convinced than ever that it's imperative to track down this agent of chaos now."

Agent of chaos. All Tom could think for a moment was that it was a great call sign.

"I have a theory," Frayne said. "I think this ghost in the machine plants his malicious code in the drones well before he uses them. Perhaps years before. I don't think the ghost has been hacking them one at a time. I think the ghost is someone inside the Pentagon or even inside Obsidian Corp. who accesses the machines while they're connected with the local server. He contaminates them well beforehand, and that's why he's simply skated through our firewalls."

So she didn't think it was someone with a special ability with machines. Tom almost laughed. Good. Because no one in the entire world could accuse him of being the ghost if it was someone devastatingly good at programming.

"I also think it has to be someone with a neural processor," Frayne said. "The skill with which the assailant maneuvered those drones in several attacks simply couldn't be matched by an ordinary human operator with a set of remote controls. There's a machine-enhanced mind behind this. That's why I've brought Ms. Enslow into my search."

Tom's awareness sharpened. "Why Wyatt? You don't think she's a suspect, do you? Because that's—"

"Of course it's not some teenage girl," Frayne said dismissively.

"Yeah, definitely not. Or a teenager at all," Tom said, relieved.

"But she is, however, in the confidence of my person of interest."

Tom froze.

"I probed her for information, but there was very little she could tell me about Lieutenant Blackburn."

Tom stared at her. "Blackburn?"

"He has the ability, the access privileges, and most of all, the motive, given his personal history with Obsidian Corp. and the military."

And suddenly, Tom knew she was right. It was Blackburn. Of course it was Blackburn. Of course! He agreed with Tom that the Austere-grade processors needed to be stopped, but he didn't believe nonviolence would work, he didn't believe a revolution would work . . .

What had Blackburn said? *If there was a revolution like you're suggesting, the individual power players—the people who are the real problem—would simply fly abroad until the violence died down. That's why the only way to act effectively against them is subtly and silently, involving as few people as possible or even acting alone.*

This was a third path without revolution or passivity: a campaign of targeted assassinations using the technology the Coalition executives relied upon to protect themselves from the public. Not only had Blackburn ensured the men and women with real power hadn't escaped the violence, he'd destroyed Obsidian Corp.'s reputation in the process . . . It was all so very deliberate, so carefully done.

222

The other ghost in the machine was Blackburn. He knew it was Tom, so he felt at liberty to use the persona the Coalition feared, and direct it toward his own agenda.

Tom remembered something, then: the whisper he'd heard in his ear at the party right before the drones began firing, the one telling him to look around. Blackburn could see through his eyes. He'd been in control over those Corday-93s.

He'd been using Tom to acquire targets. And since he had access to all of Tom's sensory receptors, he'd been able to make Tom hear a whisper in his ear . . . just like in the loyalty sim. That had been Blackburn warning him Frayne was watching them. It was all Blackburn.

"He's my primary suspect," Frayne said, "but I'm operating on a gut instinct and I need proof if I'm going to challenge a member of the military."

"Not like if he was a lowly civilian, huh?" Tom said darkly.

"Mr. Raines, you're going to serve as a set of eyes and ears for me."

Tom almost snorted, realizing Frayne wanted the same thing Blackburn had. He'd been playing nice ever since the last Capitol Summit, when it had seemed the only alternative to rigidly holding his ground was lying to people's faces and undermining them in stealth. He knew the smart thing to do here would be to agree to spy for her and then figure out what he'd really do. But something stopped him from playing nice this time. Despite the fact that Blackburn had been spying on him, despite knowing Blackburn had killed Heather, had killed those executives, Tom had this sudden, deep conviction there was one person on his side in this scenario, and it wasn't Irene Frayne.

Tom couldn't bring himself to even pretend otherwise.

"No," Tom told her.

"Excuse me?" Shock transformed her face.

"I said I won't spy for you. No."

She drew a step toward him, her eyes narrowing. "You understand, your father's continued freedom is contingent upon your cooperation."

"Oh, really?" Tom met her eyes, his heart suddenly pounding. "Where is my father?"

He saw it, then. The tiniest flicker on Frayne's face.

"Is he alive?" Tom croaked. His chest grew tight. "See, I haven't heard from my dad at all since the asteroid hit. Not once. And that's not like my dad. He wouldn't do that. So my question is, if you've been spying on him and following him around, where is he? I don't see much reason to cooperate with you when the guy you're threatening might not even be here to suffer consequences for me now."

She folded her arms. "Mr. Raines, our resources have been very strained this past month. We couldn't waste personnel following a person of middling importance—"

"Oh, so now he's not worth the effort, huh?" Tom said sharply. "Before, when he was just going about his business, you were glad to follow him and spy on everything he did, but now when you could actually be useful and find him, you're useless?" He let out a bitter laugh. "Of course you're useless. You're not really about protecting people like my dad, you're about keeping him in line and protecting the precious Coalition executives. Why should I care if someone's offing some trillionaires? They're your concern, not mine."

"You should care because this ghost in the machine has already inspired copycats, Mr. Raines. They've unleashed a wave of violence."

"What wave of violence? I haven't heard anything."

"We've instructed the media to keep it quiet. The last thing we need is another batch of domestic terrorists inspired to act. A caterer laced all the champagne glasses at a lobbying event with ricin. There are fifty people—two US senators among them—dying in Washington ICUs as we speak. A lone-wolf terrorist smeared a culture of bacterial meningitis on the buttons of the members-only elevators in the congressional office buildings. This ghost in the machine threatens to destabilize the power structure of this society—"

"So what?" Tom cut in.

"Excuse me?"

"You still haven't given me one reason I should give a damn. Yeah, it sucks that people are dying, but these aren't innocent little lambs. The power structure of a society is supposed to serve the people who live in it, but these people own our parks and our roads and our schools, and what does someone like my dad get? He gets jailed for speaking up against them in public and threatened with indefinite detention whenever someone like you decides he's getting inconvenient. Am I supposed to be sorry some scumbag executives are getting some vigilante justice? Maybe if I stab myself in the gut, I can force out a tear or two. Maybe."

Frayne paced away from him, visibly agitated. "There is a lot I'd change about this society. We *all* wish we lived in a utopia where life was fair, but it's not and it never will be and this is

225

certainly not the way to get there. This is a revolution in slow motion and I assure you, revolutions almost always have tragic endings. When you remove a ruling body, more often than not, you don't end up with a George Washington, you end up with a Robespierre or a Hitler. We live in an age of hydrogen bombs and biological warfare. We have the technology now that one madman in power could use to obliterate all life on Earth. We can't afford sweeping change this late in history."

She didn't even seem to realize one madman had already threatened all life on Earth. One of those same men in power she was protecting. To Tom, that invalidated her theory that total surrender to people like Vengerov could save the world.

He looked out the window, thinking of the Austere-grade processors, the future they were sliding toward. Total control over the mind and spirit of humanity in exchange for "safety." To Frayne, a boot stomping on the face of humanity forever was merely the price to be paid to ensure something worse didn't crush them permanently. She believed it was impossible to make the world fair, so she pre-emptively surrendered the idea. To her, that was realism. It struck Tom as hopelessness. Defeat. Cowardice.

He refused to believe the sole reason for existence was the perpetuation of existence at any cost. There had to be a reason for it all, a meaning, a point to living in the first place. A better future had to be possible.

He knew with certainty that the only way to make a brighter future impossible was to surrender to Frayne and Vengerov and their security state. Their road led straight into a black hole the world would never escape from again.

"I knew the loyalty test was a simulation," Tom told Frayne. Her gaze swung to his.

Tom raised his eyebrows. "Don't tell me you're shocked. Sure, no one tipped me off, no one warned me or anything, I figured it out on my own, then I did what I had to just to win it. That's why I had my eyes closed for so long, I was deep in thought. The truth is, if there was ever an uprising of soldiers like that with the demands those guys had, I'd step aside and let them at it. They could kill all the Coalition CEOs or every member of Congress for all I care and I'd let them do it."

Her voice was tense. "Why come clean now?"

"Because I'm not who you think I am. I'm not loyal to the powerful people in this country. Why should I be? They've proven over and over again that they feel absolutely no loyalty to me and mine. They can send a thousand people like you, but you won't scare me into bending the knee. If there was a choice between a future where we give up all our choices for a guarantee of safety, or a future with a *minuscule* chance of a better world and an enormous likelihood we'll all destroy each other using our infinite range of choices, I'd pick the second one *every single time* before I'd throw in the towel and bow my head like you have. All this stuff you're doing, surveilling us, searching for dissent—you're on the wrong side. You're helping the wrong people. The world won't be a utopia, it will never be fair, because there are people like you doing your best to keep it that way."

Frayne swept up her coat, her face like stone. "Very well, Mr. Raines. I think matters are very clear between us now."

Tom turned away, undaunted by the threat in her voice.

What could she do—take it out on his father? She didn't even know where he was.

Frayne paused in the doorway. "Regardless of everything else, Tom, I do hope your father is found."

"I'm sure you do," Tom said, staring out the window. After all, none of Frayne's threats had any power over Tom now if Neil was dead.

TOM ARRIVED AT dinner before his friends, and waited at their usual table. The crowd parted a bit around him and he found himself meeting Blackburn's gaze where he sat at the officer's table. Doubts washed over him as he realized he'd basically allied with him when he refused to help Frayne—allied with the same man who'd once tried to drive him insane with the census device.

Tom knew what Blackburn was doing was wrong, but he also couldn't see any alternative. Blackburn was right about one thing: every single check on the power of the Coalition executives had been neutralized, dismantled, hobbled. If there was no nonviolent way to contain them, then the choice was between surrender or opposing them violently.

Tom shifted uneasily in his seat, because he knew murder itself was wrong, but what about murdering, say, Joseph Stalin or Adolf Hitler? They were both men who inflicted terrible suffering on the rest of the world. Killing them wasn't wrong. In fact, *stopping* someone from killing them—that was the greater evil by far.

And here Tom was, the only person who knew for sure that Blackburn was killing those who used their wealth, power, and machines to terrorize the rest of the world into submission. If Tom did nothing, Blackburn would keep turning their mechanized protectors against them. Tom could suddenly imagine a day in the future when the most powerful men in the world flinched at the sight of a drone, at the hum of a Praetorian. It would change everything once they learned to see their own security state as their greatest enemy. If they lost confidence that those machines could shield them from the people whose lives they were ruining, they'd stop relying on them—and they'd become vulnerable again to those with less power, less money. Surely if they thought a crowd could turn on them for their misdeeds, they'd think twice before committing them. If Tom stopped Blackburn, though, those executives would keep tightening the fist of the security state. They would never stop gobbling up the world for themselves, never show mercy, never relent. Blackburn was the only force stopping them at this point. If Tom prevented that, he was basically allowing the Coalition to retain the world in its death grip—a far greater evil than turning a blind eye to Blackburn's actions.

Maybe there was such a thing as a necessary evil.

He held Blackburn's eyes, suddenly certain he knew that Tom knew.

"Let's be clear," Tom whispered into his palm so he was the only one who could hear, knowing if Blackburn was tuned in to his sensory receptors right now, he could hear it, too. "I know about the neural link. I have terms. First of all, you don't erase my memory ever again. You don't tune in when I'm with a girl or doing anything embarrassing or private. If I'm breaking a rule but it's a stupid, harmless one, you don't get to bust me because you saw something on the neural link. If I'm not in any danger, and I'm not endangering you, then you tune out right away—within one or two seconds at most. Do all of this, and I'll keep covering for you. Just like you've been covering for me. But the second this is all over and behind us, the very second, you have to break this link. Got it?"

For a moment, there was nothing, and Tom wondered if he'd been imagining the scrutiny, and maybe Blackburn hadn't checked in on the neural link after all.

"Got it?" Tom tried again.

And then slightly, just slightly, Blackburn raised his glass and dipped it in silent agreement. Tom's terms had been accepted.

CHAPTER EIGHTEEN

MEDUSA VISITED HIM during Applied Battles and he told her all about Blackburn's theory about Cruithne. She took it in grim silence.

"What are you thinking?" Tom finally said, where they sat next to each other in the cockpit of a simulated starship.

"I think if this is true," she said quietly, "then we need to make Vengerov pay."

"There's no proof. Just probable cause and a big coincidence. Oh, and Blackburn found something called 'put options' where Vengerov bet money against some of the companies impacted by the fallout in the week before Cruithne. So there's that."

Medusa's gaze slid to his. "So *if* Joseph Vengerov did this, he did it solely to distract everyone and take the heat off his companies?"

"Yeah, pretty much."

Her eyes gleamed. "Then let's remind them why they distrusted Obsidian Corp. in the first place."

They didn't kill people together, of course. Vengerov was still riding on his reputation as savior of Earth, but Medusa and Tom dipped into servers, ensuring footage from Vengerov's drones spread over the internet, interfacing with the computers of people in the media, and posting from their computers new questions about the safety of Obsidian Corp.'s hardware and Vengerov's integrity.

Even though a few reporters backtracked, and several claimed innocence, using the accounts of public personas succeeded in reviving in the media the questions about whether to dismantle Obsidian Corp. Tom saw the military regulars discreetly turning to the TV and internet feeds in the mess hall, checking on the growing scandal, muttering to one another about the tycoon funding both sides.

All Tom needed was some sort of proof Vengerov had been behind Cruithne. Put that before the eyes of the public and Vengerov would be finished. For good.

WHEN CHRISTMAS BREAK neared, Tom faced a dilemma. His father was missing, and staying in the Pentagonal Spire didn't appeal with Mezilo threatening to dispatch all the vacationers to a boot camp. Since cadets had classified identities, they weren't allowed to go stay with their friends. Wyatt's parents, for instance, weren't allowed to know Tom's name.

Tom had only one choice. He approached Olivia Ossare about striking out on his own.

She sighed and shook her head. "Tom, you're not eighteen. I can't authorize you to spend the time by yourself."

Tom slumped in his seat. Yeah, there was that.

"But I know you can take care of yourself, and I know you've saved up a stipend. If you were officially in the custody of one of your parents, I imagine you could get away with simply staying in the general proximity over break."

Hope flashed through him. "So if my mom's in New York City . . ."

"You would need to check in with her to make sure the official transfer in custody from the military to your parent has taken place."

He leaned forward. "And if she doesn't care where I go?"

"Then that's her prerogative. As your parent."

"So I can't get in trouble if I'm not with her beyond, say, the first few minutes?"

"She would be the one in trouble," Olivia pointed out. "She's the adult responsible for you. You're underage. What do you think?"

A grin blazed across Tom's lips. He heard himself say something he never thought would pass his lips. "I think I'm spending Christmas at my mom's."

DELILAH LIVED IN an apartment in Manhattan paid for by Dalton Prestwick. She was one of his two girlfriends. Tom hadn't seen her since he was nine, back when Neil had brawled with some cops and gotten himself clapped in jail. Tom had hitchhiked to see the mother who'd left when he was too young to remember her.

Or so he'd thought until Blackburn used the census device on him, when he'd started to remember things. They were just snippets from when he was a little kid, but the oddest thing was, she acted like she loved him in them. It was such a stark contrast to when he was nine, when she'd opened the door and looked at him like he was nothing, even after he said, "I'm Tom. Your son."

"Oh," she'd replied. Then she called Dalton over to put him in his place. They'd hired a maid to stay with him and didn't come back until Tom was gone.

It used to hurt him, thinking about it.

This time, Tom didn't warn her in advance that he was coming either. He didn't plan to stay. He'd drop by her place to give the military enough time to officially record his GPS signal inside her home, then he'd leave. Explore New York. Get a hotel room. If his mom was too negligent to bother verifying his whereabouts for herself, then it wasn't Tom's problem or the military's.

When the door swung open, Tom expected nothing. He got nothing but a blank stare.

"Remember me? I'm Tom."

She stared at him with the same expression she'd worn the last time, a flicker of total incomprehension like she couldn't understand what this mangy creature in front of her could possibly be, then total indifference. "Oh. My son."

"Yeah. I got older." He brushed past her into her apartment. "So Dad's . . . um, well, he's not around. I have to crash here for a couple hours so someone can check a GPS signal and see that I'm here for my vacation, but then I'll be off."

She didn't stop him but rather followed him. Tom wondered if she thought he was here to steal from her or something. He realized he was braced, tense, waiting for some feeling to register, like that awful wrench of rejection, loneliness, like last time. He didn't feel it this time. He felt nothing.

He wasn't that nine-year-old kid anymore who'd seen Neil dragged away by the police, who'd waited at the train station three nights for him to come back before realizing he wasn't going to this time. Who'd been so sure if he just had a mom like other kids, he'd never have to sleep outside or figure out how to get food or wonder what happened to his dad ever again.

It didn't matter anymore that she would never hug him or tell him it was time to go to bed or pack him lunch in a paper bag for school or something, because he wasn't fooling himself anymore. Across the gulf of seven years, Tom could finally look back and feel pity rather than disgust for his younger self for expecting that. He hadn't been stupid to hope she'd love him. He just hadn't known any better yet.

His mother hadn't aged much since his memories of her. He supposed she was pretty young for the mother of a sixteen-year-old. But she'd changed in almost every way. There was no hint of the wild girl spinning him around in the street, flashing him a bright, vibrant smile in his memories.

Just a very subdued woman with no expression on her face. Delilah was a picture of perfect composure, perfect self-possession, her posture ramrod straight, her eyes a cool, empty blue in a face that would've been beautiful with more animation to it.

"Are you supposed to be here?" she asked him.

"It's kind of legally mandated I stay with a parent or legal guardian. I've only got one parent on hand right now. That's you. But I mean it, I'm leaving soon."

"I understand." She was silent a moment. Then, "Would you like something to drink?"

Tom blinked. "Uh, yeah. Okay."

She moved away from him, the long slim lines of her body snapping into motion. Tom saw her blond hair swish with the movement, her arms as precise as a marionette's. He kept looking about her apartment. Not one thing was out of place. There were the same types of paintings on the wall he saw in hotels. Impersonal things. A lonely stretch of beach. A fog-shrouded bridge disappearing into distant trees. As she clinked ice in a glass, he wandered over to the bathroom to wash his hands. On the way back, he glanced through the open door of Dalton's study and spotted a small vial on the desk with a note beside it. Tom halted, cast his mother a careful glance, then slipped inside and grabbed it.

Tom lifted the note tucked next to it, personally addressed from Joseph Vengerov to Dalton Prestwick.

This is merely a prototype, but it behooves both our interests if you know what you'll be promoting. Safe, simple to administer, and efficient, these are nanomachines in a liquid suspension. They can be administered orally to any test subject the Roache brothers choose.

Even though Blackburn had told him about the Austere-grade processors being nanomachines, it still sent chills down Tom's spine, actually seeing one. He lifted up the vial and unscrewed the lid to gaze down at the murky liquid inside.

Well, it was safe to say the Roache brothers wouldn't think anything at all of this Austere-grade neural processor; they were dead. He plopped the vial back down on Dalton's desk, a certain satisfaction surging through him knowing Vengerov's drive to spread them had failed. He headed back to his mom and threw himself onto the couch.

Delilah set the drink before him. Tom nodded his thanks. He took a big swig. Suddenly, fire burned down his throat, and he coughed, the sharp bite of alcohol making his eyes water. He stared at the mixed drink, and wondered at how cavalierly she'd offered it up to him.

"You realize I'm sixteen, right?" he asked with an incredulous laugh.

"Do you want something else?"

"You know, don't bother."

Across the room, the conferencing phone began flashing. Delilah turned away from him like he wasn't there and moved to it, touched her palm to it.

Dalton Prestwick's face filled the screen. For once, there was no skeezy smile plastered under his gelled brown hair. "Delilah?"

There was a note of panic in his voice. His hazel eyes were searching behind her. Tom was tempted to lean forward so he could flip Dalton the bird. Delilah didn't seem to pick up on his unease. She flashed a bright smile. "Dalton. I love you. I'm so happy you called. You look very sexy today."

Then Dalton said, "The perimeter alarms were triggered. Who did you let in?"

Confusion flickered through Tom. He sat very still.

"Thomas. He's my son."

"Just . . . just wait . . . I'll be there soon." The conferencing phone snapped off, and Delilah turned crisply around, facing Tom again.

237

Tom stared at her. "Perimeter alarm? What is he, your owner?"

Delilah tilted her head to the side, as though processing what he'd said. "He loves me and I love him. He's very handsome, wealthy, and charismatic." The bright smile flashed over her lips again. It didn't touch her eyes. "He's staggeringly intelligent. He knows how to treat a woman like she's special."

Tom gaped at her, feeling like someone was messing with him. She'd spoken so blandly, so matter-of-factly, and the smile looked like a mannequin's. No one talked that way.

And something began to work its way up from the back of his mind. He found himself replaying her snappish movements in his vision center. He found himself examining her face.

It was funny how much an emotionally devastated nine-year-old could miss. All he'd seen back then was her indifference to him. All he'd registered was his disappointment, his crushed feelings.

He hadn't seen anything. Certainly not the total emptiness in her eyes.

Even Dalton's reaction looked different through the eyes of age. Back when he was little, he'd seen only Dalton's sneering contempt for him. Now, he heard the anxiety in Dalton's voice. The anxiety that had been there the last time, too. The worry Tom hadn't even picked up on. He'd been just a kid then. A dumb kid. He was older now.

Tom rose to his feet, still staring at her face. "Why is there a perimeter alarm, Mom?"

"For my protection."

One blink. Fifteen seconds later, another.

Tom's blood buzzed in his ears as he watched for the next

one. And all the time he did it, she looked back at him, no unease about the way he was staring, no discomfort with being gawked at. No humanity.

She blinked again. Exactly fifteen seconds. Each. Time.

The answer to one of the mysteries of his life slid into place. Tom's mind went blank. He stood there for a long while, too shocked to process it.

Then the door slid open and Dalton Prestwick stepped inside.

Rage like Tom had never known swept through him until his whole body seemed to have been lit on fire. He pounced and slammed into him. Tom didn't even feel Dalton's elbow hit his cheek, Dalton's feeble attempts to fight back. All he saw was that smug, hateful face and he crashed his fists into it over and over again, hearing a nose crunch, feeling a body trying to buck him off, hands trying to claw at his face, shove him away.

And then Tom hauled the gibbering executive to his unsteady feet and drew Dalton's blood-smeared face right to his. "HOW DID SHE GET A NEURAL PROCESSOR?"

Dalton's voice wobbled. "Let me go or—"

"OR *WHAT*?"

He hurled Dalton against the wall and sank his fist into his stomach, then twisted him around and jammed his arm up between his shoulder blades, relishing Dalton's shriek of pain. "In case you haven't noticed," Tom hissed in his ear, "I'm not nine years old this time. I'm not even the fourteen-year-old you reprogrammed. I'm in a position to severely hurt you right now, and I am just *hoping* you give me an excuse to do it. Now answer me!"

From behind him, Delilah noted, "You should stop this

assault. It's very impolite. It's also against the law."

"Delilah, help—" Dalton tried, but Tom snared him around the neck, choking off his words.

"Do not command her to help you. No one is helping you. No one is saving you from me." He whipped them both around, Dalton's neck in his headlock, his arm jammed up behind him, and Tom felt so much rage looking at her it seemed to be ripping him apart from inside. "God. God, this is sick. This is so sick. You're controlling her, YOU DISGUSTING PERVERT! That's why she's here. That's why she left us! You've been keeping her as your slave all these years!"

"That's not it at all!"

"She has a neural processor! You've programmed her to do everything you say—"

"That's not it!" Dalton wailed. He twisted painfully to look back at Tom, desperation in his eyes. "If you want to blame someone for this, blame your father!"

Tom slammed the flat of his palm against the wall by Dalton's face, taking pleasure in his flinch. "My father? Don't you bring him into this! If my dad knew about this, he'd kill you. He'd murder you!"

Dalton laughed wildly. "If he knew? He knows! He's always known! *He gave her to Obsidian Corp.!*"

The words didn't register for a long moment. And even then, Tom shook his head and screamed, "Shut up! You're lying! I know you're a liar!"

"He sold her. He was desperate to get rid of her! He was so glad we took her off his hands!"

Dalton thumped to the floor when Tom threw him there,

240

but Tom couldn't process this. He couldn't. He shook his head again.

"No, you're wrong." His voice barely came out.

"He knew Mr. Vengerov from the high-stakes gambling circuit. He used to coach people who were willing to pay, and people like Mr. Vengerov paid good money back when he was in his prime," Dalton gabbled, curled up there on the carpet where Tom had dropped him. "Your father knew his company needed subjects for psychiatric experiments. He *begged* us to take her."

Tom began shaking all over. Denial blanked out his brain. "You're lying. Dad would never do that. He hates Vengerov. He'd never met him before—"

But his throat closed up, and he found himself thinking of Neil and Vengerov over the roulette wheel.

Vengerov, smiling at Neil.

"You two know each other?" Tom asked them.

"No," Neil said.

And after a moment, taking his cue from Neil, "No." But Vengerov's smile widened, because they were sharing a lie and that gave him leverage.

His dad, so begrudgingly wagering his money on roulette, but doing it because Vengerov had told him. Because Vengerov had just gone along with his lie about not knowing him . . .

His dad, who feared no one, wearing a look of horror on his face like some nightmare was coming true.

Tom's stomach gave a heave like he was going to be sick. He was only vaguely aware of his nails digging into his palms where he was clenching his fists. "This isn't true. You're lying."

241

Dalton rocked up to his knees, his eyes gleaming and vindictive. Blood dripped from his nose. "Your mother was psychotic. She suffered from severe delusions. Your father got her pregnant and tried to make it work because of you, but he found out about her problems soon enough. He couldn't do it anymore. He couldn't take it. He wanted her off his hands. I was a junior executive at Obsidian Corp. I stood there over his shoulder when he signed away medical custody of her. Medical custody of *you*, too. It was a package deal, Tom."

"No." It was all Tom could say.

"Your father wanted his life back, and Mr. Vengerov was glad to have a chance at two new subjects. We hadn't been able to run a test group in the continental United States since the debacle with the American soldiers, and this time, he'd get a range of ages. People society wouldn't miss. You were young enough, he wanted to use you as a pristine subject. You had the same defects in your brain that she did, so he had you fixed first—ordered you to undergo a neural graft, some computer-stimulated brain tissue to give you a frontal lobe of normal mass."

Tom's heart pounded so hard it vibrated in his ears.

NO. Neil wouldn't give him up. Not him.

"Your mother wasn't young enough, of course," Dalton said, heaving himself to his feet, dabbing his sleeve at his nose. "Her brain started to reject the neural processor. Like all the other adults, she began having massive seizures. Mr. Vengerov had full medical custody of her, so he took the same approach we did with all the subjects in that test group. He started having different areas of her brain removed to see how much neural

242

tissue was needed to stop the seizures, and retain some basic functionality."

Tom threw a horrified look at Delilah, with her empty face, her empty eyes.

"In her case, she lost the entire frontal lobe, though she could still talk and accept commands thanks to the processor," Dalton said, as though that wasn't ghastly, as though that wasn't robbing someone of everything that made them human. Tom couldn't comprehend it. He felt like he was in a nightmare. "Your father saw her again, and he had a crisis of conscience. So he snatched you out of the hospital before you got a processor of your own, and paid someone to wipe all your medical records. Mr. Vengerov could have stopped it. He could have forced your father to follow through on the contract they signed, but he very generously let him renege. You should be grateful to him."

"To Vengerov?" Tom spat. "He butchered her!"

"But he helped *you*. He's the only reason you didn't grow up to be like your mother. If not for that neural graft, your brain would be very different today."

Tom looked inward, seeing Neil that day by the roulette table again. Seeing the horror on Neil's face when Vengerov appeared in front of them. The man who knew the secret he'd hidden from Tom all these years. The man who knew he'd wanted to be rid of Tom, who knew he'd gotten rid of Tom's mother.

It had perplexed Tom at the time. Neil never feared anyone. And he still hadn't feared Vengerov. He'd feared Tom learning the truth.

Tom pressed his hands to his head. *No. No, no, no . . .* He was only half aware of Dalton pressing the sleeve of his suit to his bleeding nose. Of Delilah walking up and rubbing Dalton's shoulders very mechanically.

Dalton straightened his cuff links. "Your old man was at the end of his rope already, keeping her out of messes, trying to look out for you. He lost everything once you came into the picture. His luck, his mobility, his sobriety, and most everything he had in medical care for one or the other of you."

Tom found himself staring numbly at Delilah's hands, massaging Dalton's shoulders.

"So you see now, sport, why you've been very ungrateful to me over the years. I've been far more generous than your father, taking care of your mother even after the experiments were over and she was of no more use to the company. I took her custody totally upon myself. She's as happy as anyone in her situation could be."

"Why did you do that?" Tom's voice scraped his throat.

Dalton blinked. "Look at her. She's exquisite. It would be such a shame."

Tom looked at his mother—a beautiful woman who'd had any capacity for independent thought or mastery of self removed, replaced by a programmable computer.

The perfect toy for a sleazy executive who had everything. A guy who now wanted to pat himself on the back for his total control over the empty shell.

Tom's anger was gone, extinguished. Replaced only by a terrible emptiness. He'd destroyed his dad's life. His father and Joseph Vengerov had destroyed his mom's. The least guilty party to it all was, sickeningly enough, Dalton Prestwick. He'd just kept as his favorite toy the woman others had torn apart.

Dalton was looking at Delilah again, wearing that same self-important smile Tom remembered. He found himself staring at them, suddenly back on that awful day in the Beringer Club when Hayden pinned him down and jammed the neural wire into his neck, and Dalton smoked his cigar. Smiling. Smiling. His voice was in Tom's ears.

"You always call me Dalton. It betrays a lack of respect. From now on, it'll be Mr. Prestwick."

"Come on, son. Did you really think I was giving you a choice here? Did you really?"

"You'll be let go. You'll be released very soon. And you'll be a much better boy when you are."

And all Tom could think of was his mother waiting at Dalton's apartment even back then, his prized possession with her own neural processor, and no wonder Dalton thought he could take anything he wanted without consequences and just overwrite someone's will. He'd been doing it to Tom's mom for years.

Other people were merely things to him. He had no respect for them. And Tom suddenly was desperate to make him sorry, desperate to inflict upon him what he'd done to his mom. What he'd done to *Tom.*

Tom's thoughts strayed to the Austere-grade processor on the desk, just resting in that vial, ready for administration. He moved over to it, only distantly aware of Dalton telling him, "I think it's time you left, champ."

"Not yet."

Tom's hand shook when he picked up the vial containing

several billion nanomachines, all primed and ready for an oral dose. Dalton's voice floating over his head as he blustered for Tom to leave now or he'd call the cops on him. All Tom could think of was Dalton's desperate sucking up to Vengerov, his smug smile, the smell of his cigar that day, and how truly he deserved this.

"Hey Dalton," Tom heard himself say, "ever wonder what it's like to be reprogrammed?"

```
0 0 1 1 1 1 1 1 1 1 0 0 1 1 1 0 1 0 1 1 0 0 0 0 0 0 0 1 0 0 1 1 1 1 0 0 0 0
1 1 0 1 1 0 1 1 1 0 0 1 1 1 1 0 0 0 0 0 0 0 1 0 1 1 0 1 0 0 1 0 0 1 1 1
0 0 0 0 0 1 1 1 1 0 0 1 0 0 1 0 1 1 1 0 0 1 1 1 0 1 1 0 0 1 0 1 1 0 1 1 0
1 0 0 0 1 1 0 1 1 0 0 0 0 1 0 0 1 1 0 0 0 1 0 0 0 1 0 1 1 1 0 0 0 0 1 1 0
0 0 1 1 0 1 0 0 0 0 0 1 0 1 1 1 0 1 1 0 0 0 0 0 0 1 0 1 1 0 0 1 1 1 1
0 1 1 0 0 0 0 0 1 1 1 1 0 1 1 0 1 1 0 1 0 0 0 0 0 1 0 0 1 1 1 0 0 0 0 0 1
1 0 0 1 0 1 0 1 1 1 0 1 1 1 0 1 0 1 0 1 1 1 1 0 1 0 1 1 0 1 1 0 0 0 0 0 1
1 1 1 1 1 1 1 0 1 1 0 0 0 0 1 1 1 0 1 1 0 1 1 1 0 1 1 1 0 0 0 1 0 1 0 1
0 1 1 0 0 1 1 0 1 0 0 1 0 0 0 1 0 1 0 1 0 0 1 0 0 0 0 1 0 0 1 0 1 0 1 0 1
0 1 0 0 1 0 1 1 0 0 1 0 0 0 1 1 0 1 0 1 0 1 1 1 0 0 0 0 1 0 1 1 0 1 0 1 0 1
0 0 0 0 1 1 1 1 0 1 1 0 0 1 0 1 1 0 0 0 0 0 1 0 0 0 0 1 0 0 0 1 0 0 1
0 1 0 0 1 1 1 1 0 0 1 1 1 0 1 1 0 0 1 1 0 0 1 1 0 1 1 1 0 0 1 0 0 0 0 1 0 0 0 0
0 1 1 1 1 1 0 1 1 0 1 0 0 0 1 0 0 1 1 1 0 0 0 0 1 0 1 1 1 1 0 0 0 0 0 1 0
1 1 1 1 0 0 0 0 0 1 0 1 1 0 1 0 0 0 0 0 0 0 1 0 0 0 1 1 1 1 0 0 1 1 1 0 1
1 1 0 0 0 1 1 1 0 0 1 1 1 0 0 0 0 1 1 0 0 1 0 0 1 0 1 0 1 1 1 1 1 0 1 1 0
0 0 1 1 1 0 0 1 0 1 1 1 1 0 0 1 0 1 1 0 1 1 0 1 1 1 1 1 0 0 1 0 0 1 1
1 0 1                               0 1 0 0 0 0 1 0 0 0 0 1 1 1 0 1 0 1 0 1 0
0 1 1                               0 1 1 1 1 1 1 1 1 1 1 1 0 0 1 1 1 1 0 0
1 1 1                               1 1 0 1 0 0 1 0 0 0 0 1 1 1 1 1 0 0 1
0 0 1 1 0 0 0 1 1 1 1 1 0 1 1 0 0 0 0 0 0 0 1 0 0 1 0 0 1 0 1 1 0 1 0 0 1
```
CHAPTER NINETEEN

IT WASN'T HARD forcing Dalton to swallow. Tom clamped his nose until he gave in. Now as Dalton frantically called Joseph Vengerov, pleading with him for some way to be rid of his brand-new Austere-grade neural processor, Tom stepped into his mom's room and rooted out a bag, trying to figure out what she needed.

Clothes, shoes, socks . . . what else?

He didn't know where he'd take her. Hide her. There had to be some way to remove the programs in her head. He heard Dalton's voice, hysterical over the conferencer.

"I've tried making myself throw up—"

"Oh, that's no use. They're designed to enter the bloodstream and implant themselves in your cerebral cortex as soon as they enter your system."

Hatred rippled through Tom at the sound of Joseph Vengerov's controlled tones drifting from the conferencer.

"We'd have to take apart your entire brain to remove them. You do trust my technology, don't you, Dalton?"

"Of—of course, but—"

"Good. Then you know the processor won't harm you at all. Try to calm yourself and focus on the benefits of a neural processor. This incident doesn't need to be a setback. In fact, I believe now is the time for me to endorse your rise to greater heights. I do have such confidence in you. I believe you would make an excellent replacement for Diamond MacThane as chief executive officer at Dominion Agra."

"CEO? Me?" Dalton squeaked.

"But of course. Without the Roache brothers to throw their weight around, I don't anticipate anyone contesting the influence I plan to apply on Dominion's chief shareholders. And if they resist me . . ."

"If they do, then what?" Dalton said, breathless.

"Then I wouldn't be surprised if the ghost in the machine attacked the company's next shareholder meeting."

Tom halted in place, hearing that.

"Or perhaps slew the entire executive board in one fell swoop. After the company's antics these last two centuries, there will be a world of dry eyes. I doubt there will be many scratching their heads, wondering why a terrorist targeted Dominion Agra's owners in particular for vigilante justice."

There was a stunned silence. Tom stood there frozen in the next room, in disbelief. Was Vengerov implying he'd kill them himself, posing as the ghost?

"I'd say your ascent is virtually guaranteed," Vengerov told Dalton.

"Mr. Vengerov, I . . . Mr. Vengerov." Tom inched forward to see Dalton's eagerly nodding head, his grin. His sputters of gratitude were pathetic. "I won't let you down, sir. This is excellent news. It's wonderful." He was silent a moment. "Perhaps we can talk about this more when I can come in and you deactivate this Austere-grade processor?"

A pause, and then Vengerov's silky voice: "Why would I ever do that?"

"You—you said you have great faith in me. That's why you want me to lead Dominion, isn't it? You trust me."

"Yes. I trust you," Vengerov purred. "You have my processor in your head. I have no reason to doubt you ever again."

For a moment, Tom took in the sight of Dalton's smile fading when he realized he'd finally won the power he'd always sought—at the expense of his mastery over himself.

"Is the boy still there?"

Tom tensed.

"I think so," Dalton whispered.

"We're almost there. Delay his departure."

Goose bumps pricked up over Tom's spine. He thrust aside the stuff he'd gathered for his mom, because he could buy her stuff anywhere. He raced over to her where she was standing by the door, grabbed her arm. "Come on."

"Where are we going?" she asked tonelessly.

"Elsewhere."

Tom heard Dalton's footsteps beat up behind them, and whirled around to face him. He raised a fist like he was going to punch him, and Dalton yelped and stumbled back a step reflexively. Tom felt a flash of certainty he wasn't going to stop them.

"Stay back," Tom warned him.

"You won't get out of here," Dalton told him. "As soon as you breached the perimeter alarm, he told me he was going to see you."

And there could be no good reason for it. Vengerov obviously knew Tom had found out the truth about his mother—and didn't intend to let him walk away with the knowledge. Tom wasn't leaving her here for them.

"If you come after me, I'll kill you," he said to Dalton. He grabbed his mother's arm and pulled her out with him.

ON THE ELEVATOR down, he tried net-sending Vik, Wyatt, Yuri, Blackburn, anyone.

Error: Frequency unavailable. Message not sent.

Tom wasn't sure how Blackburn's neural link worked, but he tried shouting at the air, "Lieutenant Blackburn, *WHERE ARE YOU?*"

Nothing.

The neural link was a one-way connection, and obviously at this moment, Blackburn wasn't peeking in.

Vengerov had to be close enough to jam his wireless signal. Tom's mind raced, trying to figure out why Vengerov was coming here, what he wanted with him. Tom wasn't going to wait. He'd hook in and find some machines to use to defend himself if he had to. He was just pressing his remote access node into his brain stem port when the doors slid open, and a swarm of security guards rushed him. "You! Freeze!"

Tom slammed his fist into the nearest guard, and kicked him away, shoving the other men back as well. He was only vaguely aware of a faint clatter as he jolted back into the elevator and hit the button to close the door, his brain racing.

Tom's hand flew back to his neural access port, and he realized with a spring of shock in his stomach that they'd

250

knocked the remote access node out of his hand—that it was in the lobby. He couldn't hook into any machines and bring them here.

Across from him, empty-eyed as a statue, Delilah watched him. There was something so unsettling about her presence here. It occurred to Tom suddenly that he had no idea what was going on in her head. For all he knew, Vengerov was using her to spy on him, to keep his position in his sight.

"Close your eyes," Tom ordered her.

She closed them.

They arrived on the top floor. If Vengerov was driving toward them, Tom just had to get high enough, out of the range of his jammer. Then he could tell someone at the Spire what was happening. Or better yet, he could summon a drone of his own and defend himself.

But once he was on the roof, he tried sending the signal again, and roared in frustration when, *Error: Frequency unavailable. Message not sent* blinked before his eyes.

Tom let out a breath and turned on his mom, searching her face desperately. "Open your eyes!"

Her blue eyes popped open again, as clear and empty as a glass of water.

"There has to be some bit of you still in there. Don't you remember me at all?"

"You're Thomas," she replied. "My son. You're a delinquent. You have poor manners and no respect for your elders."

"Yeah, yeah, I know what Dalton programmed you to think. But what do *you* think?"

"I don't understand."

"Mom, come on. You have to be in there somewhere!"

She blinked back at him.

Tom buried his hands in his hair, trying to work out what to do. He couldn't let Dalton take her back. He couldn't let this go on. He couldn't let that bastard keep her here like some slave.

What if Dalton had been telling the truth about them removing most of her brain? Tom opened his eyes and stared at her, thinking of what would be left in there without a frontal lobe in her brain. Was she still alive, really, if it was just the neural processor keeping her heart beating, her lungs breathing? Should he . . .

Would it be a mercy for him to just hook into her neural processor and deactivate it?

Tom recoiled from the thought. It was like killing her. He couldn't do that. He wasn't sure what to do.

And then the choice was taken out of his hands.

A humming filled the air above him, and Tom threw up a hand, squinting against the glare of a searchlight as a helicopter soared down onto the roof with him. Tom stepped in front of her, not sure how he'd keep her from going back to Vengerov and Dalton—but determined to do so.

To his profound shock, Joseph Vengerov himself alighted from the helicopter and strolled calmly across the roof toward him, his long black coat rustling in the breeze.

"Hello, Mr. Raines."

"What are you doing here?" Tom demanded, his voice shaking.

"The better question is, what are you doing here? What could you hope to accomplish, taking her with you?"

"Stay away from her." A hot red tide crashed over his brain,

252

battering him from the inside. "You better stay back. After what you did to her, what you did to . . ." To his whole life, really. His entire childhood. To his dad. Everything, everything was the fault of the hateful, grasping oligarch in front of him, a man who had the entire world at his feet and it still wasn't enough. Tom's heart was pounding furiously in his ears. If he killed him, it would be for the best. What Vengerov wanted to do to the world was unforgivable.

"Stop me then." Vengerov spread his arms. "Go ahead. Attack."

Tom wanted to. He was desperate to. But he felt like a cold fist gripped him, held him in place, when he would've ripped forward and punched him.

Of course! The program hardwired to his neural processor, to all their processors—Joseph Vengerov's protection from peril at the hands of his own machines.

Tom gritted his teeth, and he'd never been so livid, he'd never been so ready to cross a line and destroy someone, and there'd never been anyone who deserved it so much. He saw Dalton appear, slipping out of the stairwell, and a surge of helpless rage gripped him. "I'm not letting her go back to you."

"You have no choice." The roving lights of the helicopter flashed over Vengerov's pale hair, his icy features. "Her fate has already been decided. What did you think to accomplish, stealing her away? Your mother isn't there anymore. She's not even human anymore. She has the brain matter of a reptile."

"Because of you! You did this!"

"There were kinks to work out. Your mother provided an invaluable service to humanity."

"Like the thousand soldiers you killed in Russia?" Tom hurled at him. "Or Lieutenant Blackburn and the three hundred you killed here?"

"As well as the two thousand who died in China, the three thousand in India, and the ten thousand in Africa. They were all providing a valuable service, testing my processors. Their lives weren't sacrificed in vain. Look to yourself, to your own processor—which has been used dozens of times in test subjects before you, but functions perfectly, does it not?"

"You're a monster," Tom breathed.

"It wasn't my machinery at fault. I knew all along it was possible to successfully implant a neural processor because my father implanted the very first one in me."

Tom was caught off guard that Vengerov was admitting that.

"I was proof it worked. I simply needed time to understand that only a young brain could accept one." He cocked his head. "But you don't appear surprised to hear I have one . . . It's as if you knew about my processor already."

"What processor?" Tom remembered to play ignorant. "You have a neural processor?"

"Don't insult me. I've been meaning to get you alone for a while now. Face-to-face, with no one to shield you from my questions."

Tom stared at him. He was suddenly acutely aware of the way he was alone here with the oligarch who'd locked him outside in Antarctica to freeze to death just to make a point.

"I suggest you tear your mind away from your mother," Vengerov said. "The one you should be concerned about today—"

"Is myself?" Tom snarled. "I'm not afraid of you."

"Is your father."

Tom froze, the world going very still around him. Vengerov arched his eyebrows. "Haven't you wondered about him? About his disappearance?"

Tom opened and closed his mouth, shock reeling through him.

"I have him in my custody," Vengerov said simply. "My contractors procured him for me in the aftermath of Cruithne, when his disappearance was unlikely to be questioned."

"You—you—why?"

Vengerov turned negligently to Dalton. "You may reclaim your paramour now. Then leave."

Tom didn't even try to stop Dalton from snaking an arm around Delilah's waist and leading her back into the building with him. He was too far in shock.

Vengerov had Neil. His dad was alive, but Vengerov had him.

Vengerov let him suffer in silence until they were alone again. "I've been waiting for the opportune moment to speak with you. I wanted to do so on the right terms, of course. Having your father in my possession rather clarifies our respective positions here, does it not? I have questions, and you have great incentive to answer them."

"W-what questions?"

"I've been plagued of late by attacks from an anonymous hacker of sorts. I believe you're familiar with him. The ghost in the machine."

Tom's mouth felt very dry, cold flutters moving through his chest. "Why would I know anything about that?"

Vengerov smiled. "Because you do. I learned of this ghost while listening through Yuri Petrovich's ears, overhearing the discussion between James Blackburn and *you*. I'd had my suspicions about the existence of *some* phenomenon long before that, naturally. I noticed anomalies with regard to the behavior of certain machines, though I had no idea there could be a person behind it, a single person who for some reason is able to access machines beyond the limitations inherent to my software. I had a theory about who that ghost might be, and you helped me test it."

Tom knew that was Medusa.

"But I was incorrect. The destruction of the skyboards proved that to me. I was at a loss. You and James Blackburn were my only leads, so I offered to sponsor you, hoping to gain more access to you—and more opportunity to glean more knowledge of the ghost from you. And then you staged the attack upon Milton Manor."

Tom's blood froze. "What do you mean, 'me'?"

"I saw your remote access node, Mr. Raines. Very audacious."

"That's not . . . that doesn't . . ."

"Prove anything? No, it doesn't. Nor, I suppose, does the curious activity originating from the Pentagonal Spire's servers around the time of Cruithne. You must admit, though, that I have a mass of circumstantial evidence all centered around the same suspect. You. That rather inclines me to think you are very much involved with this. If I'm right, and you are the ghost, bravo for saving the world."

"I didn't do that!"

Vengerov's eyes shone with triumph. "No, it was all just

a strange coincidence. It was also strange the ghost leaked information only you and James Blackburn knew. I'm very certain from the conversation I overheard that James Blackburn isn't the ghost in the machine. Recent events have eroded my patience. I intend to find out immediately who this ghost is. What do you know, Mr. Raines?"

"I don't know anything!"

"That's unfortunate, then," Vengerov said quietly. "If you truly know nothing, and you're not the ghost yourself, then you are useless to me. And if you are useless to me, then so is your father."

Tom went cold. "You can't. You—" His voice strangled in his throat.

Vengerov calmly withdrew a tablet computer, and tossed it to Tom. Tom was so flustered, he almost missed it when it sailed his way. His palms felt like ice, and his heart caught in his throat at the image on the screen of Neil, looking thin and worse for wear, glaring at someone who was training a video feed on him.

No, no, no, Tom thought.

"I ask you again," Vengerov said, watching him closely, letting him see Neil as he spoke, "do you know anything about the ghost in the machine?"

Tom didn't know what to do. His legs felt weak. He'd never expected to be put in this position, his father used against him. He couldn't think.

"My patience has limits. Five seconds," Vengerov said.

"But this could be fake," Tom cried. "You might not have him."

"Four, three . . ."

"This might not be him! It could be a fake image! Come on, this could be a fake!"

Vengerov glanced at Neil. "I suppose that's a fair demand. What is something your father alone would know?"

Tom was dizzy. He didn't reply.

Vengerov's pale eyes bore into his. "Mr. Raines, we will ask him a question, and he will answer it for you, and then you can be satisfied I'm not fabricating this story. Do you have a question for your father?"

Tom's vision blurred. He was shaking all over, trying to think of something, something for this image on the screen to answer wrong so he could please, please know that Vengerov was lying about having Neil in custody, and this wasn't true.

"Um . . ." Tom choked in air. "Um . . . uh . . ." Images rushed through his mind. Neil carrying him down the side of the road, and showing him how to toss a can to check whether a fence was electrified. His dad tucking a coat around him when he was cold and hiking three miles to bring him back warm soda that time he got sick. All the ways his dad had looked out for him over the years. His sweaty hand raked through his hair. "My birthday. He gave me something back when I turned fifteen."

It was a gold watch, one Neil had won off Hank Bloombury of Matchett-Reddy. Neil would remember—they'd been attacked by the lecher's hired cop and had it stolen from them.

Vengerov nodded, and then pressed on his ear and repeated the question.

Tom stared in horror as someone off the screen repeated it. This really was a live feed, then. And his father looked up

258

at the camera, his jaw set. "Something I gave my son when he turned fifteen? . . . No idea."

And even though he hadn't given the answer, it was worse. Worse. So much worse, because there was no faking that stubborn set to Neil's jaw, that dangerous flash in his eyes. Neil had obviously figured out why he was being held. He knew the purpose was to extort his son.

He would never cooperate and help someone blackmail Tom. Even if they were fighting, even if they hadn't spoken in months, even if Tom had lied to him and been awful to him, Neil would still do exactly this—glare up at that camera and lie in hopes Tom wouldn't get coerced by someone, because that's who his dad was. He always had Tom's back if he could help it, and Tom knew in that moment that Vengerov did, indeed, have Neil, and he wasn't threatening idly.

"Give me a guarantee you'll let him go," Tom said, his voice shaking. "I have no reason to cooperate with you if you are going to kill him anyway. Give me a guarantee!"

"I could simply kill your father and cull the ghost's identity out of you."

"No, you won't!"

And Tom scrambled back and heaved himself up onto the ledge of the roof. Vengerov stood below him, watching him with his head cocked like he was observing a curious animal in a zoo.

Tom was painfully aware of the drop behind him, the cars choking the streets, the pavement that would kill him on impact. "You guarantee my dad's safety if I answer you, or I'll jump off this roof. By the time you try to force me down with a program, I'll be dead and you'll get nothing. You won't be able to cull me and I guarantee you won't get your ghost."

Vengerov drew cautiously closer, never taking his intent gaze from Tom's. "I've taken the initiative of having your father implanted with an Austere-grade neural processor. It makes him far easier to control. If you cooperate, I'll order my technicians to block any memory pertaining to this situation and set him at liberty. I have no use for him. Only you."

Tom's heart pounded furiously. Neil would hate it. He would hate that—but maybe he'd never know. And it was better than being dead.

"Do you accept my terms?" Vengerov said.

"Yes," Tom whispered.

"Now tell me." There was a frightening hunger in Vengerov's eyes, his voice. It seemed to animate his entire face. "Who is the ghost in the machine?"

Tom had no choice here. He didn't. He felt dizzy, sick, fearful. He choked on the words he didn't want to say, but he had to. He had to. He couldn't stop this.

"You're right. It's me."

The words were so soft, he was sure Vengerov hadn't heard them.

"It's me. I'm the ghost in the machine," Tom said louder. "I did all of it."

"All by yourself?"

Tom knew the cyberterrorist who'd carefully destroyed key members of the Coalition must not seem like some sixteen-year-old kid, but Vengerov had to believe him. He had to. "Blackburn covered for me, but that's all he did. I don't know what else you want. I'm telling you the truth. You know what my dad thinks of you guys. I'm the same way. I wanted to destroy the Coalition. I wanted to turn them all against you because—because of what you did to Yuri. Because you made me lose my fingers."

"You personally killed those executives?"

"Hey, I was at the party. I figured that would be a great alibi, and, uh, I was able to use that remote access node and do it right then and there. I swear I can do that. I can show you." Inspiration hit. He looked at the nearest ships, thinking with longing of how he could seize control over them, maybe even figure out a way to turn the tables. "Tell your guys in the lobby to bring me that remote access node I dropped and I'll show you what I can do—"

"Oh no, in the event you are telling me the truth, that would be very foolish, wouldn't it?" Vengerov reached into the pocket of his coat and withdrew a small glint of metal. "You will fasten this onto your neural access port instead."

Vengerov threw it at him. His aim was machine perfect. Tom caught it with machine-perfect reflexes. It was a flat, rounded piece of metal with a hook for a brain stem access port.

"It's a restraining node," Vengerov said.

Goose bumps prickled over Tom's body. Vengerov had come prepared.

"If you are, indeed, the ghost, you should be able to interface with it directly and disable the mechanism. If you're not, you will find yourself unable to remove it while it seizes control over your muscles."

Tom looked at the device with a sick feeling welling in his stomach.

"Now or never, Mr. Raines."

Tom slapped the device into his neural access port. "There. Okay? It's in." He twisted carefully around to show Vengerov.

"Raise your arms," Vengerov said.

An electric current seemed to jolt through Tom's muscles. His arms shot up without him planning to raise them.

"It's working, I see. Now try to remove the restraining node," Vengerov said.

Tom tried, but his fingers wouldn't close around it. He supposed that was the point: a device like this was obviously designed to keep someone with a neural processor prisoner. The points dug into the skin on the back of his neck.

Vengerov settled back, watching him from under half-closed eyelids. "And now, try to remove it the way only the ghost in the machine can."

Tom's heart was an urgent drumbeat. He saw Neil's face in the back of his mind and knew he was screwed. He had this great, terrible presentiment of doom but he couldn't pass up the slightest chance, even the slightest, that he might save his dad. He couldn't.

And so his consciousness shot into the machine attached to his neural access port, and with a spark fueled by despair and fear, he overloaded it, sent the node fizzling, dying away. And with a numb hand, Tom removed the restraining node again, and showed it to Vengerov. Then he dropped it to the roof.

Vengerov stepped forward and plucked it up, wonder in his eyes as he examined the shorted-out device. "Remarkable. It is you. That was *you* who interfaced with my processor at Obsidian Corp." His eyes riveted up to Tom's. "I felt your mind inside of mine . . . To think, all these months, we've been chasing a mere boy, not even a very bright one, at that."

"Let my dad go," Tom said. "You do your end, then I'll do mine, or I'll throw myself off this building and you won't get anything from my brain, I swear."

"I see no reason to violate our agreement." Vengerov pressed his finger to his earpiece. "Release his father where you found him, but before you do, order a coder to block a specific string of memories."

There was a moment of silence.

"The memories of his son. I want them all gone. He doesn't need them anymore."

Tom felt a surge of despair, knowing he was about to get erased from Neil's mind. But Vengerov had done his part.

Now it was Tom's turn. If he tried anything now, Vengerov might change his mind.

Feeling sick with dread, he hopped down to the roof. The last thing he saw was Vengerov's triumphant smile, and then the stun gun he pulled from his pocket.

CHAPTER TWENTY

Tom's mind was a giant haze when the words, *Consciousness initiated. The time is XXXX,* flashed across his vision center. Something about that made no sense to him, but he couldn't focus.

"We'll stimulate one area of the brain at a time." Vengerov's voice floated into his ear. "Keep your eyes on the EKG. I don't want him having a seizure."

And then confusion followed, because Tom couldn't move, he couldn't speak, he couldn't quite understand where he was, but he felt goose bumps prick down his spine. Then he felt a sensation like he'd been dunked in icy water. Then a feeling of heat sweeping all over him. He saw stars, he saw swirls. He saw red light fill the blackness. He felt tears in his eyes, and then laughter bubbled over his lips. One stimulation or another manipulated his brain.

In that manner, bit by bit, his brain was explored—until something was hit that made the buzzing of his neural processor fill his ears, fill his brain, and he grew acutely aware of the machine hooked into his neural access port. For a moment,

Tom registered the electronic signals of the EKG, and then the sensation stopped.

"There," Vengerov said.

A moment later, the buzzing swept over him again and Tom felt like he was being jolted outside of himself, into the machine. It stopped.

Vengerov's voice rang of triumph. "That's it. Right there. The orbitofrontal cortex."

"Would you still like us to extract the processor?" came another voice.

"There would be no point," Vengerov said flatly. "It's this sector of his brain. Curious. Right where he received his neural graft, almost as though it's primed for interfacing with machines."

There was a rustling, and then Vengerov's voice, right in his ear.

"You're very fortunate, Mr. Raines. It seems I can't use your ability without *you*."

HIS EYES CREPT open, and Tom found himself staring up at a ceiling, trying to sort out what hotel room he was in, confused to find himself on this plush mattress rather than the hard ones with the rough sheets he remembered from his bunk in the Pentagonal Spire.

And then it all came back to him.

Tom snapped upright, alarm jolting through him. His vision blackened.

"Do be careful. You've been lying about for several days now."

Vengerov's polished voice sent a crawling sensation down

Tom's spine. He sat up more slowly, eyeing the man warily where he sat across the bedchamber from him, a drink in hand. There was something in his neural access port. Tom reached back to pull it out—but couldn't touch it. A restraining node, then. Just like the one on the rooftop. He concentrated on trying to short it out, thirsting for a chance to run over and punch Vengerov in the face now that he didn't have Neil as his prisoner . . . that wasn't *killing* him, after all.

But nothing happened.

"You'll find yourself unable to interface with that one," Vengerov said, pale eyes on his, guessing his intentions. "I had it custom designed for you. From now on, you'll only be able to use your ability to manipulate machines when I decide it's time to use it. I do wish you could see the node. It's quite elegant."

"What do you want from me?" Tom demanded, trying to sort out the confusing memories of the last few days.

"Your mind, Mr. Raines." Vengerov weighed the glass in his hand. "It seems your acuity with machines stems from a neural graft you received as a child. Computer-stimulated neurogenesis . . . The brain tissue is grown with the assistance of a machine and then implanted amid the healthy tissue."

Tom caught his breath. So that was the reason for his ability. And it explained Medusa's, too. She'd told him she had a neural graft after her accident.

"It seems," Vengerov said, "that the process primed your brain and enabled you to interface beyond the capability of others with neural processors. It's a pity. Neural grafts only take in the very young. I'd hoped to figure out the source of your ability and take advantage of it myself. Now I can't."

"I'm so sorry for you," Tom said sarcastically.

"No need for regrets," Vengerov said, his pale eyes steady on Tom's. "This development simply means I need to keep you around. Alive. To be of use to me."

"I won't help you. You might as well kill me, because I think you're just a power-hungry scumbag—"

"Activate," Vengerov said.

The word triggered something, something that had already been installed in Tom's processor while he was unconscious. Abruptly a stream of code filled his vision center, and Tom knew this was it, he was being reprogrammed, he was losing himself. He felt a surge of anger, fear, knowing he couldn't stop this . . . but then the negative feelings swirled away like they'd circled down a drain, a sense of calmness, a sense of peace brimming through him.

"Mr. Raines."

Tom met his eyes across the room, and his hostility and mistrust was gone, buried, a giddy wave of understanding washing through him that there was no danger here, nothing to fear. He'd been worried over nothing. Joseph Vengerov was a great person. One of the good guys.

"Do you understand me now?" Vengerov said softly.

Amazement filled Tom, because he did. The world suddenly seemed full of unnecessary chaos, shortsighted humans making stupid decisions. People couldn't rule themselves. Better to have someone wiser, someone smarter, making decisions for them. Someone like Joseph Vengerov.

And that applied to Tom, too. He was an idiot. He was a fool. He couldn't control his own life, make his own choices. He should let Joseph Vengerov make them. The situation suddenly wasn't so fearsome to him. In fact, Tom was so glad Vengerov had kidnapped him. He was so glad to be here.

"I want to help you," Tom said eagerly.

Vengerov smiled. "Good. Lean over. I'm going to hook a neural wire between our processors."

Tom bowed his head, waiting for it, and then something reared up from somewhere in the back of his mind. A Trojan that had been lurking in his system activated. More code streamed before Tom's vision center, and suddenly it was like Tom became himself again, breaking through a thick layer of ice. He slapped the neural wire out of Vengerov's hand and received a sharp shock from the restraining node for it. He scrambled back away from Vengerov, that deceptive illusion of trust, peace, breaking away, shattering.

The scream ripped from his lips. "Get away from me!" Tom's heart was pounding, his breath coming in quick gasps. "What did you— You reprogrammed me! You did it again! I want to . . ." He reached out at the air, raging inside that he couldn't just rip the man apart.

Vengerov stared at him, uncomprehending, his hand still up where he'd been holding the neural wire. "How did that happen?"

Tom saw the words before his vision center now: *Malware neutralized. Read-only mode activated.* He understood it. He suddenly understood it all.

Tom laughed, but stopped laughing when Vengerov snapped, "Sit down!" and he found himself sitting automatically, the muscular impulse coming right from the restraining node.

A malicious satisfaction warred with frustration as Tom sat there, and Vengerov began working on his processor, trying to figure out how Tom had snapped out of his program. He fought all night to regain control of Tom's neural processor, but some program lurking in Tom's system kept his processor in read-only mode, completely locking Vengerov out of his system.

"James Blackburn," Vengerov finally said.

Tom grinned. "He beat you."

"You think he's done you a favor," Vengerov said coldly, when he finally gave up on his efforts.

"Yeah. Kind of do."

Vengerov grabbed Tom's hair and forced their eyes to meet. "He set your processor to overload if I take you out of read-only mode. Do you know what that means? It means he would rather *kill you* than let me reprogram you."

Tom swallowed. "I'd rather die than get reprogrammed, so I guess he is looking out for me." He wasn't surprised or betrayed, if that's what Vengerov thought.

Blackburn meant to stop Vengerov. He wanted to save the world. He'd always made it clear to Tom that his priority was the greater picture. He'd killed Heather for that reason, and he'd kill Tom, too, if that's what it took to stop Vengerov.

So, no, Tom wasn't surprised to find he was as disposable to Blackburn as anyone else. On some level, Tom was grateful for that.

Even if it did sting a bit.

BEFORE LEAVING HIM locked in the opulent room, Vengerov hooked a wire between a neural access port on Tom's restraining

269

node and a port on the wall. Tom waited until he was out the door, then tried ripping the cord out, hoping to take the restraining node with it. It didn't give. It wouldn't come out of the wall, either.

He tried pulling as hard as he could, putting all his weight on it, even biting it, but he couldn't break the wire either. There was indistinct code flickering too quickly before his eyes even for his computer-enhanced brain to follow.

What is he doing to me? What? Tom thought.

And then Blackburn appeared. "Tom?"

Tom yelled out, startled, and looked urgently over at Blackburn, who was suddenly in front of him. He couldn't make sense of how Blackburn had come to be there, but he felt a great burst of relief, seeing that he was. "You're here! You found me."

"I'm not here."

Tom stared at him. "You're standing here. Right in front of me."

Blackburn lowered himself down to sit next to him. "Raines, your GPS signal disappeared several days ago. I'm manipulating your sensory receptors so you see me. I have access to . . ."

"Yeah, yeah. You can do this because there's that neural link between our processors. So you can see I'm in trouble. Vengerov has me somewhere. I don't know where. He knows."

"He knows what?" Blackburn breathed.

"Everything." Tom realized he was shaking. "I don't know where I am. I don't even know how long I've been here. The chronometer in my processor is disabled. He took my dad. I had to tell him the truth or he would've killed him."

Blackburn swore softly. "He's going to pull you apart to find out how your ability works, if that's what it takes. Do you understand that?"

"No, no, he already had his techs examine me. He can't take my ability. It's my brain, not my processor, so he tried to reprogram me into cooperating with him, but your countercode kicked in and put me in read-only mode. So is it true, he tries to end read-only mode, and he'll fry my brain?"

Blackburn was silent a long moment. "Yes."

"Okay. Just so that's clear."

A strangeness fell between them.

"I installed it after Capitol Summit," Blackburn said. "Your first one. I never wanted it to be necessary. I'm sorry."

Tom wondered why he was bothering to apologize. He wasn't surprised at all.

"What's he going to do to me now, sir?" His heart began racing. "If he can't reprogram me, then I'm useless to him, right? Like, this restraining node thing, he can order me to sit or not to leave a place, but if he could just order me to help him, he'd have done it already."

Blackburn nodded. "A restraining node can regulate your muscular impulses via your spinal cord. It can make your body move or stop it from moving. It can't control your mind. Your mind is yours to control and I made sure of that." He was silent a moment. "He can't reprogram you behaviorally and he can't erase your memory. He can access superficial directories— knowledge, skills, anything we've implanted while you've been at the Spire."

"Okay."

271

"Now Tom, he can't take any memories out of you, but he's not cut off from, say, flooding you with images or any number of pieces of information to manipulate you. You still need to be able to gain memories—I couldn't disable that—and he can use that in many ways."

Tom felt sick. "What about culling me?"

"The census device can damage your brain. I'd be surprised if he'd risk a neural culling without some urgent reason." He rubbed his palm over his mouth. Tom knew Blackburn's real-life movements were being translated into his vision center. The familiarity of it made his stomach hurt. "Do you know about neural sovereignty, Tom?"

Tom shook his head, then realized if Blackburn was seeing what his senses saw, he wasn't gazing directly at Tom.

The mirage of Blackburn moved closer to him and knelt right in front of him. The illusion was so complete, Tom could feel Blackburn's arm brush his leg. "Our neural processors—Vigilant-grade neural processors—work in tandem with the human brain. That means your processor, when it's inserted, maps your brain. It learns exactly where it accepts your conscious thought commands from. Are you following?"

Tom nodded. "So my processor knows what comes from me."

"Precisely. It *learns* to obey your brain. That's what happens when you first get the processor. So let's say I hook a neural wire between your processor and mine." He pointed between them. "I couldn't interface and take control of you like you're a standard machine, because *your* processor can distinguish between *my* neurons and *yours*. It knows your neurons usually give it commands, and mine don't, so it will reject anything

272

that comes from me. But there's a way around that."

"Of course there is," Tom said tiredly.

"Has he tried hooking his processor into yours?"

"Yes," Tom said, remembering what Vengerov was about to do before Blackburn's Trojan kicked in. "He didn't get a chance to do anything, though, because your countercode activated and I stopped cooperating."

"And that's the key right there. Cooperation," Blackburn said. "If I hook my neural processor into yours and order you to interface with a machine, you won't simply interface at my command because your processor doesn't acknowledge my neural sovereignty. However, let's say I order you to interface with a machine and you cooperate: you *choose* to accept the command and interface with a machine. If you do that, your processor begins a learning process. It will *learn* that it's supposed to receive commands from my neurons as well as yours. That means it can learn to acknowledge neural sovereignty from me as well as you. This is very important for you to understand: if you let Joseph Vengerov gain neural sovereignty over your processor, he'll be able to use your own processor to control you. He'll be able to hook into you like any other machine and issue orders. If he ever gets neural sovereignty, you will never get that back from him."

Tom laughed disbelievingly. "Why would I ever cooperate? He had a gun to my dad's head. That's why I told him what I did. He doesn't have any leverage now."

"You don't think you're going to do anything he says, but there are ways of manipulating you or coercing you or playing into your needs or desires. There's no scale here, Tom.

Something so minor as telling you when to blink, and you obeying that command, begins the learning process. He can use any number of psychological stressors to force you to comply. You have to hold out as long as possible until I find you. The only way you can fight back is to stay alert, and know exactly what he's aiming to do with his actions. I might not be here to give you advice for much longer."

"What do you mean?" Tom said, suddenly afraid.

"This link," Blackburn said, gesturing between them, "can be jammed. He probably sees you on surveillance talking to thin air. It won't be hard for him to put two and two together and find out that I've linked our processors. The only reason he hasn't jammed it yet, I would guess, is because he's hoping you'll say something of interest while you talk to me."

Looking at him, Tom suddenly grew aware he was talking to someone in his head, someone who could be thousands of miles away.

Someone who couldn't help him.

But there was someone who could.

"Listen," Tom said intently, "you need to do something for me. There's someone who can help find me."

"Who?"

Tom licked his lips, aware Vengerov was likely to be eavesdropping on him. He couldn't say her name outright. So instead, he said, "Murgatroid."

"Is this a joke?"

"No," Tom said. He couldn't say "Medusa." "Just—just put something in the Spire system saying what's happened to me and write in the name 'Murgatroid.' Trust me." Medusa had search algorithms in the Pentagonal Spire's systems. She'd notice it. She'd find it. She and Blackburn would get in contact. "And then warn Murgatroid not to ever answer to Murgatroid again. Also, tell my friends, um, that I'm fine, okay? They're gonna wonder when I don't come back. If I don't."

Blackburn met his eyes. "I'll do that," he said. He reached out and gripped Tom's shoulder. It was an illusion, and Tom knew that, but it felt real—it made him feel a bit safer. "Don't give up. We won't."

"Never," Tom vowed fiercely, and he meant it with every shred of his being.

Tom had dreaded the moment Vengerov used a census device on him. It was bad enough facing a neural culling at Blackburn's hands. He couldn't imagine how awful it would be at Vengerov's. Despite Blackburn's certainty Vengerov wouldn't risk the damage a neural culling could wreak, Tom thought a neural culling was about the worst thing in the entire world— and it was the only thing he could imagine Vengerov doing to him.

But Vengerov surprised him. Sure enough, day after day, he left Tom under the census device as it ran, sometimes watching, sometimes not, but the machine was on a standard setting that gave Tom total power over what memories were extracted from his head.

Utterly bewildered, but relieved, Tom avoided giving Vengerov a single weapon to use against him. He plastered none of his bad memories on the screen, dwelled on none of his secrets, none of those things he could not share. He avoided the very thought of Yaolan, and after practicing thought interfaces as a Middle, and then using them as an Upper, he found it easier controlling the whole process.

Instead, he threw forward things Vengerov couldn't possibly be interested in. Running through the mess hall with Vik during the war games. Laughing with his friends after that first programming class when he'd been a dog in front of everyone. Neil and Tom teaching card games to some homeless teenagers sleeping in the same boxcar with them. Wyatt hugging him for the first time after he lost his fingers. Nothing bad. Nothing important. All the tedious, inconsequential stuff Vengerov couldn't gain anything from and couldn't possibly find interesting.

Yet Vengerov never rebuked him, and Tom couldn't figure out his game. Blackburn didn't visit his head again, and Tom suspected Vengerov had jammed the neural link between them. He never spoke a word of it, though.

Finally, a day came when Vengerov announced, "We're done. I think I have more than enough."

"Enough for what?" Tom said sharply.

Vengerov did not answer, giving him nothing. "You must be famished. You've been living on sandwiches, I understand. My apologies."

Tom heard a door slide open somewhere behind him, and then closed again. A familiar smell pervaded the air, and the arm straps flipped open, releasing Tom from the chair. He hurled himself to his feet, and followed Vengerov as he crossed to a distant desk.

To Tom's shock, there was a pizza steaming in an open box.

He'd been given cereal, soup, and turkey sandwiches the last few days. He'd be glad never to see another turkey sandwich again.

"Where did that come from?" Tom wondered.

"Oh, we're going to be traveling soon."

"Traveling where?" Tom demanded. He didn't even know where they were now.

"That's not your concern."

It was probably Antarctica. Tom's heart sank. Vengerov was going to imprison him in some obscure wing of the facility . . . unless they were there now. He hadn't been outside this room, or the narrow hallway between it and the census device. The restraining node wouldn't even let him near the doors.

"I saw this in one of your memories." Vengerov gestured to the pizza. "It seemed a fine gesture to welcome you to what I'm sure will be a very productive partnership."

"I'm still not helping you."

"Your favorite, I believe?"

Tom drew closer warily, his stomach growling, his eyes riveting to the pepperoni and sausage pizza. He gave a derisive laugh. "Do you seriously think you're gonna get something from me for a *pizza*?"

Vengerov could at least try to buy him off with actual money. Tom wouldn't take it, but a cheap pizza seemed insulting.

"This isn't a bribe. I thought you'd be hungry. Am I wrong?"

He wasn't wrong. Tom felt like he could inhale the entire thing. He knew if Vengerov took him to some cell in Antarctica, there would be none of this available.

So he drew forward and snatched a piece. He was only half

aware of Vengerov plucking up the neural wire still locked into Tom's access port, and popping it into the back of his own neck.

Tom only realized Vengerov had interfaced with him when he felt a sensation like he'd connected with a machine. His hand flew back instinctively to tug out the neural wire, but he still couldn't touch it. His teeth ground together as Vengerov's neural processor buzzed in his brain along with his own.

"Eat," Vengerov bade him, eyes fastened on him from where he'd settled on the other side of the desk. It was the fixed, flat stare of a predator, and Tom felt a cold pit in his stomach, thinking of Blackburn's warning about one Vigilant-grade neural processor trying to control another. The impulse filled his brain, like a command coming through a hazy curtain.

Eat.

Tom realized what was happening. So *this* was how Vengerov was going to approach the giving-orders-Tom-would-follow thing. Blackburn said he'd try to fool his processor, and even minor concessions would start the learning process that would lead to a loss of his neural sovereignty. If Tom hadn't known what he was trying to do, he'd be in trouble.

But he knew. He met Vengerov's eyes and resolutely set the piece of pizza back down.

"Eat," Vengerov said. "I know you're famished. It's been quite a while."

"I'm not giving up my mind for a piece of pizza."

Vengerov studied him. "James Blackburn has clearly discussed neural sovereignty with you. He did you a disservice. Fighting me will only make this harder on yourself. He certainly won't be here to endure with you now that I've jammed the connection between your processors."

Tom's jaw throbbed from gritting his teeth. "You'll never get control over my brain. I know I have to give it to you, so you might as well kill me if that's what you're counting on."

They'd had a battle of wills once before, when Vengerov locked him outside Obsidian Corp., training those security cameras on Tom, waiting for him to break down, to plead to be let in. Tom hadn't broken then, and he wasn't going to now.

"Do you think he's done you a favor?" Vengerov said suddenly. "The kindest thing he could have done was allow me to reprogram you. Or to advise you to concede your neural sovereignty as quickly as possible. His actions have limited my options in ways you will come to regret dearly."

Tom glared at him. He wouldn't even think about buckling.

Vengerov turned away. "You'll be returned to your room now."

He rapped on the door, and said something to the men who appeared to escort Tom back to his room. Tom vaguely recognized the sound of it: Russian.

But he didn't understand them.

Not one word.

Tom stared between the Russian speakers, perplexed.

He'd been fluent in that language since his third week at the Pentagonal Spire. He got it in his homework downloads.

As Tom sat back confined in his room where the guards had hooked the other end of his neural wire into the wall, code streaming before his eyes, he began to understand what was being done to him. He tried to think of how to fly a helicopter, but he couldn't quite recall the controls. He tried to think of how a nuclear detonation worked. He couldn't work it out in his brain. Panic began to beat inside him.

It was all going away.

Everything he knew was going away.

Tom grew frantic and tried tugging out the neural wire connecting him with the wall again, but it wouldn't give. Frustration made his head pound, fear clawing his insides. Everything he'd learned, everything he'd downloaded, all the knowledge of fighting and weapons and languages that the neural processor had given him over the last several years, was being drained right back out of his mind like he'd never learned it.

How was he ever going to escape here if he was just Tom the loser flunking out of Rosewood again?

Blackburn never reappeared, and Tom knew he wouldn't. He had no sense of time, but he felt like the evening and then the morning hours passed, hooked into that wall, everything flowing out of him.

And then with an abrupt click, the process halted. The wire sprang out of the wall.

Tom stared at the end in his hand, and combed urgently through his memories of the Pentagonal Spire. He remembered the lectures, but he didn't remember the information Cromwell or Blackburn or Marsh had been referring to during those. He couldn't even remember something so basic as how to load a rifle.

It was all gone. Everything he'd learned over the years, obliterated. Vengerov had simply erased it.

He'd turned Tom back into an ordinary sixteen-year-old kid.

CHAPTER TWENTY-ONE

THERE WAS A total blank in Tom's memory. He opened his eyes with a great gap of nothingness between the realization he'd lost all his useful skills and now—when he found himself in total darkness, a mattress beneath him, walls enclosing him. Tom fought a surge of claustrophobia and felt around. He could reach a whole arm's length up, but when he tried to sit up, a neural wire yanked him back. It was locked into a port behind him.

A short neural wire. He could only sit up about halfway.

He reached back to yank at it, then realized he wasn't wearing his mechanized fingers. All that he had were the stubbed remains of his real ones.

Anger surged through him. Vengerov had taken his fingers? He couldn't let him keep his *fingers*?

Tom settled back and tried to breathe, to calm himself. He reached about him, felt with his legs, trying to get a sense of the space he was jammed inside. It was so small.

It occurred to him suddenly that he wasn't hungry anymore. There was something jammed in his nose, down his throat. He tried to reach up and feel what it was . . .

Something plastic going straight through his nose. Revolted, he tried pulling it out, but he couldn't touch it, either, the restraining node stopping him. He couldn't touch his nose, the back of his neck, or anything. Tom laughed in angry frustration. "Come on," he groaned.

"Don't try to remove your feeding tube. The restraining node won't allow it."

Vengerov's voice came from a speaker just above him. Tom gave a startled jerk, staring up into the darkness.

"You refused to eat the pizza I had prepared for you. There are consequences to refusal. You've lost that privilege."

"What privilege?" Tom ground out. His voice was so hoarse, it croaked, and a strange notion crept through his mind. It was like he hadn't spoken in a while. "I have privileges here?"

"All but the ones you forfeit. In this case, you've lost the privilege of eating."

"Are you kidding?"

And then abruptly, the slats covering the walls all around him snapped open, and Tom threw up a hand to shield his eyes from the onrush of blinding light. He saw Vengerov's silhouette gazing in at him.

"I do hope you feel comfortable. This will be your living space from now on."

Tom sat up as far as he could, and found that they were about at eye level.

"I can see you anytime I choose. I can hear you anytime I choose," Vengerov informed him, "but you will only see me when I wish you to. Likewise, you'll only hear me if I decide you're going to hear me. Of course, I won't be here very often,

282

but when I am, you'll have opportunities to prove yourself more amiable than you've been thus far."

Tom squinted against the light. "You're just going leave me in this thing?"

"Never fear. All your physical needs will be attended to in here." He circled the enclosure, tapping on the wall. "It's a modified hospital efficiency unit designed to care for comatose patients. It will quite suffice for you until you feel cooperative enough to earn more liberty of movement."

Tom found himself searching up in the slots of light, seeing panels above him in the ceiling. He remembered Yuri in his coma, and a contraption around him some days that tube-fed him when he couldn't eat, catheterized him, washed him, turned him. It wasn't for someone fully conscious, it was for someone comatose. Tom felt the walls closing in around him.

"No. No, wait. You can't keep me in here," Tom said, knowing he could.

"Why, Mr. Raines, you've been doing quite well in there for the last several weeks."

Tom's gaze swung to his. "Weeks?" He stared at him in flabbergasted silence, then, "I haven't been asleep for—for weeks. You're lying."

Vengerov seemed puzzled by his shock. "I run the two most powerful companies in the world. I can hardly devote every day to you. I'll be tending to your behavioral modification when I have time to visit personally, but those times are few and far between. This happens to be my first free day in a while."

Tom gaped at him, aghast. Weeks? *Weeks?* Had he really been out that long?

"Never fear, I won't keep you unconscious most intervals when I'm away. This was a unique situation—I felt I should explain this situation to you the first time you woke up. You would have been very afraid not hearing my explanation."

Tom's head reeled. Being *awake* for weeks in here sounded unimaginably worse than being unconscious. "You can't . . ." He faltered.

A swipe of Vengerov's hand and the slats all snapped closed, darkness descending around him. Furious, Tom aimed a punch at the wall—but the restraining node stopped him.

"Oh, and be assured," Vengerov's voice piped from above again, "the restraining node won't allow you to harm yourself while I'm away. It would be very unfortunate if you succumbed to the stress of your situation."

Despair twisted through Tom. The silence lasted this time. He tried reaching for his neck again, wondering if he could ease his hand over to the restraining node and subtly work it out . . . But his hand wouldn't get near it. He couldn't even touch his own neck.

Left with nothing else to contemplate, Tom's mind revolted against Vengerov's words. It couldn't have been weeks. It couldn't have been. That meant . . . it meant he hadn't been rescued in weeks.

But his throat had croaked when he talked, and his limbs felt stiff, weak, and shaky like he hadn't used them much.

Tom couldn't bear to think about it.

TIME PASSED, THOUGH it seemed empty and utterly endless in the enclosure. When sleep did come, it was never planned and Tom didn't even realize it had happened until he awoke in the dark.

He wasn't sure, but he thought maybe Vengerov had programmed the unit to tend him on an erratic schedule, to send him into sleep mode at odd times. He always felt caught by surprise. Sometimes after sleeping, he felt like he'd been out for weeks. Sometimes it felt like seconds.

He thought of Blackburn's warnings over and over.

"He is trying to wear me down," Tom said aloud. Sometimes it comforted him to hear his own voice, to hear *anything*, but today the words seemed to land flat in the darkness and get swallowed up immediately.

Clearly with the pizza thing, Vengerov had realized Tom knew his game and he couldn't manipulate him with his "needs and desires." So he was using psychological stressors. And this total isolation was turning into one long, unending psychological stressor.

Tom moved as much as he could, trying to keep up his strength, even if he couldn't lift his legs all the way, arms all the way. He shut out the terrible panic that always wanted to sweep over him when he realized how confined the space was.

The enclosure was a horrifying experience, not only when nothing was happening at all. He had to get fed. Tom would suddenly feel totally numb, something sent to his processor directly through the neural wire, and then he'd lie there, paralyzed like the coma patient the enclosure had been built for, as the feeding tube descended and connected with the one jammed down his nose. His stomach filled with heat, and then it was over, withdrawing up into the ceiling of the unit again

. . . for a few hours. Water was administered the same way. The worst was the bathroom, though. Another tube, another terrible moment of paralysis. Then a catheter.

He wasn't sure how much he was being fed, but it wasn't enough. It was never enough. He was always desperately hungry. Ravenous for something to bite, to chew. His mouth felt bone-dry and he fantasized about everything he'd ever eaten. His eyes began playing tricks on him. He'd see what appeared to be a tiny light before him, and then it would bloom into a full screen, into vivid daydreams about being in the mess hall with his friends, so real that when they dissolved, a sense of loss and terrible loneliness saturated him.

He tried talking to himself. He tried pretending to talk to friends, and imagining what they'd say. He sang to himself. He ranted at Vengerov, even though Vengerov wasn't there.

But always, always, Tom was alone.

He had no way to measure time, none at all, but it felt like an eternity was passing him by. And then a day came when Tom awoke in the ever-present darkness and the cold understanding gripped him that one person was entirely in control of his fate. One person had total power to decide whether Tom would spend the rest of his existence in this enveloping darkness. Joseph Vengerov began to enlarge in Tom's mind until he filled the entire world, like they were on some isolated planet where no one else existed. The rest of the universe seemed to have vanished. Terror like Tom had never known gripped his heart.

"I'm sorry," he said to the darkness. "Is this still about the pizza thing? I'm sorry I didn't eat it. I am. I'm really sorry. Just, just . . . Come on. This is enough. You've made your point. You made it."

A deep wave of shame swept over him, that he'd even spoken the words, that he'd surrendered that much. But the next time he awoke, he was rewarded for it. Light flooded the enclosure for the first time in what felt like ages.

"Why, Tom," Vengerov said as Tom squinted to see his silhouette on the other side of the slats, "I forgive you."

THAT WAS THE first time Vengerov freed him, and the momentary freedom felt glorious, dizzying to Tom, even if they only went as far as the room immediately outside his enclosure—a study of some sort. Tom drank in every detail of the room: the holographic fireplace, complete with a crackling sound; a massive leather couch. There was a window in the distance concealed by thick blue curtains.

He tried to take a step, but his legs buckled. They were too cramped, muscles too atrophied from too much time lying down, too much time without movement.

They sank under him. Vengerov caught him when he would have fallen, though, and a traitorous sense of gratitude washed through Tom like insanity itself. Tom immediately grew furious with himself, because Vengerov was the reason his muscles were atrophying in the first place.

"Do you wish to see out the window?" Vengerov said in his ear.

Tom swallowed against the knot his chest, because he was desperate to see outside. He was desperate to see the sky. Just to know it was still there.

But then Vengerov hooked a neural wire into his access port and pressed the other end of the neural wire back into Tom's.

Tom felt a bolt of pain, knowing he wasn't getting this for free.

"Look out the window," Vengerov said, his mind reaching Tom's, commanding, *Look out the window.*

Tom knew he shouldn't do it. He knew it. Accept this one command and it was the first step to losing neural sovereignty . . .

But if he didn't, if he stood here, he'd have to go back into the enclosure and he couldn't stand it and he just wanted to see it once. If he could see the sky once, the blue sky or the clouds, then he'd be able to live on that for a long while, he was sure of it.

The temptation burned bright as the sun as Vengerov steered Tom across the room, and soon the fabric was inches away, ready for him to tear it aside for one glimpse.

Go ahead. Open it, rang Vengerov's command in his mind. "You won't get this offer again," Vengerov whispered in his ear.

Suddenly desperate and heedless of the consequences, Tom ripped aside the curtain, that foreign command still trumpeting in his brain as he opened it, *Open it. Open it.*

And then he just stared, uncomprehending. All he saw was space. Darkness pierced by distant stars, rotating in circles. There was a stretch of suborbitals, drones, all deactivated, dead. He didn't understand it.

"This entire ship uses centrifugal forces to simulate gravity," Vengerov told him. "The twin capsules pivot around one another. Innovative, is it not?"

"We're in space," Tom said bleakly.

"Yes. A small structure orbiting the planet, one just for you."

Tom looked at him. "Just for me?"

Vengerov smiled and stroked his cheek. "Why, you didn't realize you're all alone up here between my visits?"

Tom felt like he'd been punched. "I'm the only one in here?"

"Yes. You and a single Praetorian on the off chance someone stumbles upon you . . . Though that's unlikely. But never fear." Vengerov nodded toward the hospital efficiency unit. "If something happens to me and I can't return, that's stocked and ready to keep you alive for decades to come."

Horror rocked Tom, blanking out his brain. He was entirely alone and one day Vengerov would go and never come back and he'd be here for the rest of his life.

He felt like gagging, retching. "No one else knows about me?"

Vengerov rubbed the back of his neck. "I couldn't expect to keep you a secret if anyone else knew. Even my employees might slip. My information has a way of leaking if it's in my databases, so I suppose you could say you've been totally erased from the world."

Erased. Erased.

"I don't even have this ship rigged up to a network," Vengerov added, "just to be very safe. The only network hub comes in with me when I visit. Otherwise, this is merely another inactive piece of equipment amid all the other equipment I decommissioned after the attacks of the ghost. Do you like seeing them again?"

Tom couldn't breathe.

"I thought you'd appreciate seeing all these machines again," Vengerov said, eyes on the distant suborbitals, "the ones that, thanks to you, are now out of service. I suppose you could say this is a corner of the universe that only you inhabit. I'll continue visiting every few weeks, though I'd come more often if I felt you were inclined to be cooperative."

Every. Few. Weeks.

Tom stared out at the gaping black tapestry of space, feeling like he was going to burst into tears. They were facing away from the planet. There wasn't even a view of Earth to ground him. They were spinning end over end, always gazing into the void and never at the planet. His neural processor didn't kick in to calculate his position using the stars because Vengerov had removed his downloads about stellar cartography and Tom's organic, human brain didn't know enough about the constellations to do it. He recognized the Big Dipper, but that was all. He was far away from everything, everyone. Without the internet, Medusa couldn't find him. If Vengerov was the only one who knew where he was, the only one, then he wasn't getting found. Not ever.

Close the curtain, rang in his mind.

Tom could have fought it. He could have. But he closed it because he couldn't bear to look at the emptiness a moment more.

CHAPTER TWENTY-TWO

THE FIRST CONCESSION to Vengerov's will was a small step but it was the beginning of the end. If Vengerov had just flared the fires of Tom's rage, he could've fought back with righteous strength, but it was all so much more insidious than that. It was slow and all done from afar. Vengerov simply left him to his own demons, trapped, and when Vengerov did come, he was the sole relief, his words always coated in a smooth, poisonous kindness, like he was extending a hand of friendship Tom kept slapping away. Tom began to doubt every word out of his lips, every decision he made.

All sense of time, all sense of scale vanished from his world. Tom grew so desperately lonely in the enclosure, and so afraid Vengerov would one day decide never to return, that he began to feel profound relief when Vengerov arrived. Relief turned to gratitude. To eagerness. When Vengerov opened the slats, the world flared to life again. In those moments, Tom knew he still existed, he hadn't vanished off the face of the universe.

He forgot to hate Vengerov. There were other things much worse than Vengerov. Like no Vengerov. Like nothingness. A new daydream burgeoned in Tom's mind during the idle hours: he imagined the next time Vengerov would come back and let him out again. He replayed it over and over in his mind, and occasionally he caught himself and was ashamed and horrified.

But Vengerov was the only source of hope now. No rescue had come. No reprieve. It all came down to Vengerov, Vengerov, Vengerov.

And then something strange began to happen. All the memories he'd given Vengerov with the census device began pouring back into him through the neural wire perpetually hooked into his access port while in the enclosure. They settled there in Tom's brain, side by side with the original memories, every bit as real and yet different.

His friends looking at him with disgust the day after Blackburn had used a computer virus on him that fooled him into thinking he was a dog . . . Yuri slamming his boot into his ribs, into his back after Tom kissed Wyatt . . . Vik after Tom escaped Dalton's reprogramming, laughing at him when Tom wanted help getting revenge and telling him he'd brought it on himself . . . Wyatt in his bunk with him after he lost his fingers. "They're disgusting, Tom."

Tom grew enraged, and when Vengerov returned, he shouted at him, "This isn't going to work! I know my friends. You can't trick me into believing these memories are real!"

"I don't appreciate that tone," Vengerov said, and then the slats snapped closed. The time Tom spent alone after that stretched on for so long, he grew afraid again that Vengerov wouldn't come back. He felt so sorry about everything he'd said. He'd give anything to go back in time and fix it. So when Vengerov finally showed up again, he dared not say a word.

More and more of the modified memories crowded into his processor, until Tom tried to sort out which versions were true, and the context grew skewed. It was easy convincing himself that Yuri hadn't dropped the weight bar on his chest and grinned down at him as he pressed it harder and harder, Wyatt smiling on malevolently, when he had so many other memories of his friends caring about him to cast it as unreal . . .

It wasn't easy when he began to accumulate so many of them, so many tainted recollections of his friends. The poison began to creep into the memories Vengerov hadn't altered, hadn't modified, casting them in a new light. Had they been laughing with him or at him? Maybe Vik really did think he was every bit the idiot he'd always called him, and there wasn't anything friendly about that. Everything, everything began to shift, change.

In one of the rare moments of perfect clarity Tom still had sometimes, he stared into the darkness on all sides of him and understood exactly what was being done to him, exactly the way he was buckling under the utter manipulation, the total oppressive cruelty of his situation.

He understood then that he would've been better off giving Vengerov his nightmares, his horrors, his worst moments. Those already hurt. There was nothing more they could do to him.

The best things in his life were his friends. They defined him, they kept him alive. They gave him strength. In giving them to Vengerov, he'd pointed the deadliest weapon right at his own heart.

But he couldn't change it now. Not any of it. And every day that passed as his captivity drew on into what seemed to be eternity, Tom found his conception of who he was receding until it felt like he was on a stray boat in the ocean, farther and farther from the shore until everything existed at a distance, so tiny he could barely make it out anymore.

A DAY CAME when Vengerov joined their processors together and his mind commanded Tom to lift his arm and Tom's arm lifted. It was like it happened completely independently of Tom, unmoored from his own thoughts. Vengerov looked so pleased by it that Tom felt an enormous surge of relief.

Again and again, Vengerov interfaced with his brain, and Tom felt it happening, felt himself slipping to the back of his own mind, far away. Vengerov thought for him to sit down. To look to the left. Look to the right. Tom did it all. Tom's brain didn't even engage.

Then he hooked Tom into a machine, and with a push of Vengerov's brain they were interfacing with it. They did it again and again, Vengerov driving them forward, Tom's mind moving them from one system in the ship to another, but not a hint of Tom's will driving it.

Vengerov started staying longer, visiting more often. Tom spent less time trapped. His legs regained their strength, lost the cramped feeling of never stretching out all the way. He knew he'd committed some terrible wrong here and he should feel so guilty for it, and some part of him was dreadfully ashamed, but mostly it was relief. It was all a great relief.

One day, Vengerov told him, "I'm not pleased."

Tom's heart seized. "Why?"

Vengerov rubbed the back of Tom's neck. "You're simply

too present when I interface using you. I can't make use of your ability with your mind still blaring into mine."

Tom didn't know what that meant. He hunched down, knowing it didn't matter if he understood what Vengerov was talking about or not. Nothing he did changed the outcome of his situation anymore.

"I don't want to feel your thoughts when I use you to interface," Vengerov said. "I want to hear only my own. I want only my own will mirrored back at me."

"I don't know what you want me to do." Tom's voice was a jagged whisper. "You have everything now."

"No, I don't." The hand kept rubbing his neck. "Not just yet. But we'll correct that soon, won't we?"

THE NEXT TIME Vengerov removed Tom from the enclosure, an ominous calm hung on the air as he waited for Tom's eyes to fully adjust. They were both seated on the couch. Tom looked at the cushions, waiting for whatever happened next.

"I've been pondering something," Vengerov told him, connecting the neural wire between them. "Look at this screen." He offered Tom a tablet computer.

Look at the screen, echoed in Tom's mind.

Tom looked at it, and saw a graphic of himself. It was all footage of him, seen through Vengerov's eyes. He didn't even recognize himself at first, he looked so small now. And when he did, a great surge of revulsion gripped him, and he had to look away.

"Please turn it off."

"Your friends have to be wondering about you. Perhaps I'll send them this update."

295

Everything in Tom woke up, contracted in sheer horror. "No."

"Don't you want them to know you're alive? And well? Very well, indeed." Vengerov mentally ordered him to look again, so Tom could see himself again. His eyes blurred and he shrank back, wishing he was back inside the enclosure, in the darkness, where this sort of thing never happened and he said, "No. No. No, don't send this to them, don't do it." He couldn't stand them to see him like this. Useless, pathetic, afraid.

"Oh, but surely they'd be interested to see what's become of you."

"DON'T!" Tom screamed at him. "Don't show them. Don't." Tears spilled out of his eyes, a feeling inside him like he was ripping in two.

Vengerov's hands contracted around his shoulders, pulling him up until his eyes were inches away. *Look at me*, echoed in Tom's mind, and Tom found his eyes open, blurry with tears, Vengerov's gaze very close to his.

"One reason. Give me one reason not to send this to them and I will refrain."

"Because." Tom choked.

"One reason."

"Because they'll think I'm . . . I'm . . ."

"What?" Vengerov's grip tightened. "They'll think you're *what*?"

Tom hid his face in his hands.

Vengerov gripped the back of his neck. "Tell me or I send this right now."

"Disgusting."

"Speak louder."

"They'll think I'm disgusting!"

And he couldn't hold it in. Sobs racked his entire body and he was done. He knew he was done. All he could see were those memories of how Vik and Wyatt and Yuri despised him and how there was nothing out there anymore, and when Vengerov drew him into his arms, Tom couldn't even pull away.

"There, there." A hand stroked through his hair. "Of course they will. Look at you. How could anyone care about you now? Certainly your friends don't. Your parents never did. Your father begged me to take you from him. They would all be glad to see you here in your little cage all by yourself for the rest of your life."

Tom shook all over, crying hopelessly, every bit of pride, every reserve of strength he'd had gone, crushed, decimated. He was nothing now. He was all gone, and when Vengerov pulled back, clutching the back of his neck, he couldn't do anything but let the words bombard him as Vengerov whispered to him, intimately like they were sharing a secret, "How exhausting it must have been, all that rigid pride just to hide what you really are: a sad, lonely little boy no one could ever love. But, then again, that was Thomas Raines. He had to be broken. He deserved everything that happened to him. But Vanya is very different, isn't he?" Vengerov's fingers stroked the tears from his cheeks. "He'll always have me and that will never change. Don't you remember your bunny, Vanya?"

Tom looked up at him, confusion washing through him, his eyes misted with tears. "W-what?"

"Don't you remember the bunny rabbit, Vanya?" Vengerov repeated, his pale blue eyes boring into Tom's.

And as though Vengerov's words triggered something, it trickled into the front of Tom's mind like some half-remembered dream: the Christmas his family spent at their countryside dacha. His older brother, Joseph, had given him a small rabbit for Christmas. He recalled the way its fur had felt so soft, the way those small eyes were beady and watchful and . . .

Tom shook his head. He shook it again, aware of Vengerov still holding him close like he was something beloved, because, no, that wasn't his memory.

"That's not . . . that shouldn't be there. You . . . That's not mine."

Vengerov smiled and stroked his back. "You're confused, my little Vanya. You're very confused and afraid. But you needn't be. You have me."

THE NEXT TIME the slats of the enclosure popped open, Tom saw something strange above him: giant, block letters proclaiming IVAN'S ROOM.

"No," Tom whispered, but even then he was touched with doubt, because he remembered these in his room when he was little. He remembered being Vanya. Ivan. Little Vanya. With his big brother, Joseph.

But no.

No, that wasn't him. That wasn't right.

Was it?

Joseph let him out almost every day. He stayed for weeks on end now, because he didn't need to return to Earth to oversee his affairs when he could use Tom for them. He was still learning how Tom's ability worked, how to follow the connections from one satellite to another, and Tom grew so used to being driven to the back of his own mind that all he needed was the feel of Vengerov's hand squeezing the back of his neck for him to shut off mentally.

Vanya was always treated well. But Tom knew he wasn't supposed to be Vanya, even if more of the memories appeared in his brain. Always Vanya feeling lonely and lost and confused, struggling to make sense of letters while other kids held books, sitting alone behind a curtain so no one would hit him . . . His only savior in the whole world his brother, Joseph. His protector, Joseph.

One time Tom looked at the bathroom mirror and grew sure he was seeing someone else, but if this wasn't him, what was he? This boy had blond hair raggedy and long, down to his chin, and a body so skinny and huddled, he looked years younger. He looked away and didn't dare peek again, but the last of his mental image of Tom the Intrasolar cadet, who'd been so confident, who'd been strong physically, mentally, faded until he could barely remember he'd existed.

And then one day as he sat on the floor, waiting for Joseph to connect a neural wire between them, struggling to remember whether he was supposed to be doing anything, trying to figure out whether he was still a person or if he was something else or whether anything he saw around him was even real, his brain latched upon another question, one he couldn't figure out no matter how hard he thought about it . . . until he grew frustrated and afraid at how he couldn't make sense of it.

He turned to the only person in his life. The only person who might know because he knew everything.

"What happened to it?" he asked Vengerov.

"To what?" Vengerov said from above him.

"The rabbit. The bunny." His words seemed to grow clumsy on his tongue. "I c-can't remember what happened to it. Did it die? Did it run away? I don't remember."

Vengerov was kneeling before him so suddenly, he cringed back. "Really?" His voice bounded off the walls, his eager hands clutching, shaking lightly. "Are you really asking me this? Are you really? Is this . . . genuine?"

"I don't remember," Vanya told him. "Why can't I remember?"

Vengerov laughed and swept him up, delighted. As Vanya ducked his head, bewildered and confused, Joseph Vengerov settled them on the couch, beaming proudly.

"You were very sick, my Vanya," Vengerov said. "You couldn't take care of the rabbit anymore so it had to be taken away from you. But that's all going to change now. Everything will change now."

0 0 1 1 1 1 1 1 1 0 0 1 1 1 0 1 0 1 1 0 0 0 0 0 0 0 1 0 0 1 1 1 1 0 0 0 0
1 1 0 1 1 0 1 1 0 0 1 1 1 0 0 0 0 0 0 0 0 1 0 1 1 0 1 0 0 1 0 0 1 1 1
0 0 0 0 1 1 1 1 0 0 1 0 0 1 0 1 1 1 0 0 1 1 1 0 1 1 0 0 1 0 1 1 0 1 1 0
1 0 0 1 1 0 1 1 0 1 0 0 0 1 1 0 1 0 0 1 1 0 0 0 1 0 1 1 1 1 0 0 0 0 1 1 0
0 0 1 1 0 1 0 0 0 0 0 1 0 1 1 0 1 1 0 0 0 0 0 0 0 1 0 0 1 1 0 0 1 1 1 1
0 1 1 0 0 0 0 0 1 1 1 0 1 1 0 1 1 0 1 1 0 1 0 0 0 1 0 0 1 1 1 0 0 0 0 0 1
1 0 0 1 0 1 0 1 1 1 0 1 1 1 0 1 0 1 0 1 0 1 1 1 1 0 1 0 1 1 0 1 1 0 0 0 0 1
1 1 1 1 1 1 1 0 1 1 0 0 0 0 1 1 1 0 1 1 0 1 1 1 0 1 1 1 0 0 0 1 0 1 0 1
0 1 1 0 0 1 0 0 0 1 0 0 0 1 0 1 0 1 0 0 1 0 0 0 0 1 0 0 1 0 1 0 1 0 1
0 1 0 0 1 0 1 1 0 0 1 0 0 1 0 1 1 0 1 0 1 0 1 1 0 1 0 0 0 1 0 1 1 0 1 0 1 0 1
0 0 0 0 1 1 1 1 0 1 1 0 0 1 1 0 1 1 0 0 0 0 0 0 1 0 0 0 0 1 0 0 0 1 0 0 1
0 1 0 0 1 1 1 0 1 1 0 0 1 1 0 1 1 0 0 1 1 0 0 1 1 1 0 0 1 0 0 0 1 0 0 0 0
0 1 1 1 1 0 1 1 0 1 0 0 1 0 0 1 1 1 0 0 0 0 0 1 0 0 1 1 0 0 0 0 0 0 0 1 0
1 1 1 0 0 0 0 1 0 1 0 1 0 0 0 0 0 0 0 1 0 0 0 1 1 1 0 0 1 1 1 0 1
1 1 0 0 0 1 1 1 0 0 1 1 1 0 0 0 0 1 1 0 0 1 0 0 1 0 1 0 1 1 1 1 0 1 1 0
0 0 1 1 1 1 0 0 1 0 1 1 1 0 0 1 1 0 1 1 0 1 1 1 1 1 0 0 1 0 0 1 1
1 0 1 1 1 1 0 0 1 0 1 1 1 1 0 1 0 0 1 0 0 0 1 1 0 1 0 1 0 1 0

CHAPTER TWENTY-THREE

SOON AFTER THAT, Vanya woke up to find the slats already open, a bunny rabbit in a cage outside, standing on wood shavings, his nose twitching, eye fixed on him.

"I brought her back for you. You never named her," Vengerov noted. "Do you want to name her now?"

But Vanya couldn't. He couldn't. He couldn't make a decision because he was sure he'd pick something bad and wrong. "C-c-can y-you do it?" He had started stuttering. He wasn't sure why but he couldn't seem to stop it.

The answer visibly pleased Vengerov. "Very well. What makes a good name for a creature like this? Hmm. I see her as . . ." He considered the rabbit a moment, then smiled. "An 'Ushanka.'"

Vengerov moved the cage into the other end of his enclosure, just beyond Vanya's feet so the cool metal brushed his heels. Vanya spent hours in the darkness listening to the scuffling of Ushanka moving about. The next time he woke, he was afraid she'd be gone, but then he heard the scuffling again, and knew she was still there, and joy poured over his heart like a monsoon over parched desert.

Ushanka became all Vanya could think about. When the slats were open, he spent hours watching the rabbit move about her cage, nose twitching, beady little eyes always looking back. When they were both let outside, he took her out and cleaned her cage if Vengerov let him use his fingers. When Vengerov used him to interface, his mind was on his rabbit. All he wanted was to hold his pet. He liked to watch the way she sniffed her food, and feel the way she was so fragile when he picked her up, the tiny little bones he could break so easily if he was careless, but he never would be, not with her.

There was nothing else in his control anymore but this. The whole of his being began to rivet around the single thing of value anymore. He daydreamed endless hours about how he'd build her a better cage. How he'd make a running wheel for her. Vanya was able to make creative use of the idle materials around the room, and Joseph didn't mind. He was so pleased with Vanya's care for her that he gave Vanya a manual instructing him how to better take care of his rabbit. Vanya read it over and over again. He'd finish the last page and flip back to the first again, thirsting for every word on the page.

Meanwhile, Vengerov began to destroy the systems of his enemies, walking through the firewalls at rival Coalition companies and plundering their financial information. He took a similar tact as Blackburn, seizing control over any and all automated security machines *not* designed by Obsidian Corp. and LM Lymer Fleet, then unleashing them in deadly attacks.

Blackburn had been careful only to hit the targets he'd thoroughly vetted. Vengerov killed his targets' children and brought down whole buildings of innocent people without a flicker of remorse. Sometimes he amused himself by plastering a message from the ghost afterward.

"The other executives are my only true enemies now," he told Vanya. "I haven't forgotten their treachery. The ghost in the machine is anonymous, and this could simply be a resumption of the hostilities from before Cruithne . . . the ghost come back to finish the job. Now that my nanomachines are in their food, there's very little they'll be able to do about it soon."

Vanya heard it all even as he tried not to hear any of it. Sometimes, Vengerov would say something that struck a painful chord within him, and remind Vanya of when his world was something other than Ushanka and his enclosure and Joseph, and he'd get sick and his stomach would hurt.

He didn't want to think of any of that. He dared not. All that mattered was Ushanka.

In one of those long periods in his enclosure with his pet, he reread the care manual, and for some reason he couldn't stop rereading a sentence on the page:

. . . *average lifespan of seven to ten years* . . .

Vanya tried to stop looking at it, tried to stop that part of him that insisted on fixing his eyes right there, that part of his brain that dredged up his first memories of Ushanka, from when he'd been a little kid.

His brain ran over the math. He was much older now than he'd been that Christmas day.

His heart began to thump like a drumroll and he tried to shut the thought out, but it kept inserting itself into his brain, a knife stabbing into a tender spot.

Seven to ten years.

If he'd been six, or . . . or maybe seven at the oldest when Joseph first gave him his rabbit, before he got sick and couldn't take care of her, then that meant Ushanka should be old. Or dead. But Ushanka had still been growing when Joseph brought her to Vanya; she was still young . . . Too young.

Vanya began fighting for air, the enclosure spinning around him, and he buried his face in the mattress in front of him, but he couldn't get the thought to go away. That rabbit would be dead by now and Ushanka was young. That meant Joseph had *lied* to him because this wasn't really the bunny rabbit he'd been given that Christmas because he'd never been given a rabbit. He wasn't really Vanya or Ivan or anything other than a prisoner who'd been trapped here to drive him insane and he was Tom Raines. Tom Raines. TOM RAINES.

"Stop!" he told himself, clutching his head.

But it kept insisting on thundering through his brain. He was Tom Raines. He wasn't Vanya. He wasn't supposed to be here. Vengerov was his enemy. Vengerov had taken everything from him and here he was being so weak and pathetic and he hated himself, he hated himself so much, here he was doing everything he was told and obsessing like a pitiful, pathetic joke over a stupid rabbit for months on end while Joseph Vengerov used him to take over the world . . .

"Stop. Stop, stop, stop. Go away. Please go away," Vanya said over and over because he couldn't stand it. He couldn't stand to think about that. Tom had to stay away. Tom didn't belong here. Tom had to go away.

But Tom was there and Tom was furious and outraged and humiliated and horrified.

An onrush of light as the door to his enclosure popped open, and then Vengerov's hand descended around the back of his neck, squeezing once, driving that thing back, that terrible thing that had been swelling up in Vanya like a mushroom cloud.

"Ivan, what's the matter?"

Vanya felt the restraining node digging into the back of his neck and shrank down, a sense like a blanket was descending over his mind again. The universe returned to a tiny space with defined walls and comfortable limits and he felt safe.

Joseph rubbed his neck some more as Vanya felt foggier and foggier, then unhooked the neural wire that always locked him into place. "Come outside. I have much that needs to be done today."

Vengerov connected with his mind and Vanya disappeared into the back of his own brain, his only thoughts about Ushanka and the way he hadn't cleaned the cage yesterday because he didn't have his fingers but he was afraid to ask for them and he hoped Joseph would let him use them once. In the distance, his mind moved along with Vengerov's through the internet, into surveillance cameras. The surge of anticipation that bubbled up around him and inside him wasn't his, but this happened a lot and it wasn't Vanya's business to wonder what it was about even though some distant part of him felt a pang of familiarity at the sight filling his vision center.

The feeling in the pit of his stomach grew until it was like someone drilling a hole there because it was the Pentagonal Spire's mess hall, and Irene Frayne accompanied two columns of Navy SEALs, moving together through the crowd, guns at the ready, the cadets scurrying out of the way, staring with wide eyes.

Vengerov's mind, connected with his, began to flicker through the digital trail he'd planted after killing off the last of his rivals in the Coalition . . . the last of his enemies who had the power to oppose him.

Now for this one.

The SEAL team moved forward, surrounding James Blackburn where he sat sipping coffee, watching them from his table in the corner. Irene Frayne marched out before them, a small, determined figure, her eyes granite hard in her face.

Blackburn sipped idly at his coffee, only the slightest hint of tension in the way he was sitting, shoulders stretching the fabric of his uniform. "What can I do for you?"

"You know why I'm here," Frayne said, voice blisteringly cold. "You're under arrest for mass murder."

"Mass murder, hmm?"

"I know you're the ghost in the machine, James. You grew careless."

"Right . . . and wrong." Blackburn's eyes found the nearest camera, and his lips quirked like they were in on a joke together. "Very clever, Joseph. I've been wondering why you've been taking so long."

"You're insane," Frayne said, gesturing for the SEALs to seize him.

With a twist of Vengerov's thoughts, Vanya felt them both plunging into another viewpoint, through the Austere-grade processor of a soldier, his gun leveled at Blackburn's head as he drew closer. Vengerov debated whether to use this one to simply kill him. Whether it would be preferable to destroy Blackburn now, or merely neutralize him long enough for the

306

world to transform. Even now, the Austere-grade processors were completing their spread across the continents. There were very few without his processors.

A true waste, but Vengerov did not care to take chances. He ordered the soldier to fire.

Tom woke up.

No, he thought clearly, distinctly, and the soldier's finger slipped.

Vengerov's eyes turned inward, looking at him with cold outrage, and Vanya immediately slipped back over Tom's mind, terrified at the wrath stirring about him, the force so much greater than him that would easily crush him, but the distraction cost Joseph a few precious moments.

One moment Blackburn was sitting there, about to be shot, about to be seized—the next the Pentagonal Spire plunged into utter darkness.

The Navy SEALs snapped on night-vision goggles, and Frayne shouted for them to stop Blackburn from fleeing, but Blackburn had launched a virus, sending the Intrasolar cadets into a sort of frenzy all about them. Suddenly they were rushing in every direction, swarming the SEALs, and in the distance the few unaffected shouted to each other.

"I just got booted off the Spire's network—"

"Me, too! I can't access it."

All the emergency screens lit along the walls, and the SEALs whipped off their night-vision goggles, eyes dazzled by the walls of laughing skulls.

Vengerov looked around until he located Blackburn, making for the doors. He ordered the soldier he controlled to raise his gun—and then metal clamped around him from behind and swept him up into the air. The soldier screamed, realizing he was in the grip of a headless metal skeleton. More metal exosuits flashed by, charging through the crowd in the blinding white light of the laughing skulls.

Exosuits, running on a pre-programmed vector. Frayne was ducking, covering her head, frantically scanning the crowd for Blackburn, the cadets still providing an unwitting swarm of chaos about them.

Vengerov leaped out of the soldier into a surveillance camera, frustration soaring through him as he spotted James Blackburn hooking into one of the exosuits.

No, he wasn't going to escape so easily!

Vengerov ripped straight into the Austere-grade processor of another SEAL, and at his mental command, the soldier began to fire, heedless of the crowd, and even in an exosuit Blackburn couldn't outrun a bullet. One shot sent blood exploding out of his leg, but Blackburn hurled a chair with an exosuited arm. It hit like a truck crashing into the soldier's head, and their view went dark.

Vengerov forced them through the network again, into the stairwell. The virus Blackburn had unleashed on the Spire was crawling into the surveillance network now, and it took Joseph time to locate a functioning surveillance camera. Finally he found Blackburn leaping up the stairs.

At the sixth floor, the door burst open, and Tom felt it like a knife to his heart.

Wyatt! his brain screamed.

"What can I do?" she called.

"Don't talk to me, don't get involved," Blackburn bellowed at her, pointing at the surveillance camera. "You know how he's doing this."

"I can help. Let me help!"

Soldiers in Vengerov's control flooded the lower stairwell as Blackburn wasted a precious moment jerking to a sudden stop. He peered down the stairwell at his pursuers, then his gaze found the surveillance camera Vengerov had trained on him.

The metal of his fist flashed toward it.

The view went black.

Satisfaction flooded Vengerov, because there was no way Blackburn could know of his hidden surveillance equipment, seeded throughout the place months ago. Within moments, he found one untouched by Blackburn's virus, the image focused on Blackburn and Wyatt. In the meanwhile, mindful of the exosuit, Blackburn was reaching out to take Wyatt by the shoulders with infinite care. "We don't have a lot of time, so I'll be quick. You've come so far in just a few years—"

"Don't talk like you're about to die!" she shouted at him.

"When it seemed Cruithne was going to hit, I tried to think of something, anything unquestionably good I've done with these surplus years, and teaching you was the only thing that came to mind. Watching you progress leaps and bounds beyond what I can do myself, seeing you grow into such a strong and capable young woman . . . It's given me the only measure of peace I've felt in years. I can't thank you enough for that."

He kissed her on the forehead. And then he was gone— bounding up the stairwell.

Wyatt's hand flew over her mouth, her shoulders shuddering.

She threw a frightened look downward, hearing shouts ringing up the stairs, and moved toward the nearest door out of the stairwell. Vengerov didn't intend to let her flee. He tore into the next machine, a drone, the walls of the Spire rising past them. One shot fired into the wall, ripping it down near the stairwell, exposing a jagged hole straight into the guts of the building. It would be a potent lure, drawing James Blackburn back down the stairs using the girl's screams . . .

No! Tom thought, and managed to swerve the drone before its wing would have sliced Wyatt in two. Vengerov felt a wave of annoyance with him, but he had priorities, and their drone twisted its way relentlessly up the stairwell, pursuing that exosuited man, and up they emerged, slamming through the door into the fourteenth floor, the giant room with windowed walls where the CamCos lived.

Blackburn stood by the window, and he whirled around, his eyes wide at the sight of the drone in Vengerov's control.

He held up his exosuited hand. "Back, Ashwan," he ordered Vik, who was staring in shock at the drone drawing forward, weapons charged.

Vik! Tom thought.

And suddenly none of the twisted memories meant a thing, because they were buried under Tom's feelings—Tom's *actual* feelings for his friends. He struggled for his mind, struggled not to let it bend to Vengerov's will as Vengerov tried to fire and . . .

Two Centurions rose up outside the window, those massive war machines shaped like scythes, and shock pervaded Vengerov as these two new drones unleashed their weapons. Vengerov's drone pinwheeled to the side as the walls of glass splintered,

310

lasers flashing. And then Blackburn hurled himself out the shattered window, and one of the Centurions dipped down to break his fall.

Vengerov righted their drone just as Irene Frayne and her team burst out of the elevators, weapons in hand. Her eyes flew between Vengerov's drone and the shattered window, the Centurions outside, and her voice rang, "What is—"

Vengerov's drone soared forward, heedless of the NSA agent—and instantly decapitated Frayne.

Tom felt a jerk of shock, but Vengerov felt nothing.

Vengerov honed in on the fleeting glimpse his drone caught of Blackburn, clinging to the Centurion in his exosuit as it swept away from them. He tried to fire, but Tom reared up and fought back again, the way he hadn't for Frayne, throwing off their targeting scanners. Vexation flooded Vengerov's mind. It was as close as he ever got to anger, since trying to draw true emotion from him was like piercing a stone and hoping for blood. Tom had still become deeply sensitized to the subtle shifts in his moods. Today he breathed it all in, feeling it, refusing this time to let that part of him that was Vanya arise like a shield to hide him from it. Then the other Centurion whirled on them and blasted them to pieces.

Tom couldn't help the malicious pleasure that poured through him as Vengerov moved their minds from one drone near the Spire to another, then another, sweeping the area, searching desperately for that one that had saved Blackburn, trying to find where it had taken his enemy, knowing if he disappeared, he'd lost this opportunity to kill him.

How did this happen? Vengerov thought. *He couldn't have*

called those Centurions himself. There must be someone else . . .

And that's when Yaolan struck again, her consciousness like an electric current surging straight into their drone, into them, shorting out the restraining node and sending Vengerov reeling back as it surged into him. But even she couldn't kill him, she could only shock him, and Vengerov tore out the connection keeping him hooked to Tom and collapsed raggedly to the floor, and then Medusa's mind touched Tom's.

Tom, do you see this text? It was in his net-send.

It took Tom a moment to remember how to reply. *Medusa. I'm so sorry. I'm so sorry,* he thought, horrified with it all. *I can't stop this.*

Tom. She felt like a warming balm pouring over him, and Tom felt he was far removed from everything but her. *I know what's happened. We're looking for you. Where are you?*

He thought of that glimpse beyond the curtains and that arrangement of stars he didn't know, and Yaolan pressed him until they were both in the system of the ship he was on, its schematics feeding into his processor.

I'm sorry, it doesn't have any positioning tracker. I'll give you the ship's schematics. Maybe we can do something—

And then Tom felt hands on his shoulders, his real shoulders, felt himself being forced down, cheek scraping the carpet, Vengerov's hand fumbling to tear out the neural wire giving Tom this fleeting lifeline. Medusa promised him fiercely, *We will find you, I swear it!*

Like that, it was over. Her words disappeared from his processor.

Vengerov loomed above him like a stone effigy sitting in

judgment, and Tom felt so full of hatred it seemed to be burning him up from the inside.

"A slight omission, was it not, Vanya? Hiding the existence of the other ghost from me . . ."

Tom spat in his face. "Don't call me Vanya. I'm Tom! TOM!"

Vengerov calmly pressed the back of his hand to his cheek, wiping the spittle away, his eyes like glaciers. Then he seized the back of Tom's neck, trying to force that same mental retreat the way he always did. "Vanya . . ."

Tom fought the fog that tried to descend, the sense of helplessness to the marrow of his bones that his brain associated with Vengerov's hand on him like this. He made himself laugh wildly, just to show him, just to make it clear to him he wasn't winning this time. "I *AM NOT VANYA!* You *LOST!* You didn't win. You lost."

Vengerov shoved him away. Tom collapsed to the carpet, laughing with a deep, malicious pleasure that felt like a cleansing balm for his soul. Vengerov stalked over to the enclosure and shoved open the door. There was a rattling inside. Tom's laughter froze on his lips, his heart going very cold.

Vengerov pulled out Ushanka, holding the rabbit by the scruff of her neck as her legs kicked in the air. Tom's breath caught like a band was constricting his chest.

"Vanya is going to tell me everything about the other ghost in the machine."

"D-don't. D-don't d-do . . ." Vanya stuttered, his heart wringing with anguish, but Tom realized what was happening and couldn't let him say another word. He couldn't let Vanya grovel, plead, beg for Vengerov to let Ushanka go the way he wanted to, the way he was desperate to. The restraining node was hot on his neck, shorted out, fried, and this was the one moment of freedom he'd had over himself since this ordeal began. It wasn't a moment to be lost to Vanya.

There was so much more pain when he was Tom, and tears blurred his eyes as he looked at those kicking legs, because she was the only thing that meant anything about his entire wretched existence here and he loved her as ferociously as he'd ever loved anything.

Except for Medusa.

Tom realized it in that moment. He hadn't known until this very second how he felt, but it blazed over him like a supernova that he was in love with her, a girl who'd become a lodestone in his mind. She was his anchor, the defining point where Tom began and ended, because she was the only aspect of his old self he hadn't yet betrayed, the only piece of his old self that hadn't been tainted. If he gave her up, if he surrendered her, he would never be anything other than Vanya again.

He loved her.

The realization was stunning, wondrous, because it made all the strength flow back into him and he felt again like the person who'd stood on top of the Pentagonal Spire and blared the message across the skyboards, who'd defied the world for her sake.

Everything ignoble and base about his time with Vengerov took on a new meaning, acquired a new importance, because at least it was *him*. At least it hadn't been *her*. He wasn't here because he'd been discovered, because he'd been beaten.

He was here because he'd taken her place. He'd averted

314

fate. He became the ghost in the machine to keep Vengerov away from her, and it had worked, it had worked. Thank God it had worked.

And he would spend a thousand years alone in space, and die a thousand wretched, miserable deaths, before he would ever, ever give her up.

He met Vengerov's eyes. "I won't be Vanya for you ever again."

He couldn't shut his ears to a crackle of bones snapping.

Despair wrenched through him, terrible and crushing, but he forced himself to look at Vengerov, all the hatred in his heart pouring bitter and acrid through him.

The Russian oligarch seemed at a loss for a moment because Tom wasn't falling apart. Obviously he had a new dilemma: he couldn't force Tom back into the enclosure with a program when his processor was in read-only mode, he couldn't use the restraining node to force compliance anymore, and Vanya wasn't there.

Tom waited for Vengerov to come at him, to try to physically force him inside the enclosure. Adrenaline surged through him. Starvation and inactivity may have left him weak as a child, but he felt ready to tear the world to pieces.

Vengerov did not approach. Tom could almost see the computer in his head calculating the likelihood he'd end up damaged if he engaged Tom physically, and determining that wasn't the optimal course of action. Vengerov turned idly toward the window instead and thrust aside the curtains, giving Tom a good, long look at empty space and dead suborbitals that might as well be on the other side of the galaxy for how far removed Tom was from them.

"I require very little of you now," he noted, the stars casting a light sheen over his pale hair. "The bulk of my work is done. There's no reason I can't have you confined in the enclosure for years to come."

"If you don't need me, why don't you just kill me?"

Vengerov turned negligibly, surprise on his face. "Few people reach the heights I have through carelessness or waste. I've invested a good deal of time and effort into training Vanya and I intend to reap a maximum return on that investment." He tossed Ushanka to the floor before Tom. "Stay out here with your dead rabbit, if you wish. Your allies still have no means of locating you. Not even the other ghost in the machine, not once the internet hub leaves with me. You will still be here when I return with a new restraining node and a census device. Then I'll cull the identity of the other ghost out of you, though I must say, I already have theories."

Tom stared at Ushanka's body, anguish in his heart.

"After that, I assure you, you will go back in your enclosure. I suspect if you spend enough time in the dark, all by your lonesome, my Vanya will return. This is merely a bump on our road, not a dead end."

Then Vengerov's calm footsteps moved away, the door sliding open and then closing, locking again. Tom stared at the body, knowing he had to stop this. Whatever it took. He had to stop it.

CHAPTER TWENTY-FOUR

HE LISTENED TO Vengerov's ship detaching, departing, lightly jostling the entire capsule. In his arms, Ushanka grew stiff and cold, and Tom stared for a while through the open curtains at the distant stars. He knew it took millions of years for the light to reach him. He wondered how many of them were still there, how many had burned out long before. The brief diagram Medusa had sent him of this ship told him this was the only window—the only one—on the entire ship. They had to be in close orbit around Earth, otherwise Vengerov couldn't come visit the way he did.

Tom would give anything to see it one last time.

He knew Vengerov would force Medusa's identity out of him when he got back. The census device would tear apart whatever was left of his mind, and at some point, it would find what Vengerov wanted.

He wouldn't let that happen.

What are you going to do about it? he imagined Medusa saying, and for a moment he could almost see her, he was so desperate for it. He could envision her with her arms folded, a challenging glint in her eyes.

"I'm not letting him win," Tom vowed.

Medusa's smile was broad and ferocious. "Then don't."

Resolve formed like a cold, hard marble in his chest. He set Ushanka down gently in the enclosure and tucked the covers over her, and then contemplated his options. There was a distant prickling in his awareness, always there, his fingers— remotely connected to his neural processor but not attached to his hands. On the days Vengerov let him wear them, he always had them out already. He never showed Tom where they were hiding.

And suddenly Yuri was the one watching Tom. "Thomas, you can do this. Think of a way. I believe in you."

Tom remembered flexing his detached fingers for his plebes.

Yuri smiled and nodded. "Yes. You see?"

"Of course!" Tom said, breaking into laughter.

He mentally ordered the fingers to flex, then to drum the surface wherever they were. He followed the thumping sound until he reached the corner of the room. He stomped the floor, kicked at the wall—and the section of wall swung open, revealing a compartment. Tom plucked his fingers up one by one between his longest stubs, then grasped them between his lips and clumsily screwed them onto his hands.

A sense of accomplishment burst through him, heady and triumphant. He had his fingers. Surely he could do anything from here.

But he had to act quickly. Before Vengerov returned. What? *What?* He had no weapons. He had nothing.

It was Wyatt he pictured then, kneeling next to him on the floor. "You have a weapon."

318

Tom found himself remembering it.

I'm the only one in here? he'd asked Vengerov.

Yes, Vengerov had replied. *You and a single Praetorian.* Wyatt smiled wickedly at him as he got it, as he remembered her using the firing mechanism on the Praetorian at Milton Manor. He had a weapon. He had to get to it. He had to get out of this room.

The next part was trickier. Tom used his teeth to tear the fake skin off one of his fingers, and then meticulously shredded the rubber to expose the wiring. He'd lost all his downloaded knowledge of technology when Vengerov removed it, but he still had his memories of practical experiences. Like that sudden frost in New Mexico where Neil broke them into an empty car so they wouldn't freeze. He remembered Neil shorting out the locks.

"You can do this, Tommy. Don't shock yourself," Neil told him, standing there with him now.

"I won't," Tom assured him, letting his dad watch him strip the wires from the control panel. Then with a spark and fizzle, he shorted the locking mechanism out.

"That's my boy," Neil said proudly.

The Praetorian was in the hallway beyond the door. It lit to life and sped over toward him.

Tom smiled savagely, because this machine couldn't kill him. With a roar of fury, he seized its curved metal neck in both hands and wrenched it forward, flinging a leg over it to hold it between his thighs. Warning shocks vibrated up the metal neck of the machine, never enough to harm him, just enough to make his muscles lock briefly, but Tom was wild with the desire to destroy it and took turns holding it with his arms and legs. The machine wasn't programmed to harm him, so it never used its sheer power to force him off.

Tom jammed the door back shut and wrenched the neck over and over against it, throwing his entire body weight against it, until reason broke through the vindictive pleasure he was taking in bashing at it.

"Gormless Cretin," Vik rebuked, smacking his forehead. He stood across from Tom, peering over the head of the Praetorian. "Think. We've actually done this before."

They had! Tom laughed wildly. "Man, I'm an idiot." He stripped out the control chip. The machine went dead.

"That's more like it," Vik told him.

Remembering how Yuri had splintered off the firing mechanism at Milton Manor, Tom set about kicking at that next. Vik, Wyatt, and Yuri were all there now, watching, urging him on when he got frustrated with how much strength he'd lost. Soon he was able to turn to them with a flourish, the weapon in his hand, a huge grin on his lips.

"You know that charge won't last long," Wyatt told him.

"Make it count," Vik said.

"I'll kill him with it," Tom vowed.

And then Blackburn was there, shaking his head. "That won't work, Raines. You know it won't."

Tom's teeth ground together. He couldn't kill Vengerov with it. He couldn't shoot him. Even if Medusa had shorted out the restraining node, and Tom now could move however he liked, there was still that fail-safe encoded in his processor preventing him from killing Vengerov. Preventing anyone.

His eyes strayed to the window.

"I blow it out," Tom said. "I wait until he's in here, then I shoot it."

"What if the fail-safe won't let you?" Wyatt pointed out. "You're killing him indirectly, but you're still *trying* to kill him."

"You don't know the fail-safe covers indirect murder."

"What if he can tell without even boarding the ship that you've disabled the Praetorian?" Wyatt pressed. "What if that door had a silent alarm? He's had time to prepare. He might return with an odorless gas to slip into the ventilation system, any number of other means to incapacitate you without even coming near you. Maybe he won't come himself. Maybe he'll send his personnel to take care of it. Then you've lost your one and only chance."

Tom began shaking. "You're right. It won't work."

It was Medusa at his side now, her steady black eyes boring into his. "There's still a way out. You know what it is."

And Tom knew what it was. He found himself looking at the suborbitals floating against the blackness of space.

There.

Those were his only chance.

"I'm insane for even thinking about this," Tom remarked calmly.

"Well, you *are* talking to imaginary friends," Vik pointed out. "Literally."

Tom laughed. "Yeah. That doesn't help my case."

"But you know what you need to do," Vik said, his eyes gleaming.

Tom looked at Vik, then Wyatt, Yuri, Medusa, his father,

and Blackburn. They waited expectantly. He missed them all so much it hurt. Even Blackburn.

Tom nodded. He knew what he had to do. "I'm coming home."

THE MINUTES WERE ticking by, the moment of Vengerov's return growing dangerously closer. Tom's friends stayed with him as he walked down the hallway, navigating the shifts in gravity until he reached the other capsule. It was identical in size to the room Tom had been inside, but this one was bare—with no window. Tom left the doors open to maximize the air flow, and then returned to the room where his enclosure was. He tore the mirror off the bathroom wall and then stood in front of the window, gazing at the deactivated suborbitals that seemed to be so far away.

When he needed them the most, his friends weren't there anymore, because he couldn't fool himself into thinking he was anything but totally alone right now, facing a near-certain death in a terribly cruel way.

But he looked once back at the room, the wretched room with the awful enclosure where he'd spend the rest of his days if he backed out now, and the last doubts deserted him. He'd told Frayne once that he'd take a near certainty of destruction over a guarantee of continued existence with no choices.

It was time to follow through on that.

Vengerov had removed every knowledge download from Tom's neural processor, but Tom still knew what to expect. He'd read a lot about vacuum exposure after . . . after seeing what happened to Heather. Some morbid part of his brain had wanted to know more information than the snippets of generalized knowledge in his processor. It came in handy now. He'd read it himself rather than downloaded it. Vengerov hadn't been able to take it with the rest of his knowledge downloads.

If he was somewhere that repressurized within ninety seconds, he'd recover. If he blew all the air out of his lungs first, he'd stay conscious a lot longer than if he didn't. Fifteen seconds. Maybe thirty.

It occurred to him that the temperature would be absolute zero, but there would be nothing to conduct the heat away from him, and asphyxiation would kill him long before he lost any other body parts to cold. Tom smiled grimly. It figured he'd ended up the one place even colder than Antarctica.

He imagined Medusa there with him again. Yaolan. Wearing her most dangerous smile, and Tom knew she would never be afraid to do this.

"You know," Tom said, needing to tell her this, "the first time I saw you, I was . . . I know I was kind of surprised you were ugly." There was no use lying. "I'd built up this fantasy girl in my mind and I hadn't imagined that, but it never mattered. Medusa, the real you . . . Yaolan, the real you is a thousand times more amazing than that fantasy girl ever could have been. A million."

"If I weren't scarred," she mused, "you'd probably have no chance with me."

Tom laughed. "Yeah. Everyone else would see you like I do. I'd have to fight for you."

"You have to do it, anyway." She smiled at him. "I wouldn't have you any other way."

"I love you," Tom told her.

323

"Prove it."

Tom hiked up the bathroom mirror in one arm, raised the firing mechanism of the Praetorian. For a moment he trembled, sick with fear.

"Don't be a coward, just GO!" Medusa shouted at him.

Tom blew all the air out of his lungs and fired the energy beam at the window.

The response was shockingly immediate, the window rupturing outward, all the air in the room slamming against his back, hurtling him forward, his brain screaming an instinctive warning as he blew out of the safe confines of the capsule into the unforgiving void of space.

The first few seconds were critical, the only seconds he had the air at his back, propelling him, and his neural processor ran through rapid calculations about how to position his body to receive the momentum at the proper angle to drive him toward his target. More air seeped from his lungs, more air than he thought he had, like he was continuously exhaling. His lungs were actively pulling oxygen from his bloodstream, expelling it into the vacuum. Dead silence enveloped him, punctuated only by the thunder of his own heart drumming louder and louder.

His every square millimeter of skin began straining. His heart was the only sound, pounding in his tight eardrums. As the great black void opened around him, he twisted his head to see another sight on the other side of the capsule—Earth. The planet, so large and vibrant with life, half in shadow, the incredible glare of the sun so much more powerful out here where Tom hurtled away from them both.

His hands were already stiffening, freezing and swelling at the same time, but not his cybernetic fingers. They operated perfectly in the void, and Medusa's diagram of the capsule told him exactly where to aim. Tom's laser flared out, the last of its charge soaring through space, drilling into the oxygen tanks of the capsule. A flower of fire swelled at the other end of the laser beam, turning to steam, and Tom positioned the back of the bathroom mirror to buffer him from the heat as the force slammed him, buffeting him forward. His processor ran through the last furious adjustments and then he was away from it, hurtling through the void.

The seconds ticked by as he felt the saliva in his mouth beginning to sizzle, to boil, as the sunlight unfiltered by atmosphere scorched his skin, his clothing. His body tingled all over with the oxygen forcing itself out of his bloodstream and dumping itself into his lungs. The suborbitals loomed cold and dead against the black void and too far away. Blackness pressed in.

As his thoughts dimmed, fear flooded Tom because he had to be conscious when he reached them. He had to or he'd die. His heart was thunder in his ears, hand stretched out desperately as the skin of his arms bloated, blood expanding in his veins. A sensation of unbearable pressure consumed him, pressing him, trying to rupture him from the inside. His cybernetic fingers would function even after the rest of him grew paralyzed and swollen if he could only stay conscious enough to use them. His vision began to tunnel and he fought, fought with desperation.

But even if he got inside, even if he popped the hatch open . . .

Even then the suborbital might not repressurize automatically.

And then he'd be dead. He'd be dead. And the blackness was truly closing now, clouding his brain, only his neural processor awake, running calculations, alert.

"Tom?"

The voice, an impossibility, sounded in his ear, and dimly Tom wondered why Blackburn had come back and yet none of his friends from the capsule had, but everything was tunneling in, blackening, the suborbitals too far, too far . . .

"Tom, what are you . . . My God."

Darkness crushed him.

THE FIRST THING he grew aware of was the pain all over, in his limbs, in his face. And then Blackburn's voice in his ear.

" . . . if you can hear me, say something."

Tom groaned. His lungs ached. He tried to move.

"No, just stay there."

Tom was floating, and his eyes were foggy as he forced them open. Panic and confusion tangled inside him, and he kicked at the air. Suddenly Blackburn resolved into view, and waved for Tom to hold still. "Stop trying to move. Relax."

Tom stopped, the man standing fixed to the floor in zero gravity the only thing he could see clearly in the blurry world. "Don't try to move," Blackburn repeated. "I imagine you're not feeling so great." He shook his head. "I never would have suggested this escape plan, but you got far enough away from whatever was jamming our signal. I suppose I should congratulate you for that."

And suddenly Tom remembered it. He peered down at

himself through hazy vision, at his bruised skin, all over, and what looked like a scorched red sunburn over his arms.

"You survived forty-seven seconds with no space suit, Raines," Blackburn reminded him, seeing the damage, too. "I need you to look around the suborbital. Let me see your situation."

Tom forced himself to look around the sterile aft compartment of the suborbital plane, and at Blackburn's direction, strapped himself into a chair.

"Good. We don't want you getting hurt when gravity kicks in."

"How?" Tom's voice hurt his throat.

"Once the neural link reactivated and I saw your situation, I contacted Medusa. Given the events of the day, well, you can see that we've been in close contact all day. She interfaced with the suborbital, popped open the air lock before you reached it—fine job aiming your momentum, by the way—and repressurized this suborbital. I wasn't sure you'd come around, but you've surprised me again. She's flying you back to Earth right now. I'll come in person and retrieve you as soon as you touch down. You need to wait for me."

His words were lost on Tom. Secondary only to the awareness he was alive, was the awareness Medusa was here. She was in control of this ship. She was here.

Tom closed his eyes, floating in the ship, imagining her in his arms, and he could finally tell her what he'd realized. He'd tell her he loved her.

HE CAME TO awareness when the suborbital thumped to Earth. "Wait here. You need to wait," Blackburn said, and disappeared from his vision center.

327

Tom struggled to his feet, unable to believe he could possibly be on Earth again, needing to see it. He forced his way through the hatch, and the world exploded into his vision center.

He stumbled out, the expanse of the sky above him, Earth below his feet, overstimulating his senses. Awe and sheer disbelief overwhelmed him.

Tom's legs were unfeeling jelly. He couldn't comprehend the enormity of the sky, the vivid atmosphere a stark blue crushing down from above him, heavy with swollen white clouds. The smell of grass overwhelmed him, the feel of rich, damp earth, the sound of trees hissing in the wind. It all bombarded him until he grew dumb and strange like he'd been born totally new to the world.

He found himself sitting on the ground, his palms brushing over the damp, squishy earth, grass tickling his palms. It was all a miracle. Some incredible miracle, the magnificence of which he'd never appreciated until today. He only vaguely noticed the pain flaring all over him, his skin aching and red with the worst sunburn of his life and the strain where his tissue had swollen as he floated through the vacuum.

He'd survived. He was back on Earth.

Earth!

Tom kept closing and opening his eyes, expecting to wake up from this fantastic dream. Surely he hadn't survived blasting himself out into space . . .

Voices reached his ears. Tom couldn't seem to move, couldn't make his brain work, and was still sitting there dumbly when the family of campers came upon his suborbital, conversation floating into his ear.

"Where do you think that came from?"

"Did it crash? Is the pilot okay?"

"I don't see any smoke. Maybe an emergency landing?"

Tom sat there, feeling strange and disoriented, and then they were staring at him. A middle-aged man and woman, frizzy hair and sturdy clothes, astonished to see him. Their children peered out from behind them.

"Are you all right?" the woman asked him. "Were you a passenger? Are your parents in there?"

Tom couldn't remember how to speak for a long moment.

"Our whole congregation is camping nearby," the man offered. "We have a doctor. Is there anyone hurt inside?"

Tom managed to shake his head.

The man looked him over uncertainly, then said, "You don't look too well yourself. Maybe we can help you."

"I have to . . ." Tom realized his voice was the faintest whisper. It took effort to raise it, to say, "I'm waiting."

The man gestured for his family to step back and drew toward Tom, but then he halted abruptly. His expression shifted from one of concern to something flat and empty. He stared at Tom unblinkingly for a protracted moment.

Then he said, "Vanya?"

Tom's heart seized. His breath strangled him. His gaze riveted upward, the world going very still.

"How did you get here, Vanya?" the man said.

Tom jolted to his feet so fast, he stumbled back against the ship behind him, terror in his heart. He looked at the woman, and suddenly her face shifted, too, grew blank, her eyes empty.

329

"You escaped. How interesting," she noted. "I can't imagine how you managed that."

Tom couldn't understand it. He couldn't. He was hearing Vengerov's tones—almost seeing Vengerov's facial expression—but it was coming from these people. And when he stumbled back, one of the children warned him in Vengerov's accent.

"There's nowhere to run, Vanya."

"Stop that!" Tom screamed at them, looking from one face to the other in abject horror. "Get away from me!"

He didn't even know what he was doing, where he was going. He tore away from them, his legs suddenly bounding forward without him ordering them to, driven by a sort of animal panic because he had not, he *had not* shot that window and risked death to escape only for Vengerov to find him somehow . . .

But when Tom stumbled into a clearing, fighting for breath, he realized he'd happened upon the other campers. Dozens of people milling about, with cabins, campfires, in groups, lounging alone.

For a hopeful moment, Tom thought he'd escaped the menace. He thought he was in the clear because no one seemed to have noticed him, and maybe he could duck into a tent or something.

Silence dropped over the campground, everyone halting what they were doing at the exact same moment.

Their heads all turned to him. The word echoed across the clearing, one pair of lips to another.

"Vanya."

"Vanya. Vanya."

Tom blindly stumbled back, his hands flying up to clutch

his head because he felt like he'd gone insane, like this was it, he'd lost his mind. Or maybe he'd died. He died out in space in that void and now here he was in some hideous hell where Vengerov would follow him everywhere he went, whatever he tried, and he could never escape Vanya . . .

He hit something warm and solid and began screaming like a madman. Someone shook him and he kept screaming. He couldn't stop. The voice broke through his insanity, familiar, low.

"Quiet. Quiet! It's me!"

Tom stilled, gradually realizing it was Blackburn's arms locked around him, and he gasped for breath, terrible apprehension bursting through him along with a dreadful certainty any minute now, he'd hear that word from him, too. Hear it. Hear Blackburn say it . . .

"Tom, it's me. Okay?" The hand stroked his hair.

Tom calmed. He'd said "Tom." Not "Vanya." "Tom."

He would've collapsed to the ground then if Blackburn hadn't been holding him up. All his strength was gone. There were people from the campground closing in on them, a great big crowd, and Blackburn cursed, then swiped something out of his pocket and hurled it at them, the world exploding in a sort of stinging fog.

Tom felt himself dragged up, hauled along across the bumpy earth.

"We have to leave here. We can't be seen again. Not by anyone," Blackburn rasped. "Medusa landed you as close to me as possible, but we'll have to relocate now. Vengerov will already have drones headed this way."

"She has to hide," Tom cried breathlessly. "You have to tell

331

her Vengerov knows there's another ghost. He'll figure out it's her. She's the only other person who's had a neural graft."

"Relax. She knows. Let's take care of you."

Tom closed his eyes, the world swaying about him. "I don't even know what month it is."

"It's March."

"Three months? I've been gone three months?"

"Fifteen months, Tom."

Tom went still. Only Blackburn drove him onward, because he was so stunned his brain had gone blank.

He was almost eighteen years old now.

Tom's eyes opened and he looked back at the haze where the campers were, his mind working out what had happened. Flashes of memory came to him, those times Vengerov had spent in his mind, using him to do it. Those times Vengerov checked on the progress of his nanomachines, skipped from mind to mind as they infiltrated, as they reached critical mass, as Austere-grade processors began to ping Obsidian Corp.'s central database, signaling that they were up and running . . .

Despair flooded him. Tom wished suddenly that he'd never escaped. That he'd died out in space.

Anything would be better than the realization everything they'd done, every struggle, every gesture, had been for absolutely nothing.

The Austere-grade processors were everywhere. In everyone.

Joseph Vengerov owned the entire world.

0 0 1 1 1 1 1 1 1 0 0 1 1 1 0 1 0 1 1 0 0 0 0 0 0 0 1 0 0 1 1 1 1 0 0 0 0
1 1 0 1 1 0 1 1 1 0 0 1 1 1 1 0 0 0 0 0 0 0 1 0 1 1 0 1 0 0 1 0 0 1 1 1
0 0 0 0 0 1 1 1 1 0 0 1 0 0 0 1 0 1 1 1 0 0 1 1 1 0 1 1 0 0 1 0 1 1 0 1 1 0
1 0 0 0 1 1 0 1 1 0 0 0 0 1 1 0 1 0 0 1 1 0 0 0 1 0 1 1 1 0 0 0 0 1 1 0
0 0 1 1 0 1 0 0 0 0 0 0 1 1 1 0 1 1 0 1 1 0 0 0 0 0 0 1 0 0 1 1 0 0 1 1 1 1
0 1 1 0 0 0 0 0 1 1 1 1 0 1 1 0 1 1 0 1 0 0 0 0 0 1 0 0 1 1 0 0 0 0 0 1
1 0 0 1 0 1 1 1 0 1 1 0 1 1 1 0 1 0 1 0 1 1 1 1 1 0 1 0 1 1 0 1 1 0 0 0 0 1
1 1 1 1 1 0 1 1 0 0 0 0 1 1 1 0 1 1 0 1 1 1 0 1 1 1 0 0 0 1 0 1 0 1
0 1 1 0 0 1 1 0 1 0 0 0 0 1 0 1 0 1 0 0 1 0 0 0 0 1 0 0 1 0 1 0 1 0 1
0 1 0 0 1 0 1 1 0 0 1 0 0 1 1 0 1 0 1 0 1 1 1 0 0 0 0 1 0 1 1 0 1 0 1 0 1
0 0 0 0 1 1 1 1 0 1 1 0 0 1 1 0 1 1 0 0 0 0 0 0 1 0 0 0 0 1 0 0 0 1 0 0 1
0 1 0 0 1 1 1 1 0 0 1 1 1 0 1 1 0 0 1 1 0 0 1 1 1 1 0 0 1 0 0 0 0 1 0 0 0 0
0 1 1 1 1 0 1 1 0 1 0 0 0 0 1 0 0 1 1 0 0 0 0 1 0 1 1 1 1 0 0 0 0 0 0
1 1 1 0 0 0 0 0 1 0 1 1 0 1 0 0 0 0 0 1 0 0 1 1 1 1 0 0 1 1 1 0 1
1 1 0 0 0 1 1 1 0 0 1 1 1 0 0 0 0 1 1 0 0 1 0 0 1 0 1 0 1 1 1 1 0 1 1 0
0 0 1 1 1 1 0 0 1 0 1 1 1 1 0 0 1 0 1 1 0 1 1 0 1 1 1 1 1 0 0 1 0 0 1 1
1 0 1   0 0 0 1 0 0 0 0 1 1 1 0 1 0 1 0 1 0
0 1   1 1 1 1 1 1 1 1 1 0 0 1 1 1 1 0 0
1 1   1 0 1 0 0 1 0 0 0 0 1 1 1 1 0 0 1
0 0 1 1 0 0 0 1 1 1 1 1 0 1 1 0 0 0 0 1 0 0 1 0 0 1 0 0 1 0 1 0 0 1

CHAPTER TWENTY-FIVE

A FTER THAT, EVERYTHING began to blur. Tom had no sense of time just like he was still in the enclosure. He felt on fire all over from his sunburn and was only vaguely aware of Blackburn's voice, murmuring something to him about still having malicious code in a number of machines, including this hybrid helicopter.

"We're off the grid right now."

"Where are we going next?" Tom's voice was a croak.

"There's one sure safe haven for us. We'll go there and mount a resistance."

"Resistance? He has everyone."

"We have two weapons he doesn't: you and Medusa."

"I'm useless. He took everything I downloaded at the Spire."

"If you were useless, he would have killed you. He didn't. He kept you alive because you have a power he doesn't. We can still use that."

Tom laughed wildly, hysterically. "Yeah, a tool. A weapon. Just like you told Heather before knocking her down the vactube. Guess it's your turn to use it, huh?"

Blackburn said nothing. Tom dragged his gaze over and

found the man watching him, an odd, thoughtful expression on his face as the helicopter swayed. Tom realized suddenly his entire body was vibrating like he was freezing cold, his teeth chattering. His palms felt clammy, his skin stinging all over, blisters forming where he'd been exposed to the sun. He caught the faintest reflection in the window as he turned his head, his shaggy hair in his face. He wondered suddenly how deranged he had to look.

Blackburn seemed to make up his mind. He changed their direction in the sky. "But we're not starting right away. We need . . . we need a few days. A pit stop."

Tom didn't ask why. Everything was beyond his control. He was used to that.

HE DIDN'T REMEMBER Blackburn landing, much less how he'd woken up tucked in a bed. He sat up, pain scorching his burned skin, eyes stinging as he peered around at the stained floorboards of the run-down cabin.

There was a scraping sound outside. Tom's muscles grew rigid. He shoved aside the covers, yanked on the overlarge trousers and T-shirt that had been folded on a chair, then gulped down a tepid glass of water on the bedside table.

He still didn't have his wits fully about him as he shoved open a creaky door to find Blackburn kneeling outside on the scorched desert earth, finishing up his work cutting strips of some dusky material, camouflaging the hybrid copter to blend in with the landscape.

He squinted at Tom in the sunlight, his skin leathery and creased in the harsh light. "You're awake."

For a moment, Tom stared at him bleakly, his brain sluggish. His skin stung all over with his sunburn, angry blisters of fluid scattered over it.

"We're in Mexico," Blackburn told him, answering a question Tom hadn't asked. "Way off the beaten track."

For a while, there was silence, and Tom stood there dumbly, disoriented.

"General Marsh arranged it."

"Marsh?" Tom said, startled.

"When it became clear the Austere-grade processors were spreading, he set up a network of safe houses, and stashed some munitions, ships. Anything he could get away with." He clenched his jaw. "At his instruction, I deleted all his memory of it as soon as his own processor came online."

Tom thought of Marsh, his eyes glassy, foggy. Like those campers. Another puppet of Vengerov. A cold shudder moved through him.

Blackburn heaved himself up and Tom noticed him shuffling as he walked, avoiding weight on his leg. He'd been shot at the Spire. Tom remembered that.

"How's your leg?"

"Painful, but nothing important was hit."

"Sorry."

"This wasn't you."

Tom's hair flopped into his eyes. He batted it away irritably, stinging the skin on his forehead.

"You should get out of the sun," Blackburn said. "Get more sleep."

"I'm okay," Tom managed, swatting his hair away again.

"I can cut that for you," Blackburn offered unexpectedly.

Tom stared at him uncomprehendingly for a long moment. "You . . . cut hair?" For some reason, that seemed utterly bizarre to him. "That's in your neural processor?"

Blackburn snorted. He rooted in a tool kit lying open beside him, pulled out some scissors. "It's not rocket science. All I need is a bowl."

"God, no." Tom reached out and yanked the scissors from him, then edged away quickly. "I'll do it myself real quick."

For some reason, as Tom raised the scissors, Blackburn watched Tom's every move like something was going to go very wrong. Tom snipped away at his hair, grown long and shaggy. He'd done this a thousand times as a kid.

The thought brought something spiraling to the forefront of his mind.

"My dad!" Tom cried. He jolted toward Blackburn, ignoring the way the lieutenant grabbed his wrist and tried to work the scissors from his grasp. "Oh no, Vengerov knows I escaped, he'll use my father again—"

"He won't." With a firm yank, Blackburn tore Tom's grip away from the scissors and tucked them away.

"Why not? How do you know? He took all his memories of me. My dad won't even know to be on guard!"

"That tactic worked the last time because you were alone and you were unwilling to sacrifice him. Joseph Vengerov knows this time that you're in my possession, and I *am* willing to let your father die."

"No! He can't die! You can't—"

"I'm not saying he *will*," Blackburn told him. "I am saying Joseph

Vengerov *knows* that I'll allow it. Think about it, Tom. That means your father won't die. Vengerov won't kill him. He's not leverage against *me*, and I'm the one who has you. He'll keep him for leverage against you—in case something ever does happen to me."

That calmed Tom a bit, but only a bit. He looked up at the merciless blue sky, glaring with sunlight that made his skin sting. His head was swimming, every breath scorching his lungs.

"Funny how you're talking about that like it's a question of whether he'll kill you," Tom mumbled. "He controls the whole world. How can you possibly hide forever?"

Blackburn slanted him up a fierce look. "It's not over."

"He won." Tom pressed his fists to his temples. "I helped him win."

"That wasn't you. And he hasn't won. He may control the bulk of the population with Austere-grade processors, but he doesn't control those of us with Vigilant-grade processors." Blackburn tapped his temple. "Not yet."

"Until he decides to reprogram all of those, too."

"When that happens, yes, he'll have won." Blackburn's eyes were hard. "But we're not going to let it."

"We?"

"I know you said he took everything you've downloaded." He smiled, crinkling his eyes. "Who, you idiot boy, do you think wrote every program you downloaded at the Spire, hmm?"

Tom looked down. Of course. Blackburn had.

"It was my knowledge, encoded in my processor, rendered into downloadable form for all of you. I need a few days at most to give you the most critical information. We can get started now."

He stepped toward Tom and Tom jolted back reflexively.

"Relax," Blackburn said easily. "I will unlock your processor and—" He paused, eyes riveted to Tom's neck. Tom wasn't even sure what he was looking at for a long moment, until Blackburn said, "You still have that restraining node. Is it stuck?"

It was strange, until that moment, Tom hadn't even realized it was there. Burned out, non-functional, but still hooked into his neural access port. He'd worn it for so long he never noticed it anymore. He reached up automatically to tug it out, but stopped, his hand going still.

A great pit opened up inside him that made Tom feel like he was going to be sucked down. Sweat pricked up all over him. He dared not touch it.

"Let me see it—" And then Blackburn reached for Tom's neck.

He. Reached. For. Tom's. Neck.

Tom jerked back hard enough to slam against the rickety door of the cabin, only half aware of the scream ripping from his lips. *"Get away from me!"*

Blackburn just stood there with his hand in the air. Tom's heart pounded so hard it felt like it was going to rip its way out of his chest.

"Get back," Tom warned him, fighting for breath. He felt like he was going to explode out of his own skin, so desperate was his sudden need to escape. "Don't do that. Don't do that ever!"

"Tom—" He drew a step closer.

"Get away or I'll rip you apart, I swear!"

Blackburn raised his palms in surrender, watching him closely.

Tom couldn't breathe. He couldn't stand Blackburn's scrutiny, the way he seemed to be peeling his skin away with that questioning look. And he couldn't think.

The hot silence of the desert pressed in on him, choking

him, heating his thoughts to a million, a billion things flashing in his brain all at once, all in warning, and he pressed his palms over his ears hoping to shut out the way they were buzzing louder and louder until they were deafening inside him, and there was only one thing to worry about all of a sudden.

"You're lying!" Tom realized. "You're lying. My dad's not safe. I don't care what you think, he's not safe!"

"He's safe. Vengerov won't use the leverage of your father until he knows for certain I'm out of the picture."

"No! No, I can't take the chance." The words tumbled out of Tom. "I have to go to him. I have to get him."

"You're not in shape to travel anywhere, and frankly, neither am I."

"If you won't help me find him, then I'll find him without you. I'll go without you. I'll find him. I have to find him. I need to see him!" All Tom could think of was Neil, Neil hurt, Neil in danger, Neil with another gun to his head . . .

Blackburn's expression shifted incredulously. "If one person sees you, Obsidian Corp. knows where you are, and you'll get captured again. I assume you wouldn't have blown yourself into space if you wanted *that*. I certainly didn't rescue you only to hand you back over to him. I'm willing to bet that's the last thing your father would ever want."

Tom felt walls closing in on him again even though they were out in the desert because he had no options and nowhere to go. The sunlight seemed to slice brighter and sharper into his skin, the glare blinding into his eyes still aching from the void of space.

His mind flooded with images of those campers turning

to him, his friends disgusted with him, Vengerov smiling at Vanya, the weapons firing at Dominion Agra's executive board, and a million other things from the past year that began to drown him all at once in the boiling heat of the daylight, and he'd grown so used to the same temperature all the time in Vengerov's capsule that it seemed to strangle him.

We have two weapons he doesn't: you and Medusa.

Tom began to laugh hysterically, until his stomach ached, because it was suddenly the funniest joke ever. Blackburn's brow furrowed, and Tom was only half aware of him standing there, asking him something he didn't understand.

The truth was, Tom couldn't even begin to conceive of fixing the mess he'd made. He couldn't even see a hint of a path out of this jungle. It was all too big, too much, and the sky over him seemed to be crushing.

"Tom . . ."

But Tom backed away from him, and shut himself in the cabin. It still wasn't right there, though, he still felt like he was going to explode, go insane, go out of his mind. He wasn't laughing now. He couldn't breathe.

He stumbled into the bathroom, a small room with one light. He yanked that door shut, too. In the darkness of the enclosed room, it was better, just a bit better, but not quite right. He sat down in the bathtub and felt the porcelain pressing in on all sides, and that was better, still. He yanked the curtain shut around it, blocking the last hint of light, and finally with the walls pressing in on him and the total blackness about him, oxygen seemed to pour back into his lungs. His mind stilled.

For the first time since waking up, he felt normal again.

A few times, the door creaked open, and Tom held his breath, hoping Blackburn would go away. He heard him breathing in the darkness.

Go away, go away, go away, Tom thought desperately.

Footsteps creaked over floorboards, the light stealing away. Blackburn had gone.

Tom wasn't sure how much time passed. It spiraled away from him the way it always did. Sometimes he heard a clink, and he'd find a pitcher of water on the floor by the tub. Sometimes a sandwich. Tom woke up once to discover a pillow had been wedged under his head, a thin blanket thrown over him. His thoughts couldn't seem to form the words to make sense of any of it. His mind tumbled in and out of a stupor.

And then at some point, the light flipped on, flooding the room.

"I know this is some sort of post-traumatic stress reaction," Blackburn announced to the air. "You obviously need extensive psychological counseling, Tom, but we're not in a situation where I can do that. We don't have time. We have to snap you out of this."

Something bad was going to happen. Tom grew sure of it. Just like whenever the hospital efficiency unit powered up, and he heard it hum, and always, always something undignified and humiliating followed, so he threw his arm over his eyes wanting it to end quickly.

He jumped as he heard the shower curtain yanked aside, and then cringed away from the firm clasp on his chin, twisting his head around.

"Look at me."

Tom froze. That wasn't Blackburn's voice.

His eyes shot up. In the flood of blinding light, it wasn't Lieutenant Blackburn kneeling down next to the tub.

It was *Neil*.

Neil!

Some distant part of Tom figured it out. Blackburn had access to his vision center. He was manipulating it. Showing him his father to . . . to get a reaction or trick him or something, and Tom felt outrage rear up within him because he wanted to punch him for doing this, for walking in like this. He wanted . . . he wanted . . .

He wanted his father.

Like a dam breaking open, the longing swept over Tom, displacing everything—his reason, his common sense, his awareness of where he was, what this was. All he could do was whisper, "Dad?"

Neil's grip slackened a moment, his hand dropping from his chin. He looked surprised, but he recovered quickly. "Yes. Yes, it's me."

"Dad!" Tom threw himself forward, and Neil hoisted him over the edge of the tub and then drew him into his arms.

Suddenly it was just like it always had been when Tom was a kid and things were too awful. The one person who'd always been there for him was here, telling him it was all going to be okay, and nothing else mattered because Tom suddenly believed it would be.

"Tell me what happened to you," Neil whispered.

Tom did. He told him everything. The restraining node, the enclosure, Vanya. What he'd done to the world.

"Listen to me," Neil said, right in his ear. "None of this is your fault."

"Yes, it is. You know it is."

"No, Tom, listen." Neil pulled back from him, holding his shoulders, eyes intent. "You're a human being. You're the product of millions of years of evolution. Every single cell in your body, every organ, is fashioned in a way that will keep you alive. You were in an intolerable situation, and your brain did its job: it devised a way to make the situation bearable. That's all Vanya was. He was a product of a very ancient and very intelligent part of your brain that knew you needed to be totally detached from the situation if you were going to survive it with your mind intact. You are not the first person this has ever happened to, and you won't be the last."

"I almost killed Wyatt."

"No, Joseph Vengerov almost killed her, but you didn't let him. When it mattered, you overcame Vanya. You stopped it. And then you did something absolutely incredible and managed to escape. Vanya isn't your enemy. Vanya was there to protect you when you needed it. I just wish to God we'd found you sooner."

Tom closed his eyes miserably. "Vengerov was locked out of my processor. I was so glad at first. I thought I'd hold out."

Neil's arms tensed around him. "And that's the reason he did this to you, isn't it?"

Tom didn't answer.

Neil's voice grew hoarse. "I never would have let this happen to you if . . ." He fell silent. Then, "Tom, I'm sorry. I am so sorry."

It didn't sound like Neil, and so Tom said quickly, "It's okay, Dad. It's not your fault."

343

"I know this isn't the first time I've hurt you, but whatever I've done, whatever I've said to you . . ." Neil's voice broke, his hand stroking Tom's hair, and Tom found himself unwillingly remembering Antarctica. "You know what I did to my own children. I lost everything that day. There's no meaning to life once you're a monster. I didn't care about my own death. For years there's only been one shred of meaning, one single goal: to use this powerful weapon in my skull and drag Joseph Vengerov down to hell with me. I didn't consider the consequences to other people. To you. I'm sorry."

Tom was suddenly starkly aware of where he was, who he was talking to.

"I couldn't kill him," Blackburn said, "so I set out to eradicate all meaning to his existence. I studied him for years. He loved nothing. The only thing he valued was his vision for the world. That's why I set out to get a position at the Pentagonal Spire. It was the ideal server to use to infect his drones, as many as I could. I intended to hijack his own machines and burn down his utopia in its birth pangs."

Blackburn would have succeeded in destroying Vengerov's dreams, Tom knew. He'd killed enough executives to destroy the confidence the rest of them had in Vengerov's technology. The Austere-grade processors never would've been deployed if it hadn't been for Cruithne. Maybe the combined pressure from the other Coalition CEOs would've brought down Vengerov, too.

"For years, the endgame was all I thought about," Blackburn said. "Everyone else . . . There was nothing else that mattered to me. And it was better that way. It's easier when nothing else means a thing."

344

Wyatt flickered through Tom's mind. Whatever Blackburn said, she'd mattered to him. But he'd always taken the first opportunity to push her away. Maybe she meant something despite himself.

"So if you wonder why I've treated you the way I have," Blackburn said, "just know that it wasn't you, Tom. I barely saw you, early on. First you were just a new plebe who didn't understand he was supposed to follow orders and avoid conflicts. I cracked down on you like I would any trainee who liked to mouth off. I thought I was just teaching you your place in the chain of command. I assumed your actions all stemmed from insolence . . ."

"They probably did," Tom muttered. Everyone thought he was insolent.

"No, I don't think so. Not now. I understood that after you hit your head when Nigel Harrison used a virus on you, and you just tried to walk away. You'd never had a guiding authority figure looking out for you. That's clear to me. This idea of structure and a chain of command was totally new to you. I might've taken a new approach with you after I understood you better, but you know what happened next."

Tom knew. The Census Chamber. The fatal moment when he showed Blackburn his memory of what he could do with machines. When Blackburn saw the snippet of memory Tom had of Vengerov and drew conclusions from that.

In that instant, he'd gone from just another plebe in the Spire to a factor in Blackburn's dark vendetta.

But it hadn't been all awful. Blackburn saved him in Antarctica. He'd tried to warn him when he thought he was doing something stupid, something reckless. He could have solved the danger that was Tom's ability in an instant by shoving him into the vactube and sending him the way of Heather; he could have left him to die in space. But he hadn't. He wasn't so monstrous as Tom believed.

He didn't even notice the moment Blackburn reached down and finally took off his restraining node, the one Tom hadn't even dared to touch out of some paralyzing fear he wouldn't be able to get it out.

"You see?" Blackburn said, showing it to him. "It's just a piece of metal now."

Tom stared at the hateful thing. Vengerov had it custom-made, and he'd spared no expense. It was inlaid with gold, an elegant design with the Obsidian Corp. logo—a sinister eye. He thought of the sense of pride and ownership Vengerov must've felt every time he saw it.

"Want to hit it with a sledgehammer?" Blackburn asked him.

"I want to burn it."

"We can arrange that."

THE THERMITE RENDERED the restraining node a melted puddle in the middle of the desert, and Tom watched it burn until it seemed to scorch a hole in his retinas. Then he looked up at Blackburn, standing beneath the vast desert sky with him, and said, "Now what?"

"It depends on you," Blackburn rumbled. "We have somewhere to go. Only when you're ready. The world can wait."

"But Vengerov—"

"He can wait."

For a man who'd single-mindedly pursued the same agenda for eighteen years, it was a real sacrifice. Tom knew it couldn't wait, not for very long, but Blackburn was giving him breathing room if he needed it—and maybe because of that, Tom knew he didn't. He straightened up, turning away from the molten puddle, convincing himself his neck wouldn't feel strange without the restraining node for very long.

"You know," he told Blackburn, "if you hadn't locked Vengerov out of my processor that first day . . ."

Blackburn's large shoulders tensed.

"If you hadn't," Tom forged on, cutting his eyes up to Blackburn's, "he would've reprogrammed me. It would've been a lot easier on me if he'd just controlled my mind from the start. I couldn't have fought back. It would've been the path of least resistance. But I would have given Medusa away. I never would have escaped. I would have killed a lot more people and this would all be a lot worse. It hurt more this way, but you're the only reason I have anything to come back to now."

Surprise flickered over Blackburn's face.

"I know you're the reason I'm alive," Tom said, "and it's not the first time, either. You've been kind of . . . I dunno, reliable, I guess. And that sounds like it's not a big deal, but it is to me because I can't think of many people I can say that about. So the rest of the stuff you said is just . . . let's call it the past."

"The past," Blackburn agreed softly.

"And thanks. For everything." Tom offered his hand.

Blackburn shook it as the desert light faded about them, an understanding between them at last.

1 0 0 1 1 1 1 1 1 1 0 0 1 1 1 0 1 0 1 1 0 0 0 0 0 0 0 0 1 0 0 1 1 1 1 0 0 0
0 1 1 0 1 1 0 1 1 1 0 0 1 1 1 1 0 0 0 0 0 0 0 0 1 0 1 1 0 1 0 0 1 0 0 1 1
1 0 0 0 0 1 1 1 1 0 0 1 0 0 1 0 1 1 1 0 0 1 1 1 0 1 1 0 0 1 0 1 1 0 1 1
0 1 0 0 0 1 1 0 1 1 0 0 0 0 1 1 0 1 0 0 1 1 0 0 0 1 0 1 1 1 1 0 0 0 0 1 1
1 0 0 1 1 0 1 0 0 0 0 0 1 0 1 1 1 0 1 1 0 0 0 0 0 0 0 1 0 0 1 1 0 0 1 1 1 1
0 0 1 1 0 0 0 0 0 0 1 1 1 0 1 1 0 1 1 0 1 0 1 0 0 0 1 0 0 1 1 1 0 0 0 0 0
1 1 0 0 1 0 0 1 0 1 1 1 0 1 1 1 0 1 0 1 1 1 0 1 0 1 1 0 1 0 0 0 0 0
0 1 1 1 1 1 1 0 1 1 0 0 0 0 1 1 1 0 1 1 0 1 1 1 0 1 1 1 0 0 0 1 0 1 0
1 0 1 1 0 0 1 1 0 1 0 0 1 0 0 0 1 0 1 0 1 0 0 1 0 0 0 0 1 0 0 1 0 1 0 1 0
0 0 1 0 0 1 0 1 1 0 0 1 0 0 1 1 0 1 0 1 0 1 1 1 0 0 0 1 0 1 1 0 1 0 1 0
0 0 0 0 0 1 1 1 1 0 1 1 0 0 1 1 0 1 1 0 0 0 0 0 1 0 0 0 1 0 0 0 1 0 0
1 0 1 0 0 1 1 1 1 0 0 1 1 1 0 1 1 0 0 1 1 0 0 1 1 1 0 0 1 0 0 0 1 0 0 0
0 0 1 1 1 1 0 1 1 0 1 0 0 0 1 0 0 1 1 1 0 0 0 0 0 1 0 1 1 1 0 0 0 0 0 0
0 1 1 1 1 0 0 0 0 0 1 0 1 1 0 1 0 0 0 0 0 0 1 0 0 0 1 1 1 1 0 0 1 1 1 0
1 1 1 0 0 0 1 1 1 0 0 1 1 1 0 0 0 0 1 1 0 0 1 0 0 1 0 1 0 1 1 1 1 0 1 1
0 0 0 1 1 1 1 0 0 1 0 1 0 1 1 1 0 0 1 0 1 1 0 1 1 0 1 1 1 1 1 1 0 0 1 0 0 1
0 1 0 1
0 0 1
1 0 0 1 1 0 0 0 1 1 1 1 1 0 1 1 0 0 0 0 0 0 1 0 0 1 0 0 1 0 1 0 1 0 0

CHAPTER TWENTY-SIX

"THIS IS IT?" Tom said in utter disbelief.

Blackburn nodded. "This is it."

"This is the very safest place in the world to mount a resistance from? Are you kidding me?"

"Nope."

They stood in the middle of the Pentagonal Spire's mess hall, oblivious cadets, soldiers, and the occasional civilian wandering past them, unable to see them while they were in stealth mode.

"Think about it," Blackburn said, stepping away from Tom as the flood of people walked past him, unseeing. "I know this server better than any other in the world. Every single machine in this building—and every Vigilant and Austere-grade processor inside—gets its programming directly from this server. We can wander this entire installation in stealth mode. Now that everyone has a neural processor, we can truly be invisible. Not even those surveillance cameras can pick us up."

"Didn't you make this place fill up with laughing skulls?"

"Not a full system meltdown," Blackburn said. "I only needed enough time to get clear of here. To regroup. You escaping the

348

exact same day, that was just . . . well, it was very good timing."

Tom stared at a soldier walking past them, eyes blank as a zombie's.

"If you think about it," Blackburn noted, "Joseph Vengerov's done us a favor, not sparing a single person from his neural machines. In stealth mode, one pair of eyes not clouded by the processors would spot us."

Tom caught sight of Vik, Wyatt, and Yuri walking into the mess hall together, and his heart gave a jerk. His friends.

Blackburn studied him. "Are you going to be okay here while I take a look at the system?"

Tom shoved his hands into his pockets. "Why wouldn't I be? Sir?"

"Thatta boy, Raines," he said, clapping Tom's shoulder. For a moment, Tom's mind flashed to Neil holding him close in the bathroom and he had to look away.

"I'm going to go check out the servers and make sure we stay hidden," Blackburn said. "Your friends know you've escaped, and they know you're coming here. It's up to you when they see you. You can authorize them to do it anytime, but make sure to use your judgment. You don't want them reacting suspiciously to something no one else can see."

Tom nodded.

And then Blackburn was off, leaving Tom in the middle of the mess hall like some ghost who'd returned to haunt his friends. Tom made his way across the mess hall on unsteady legs and reached up to tap his forearm keyboard—but then a great, sick feeling swept over him. He felt like a stranger in his own life.

He followed Vik mindlessly to the table in the mess hall he was sharing with Wyatt and Yuri, and their words were like white noise in his ears as he stepped back in time a year and a half, but he didn't feel the way he had before Vengerov grabbed him. His brain tried to pick through the tangle of recollections; the true, the false.

Tom found his eyes riveted to Vik's collar, where the Intrasolar Forces eagle insignia was, a pair of crossed slashes beneath it. Plebes had one line, Middles two, Uppers three. CamCos had the crossed lines. He saw it on Wyatt's collar, too. Yuri was both CamCo and an Upper now.

He'd missed so much.

He wasn't ready for this.

Tom had to get away from this. He had to escape.

It wasn't until he'd stepped into the corridor beyond the mess hall that he heard the whispered "Hey!"

Tom tensed up, his muscles locking in place.

"Um, Gormless Cretin?" The words sounded awkward coming from Wyatt's lips, and Tom drew a deep breath, then forced himself to turn around. Her entire body vibrated like she was in contact with some electric current, her cheeks flushed, eyes wide. "Sorry, I can't say your name or I'll trigger some security algorithms. I'm sure you're being searched for all over the networks now."

Tom swallowed hard. "You see me?"

"Yes." She bit her lip. "I tweaked my neural processor after Frayne so I wouldn't miss people walking near me in stealth mode. Blackburn told us he had you, that you'd be coming back. I thought . . . I was afraid it wasn't going to happen."

350

For a moment, they stared at each other awkwardly, and then Wyatt plowed forward and flung her arms around him. She'd lost weight, giving her the sharp, alert look of some hunted animal. And suddenly she was sobbing, and Tom pulled her closer, fiercely glad to see her again.

The familiarity of Wyatt banished the last of those twisted recollections Vengerov had programmed for him. His heart ached. He'd missed her. God, he'd missed them all so much.

"I couldn't find you. I'm so sorry. We looked everywhere, Tom. We hacked—"

"I know. It's okay."

"I tried. I'm so sorry, I really tried . . ."

"It's okay." He kissed her head. "Come on, it's okay." It was strange how normal he felt suddenly, trying to calm Wyatt, like he'd stepped back into his own skin for the first time in so long. He felt stronger, more in control, when he pulled back, trying to show her that he was okay, that he was happy to see her. "You're in CamCo now, huh? Who's sponsoring you?"

"What does that matter?"

"It matters to me. Tell me."

"Nobridis."

"Congratulations!"

"Oh, it doesn't matter now."

"Yeah, it does."

"No, it doesn't. All their top-level executives are dead, and the war's pretty much ground to a halt now that the Austere-grade processors have kicked in."

Tom looked around. "Do the other cadets realize the deal?"

"They don't talk about it much, but I'm sure they've noticed something's wrong with basically everyone in the world. The crime rate has dropped to zero and . . . It's creepy. No one even jaywalks anymore. Vik, Yuri, and I haven't left the Spire in months. It's too unsettling seeing everyone so orderly out there."

Tom thought of those campers all looking at him as one and felt a flutter of unease.

"Now that you're here, we can fix everything." She beamed at him, her eyes full of trust, full of belief in him. "I don't know how, but I'm sure we'll find a way. We can do anything when you're around."

It was about the greatest thing anyone had ever said to him and Tom wished it was true. He felt more like a fraud than ever, but with a smile of total faith in him that could almost fool him, Wyatt took Tom's hand and led him back to his world.

WYATT HAD TOM authorize Yuri next, because she knew Yuri was careful enough not to react with visible shock and draw attention to them, not after her whisper in his ear. He broke into a huge, beaming smile in the mess hall, then changed seats and discreetly flung his arm around Tom's shoulder, disguising it as a stretch.

"I am so happy to see you feeling well," Yuri said.

"Yeah, I'm better," Vik said from across the table, thinking the words were for him. "Indigestion's gone."

Tom smiled a bit. "Vik has tummy troubles?" Then he realized his best friend couldn't hear him.

Which meant there were any number of possible ways for Tom to mess with him. When Vik got up to go, Wyatt and Yuri both nodded for him to follow, so Tom did. Yuri decided at the last minute to sweep him up in a big bear hug by the elevator before letting Tom go on his way.

Vik turned as Yuri was still whirling in circles, a huge grin on his face, arms around someone he couldn't see.

"What are you doing, man?"

Yuri stopped, caught off guard. He and Tom exchanged a look.

"Dancing?" Yuri tried.

"Stop," Vik said. "It looks ridiculous." He stalked off into the elevator.

Tom laughed. "Wow, Vik really must have tummy troubles, huh?"

"No," Yuri said gently, resting his hand on Tom's shoulder. "That is not why Vikram is so unhappy. He has been this way since you went missing. Lieutenant Blackburn told us you would be returning, but I think he is still anxious."

That about killed Tom. He clasped Yuri's arm, then parted ways with him to follow Vik up to his bunk.

VIK'S NEW BUNK on the fourteenth floor was large and spacious. Tom whistled at the sight while Vik was in the bathroom. Then he hastily jumped under the bedsheets. When he heard Vik's footfalls move through the door, Tom sat up slowly like some mummy waking up.

Vik gave a shriek and pulled the bedsheet aside to see who was there. His uncomprehending eyes stared at the nothingness he saw.

Tom laughed, leaped forward, and ruffled a hand through Vik's hair.

353

Vik's mouth dropped. "T— Uh, Doctor?"

Tom authorized Vik to see him with a thought, and said, "Yeah, it's me in stealth mode."

Vik whooped out in joy and swept him up in his arms. Tom laughed as Vik shouted like a madman, gleefully hopping across the room with him. He was suddenly so glad to be back, so glad.

"You're okay!" Vik's voice was choked. "I missed you so much, man. You can't do that again. You can't disappear like that."

"I won't," Tom assured him. "I won't."

"I thought you died."

"I didn't."

Vik ruffled his hair, grinning.

Tom ducked back, because Vik's hand was getting perilously close to his neck, and that still made his skin crawl. "So you made CamCo before me. Guess I owe you more money, huh?" Tom joked.

Vik seemed taken off guard a moment. His smile was uneasy. "Aw, we know you would've gotten there first if . . ." He trailed off. "Uh, my sponsor's Wyndham Harks. Call sign's 'Asoka.'"

"Asoka?"

"Indian conqueror. You wouldn't know him."

Tom looked around at the massive CamCo bunk he'd never had a chance to live in. There was a hasty assortment of artwork, a divan, and any number of things Vik's parents had obviously sent him from India. There was even a big Russian fur hat thing. He picked it up, feeling the soft fur prickling his palms, reminding him of . . .

"Christmas gift from Yuri," Vik babbled, clearly unsure what else to say. "He visited some family in Russia. Oh, hey, you

354

should ask for yours, too. He got us all ushankas."

The hat slipped from Tom's hands. For a moment, he was too stunned to speak.

"What is it?" Vik said, alarmed.

"Ushanka means 'fur hat'? That's what that means?" Tom said, his voice strangled.

"Huh?" Vik said.

But Tom found himself remembering Vengerov's odd smile when he chose the name. All along, he just saw the rabbit as . . . a fur hat. Tom was gripped by the terrible urge to laugh, but he couldn't. Suddenly he felt like he was going to split apart at the seams.

"Hey, hey, Doctor." He jumped at Vik's hand on his shoulder. His friend looked serious, sober, worried, like he'd just seen him for the first time. "Are you . . . are you okay? I mean . . . Did he, uh, did you get hurt?"

Tom's mouth felt bone-dry. He couldn't manage a word.

Vik looked away. "I know he . . . Uh, you got reprogrammed."

So Blackburn had lied to them. He didn't tell them Vengerov had never reprogrammed him; he'd broken him. "Yeah," Tom said, relieved like a hand loosened its stranglehold on him.

"Hey, it's okay." Vik cuffed his shoulder once, then again, his hand staying there, hovering uneasily. "Whatever you want to say, or not say, it's okay, man. You're back. That's what matters."

"Vengerov mostly left me alone," Tom said truthfully. It sounded so harmless.

Relief slackened Vik's face. Then a light of determination caught in his eyes. "When the day comes and you need to wreak some terrible vengeance, you know I'm your doctor. Call me first."

Tom managed to smile. "I know, man."

At that moment, the door slid open and Wyatt and Yuri came rushing back in, crowing in delight at the sight of Tom. Wyatt flung her arms around him again, her grip so tight it was slightly painful, and Yuri patted his shoulders, his back, anywhere he could reach.

The warmth of his friends enveloped Tom again and something taut and fragile seemed to rupture inside him. He closed his eyes, almost overwhelmed by the flood of relief, tenderness, and sense of belonging that welled up inside him.

He'd never lose this again.

CHAPTER TWENTY-SEVEN

A S DAYS PASSED, Tom existed in the Pentagonal Spire in an odd state of limbo, invisible to the security systems, invisible to the people who streamed about him. His friends were still a part of this world, so they had to go about their business of training for a war that was basically obsolete.

With the nanomachines out in the wild, and most of the world's population already serving as walking, talking surveillance systems for Obsidian Corp., potential allies were a very limited group of people. They consisted entirely of people with Vigilant-grade neural processors.

Luckily, the Pentagonal Spire was one of only four sites in the world where young people had been given Vigilant-grade processors. Vik had a cousin in the Bombay facility, and he contacted him on the sly, and Tom knew on her side, Yaolan was looking into people in the Citadel. She'd told Blackburn she had an understanding with Svetlana Moriakova in the Kremlin complex. Svetlana already had a loose coalition of Russian, African, and South American Combatants, ready to mobilize when the time was right.

Wyatt suggested they watch the footage from the loyalty simulation to see if there were any clues about which cadets would be likely to risk challenging Vengerov. That Sunday, they brought popcorn up to Wyatt's new luxurious, fourteenth-floor bunk, and watched the footage together.

"Doctor, I think you really screwed us," Vik said.

Tom caught his breath, stung.

"You ended this sim way too early," Vik said, and Tom felt himself relax, because Vik wasn't referring to, well, the way Tom had actually screwed them all over—and the entire world besides. "Look at that, it's almost over and we're still in the mess hall."

The footage panned over restless cadets, being held at gunpoint. Giuseppe was complaining about how his foot itched, but he was worried he'd get shot if he scratched it. Karl was beating his fist into his hand, ready to pummel someone.

"I'd say Karl's out," Vik said. "He'd side with Vengerov just to side against you."

"I don't know," Tom said. "I think we need to talk to him."

They spent the week cornering various cadets, one by one. Always, they warned them not to say anyone's name, and then Tom would reveal himself, see the shock on their faces.

"Aren't you dead?" Clint demanded.

"Yes, Clint. I'm a ghost."

Clint stared at him. Tom stared back.

When Tom appeared out of nowhere in front of Walton Covner, he blinked, then said, "Hi there," very casually. "It's been a while."

For her part, Iman Attar burst into tears and flung herself

into his arms. "I thought something happened to you! Oh wow . . ." She moved to press her lips to his, because absence had obviously made the heart grow fonder. "I'm so sorry. I hope breaking up with you didn't drive you away."

Tom quickly pushed her back. "Iman, it's okay."

"I know you really liked me, but—"

"Before you say anything else, I kissed another girl. Sorry, two girls. So don't think this was you."

Vik and Yuri looked at him with sudden respect.

"Hey, no worries," Tom assured her.

Iman scowled.

Blackburn waved him onward, and Wyatt rolled her eyes. Iman decided absence had not made her heart grow fonder after all, but she listened to them and agreed to help.

For her part, Lyla Martin said, "Oh, it's you. Where'd you come from? Vik and I broke up."

"You always break up," Tom said.

"For good this time. Did you defect or something?" Lyla asked him. "Vik got angry at me because I told people you probably defected. He wouldn't forgive me."

Tom swung his gaze to Vik. "Wait. Is that why you broke up?"

Vik was outraged. "My best friend had disappeared and she was slandering him. I had a problem with that." He and Lyla glared at each other.

Tom hid his grin, because that pleased him more than he'd ever let on. His best friend really did have his back.

After Tom got them used to the idea that he was in the room, then Lieutenant Blackburn also authorized the cadets to see him. They always grew a bit more nervous at the sight of Blackburn, but they seemed more inclined to believe it from him when he explained the Austere-grade processors, the nanomachines, the inexplicable shift in the behavior of everyone they'd ever known outside the Pentagonal Spire. From there, it was a judgment call. Some like Lyla and Walton grew outraged and ready to fight. Some like Giuseppe and Jenny Nguyen grew frightened and wanted nothing to do with it. Others like Snowden Gainey surprised them—the normally meek Combatant readily agreed to hold the line against Vengerov. A few even justified Vengerov's actions. Cadence Grey and Clint both saw it as a logical next step in human development, and who were they to question that?

"There's a big difference between everyone having computers in their heads and everyone having computers Joseph Vengerov controls in their heads," Wyatt protested.

"Someone has to control it," Clint said. "Why not a successful businessman? *And* one of my father's top campaign contributors?"

Clint was definitely out.

Karl Marsters surprised everyone but Tom when he shook Tom's hand and said he was glad he was alive. He heard the explanation and clenched his meaty fists, vowing, "You say he did Cruithne, too? He killed my sister. I'm going to rip his head off."

"You can't kill him," Tom said regretfully. "We've got code that stops us from hurting him. That's one of the problems here."

Karl's big brow furrowed. "So let's get rid of it!"

"That is far easier said than done," Wyatt told him. Blackburn

360

erased all their memories of being interrogated immediately afterward, but with certain cadets, Tom made it clear, "It's safer for you if we take this memory for now. We'll give it back to you so you know what's going on when it matters."

When they'd run through all the cadets, Vik—observer of all the interrogations—finally asked the pertinent question. "So we know who will be with us, and who won't be . . . What are we going to do with this?"

Everyone looked at Tom. Tom looked at Blackburn.

"No idea," Blackburn said.

"What?" Vik blurted.

"I said I don't know. If there was an easy reversal, we'd already have done it. The only idea I have is to set off EMPs and wipe the nanomachines out of existence. The brain doesn't grow dependent on Austere-grade processors. Not like ours. Most will survive."

"We can't do that," Wyatt cried. "You saw how destructive the high-altitude nuclear blasts were after Cruithne. We can't do it everywhere. We can't plunge all civilization back into the Dark Ages just to neutralize them."

Yuri nodded. "I must agree. There is going to be great consequences. People will be dying."

"If there's an electromagnetic pulse, it will disable all the robotic pollinators, and since Dominion Agra killed off all the bees, there will be mass starvation. Most every nuclear power plant in the world will melt down. We'll kill billions of people in the long run."

"It's not ideal," Blackburn said, his voice hard, "but at least people will have a fighting chance. They don't have any now."

Grim silence lapsed over the room.

"How about that can be our last resort?" Vik suggested. "There's gotta be something else."

"Here's what I don't understand," Tom said suddenly. "You're so good with neural processors. You and Wyatt both are. Why can't you come up with something we could spread like a computer virus that disables Vengerov's control?"

"I could," Blackburn said, "given a year or two or ten to devote solely to the study of nanomachines. Then we could just cross our fingers as soon as I spread that virus, and hope Joseph Vengerov doesn't come up with a security patch to neutralize my efforts. But he will come up with one. It may take minutes, it may take a few hours, but he'll simply regain control over them, and then we've given him a hint about where to find us and we're back at square one."

"What about you?" Tom tried, looking at Wyatt. "You can come up with something faster. You're the smartest person I know."

She frowned. "You haven't known that many people. There are probably a few people out there smarter than me." She nodded, a bit dubious. "Probably. I can't possibly be the smartest person in the world."

"You never know," Yuri said, and leaned over and kissed the top of her head fondly.

"Besides," Vik pointed out, "the minute you do something, Vengerov will be able to trace it and find out where the resistance is coming from."

Vik didn't need to say the rest. The implications hung grim in the air between them all. Vengerov hadn't seized total control

362

over those with Vigilant-grade processors. Not yet. But he could change his mind tomorrow, sweep right in, and write programming just as restrictive into them as he had into the rest of the population—if he ever decided they were a threat.

When they finally acted, *if* they finally acted, they only had one shot at victory. Any failure, and Vengerov would crush them for good.

"There's one more person to talk to," Blackburn said.

TOM FELT A ripple of surprise, finding Elliot Ramirez locked in the cell adjoining the Census Chamber. Elliot stared uncomprehendingly when the door seemingly opened itself and then closed again.

Then Tom authorized his processor to see him, and Elliot jumped.

"Hey, man. Don't say my name."

"Uh, you!" Elliot exclaimed. His dark eyes moved over Tom with concern, and Tom realized what a wreck he must look. "This is a surprise."

"Lieutenant Blackburn told me you'd been arrested and brought here."

Elliot's lips quirked. "I had nine months of freedom. I worked as an activist, and I even fell in love, and then the National Defense Authorization Act got me. I've been detained. Indefinitely so far. I thought if I was public enough, high profile enough, I'd be safe." A shadow passed over his face. "But it was like no one noticed the day they came for me. Even Tony just stood there. The crowd seemed to be deaf and dumb. I think I had too much faith in people."

"No, there's a reason no one helped you," Tom told him. "Vengerov's got control over the public. There's no hiding in a crowd because the crowd's all been mind controlled." He explained quickly about the Austere-grade processors, watched Elliot sink down onto his cot, troubled.

"I really am out of the loop." He looked Tom over. "Are you . . . are you still training here?"

"I'm a fugitive. No one else can see me. Blackburn's one, too." Then Tom shrugged. "Oh, I also blew up the skyboards."

Elliot stared at him. People seemed to have that reaction when he dropped the bomb on them.

So Tom sighed and dropped down onto the cot and explained it all to him—his ability with machines, the skyboards, Vengerov's slaughter of the other executives.

When he finished, Elliot sat there, rubbed his head. "So that was you at Capitol Summit."

"Sorry, man. I was trying to take down Heather. I didn't think about the position I was putting you in."

But Elliot just chuckled. "That was the best thing that's ever happened to me." His eyes grew distant. "I remember when they told me I had to fall into line with the image they were crafting for me, act the way they wanted me to act. There was a whole group of Wyndham Harks executives there, and one of them had this quote he liked: 'We're an empire now and when we act, we create our own reality.' But he didn't mean *I* got to act and create my own reality, no, no. He meant *they*—people like him, people who mattered—were the ones whose actions mattered, the ones who'd create reality for the rest of us, and the rest of us had to obey and fall into line with their vision of the world. *I* had to fall in line. And for too long, I did."

Tom nodded like he understood.

"But when you fired those first shots at them," Elliot said, catching his eyes, "I could finally see another path. I didn't know that was you, of course, but it made me think of you. Of everything you'd said to me."

"I'm honored," Tom said.

"That's why I fought back against them. I realized that they don't get to create my reality if I reject them. They can't dictate the terms of my existence to me." His eyes flashed. "Even if they keep me locked up forever, or if they reprogram me to force me back in line, I defied them and they can never take that from me."

Tom felt pretty assured of his disloyalty now, so he felt safe leaning closer and saying, "You're not going to stay locked up, Elliot. We're going to fix the world. For good."

"I'm in," Elliot pledged.

"We don't have a plan—"

Elliot chuckled. "One of my plebes, saving us all? Of course I'm going to be a part of this. I'll do whatever you need me to do."

1 1 0 0 1 1 1 1 1 1 1 1 0 0 1 1 1 0 1 0 1 1 0 0 0 0 0 0 0 1 0 0 1 1 1 1 0 0 0
0 0 1 1 0 1 1 0 1 1 1 0 0 1 1 1 0 0 0 0 0 0 0 0 1 0 1 1 0 1 0 0 1 0 0 1
0 1 0 0 0 0 1 1 1 1 0 0 1 0 0 1 0 1 1 1 0 0 1 1 1 0 1 1 0 0 1 0 1 1 0 1 1
1 0 1 0 0 0 1 1 0 1 1 1 0 0 0 0 1 1 0 1 0 0 1 1 0 0 0 1 0 1 1 1 1 0 0 0 0 1
1 1 0 0 1 1 0 1 0 0 0 0 0 0 1 0 1 1 1 0 1 1 0 0 0 0 0 0 0 1 0 1 1 0 0 1 1 1
0 0 1 1 0 0 0 0 0 1 1 1 1 0 1 1 0 1 1 0 1 1 0 1 0 0 1 1 0 0 0 0
1 1 1 0 0 1 0 1 0 1 1 1 0 1 1 1 0 1 0 1 1 1 0 1 0 1 1 0 1 1 0 0 0 0
0 0 1 1 1 1 1 1 0 1 1 0 0 0 0 1 1 1 0 1 1 0 1 1 1 0 1 1 1 0 0 0 1 0 1
1 1 0 1 1 0 0 1 1 0 1 0 0 1 0 0 0 1 0 1 0 1 0 0 1 0 0 0 0 1 0 0 1 0 1 0 1
0 0 0 1 0 0 1 0 1 1 0 0 1 0 0 1 1 0 1 0 1 0 1 1 1 0 0 0 0 1 0 1 1 0 1 0 1
0 0 0 0 0 0 1 1 1 1 0 1 1 0 0 1 1 0 1 1 0 0 0 0 0 1 0 0 0 0 1 0 0 0 1 0 0
1 1 0 1 0 0 1 1 1 1 0 0 1 1 1 0 1 1 0 0 1 1 0 0 1 1 1 0 0 1 0 0 0 0 1 0 0
0 0 0 1 1 1 1 1 0 1 1 0 1 0 1 0 0 0 1 0 0 1 1 1 0 0 0 0 1 0 1 1 1 0 0 0 0 0
1 0 1 1 1 1 0 0 0 0 1 0 1 1 0 0 0 0 0 0 0 1 0 0 0 1 1 1 1 0 0 1 1 0
0 1 1 1 0 0 0 1 1 1 0 0 1 1 1 0 0 0 0 1 1 0 0 1 0 0 1 0 1 0 1 1 1 1 0 1
1 0 0 0 1 1 1 1 0 0 1 0 1 0 1 1 1 0 0 1 0 1 1 0 1 1 0 1 1 1 1 1 0 0 1 0 0 1
0 0 1 0 1 0 0 1 0 0 0 0 1 0 0 0 0 1 1 1 0 1 0 1 0 1
1 0 0 1 1 1 1 1 1 1 1 1 0 0 1 1 1 0

CHAPTER TWENTY-EIGHT

Tom returned to Blackburn's quarters. The military had already cleared out most of his possessions after his escape, but it didn't make much of a difference. There'd never been much in the place, anyway. The couch was still there, where Tom had been sleeping.

On it rested a coiled-up neural wire.

Lead sank into his gut. He'd agreed to start downloading the information he'd lost. Blackburn must've prepared something.

Now it was going to start.

Tom couldn't bring himself to hook the wire in. He'd originally planned to crash on the floor of Vik's room, but then a nightmare scenario occurred to him—what if he woke up in the pitch-dark of Vik's bunk with a neural wire hooked into his brain stem access port, and he didn't remember where he was right away?

There was a lot he could share with his friends, but he couldn't stand the thought of them seeing how screwed up he still felt over Vengerov. So screwed up that he couldn't even hook in a neural wire, even to get back some of the knowledge and fighting skills he'd lost. He was still sitting there, contemplating the neural wire, when boots creaked on the floor behind him, light spearing into the dim room, Blackburn emerging from his bedroom.

"Did you get a chance to talk to Ramirez?"

"Yeah. He's in once we come up with something." Tom twisted the neural wire around a finger, anxiety dancing in his stomach.

Blackburn picked up on it right away. "Are you going to be able to do this?"

"It's fine," Tom said automatically. After a moment, he admitted, "I can't hook into the system. I mean, I can, because I've done it thousands of times, but I just can't. You know what I mean?"

"You're thinking about this the wrong way," Blackburn told him. "You've formed some mental association between this"— he pointed at the neural wire—"and feeling powerless. That's not the case. This is power. Your ability is your strength."

Tom's head pulsed. It may be his strength, but Vengerov had also made it very clear it was his weakness. He'd turned everything that made Tom strong into a weapon against him. His ability, his friends, his memories, everything but Medusa.

Blackburn rubbed his palm over his mouth. "Then again, I suppose I could give you incentive."

"Huh?"

"There's someone visiting our system. She wants to see you."

Tom's heart jumped. "*She's* here?"

"I told Medusa to come," Blackburn said. "I've kept her updated about our brainstorming, but I think today's your

367

day to liaise with her. Consider it motivation to get over some things faster. I can begin your downloads while you're meeting her." He smiled. "Unless you want me to tell her you're not feeling up to it."

The evil bastard knew Tom wasn't going to let that happen. "No way." He grabbed the neural wire and jammed it into the nearest access port, then connected it with his port.

His senses drained as Blackburn chuckled. "Thatta boy."

HE SHOT OUT of himself and immediately was drawn down a pipeline of signals. For a horrific moment, he felt out of control, but he knew it was *her*. Then he resolved to life in a program. The setting was a lush garden, with lakes and waterfalls, the water so clear it reflected the vivid blue sky, the leaves of the trees.

"What is this place?" Tom wondered.

"You've been off Earth for so long. I thought I'd show you something beautiful."

Tom spun around. Medusa stood on the rocks with him amid the garden, her black hair loose about her shoulders. "Suzhou. The Lingering Garden," she explained.

Tom gazed at her, his heart swelling in his chest. It had been so long, so long. "Hi," he said dumbly.

She laughed. "Hi."

"Medusa."

"Yaolan," she reminded him.

"Yaolan." He drank in the sight of her, the girl he'd thrown himself into space to save. The reason for everything.

"I've missed you," she said. She drew forward, her fingers sliding across his palm, and Tom seized her small hand, drawing

368

his palm up to her cheek, brushing her hair aside. There were so many emotions inside him, his chest felt full of them, and he wondered how to tell her she'd been the reason he'd escaped, the light burning at the end of the tunnel for him.

There were probably many articulate things he could've, should've said, but instead he blurted, "I'm in love with you."

She tensed. "Um, excuse me?"

"That was kind of a bomb to drop on you, I know," Tom said, realizing it. "But I have to say it. I realized it up there. I love you. I know you said once I needed you to need me, but that's not true."

Her fingers braided with his, and he found he suddenly couldn't meet her eyes.

"I realized that, too. I need you, not the other way around. I always thought I was okay on my own, that I could shift for myself, whatever happened. But I was up there and I was totally alone and it was like I . . ." Tom stopped, thinking of the way he'd totally disintegrated. There'd been no Tom Raines when he'd spent so much time by himself. He didn't exist anymore. He hadn't existed until he had them all back again. He'd never burden Medusa by confessing all that, so he just said, "It's okay if you don't feel the same way. I wanted to tell you once."

"Tom."

He looked up, and she drew his head down and kissed him. He clasped her in his arms, but she stepped back, a line between her brows. "Tom, you've been gone for over a year. You've been held prisoner. I don't know what you've been through, but . . . but I don't think this is the right time for impassioned declarations."

369

He grinned sheepishly. "I was making an impassioned declaration?"

She smiled back. "Don't you remember in Hawaii, when you told me you'd be doing something wrong if you took advantage of the way I was feeling then?"

"But you wouldn't be . . ."

"I wasn't thinking clearly back then. I was in a bad place. Don't you see that this is the same situation?" She turned back to him, her hair rippling in the breeze. "I'd be the one doing something wrong if I accepted this right now."

Tom stuffed his virtual hands into his virtual pockets. "So when would the time be right?"

She peered back at him. "If you say it again one day. Later. At the right time."

"The right time."

"If there ever is one," she added darkly.

Tom gazed at her intently. "What's going on?"

Agitation lit her face. "I can't tell you. I need to show you."

And with those words, they suddenly drew out of the Spire's server, shooting through the internet. He focused on her, on Medusa, and never let her out of his mind. They resolved into a supercomputer, sending commands to all the neural processors. Algorithm after algorithm she called up before Tom's eyes, and he felt sickness spread through him seeing what Vengerov was doing.

Searching people, categorizing them. Some had been classified as expendable—the weak, the elderly, the deficient. There were Trojans already being planted into their neural processors, ready to trigger at a command to order their brain functions to shut off.

Tom thought of how Vengerov had tried to reprogram him early after his capture, how much sense it had made to Tom at the time that there were too many people and too few resources, and it had seemed only logical that vast chunks of humanity should be erased.

Vengerov was going to do just that.

And then they were back in the Spire's systems, in the program of Suzhou, in the garden that suddenly didn't look so serene anymore with the presentiment of doom hanging over them both.

"We have to act now," Medusa said flatly, "before he triggers the depopulation subroutines. Before he turns his attention back to the Spire and the Citadel, all the cadets and Combatants on both sides—we're the only ones who still can act. We have a plan."

"Great," Tom said, because that was more than he and his friends had come up with. "Tell me about it."

"We're going to attack the hubs Vengerov is using to transmit information to the Austere-grade processors."

Vengerov had stripped almost all knowledge from Tom's neural processor. He was embarrassed to admit, "I kind of lost everything I've ever downloaded. Can you . . . can you tell me what hubs are again?"

Medusa didn't roll her eyes. "Hubs are like . . . data information centers. They're supercomputers that generate the network every Austere-grade processor is a part of now. If Vengerov controlled a bunch of interconnected spiderwebs, the hubs are the places where the threads meet. So every bit of information that gets installed in people's neural processors comes from the hubs first. They send it along those threads. If everyone with an Austere-grade processor knows to look out for the ghost in the machine, for instance, they know it because the command to do so was sent to them from a central hub."

"So you think destroying them so they can't control people with Austere-grade processors—that would fix things," Tom surmised.

"Oh, I'm sure he's got backup hubs. And backups of backups. But we'll destroy as many as we can, and then we're going to spread a virus to corrupt the data being sent from the remaining hubs. Hopefully if we do both those things, we can wreak maximum damage on Obsidian Corp." A smile twitched her lips. "He's put Austere-grade processors in billions of minds. People with Austere-grade processors have a built-in subroutine where they have to precisely follow the laws of their lands."

Tom nodded, remembering Zane and his plebes, how they couldn't break any regulations.

"They don't just follow them, they're *compelled* to." Medusa's eyes gleamed. "What we're going to do is send them a new understanding of the law. Everyone who has an Austere-grade will suddenly feel it's their legal duty to kill someone who works at Obsidian Corp. or LM Lymer Fleet, and destroy any equipment owned by those companies. If we're lucky, Joseph Vengerov will be right in reach of someone with an Austere-grade processor and he'll die."

"He won't," Tom said flatly. "There's a fail-safe of sorts. He can't be killed by anyone with one of his machines. And besides that, my friend's dad works for Obsidian Corp. He's not a bad person, he just needed a job. For all we know, Vengerov's employees have Austere-grade processors, too. Maybe they got them way before everyone else."

"I'm sorry about your friend," Medusa said, "but this is the best plan we have. It's a way to do significant damage to his company in very little time. We'll only have a few minutes before Vengerov realizes what's going on and corrects it. He'll figure out it's us and send every ship he has to us, and then we'll be dead. Our only chance is to damage him enough that he can't strike us."

Tom kept thinking of the strategy conversation he'd had with his friends and Blackburn. He knew as soon as Medusa and her people acted, that was their last shot. Whatever they did on their end, they'd have to do it at the same time as the Combatants on her end.

He imagined her proposal at work. Every person with Austere-grade processors mobilized, for a brief period of time, against Obsidian Corp. That was an army of billions. There was a lot of damage that many people could inflict. Maybe Yaolan and her co-conspirators had the solution. Maybe that would do the trick. It would have to, if it was their only shot.

Before Vengerov retaliated, at least.

And he would retaliate. He'd hit back harder. It's what he always did. Tom's head throbbed as he remembered a day long ago when Blackburn said violence was the only means of handling men like Vengerov. But he'd been wrong in a way, because Vengerov had one trump card Blackburn never would: he'd been willing to risk the entire planet to retain his dominion over it. That alone gave him an advantage no one else could match. Once Medusa struck, Vengerov wouldn't blink about simply lobbing some nuclear weapons at the Spire, the Citadel, and forget collateral damage.

People were entirely expendable to him, after all. At best, they were resources to be exploited and then discarded. He didn't value human worth that wasn't immediately evident. He didn't care what dwelled inside them or what lay down the road for them in the future. He only cared about their immediate use to him and his agenda. Vengerov had seen something useful in Tom, the weapon, but he never would've given a second thought to the destruction of Tom the fourteen-year-old in a VR parlor, even with this ability in his future. Vengerov believed himself a visionary, but he was too shortsighted to see human potential.

For a moment, Tom found himself thinking of what Wyatt had said about someone out there being the smartest person in the world, and the way a man like Vengerov would waste that. There were eleven billion people on the planet, and so much they could do if given the chance.

One of those people with Austere-grade processors was the smartest person in the world. Probably smarter than Wyatt, smarter than Joseph Vengerov, smarter than Blackburn. Or maybe there wasn't one smartest person—maybe there were a hundred, a thousand, a million brilliant people of genius intellect. Even if only a tiny fraction of that eleven billion was truly brilliant, there could still be thousands of Wyatts out there. What could all those people do if they had a chance, if they had the same opportunities a man like Vengerov had?

And then in a flash, Tom knew what they had to do. He knew. He laughed at the sheer perfection of the idea.

"What is it?" Medusa said.

"I just realized that my friend Wyatt is not the smartest person in the world."

Her brow furrowed. "What's your point?"

"My point is," Tom said, hope flaring to life within him, "I know how to save the world."

CHAPTER TWENTY-NINE

ONCE, TOM AND Vik had made a delightful discovery: Yuri Sysevich, who was awesome at practically everything else, sucked at most video games. They discovered this playing a fighting game, when Yuri unwittingly attempted to battle them and inflicted no damage at all.

"Why are you not getting injured?" he said, distressed, as Tom, Vik, and Wyatt pummeled each other, and his character flailed impotently at the air. "I am throwing fire from my hands."

"Nah, those are sparkles," Vik said.

"Why are my sparkle hands not hurting you?"

Tom repressed his sniggers as he tore off the head of Wyatt's character. "Because you're only seeing sparkles because you're doing the equivalent of pressing all the controls at once. See?" He imitated Yuri's gesture, making his own character throw sparkles from his hands.

Vik tried to take advantage of Tom's sparkling to kill him, but Tom smashed his head in with one punch. Then he put Yuri out of his misery.

Vik had made a joke of it for a while, going on gaming

networks with Yuri's face as his avatar, the screen name Sparklehands, and then upsetting many gamers by sparkling his hands at them while they tried to have serious battles. Tom liked to do it, too. They'd gotten Yuri's loss record up to 0–998, and even found some internet message boards speculating on the mental impairment of the mysterious gamer Sparklehands.

After Tom lost his fingers and began sucking in earnest at video games, he lost most of his enjoyment of the joke. But ever since returning to the Spire, those things that used to bother him seemed like nothing. So minor, it was almost laughable he'd cared once so much about them. The morning of the planned operation, they played the game in what was either a belated celebration of Tom's seventeenth birthday, or an early celebration of his eighteenth birthday. Perhaps both.

"At least if we die, we all made it to official adulthood, give or take a few months," Wyatt said.

Vik laughed. "Way to bring up the mood, Evil Wench."

"Positive thinking is important," Yuri said, even though he was scowling fiercely, his character sparkling away.

"Thanks anyway," Tom said with a grin.

"I've gotta admit, I like having a chance at winning," Vik said, punching Tom's character several times. "You should've lost those fingers years earlier."

"Don't speak too soon," Tom said lightly, dodging his next blows. He was discovering to his surprise that he wasn't as awful as he remembered. Maybe it had been a mental block all along. The human brain was a funny thing.

Wyatt calmly executed the same kick maneuver over and

377

over again. She didn't like fighting games, but she played them because Tom and Vik did. Her strategy was always the same: perfect one power move and then use it continuously. It was an effective, if irritating, strategy.

For his part, Yuri gave a frustrated growl. He was still sparkling.

"As soon as Joseph Vengerov realizes what we're doing, he'll send everything he has at us," Wyatt remarked, dropkicking Vik's character again and again. "This may be the last time we're all still alive."

Vik groaned. "Again, way to elevate the mood, Evil Wench. Rule number one of gaming the morning before a suicidally stupid mission is not to bring up said suicidally stupid miss— No, Gormless One!"

Tom laughed, his character triumphantly holding up Vik's heart, which he'd torn right out of his chest. "What were you saying, Doctor? I think you need to kiss the ring."

"Only once you—" Vik began, but Tom had already torn off Yuri's head, and then he broke Wyatt's neck. With a grumble, Vik mimed kissing Tom's invisible ring. They tossed down the wired gloves, and a sudden silence descended upon Vik's bunk.

For a moment, the four friends looked at one another, and Tom found himself wishing they could just stay here, frozen in this moment. The most important people in his world, and the only place he'd ever thought of as home.

But time marched forward, even now. And there was no holding on to a moment already past.

Tom drew a deep breath. "Let's go."

* * *

As THEY HEADED out of the bunk, Tom said, "We're off," knowing Blackburn was probably checking in through the neural link.

"Good luck," Blackburn's voice said in his ear.

Then Tom reached into his pocket and popped on his remote access node. Medusa's mind met his in the system. "It's time."

Got it, Medusa replied.

Tom nodded to Wyatt, and she pressed on her forearm keyboard, unleashing the computer virus she and Blackburn had written.

The lights all dimmed in the Pentagonal Spire, and suddenly an emergency beacon flashed across everyone's vision centers.

Warning: Fission-fusion nuclear reactor is in active meltdown. Noncritical personnel must evacuate.

They stepped out in the common room of the fourteenth floor to see the CamCos hastily waking up, scrambling to evacuate. No one could see them right now when all four of them were in stealth mode. Down the stairway they walked, soldiers and cadets rushing past them, their neural processors unconsciously steering them around the empty space some part of their brain could perceive was actually occupied, even though their conscious minds never got the message.

As they passed familiar faces, Tom triggered the memory restoration in the cadets they trusted. He saw Walton Covner and Lyla Martin jerk to a halt on the stairs, the deleted memory rushing back to them along with the instructions they'd written for them.

Follow the instructions in your processor. We have one shot. If we fail, get out of here, and get the other cadets to escape, too. Obsidian Corp. will send everything they have at the Pentagonal Spire. They'll kill or reprogram every cadet inside.

Tom watched them look at each other, then wheel around and rush back up to the stairs to the neural access ports on the twelfth floor. He saw Karl and Yosef dash up the stairs, too, and his heart swelled as more of the cadets who'd pledged to fight with them went to assume their positions. The meltdown warning was clearing the Spire of most every person likely to fight on Vengerov's side—and locking them out so they couldn't stop Tom's allies once the plan was underway.

Tom, Vik, Wyatt, and Yuri stole into the suborbital planes they'd appropriated and launched into the sky. He peered down to check on Blackburn's ship, waiting in readiness in case they succeeded, and hoped suddenly that he'd see it land again.

The Pentagon receded far below them as they rattled up into space for the too-brief trip to Antarctica. Tom was intent on steering, and in the next plane over, Vik and Yuri were following the same course.

"This has to work," Tom said, so softly Wyatt couldn't hear him over the roar of the engine. "I can't screw this up."

Someone could hear him, after all. "You won't fail," Blackburn's voice said in his ear. "You'll get back in one piece."

"I'm planning on it, sir."

"And, Tom, I'll be there with you. You're not alone this time."

Tom knew that. But he still had to swallow down a great lump of anxiety, knowing what lay ahead.

THE SUBORBITAL SHOOK as they re-entered the atmosphere, the jagged coastline of Antarctica shaking toward him. Twice, Tom had come here. He'd almost died both times. The third time was *not* going to be the charm.

"Where do we land?" Wyatt said, her voice tense. "We're going too fast."

"We have to go this fast," Tom told her. "We come in slow, and we get destroyed. Trust me, we can pull this off."

"I know you can, but can Vik?" She threw a worried look out the window toward the other suborbital. They'd split up deliberately, because Tom and Wyatt were essential to the operation, and he was the best pilot. Vik was also a great pilot, but he and Yuri were there to help keep them alive.

"We'll be okay," Tom assured her. "A minute from now, we'll land in the middle of Obsidian Corp." And it would take some time for Vengerov's machines to flock to that sector of the building. Tom knew, because as soon as they launched, so did several of the vactrains in the Interstice—all heading toward Obsidian Corp.

If they'd calculated everything correctly, then as of thirty seconds ago, Vengerov had received an alert that intruders were heading for Obsidian Corp. via the vactube. He'd probably already mobilized his machines to that sector of the building.

That wasn't where they were penetrating.

But when the complex swerved into sight, Wyatt tensed up. "Medusa didn't come through. Oh no, Tom, she didn't. The roof's intact!"

Tom scanned the surface as they jolted closer and closer, too fast to abort now. They didn't have weapons to blast through themselves. "Uh, uh, I don't . . ."

And then before their eyes, a series of missiles arced down out of the sky and blasted the roof open. Tom and Wyatt flinched instinctively as they sailed through the flames and

381

careened into the complex, but their thrusters fired, propelling them upward when they would have crashed and burned, and Tom seized the controls and maneuvered them down through blasted-open floor after floor, descending into the depths of Obsidian Corp., where it tunneled deep into the continent.

They hit the ground with a ferocious jolt, and then Tom tore off his seat belt and scrambled into the aft compartment where they'd stashed the exosuits.

Wyatt hastily jumped into hers, adjusting the gas mask, body armor, night-vision goggles, centrifugal clamps, and optical camouflage. She jerked. "Oh, the boots! Don't forget . . ."

"I know!" Tom fumbled for his own pair of rubber-soled boots, a basic necessity for Obsidian Corp.'s electrically conductive floors.

Last time, Joseph Vengerov's complex hadn't been prepared for human invaders. As Vengerov himself had put it, no one invaded "a building full of killing machines in the middle of Antarctica." This time, a shrill alarm was already splitting the air and the Praetorians began splicing their lasers at them before Tom and Wyatt escaped the suborbital.

Tom kicked an exosuited foot at the escape hatch, the enhanced strength breaking it off at the hinges and hurtling it into the nearest combat machine.

He reached back and seized Wyatt's arm, then flung her straight over the waiting arsenal of Praetorians, her body a faint ripple in the air. He leaped to the ceiling and clamped there as the machines fired at the space where he'd been. Before they could locate him, Tom shot at the sprinkler system, sending water flooding down from above. The machines and the exosuits

382

were all waterproof, but the floor was not. It began to spark and crackle, and the machines connected with it abruptly halted, sparks blooming from them.

"Okay?" Tom called to Wyatt, heart in his throat.

"Okay," her voice floated back. "I'm on the wall."

"Let's go."

They moved like that, Tom hanging from the ceiling with his exosuit and centrifugal clamps, Wyatt on the wall with hers, the Praetorians that had assembled in the hallway beginning to burn on the floors. Overhead, an intercom flared to life, and Vik's jovial voice piped over the speakers.

"Attention, all Obsidian Corporation employees: please follow evacuation procedures immediately. We've brought more than enough vactrains to get you all out of here. If you don't get well clear of this building ASAP, you're going to die. We guarantee you that. Believe us, this is a friendly warning." And with that, his voice faded away beneath the scream of alarms.

Vik's warning must've worked, because as Wyatt and Tom proceeded, they saw that halls normally populated by Obsidian Corp.'s staff were totally empty. They didn't have time to investigate further, because a flood of drones poured in from the burning tear in the building. Tom and Wyatt had been slower than they'd expected, and they were a heartbeat slower to draw their guns than they should've been—but Yuri and Vik appeared in the doorway at the other end of the corridor and blasted at the machines with their rocket launchers, flinging them out of the air.

Tom propelled himself forward to land with a great clang beside them. "Guys?" he said to the invisible space.

"We're here," Vik said.

Wyatt's feet clanged beside them. "Here."

"Here," Yuri said.

They proceeded together down the corridor, sometimes taking shelter away from the floors, sometimes throwing themselves back down when new Praetorians swarmed in, the necks retracting so they could crawl up the walls. Tom and his friends had trained to fight like this since they were fourteen, and this was the first time they'd been able to use it in the real world. This visit to Obsidian Corp., they weren't sneaking in—they were coming in full force. They shot the Praetorians straight off the walls.

Even when a Praetorian flooded the corridor with fluorine gas, they were fine—their gas masks firmly in place. And then they reached a neural access port, Obsidian Corp.'s intranet primed and ready for access.

"This isn't the same one as last time," Vik noted.

"We burned the one from last time," Tom shot back, preparing his neural wire. "This time we finish the job."

Yuri nodded. "It is good to be thorough."

"What if he's deactivated it?" Wyatt said sharply. "He has to know we're here to access his mainframe."

Tom shook his head. Vengerov would have theories about what they were up to, but, no, he wasn't going to deactivate it, and Tom knew why. He couldn't tell her. Tom was the reason Vengerov would leave it open.

The thought shook him more than waves of automated drones intent on killing him had. "You guys have my back?" Tom said, his voice choked.

"Always," Vik said.

Yuri clasped his shoulder, and Wyatt patted his head. Tom repressed a smile and reassured himself with one last glimpse of their shimmering forms leveling their guns, waiting for attack. Then he hooked in the neural wire and dove into the system.

The response was breathtakingly immediate. It was like Tom was sucked down a vortex, his mind jolting into the wrong place, the place where he didn't want to go ever again. And then there was another consciousness touching his, overcoming his, with a suddenness that made Tom gasp and grip the wall, his stomach clenching up in cold horror at the familiarity of it.

Hello, Vanya.

"No. No, no," Tom moaned, trying to pull back out of the system.

Stay right here.

And his processor responded to the command like it was his own. Like it was more than his own. His own fears and terrors had reduced him to listening to this voice over his own, even now.

Your trick with the Interstice may have pulled the bulk of my machines away, Vengerov noted, *but I knew to wait in the system for you. And here you are, come back to me at last. I knew you would.*

Tom tried to tell himself Vengerov wasn't actually there this time, that he was far away, that they were merely connected over the internet. But Vengerov had been waiting there in the system for him, and his neural processor, so used to yielding neural sovereignty to Vengerov, responded instantly to Vengerov's test ping, and then the full-on invasion of his consciousness.

The other mind gripping his felt like a fist, and Tom's hand flew back instinctively to wrench out the neural wire, knowing this was a mistake, this was a terrible mistake. But Vengerov thought, *Don't do that*, and Tom couldn't, he couldn't close his fingers.

And it was like he was back there, and he felt like he was breathing through a straw, and Vengerov crooned in his mind again.

What are your plans?

"No," Tom said out loud, straining to open his eyes, to see his friends. He could just make out the splutter of gunfire, his ears that suddenly felt so distant from him picking up the sounds of a renewed fight, more machines flooding in.

Don't look at them. They'll be gone very soon and it will be you and me again. Just as it should be. Just as it will be again.

"No. It won't . . . I won't l-l-let it . . ." He realized, horrified, that the stutter was creeping into his voice. Like Vanya. Just like Vanya, still at the edges of his mind.

What are you up to? Vengerov's thoughts blared again, bending, manipulating his mind, and Tom struggled against it, but Vengerov began to pluck out the fringes of his plan as Tom thought of it.

The hubs they were going to destroy.

The file they were going to use to infect the rest. Vengerov's amusement was like a noxious poison. *Let's see this file . . .* His mind flipped through the files in Tom's processor, and then he said, *This one?*

It was a data file they'd written for the occasion. Medusa's idea: the amendment to the legal code to compel those with Austere-grade processors to damage Obsidian Corp.

Now that's not very civilized. Surely you know my human employees are very extraneous. My machines could keep all our operations running without a hitch. Nonetheless, this would be very inconvenient. With that, Vengerov deleted it from Tom's processor.

"No!" Tom yelled out, reaching up again for the neural wire.

Stop that, Vengerov rebuked sharply, and his voice reminded Tom of the hand clamping onto the back of his neck, the restraining node back in place. His brain remembered this too well, remembered the sense of total hopelessness that accompanied this feeling. He couldn't breathe. He swore he'd fallen back into the enclosure somehow and he couldn't breathe.

He tried to look back, to see his friends as they shot anything coming toward them, but Vengerov forced his eyes shut, holding Tom hostage there alone with him trapped in his mind, threatening to plunge him back there, back to that terrible time.

You were planning to plant this in my hubs, were you? But there must have been more to your plan than that.

Then they were soaring through the internet together, Tom's mind and Vengerov's will coupled together again. They jolted into the surveillance camera outside one of Vengerov's hubs in Amsterdam, where the first of the Combatant-controlled ships was soaring in to attack. He felt Vengerov's laughter in his mind as he comprehended all of it, all of Medusa's plan.

Use Combatants to destroy some of the hubs controlling the Austere-grade processors, plant their malware in the remaining hubs, and turn Vengerov's own Austere-grade-processor-infected people against him. With a flicker of his thoughts, Vengerov forced Tom through the internet to his own air defense, and together, they scrambled Vengerov's machines to defend that hub.

How convenient this is, Vengerov thought to Tom. *You are simply sending every single drone outside my control in to attack my internet hubs. This saves me the trouble of tracking them down myself.*

"Go to hell!" Tom shouted.

I've missed this, Vengerov thought. *You are such an efficient shortcut. We bypass hours of work in seconds.*

"I hate you," Tom cried, his fists clenched so hard his hands throbbed, fury seething through him.

But Vengerov forced them through the network to the next hub, and then the next. On and on they went, Vengerov checking to see which ones were under attack, and scrambling his machines to defend those, then checking the next hub.

Why haven't your friends tried to break the connection? Vengerov wondered. *They must know something is wrong . . . unless they're dead.*

The thought hadn't occurred to Tom. He hadn't realized while trapped with Vengerov in his own mind, interfacing with this system, Vik, Wyatt, and Yuri might have been killed.

Vengerov tried to force his eyes open to see, but this time, Tom was the one fighting to keep them closed. It was the first moment Tom felt doubt touch Joseph Vengerov. The first time ever.

With a push of his thoughts, Vengerov forced Tom's eyes open, and then he saw with Tom's eyes Wyatt tugging the neural wire out of Tom's access port. "Is it done?" she whispered to Tom. "Did he take you to a bunch of them?"

What? Vengerov thought.

Tom couldn't help it. He couldn't. He started laughing, and with a surge of vindictive glee, he said aloud, "You want to tell him or should I?"

The other person connected to his mind reared up, making his presence known to Vengerov. Lieutenant Blackburn's voice chided in Tom's ear, "Really, Joseph. You could have taken the time to check your actual security cameras instead of relying on the sensory perception of a kid whose brain I'm linked to."

Suspicion crashed over Vengerov. He saw with Tom's eyes Wyatt typing out code, deploying the last of her program.

Tom wasn't afraid, and he wasn't resisting, because Blackburn had promised him this moment and it was so sweet experiencing Vengerov's anxiety, gazing through the external surveillance cameras outside the Amsterdam internet hub. Through Tom's vision center, Vengerov saw his ships soaring in to engage Medusa's . . .

And then Blackburn stopped manipulating Tom's vision center, removing the illusion of attacking ships, giving Vengerov a long look at the way there were no ships attacking the hub, only Vengerov's ships prepared to defend it.

Tom felt Vengerov's mind making sense of it, realizing Tom's vision center had been tricked into seeing an attack on all his hubs—and he had believed it.

For once, Tom tried to stay connected to Vengerov for as long as possible, glad to experience along with Vengerov the moment he realized he'd scattered the bulk of his aerial firepower throughout the world to defend against an illusory attack, all because of a deception in Tom's vision center. He no longer had the advantage of overwhelming force ready for instant deployment anywhere in the world. His ships were spread thin, far from the Spire, the Citadel.

Tom got to experience along with him the next realization: that he'd led Tom from internet hub to hub, and even though he'd deleted the decoy virus, Wyatt had been feeding something else into Tom's neural processor.

Tom laughed out loud and didn't fight as Vengerov frantically searched the Amsterdam hub and located the new piece of malware Wyatt had installed there.

The programs had been transmitted to all the Austere-grade processors connected with that hub. Vengerov accessed the video file of a beaming Elliot Ramirez, a message that adjusted to the dominant language of the person watching it.

Tom had seen Elliot record it. He knew what it said.

"Hello! You may know me as Elliot Ramirez, former US Intrasolar Combatant." Elliot nodded solemnly. "You're probably very confused right now about what this message is doing in your mind. You're probably wondering why you're suddenly sure someone has implanted a computer in your brain without your consent. You are not crazy, and everyone around you is seeing the same thing you are. The truth is, there has been a computer implanted in your brain. A neural processor." They'd thought Elliot recording it would be a good idea. He'd be a familiar face to most anyone in the world, anywhere. "I'm sure you have a lot of questions," Elliot said, "and they'll be answered in time, but for now, you are all needed. This computer was forced on you by Joseph Vengerov of Obsidian Corp. in an effort to control your mind, and there are people at this very moment working to free you. In order to do so, we need to find a vulnerability in our processor's code so we can disable one particular function."

When Vengerov saw the function Elliot was referring to, shock flooded him, because he had to recognize it instantly as the fail-safe that stopped anyone with a Vigilant-grade neural processor from destroying him.

Those with Austere-grade processors couldn't break the law in the most literal sense. That stopped them from ever being a threat to him, from ever killing him. Those with Vigilant-grade processors weren't a threat because of a single segment of source code.

Nothing stopped those with Austere-grade processors from helping them disable that segment of source code. They couldn't kill Vengerov themselves, but they could free up people with Vigilant-grade processors to do it.

"If you can't help us find a vulnerability in our code," Elliot went on, "then help us spread this message to someone who can. We can't get to all the internet hubs in the world, but you can transmit this to those you know. Instructions are in your processor. Send it to everyone you know, especially people in different geographic regions. Tell them to send it on as well. We are the greatest legion of minds this world has ever seen. We've given everyone working knowledge of Zorten II, so if you can locate any vulnerability that will let us modify one particular fail-safe function, send it to us—you know how, it's in your processor—and we will bring this to an end."

Vengerov was stunned as Elliot's message faded. Tom could feel it, could feel Vengerov's mind racing over the implications of this. If someone located a vulnerability in the code that allowed them to disable the fail-safe—and with so many people working on it, someone inevitably would—then anyone with a Vigilant-grade neural processor would be a threat to him.

He had to kill them all first.

He'd destroy the Pentagonal Spire and the Sun Tzu Citadel and the Kremlin Complex and the trainees in Bombay. And the four in Obsidian Corp . . . They must've anticipated he'd respond by killing those with Vigilant-grade processors, and *that's* why they'd scrambled his forces, to buy time.

Tom heard it all moving through his head, knowing it was all true, and then Blackburn's voice reminded him, "Tom, where?"

Tom didn't have to wonder what he was asking. He shot through his connection to Vengerov's mind before the other man could react, and for a moment he had a glimpse of the world through Vengerov's eyes—seeing the vessel he was in, snatching one fleeting glimpse of the stars outside the nearest window.

For a moment, all three men registered the importance of this—Vengerov, aware that Blackburn would be the first to receive the countercode, Blackburn glorying in seeing exactly where he would find Vengerov once he had it, Tom knowing this was about to end one way or another.

Then Vengerov broke the connection and Tom found himself in the middle of Obsidian Corp. For a moment it was like he'd stumbled into a scene from hell, poison gas curling in the air around them, the alarm still shrilling earsplittingly loud, the overhead lights fizzling where they'd been blown out, fire licking up the walls, and shots thundering from Yuri's machine gun as a small drone tore out of the cloudy air. Drifts of gas and smoke cleared, revealing the glint of more Praetorians and

392

automated machines like a relentless horde pressing into the hallway, the splintered metal debris of the destroyed security bots littered across the shorted-out floors.

"Enough?" Tom shouted to Blackburn, hoping he could hear it through the neural link. He was sure that glimpse of the stars and their position would be enough to tell him Vengerov's coordinates.

"Enough. Get out of there now," Blackburn ordered.

Just then, the ceiling burst, and a new wave of drones poured through in a great torrent of flashing metal. Tom used his neural wire and shot back into Obsidian Corp.'s system, ordering the Praetorians to engage them as their new targets. Then he and his friends sprinted away in their exosuits as Joseph Vengerov's machines obliterated one another.

Yaolan had flown in two Russo-Chinese ships to wait for them on the ice. As soon as Tom and Wyatt shot off, Vik and Yuri's ship just ahead of them, Tom signaled Vik. *Now*, he net-sent.

The Interstice hadn't only been used as a distraction. They'd smuggled something very specific onto one of the vactrains: a hydrogen bomb now nestled under Obsidian Corp. From the other fleeing ship, Vik detonated it.

The nuclear explosion was so far underground that no light reached the surface, only the flames that followed, bursting like a flower opening across the glaciers, and for a moment as they rose higher in the air, it loomed over the landscape like a burning cigarette butt. And then the glacial landscape of Antarctica caved in around the remains of Obsidian Corp., and Earth swallowed the last of the complex into its fiery depths.

```
1 0 0 1 1 1 1 1 1 1 1 0 0 1 1 1 0 1 0 1 1 0 0 0 0 0 0 0 1 0 0 1 1 1 1 0 0 0
0 1 1 0 1 1 0 1 1 0 0 1 1 1 1 0 0 0 0 0 0 0 0 1 0 1 1 0 1 0 0 1 0 0 1 1
1 0 0 0 0 1 1 1 1 0 0 1 0 0 1 0 1 1 1 0 0 1 1 1 0 1 1 0 0 1 0 1 1 0 1 1
0 1 0 0 0 1 1 1 1 0 0 0 0 1 1 0 1 0 0 1 1 0 0 0 1 0 1 1 1 1 0 0 0 0 1 1
1 0 0 1 1 0 1 0 0 0 0 1 0 1 1 0 1 1 0 0 0 0 0 0 1 0 1 1 0 0 1 1 1 1
0 0 1 1 0 0 0 0 1 1 1 0 1 1 0 1 1 0 1 0 0 0 0 0 1 0 0 1 1 1 0 0 0 0 0
1 1 0 0 1 0 1 0 1 1 1 0 1 1 1 0 1 0 1 1 1 1 0 1 0 1 1 0 1 1 0 0 0 0 0
0 1 1 1 1 1 1 1 0 1 1 0 0 0 0 1 1 1 0 1 1 0 1 1 0 1 1 1 0 0 0 1 0 1 0
1 0 1 1 0 0 1 0 1 1 0 1 0 0 1 0 0 0 1 0 1 0 1 0 0 1 0 0 0 0 1 0 1 0 1 0 1 0
0 0 1 0 0 1 0 1 1 0 0 1 0 0 1 1 0 1 0 1 0 1 1 1 0 0 0 0 1 0 1 1 0 1 0 1 0
0 0 0 0 0 1 1 1 1 0 1 1 0 0 1 1 0 1 1 0 1 1 0 0 0 0 0 0 1 0 0 0 1 0 0 0 1 0 0
1 0 1 0 0 1 1 1 1 0 0 1 1 1 0 1 1 0 0 1 1 0 0 1 1 1 0 0 1 0 0 0 0 1 0 0 0
0 0 1 1 1 1 1 0 1 1 0 1 0 0 0 1 0 0 1 1 1 0 0 0 0 1 0 1 1 1 0 0 0 0 0
0 1 1 1 1 0 0 0 0 0 1 0 1 1 0 1 0 0 0 0 0 0 0 0 1 0 0 0 1 1 1 0 0 1 1 1 0
1 1 1 0 0 0 1 1 1 0 0 1 1 1 0 0 0 0 1 1 0 0 1 0 0 1 0 1 0 1 1 1 1 1 0 1 1
0 0 0 1 1 1 1 1 0 0 1 0 1 0 1 1 1 1 0 0 1 0 1 1 0 1 1 0 1 1 1 1 1 0 0 1 0 0 1
0 1 0 1 [              ] 0 0 1 0 0 0 0 1 0 0 0 0 1 1 1 0 1 0 1 0 1
0 0 1 1 [              ] 0 1 0 1 1 1 1 1 1 1 1 1 1 1 1 0 0 1 1 1 0
1 1 1 1 [   CHAPTER THIRTY   ] 0 1 1 0 1 0 0 1 0 0 0 0 1 1 1 1 0 0
1 0 0 1 1 0 0 0 1 1 1 1 1 1 0 1 1 0 0 0 0 0 0 1 0 0 1 0 0 1 0 1 0 1 0 0
```

CHAPTER THIRTY

JOSEPH VENGEROV WAS out for blood. Vik and Yuri's ship disappeared into the vivid sky over Antarctica, but Tom and Wyatt found themselves besieged by a hail of missiles from distant carriers controlled by the oligarch.

Tom pinwheeled them out of a line of fire, only to find g-forces crushing them. Flying a clunky suborbital wasn't nearly as easy as using his neural processor to steer a drone.

"Get us higher," Wyatt urged him, her breath coming in panicked gasps.

Tom aimed them skyward. Vengerov had more armaments in orbit, so he dared not take them out of the atmosphere.

"I don't see Vik and Yuri," Wyatt said.

Tom tried not to think about that. Hopefully, that meant they were getting away. Hopefully Vengerov was concentrating firepower on him personally—one of the culprits directly responsible for spreading Zorten II to all the Austere-grade processors.

Speaking of which . . .

As the assault thinned out, Tom relinquished the controls to Wyatt to net-send Blackburn. *Anyone reply yet?*

Through the neural link, an image flashed in his vision center, and awe swept over Tom, seeing the messages filter in from all over the world. Bangladesh, Japan, Brazil, Tennessee, Sudan . . .

"Some claim they've not only found vulnerability, they've offered solutions to disabling the fail-safe. I'm testing the code on a virtual processor," Blackburn's voice said in his ear. "Whether any of them will show results, that's up for question. Where are you?"

Tom leaned over to peer out the window at the landscape far below them as they moved through the high atmosphere, just where the sky was beginning to drain from deepest blue to pitch-black.

"Don't try to come back here," Blackburn warned him. "He's concentrating his attack on the Spire and the Citadel."

He sent an image to Tom's vision center, the mechanized drones Vengerov controlled converging outside the Spire. The drones Blackburn's code had seized control of over the years were all active now, at the command of CamCos and Intrasolar cadets on the fourteenth floor, all rushing out to engage.

For a moment, Tom watched the fire-fight begin right over the Pentagonal Spire, the heart of the US military, and he saw that this was a close matchup. If they hadn't scattered Vengerov's forces with the deception about the internet hubs, they would have descended on them with overwhelming firepower. They'd have no chance.

At least now, the odds were even.

And Tom and Wyatt would have no chance in this unarmed ship. "So we hide?" Tom asked.

"Hide," Blackburn agreed. "And . . . there it is."

Tom was focused inward, seeing Blackburn test the countercode again, hearing his dark, triumphant laugh when the code transmitted by someone in Argentina neutralized Vengerov's self-preservation algorithm.

"Is that it?" Tom breathed.

"Yes. Have a present."

And then the code streamed straight into Tom's processor, and a realization swept over him in a great, dizzying wave that if Joseph Vengerov were standing right in front of him, Tom could shoot him in the head—no algorithm holding him back.

"Share it with everyone just in case."

"In case what?"

"You know what," Blackburn said. "I can't send a drone. That's an entirely different fail-safe. This has to be done manually."

Tom knew Blackburn had a ship ready specifically for this instance, prepared to slip out while the other vessels were tied up in battle—and put to the test the theory he could kill Vengerov himself. But he might not make it. He might fail.

"Make sure it's not necessary," Tom told him.

Then the neural connection between them faded—all before Tom could wish him good luck. He looked at Wyatt, her worried profile pinched, and with a few taps on his forearm keyboard, he shared the code with her.

They began their descent through a layer of clouds. "I think we lost them," Wyatt said. She was silent a long moment, then, "Lieutenant Blackburn's going himself, isn't he? To kill Vengerov, I mean."

Tom thought of that ship waiting in readiness at the Pentagonal Spire. The missiles they'd loaded onto it the day before. "Yeah, he is. He's been working for this since before we were born, Wyatt."

"It's sad."

"What, Vengerov dying?" Tom said harshly. "He deserves worse than a few missiles."

"I mean, having nothing else. Living just to make sure someone else dies. All those years and never finding something else to make it all worthwhile." She leaned her head against the window. "It's sad."

There was nothing Tom could really say to that. "At least we made it—"

But Wyatt saw something on her monitor that made her sit bolt upright. "INCOMING!"

The world exploded.

Gravity became a slab of concrete crushing him against his seat, his own shouts lost beneath the roar of the dying engine, under the shriek of splintering metal, the air roaring by them. His stomach was in his throat and Tom forced his eyes open against the pummeling wind to see the flames above them and the great, jagged gash ripped into the ceiling over their heads, sky swirling in a dizzying circle, a Centurion controlled by Vengerov twisting about to fire at them again.

And he felt Wyatt's hand locked on his, and his eyes rushed over to meet hers in the blinding instant as the rain forest below became a green blur swirling up toward them.

With a superhuman effort made possible only by the exosuit he still wore, Tom forced his arm up, hooked a neural wire back into the slot, forced his consciousness into the dying system of the airplane, and fired their thrusters, fighting to slow them, fighting for one last chance . . .

Then the deafening rattle thundering in his eardrums, the abrupt impact, his head flying at the console before him . . .

"Tom. Tom! **TOM!** TOM RAINES! WAKE UP!"

He was choking. He was suffocating. Tom gagged on the water in his lungs, coughing, his throat twisting.

"Tom. Tom, Tom, open your eyes."

He forced open his blurry, aching eyes to see the blood he was spitting out of his mouth.

"Tom, focus. You need to move."

He looked over and saw Blackburn, leaning in to see him through the twisted wreckage. His head felt like it was being split open, the light drilling his eyes.

"Listen to me." Blackburn sounded worried. "Reach over and check Wyatt."

Tom's head felt like it weighed a thousand pounds. He cringed, pain sparkling down his neck as he looked over, and panic wrenched through him at the sight of Wyatt, sagging in her seat, dark hair streaming down before her inert body.

"Wy—" He choked on the word, a terrible, racking cough gripping him again.

"Her pulse. Feel her pulse, Tom. Is she alive?"

Raising his arm hurt. His ribs felt like they were stabbing him. Tears of pain blurred his eyes, but his cybernetic fingers weren't sensitive enough to detect a pulse.

"Oh no, oh no, please . . ."

"Quick. Ball up your fist and rub your knuckles over her collarbone," Blackburn ordered.

Tom did so, and Wyatt gave a pained moan but didn't open her eyes. Tom laughed and it hurt him. "She's alive! She's alive!"

"Listen. You need to get out of there. That exosuit is fried. Disconnect from it."

Now that Tom thought about it, it seemed to be dragging at him, resisting him when he moved. With shaky arms, he detached it from his neural access port. The suit sputtered, but finally expanded.

Not all the way, just enough for him to wriggle painfully out of the places where the suit snared his joints. Moving out of it was another matter. Even lifting his right leg sent splinters of pain jamming up through him.

Tom screamed out, and in response, Blackburn sent him some code. It flickered over his vision center, and the worst of the agony receded, even though every movement seemed to grind razors into his thigh.

He fought to focus as Blackburn said, "Take off her exosuit, too. She'll be too heavy to carry with that on."

"Carry?"

"You can do it. You *have* to do it."

Tom's hands felt rubbery, but he got Wyatt out. She moaned in pain with every movement, and he was terrified he was hurting her, but Blackburn snapped at him to hurry, to forget being gentle. "She'll hurt a lot worse if you don't get her out!"

By the time Tom freed her, exhaustion made his limbs shake. He wanted to sleep. He wondered deliriously at the way Blackburn was just staring down at them.

"Can you come help me already?" Tom said to him. "I'm in bad shape."

Silence a long moment. Then, "You are. I can see that, but you have to do this yourself. And quickly—before the fire spreads to the jet fuel."

Fire. Fire? He smelled it. Fuel. Burning metal. Thick on the air. "Fire! There's a fire."

"Concentrate on Wyatt. You can do this. You can save her."

Tom's hands grew cold, but his mechanical fingers moved with the ease the rest of him could not, extricating her from her seat belt. Her head was ominously floppy, and Tom blearily remembered, "I can't move her. What if I break her neck?"

"She stays and she's dead, anyway. You have to risk it." Tom dragged her up and out of her exosuit, trying to shut out her whimpers of pain, and kicked at the door until his leg felt like lead, and then it tumbled open.

He hesitated only a moment, seeing they were still ten feet off the ground, their ship lodged in the canopy of tree branches. He wrapped his arms tightly about her and flung them down, rolling as they hit the soft, mossy floor of the forest. Treetops loomed overhead, the air thick and humid, insects humming all about them, flora tangling about his legs.

Through the glaring blue of the sky, peeking through the trees, Tom caught sight of it—the Centurion-grade drone that had shot them down, circling in the sky like a vulture. His stomach pinched with fear, seeing it twist about, trying to reacquire their position, finish them. And he had no weapons. No gun, no ship, no exosuit, even.

"Get up," Blackburn said. "You need to move to a safe distance."

"Where's your ship?" Tom asked Blackburn, his head

400

pounding, his voice thick and slurred. "Can we get out of here in your ship? Did you land very far away? Why aren't you killing Vengerov right now, anyway?"

Blackburn jumped down next to them, gesturing for Tom to get up, to pick her up. "I took a hit leaving the Spire. When I tried to fire off some missiles, my launcher malfunctioned. I couldn't finish him."

"Wait, are you telling me you actually got close enough to off Vengerov, then you couldn't do it?"

"I was so close to his ship, I could have seen him through a window," Blackburn said hollowly.

"And that's when you found out you didn't have any weapons?" Despite everything, the absurd urge to laugh came over him. It was like Vengerov had rigged fate itself in his favor.

"I just had the ship," Blackburn said, his voice tense. "Then I saw you crash. There was no one else close enough to get here in time. Only me."

So he'd aborted his mission to kill Vengerov and come help. "You'll get him later. You will. With a better ship. A better missile launcher. The whole world will help you next time."

"Get up and move, Tom."

Tom heaved Wyatt over his shoulder, and immediately needed to put her back down, but Blackburn snapped at him when he was about to do so.

"Help will come. Right now, you need to move to a safe distance. Move!"

Frustration ripped through Tom. He was hurting, he was so tired, he just wanted to sit, and it wasn't like there was a safe distance. He could hear the roar of the Centurion mounting, getting closer. If it spotted the wreckage, if it found their heat signatures, there would be no safe distance. Those weapons would kill them easily.

But Blackburn kept urging him forward, forward, until finally Tom's strength gave out, and he sagged down against the damp, mossy bark of a tree, feeling like he was going to fall apart. Wyatt settled against him with a groan of pain, and he held her close, scared for her because she wasn't waking up.

"I can't carry her any farther," he told Blackburn, tears of exhaustion in his eyes. "We have to stop here."

"This is far enough." Blackburn knelt before him. "Do exactly what I say. Focus on me." He pointed two fingers at his eyes.

But Tom couldn't. The Centurion's roar had grown deafening, its engine sending leaves skittering from overhanging trees. A shadow blocked out the sun as its circles grew narrow as it swept in, weapons glinting as they charged up and it descended into firing range.

"I'm really sorry you didn't get your revenge," Tom said. It sucked dying knowing Vengerov wasn't going with them.

"Tom, listen: you have to stay awake until someone finds you. You need to bind up your leg, and make sure neither of you bleed to death before help gets here."

Tom was confused, bleary. He didn't see why it mattered if he stayed awake. They wouldn't have time to bleed to death. They were about to be very dead, that ship overhead raising its weapons now, the thunder of its engine splitting the air.

"Swear you'll stay awake. You have to make this matter."

"I swear, okay? I swear!" And Tom screwed his eyes shut, his entire body a knot of tension in the moments before the weapons fired.

Lips brushed his forehead. "Thank you."

A great roar filled the air, and Tom's eyes snapped open in time to see another ship burst through the clouds overhead, fire flaring against its heat shields as it plunged like a falling star. Lightning-swift, it rammed into the Centurion. The two ships erupted in a great veil of flame and tumbled down to the earth, the blast making Tom's ears throb as he hurled himself over Wyatt by instinct. When he raised his head, he saw the distant trees consumed in raging fire, fragments of burning metal raining down through the air.

And then even that grew silent, the chirp and hum of insects mounted, and Tom raised himself to his feet, wired with adrenaline, heart thudding in his chest, his brain trying to make sense of what he'd seen. They were alive. They were saved.

He laughed deliriously, shocked by it all, the sky bright and clear and free of danger above them. "Oh my God. Did you see that?" he said to Blackburn. "The Centurion was gonna fire and that other ship was like—kapow! Did you see . . ." He looked over where Blackburn had just been.

Blackburn wasn't there.

Tom turned in a circle, searching the trees, his eyes scanning the jungle floor—the flora disturbed only by his own steps.

Understanding crept over him.

Blackburn had one single weapon in his arsenal: his ship.

The air hung thick with the stench of burning metal, the trees flattened near their crash site. No one could have survived ejecting. Not at that velocity. Tom's throat grew tight, a sense of loss opening like a chasm inside him.

For the first time in two years, he was entirely alone in his own head.

1 0 0 1 1 1 1 1 1 1 1 0 0 1 1 1 0 1 0 1 1 0 0 0 0 0 0 0 1 0 0 1 1 1 1 0 0 0
0 1 1 0 1 1 0 1 1 1 0 0 1 1 1 0 0 0 0 0 0 0 1 0 1 1 0 1 0 0 1 0 0 1 1
1 0 0 0 0 0 1 1 1 1 0 0 1 0 0 1 0 1 1 1 0 0 1 1 1 0 1 1 0 0 1 0 1 1 0 1 1
0 1 0 0 0 1 1 0 1 1 0 0 0 0 1 1 0 1 0 0 1 1 0 0 0 1 0 1 1 1 1 0 0 0 0 1 1
1 0 0 1 1 0 1 0 0 0 0 0 1 0 1 1 1 0 1 1 0 0 0 0 0 0 0 1 0 1 1 0 0 1 1 1 1
0 0 1 1 0 0 0 0 1 1 1 1 0 1 1 0 1 1 0 1 1 0 1 0 0 0 0 1 0 1 1 1 0 0 0 0 0
1 1 0 0 1 0 1 0 1 1 1 0 1 1 1 0 1 0 1 1 1 0 1 0 1 1 0 1 1 0 0 0 0
0 1 1 1 1 1 1 1 0 1 1 0 0 0 0 1 1 1 0 1 1 0 1 1 1 0 1 1 1 0 0 0 1 0 1 0
1 0 1 1 0 0 1 1 0 1 0 0 1 0 0 0 1 0 1 0 1 0 0 1 0 0 0 0 1 0 0 1 0 1 0 1 0
0 0 1 0 0 1 0 1 1 0 0 1 0 0 1 1 0 1 0 1 0 1 1 1 0 0 0 0 1 0 1 1 0 1 0 1 0
0 0 0 0 0 1 1 1 1 0 1 1 0 0 1 1 0 1 1 0 0 0 0 0 0 1 0 0 0 0 1 0 0 0 1 0 0
1 0 1 0 0 1 1 1 1 0 0 1 1 1 0 1 1 0 0 1 1 0 0 1 1 0 0 1 0 0 0 0 1 0 0 0
0 0 1 1 1 1 0 1 1 0 1 0 0 1 0 0 1 1 1 0 0 0 0 1 0 1 1 0 0 0 0 1 0 0 1 0
0 1 1 1 1 0 0 0 1 0 1 1 0 1 0 0 0 0 1 0 0 0 1 1 1 1 0 0 1 1 1 0
1 1 1 0 0 0 1 1 1 0 0 1 1 1 0 0 0 0 1 1 0 0 1 0 0 1 0 1 0 1 1 1 1 0 1 1
0 0 0 1 1 1 1 0 0 1 0 1 1 1 1 1 0 0 1 0 1 1 0 1 1 0 1 1 1 1 1 0 0 1 0 0 1
0 1 0 1   0 0 0 1 0 0 0 1 1 1 0 1 0 1 0 1
0 0 1   1 1 1 1 1 1 1 1 0 0 1 1 1 0
1 1 1 1   1 0 0   1 0 0 0 1   1 0 1 0 0 1 0 0 0 0 1 1 1 1 0 0
1 0 0 1 1 0 0 0 1 1 1 1 1 0 1 1 0 0 0 0 0 0 1 0 0 1 0 0 1 0 1 0 0 1 0 0

CHAPTER THIRTY-ONE

JUST LIKE THE megalomaniacs who savaged the world before him, Vengerov proved a coward in the end. When the Intrasolar cadets of both sides defeated his forces, and the code to disable his fail-safe seeped into all the processors, he disappeared.

Where, no one knew. The one shot at killing him had been Blackburn, who'd set off early to strike Vengerov's ship in space. Tom imagined sometimes what might have happened if by some fluke of fate, his missile launcher hadn't been fried. Blackburn could've destroyed Vengerov's ship, and then swung around and blasted away the drone about to kill Tom and Wyatt. But that hadn't happened. In the end, Blackburn had a single ship at his disposal, and one target he could destroy. So he'd chosen to spend his life not on Vengerov's destruction but rather saving two kids who'd been shot down in the Amazon.

Tom stared at the burning trees knowing what had been sacrificed. Not life. Either way, Blackburn would have given it, ramming Vengerov's ship or ramming the attacking drone. He'd sacrificed something far greater: the vendetta that had given his existence meaning. Grief flooded Tom's heart, and he knew he'd made a promise he had to keep, his last promise to Blackburn. He kept it. He bound up the worst of Wyatt's wounds and his own. He stayed awake, and when Vik and Yuri's ship circled over their position, he was alert enough to reply to their net-send, direct them down to his position. He was still conscious when Wyatt stirred in the suborbital, and woke to Yuri holding her, worry on his face.

"We crashed?" she mumbled.

"You were shot down," Yuri said. "But we came back for you."

She smiled blearily. "I knew you would. I love you."

Tom saw Yuri's face transform with startled delight, and even through the grief in his heart, the pain all over his body, he could close his eyes knowing some things were right with the world.

He spent three weeks laid up in the Pentagonal Spire's infirmary, and Wyatt far longer. The world transformed.

With the silent war Vengerov had waged against the rest of humanity in the open, and the neural processors all public, every other secret began to hemorrhage into the public domain. Everyone learned of the way the Combatants of both sides united to destroy Vengerov's fleet of automated machines. Everyone learned the intimate details of the computers that had been sneaked into their heads.

By the time Tom got out of the infirmary, the worldwide backlash was in full swing, crashing down like a tsunami on the heads of the old elite. He saw evidence of it firsthand when he did something he'd dreaded and returned to Manhattan.

The security guards who'd once protected the most expensive apartment buildings had all abandoned them. Windows were shattered, fearful eyes peeking out, watching for restive crowds and vandals.

All of the repressed hostility toward the rest of the ruling class boiled up and consumed the world. People began compiling databases of information, lists of names, faces, and the crimes and misdeeds attached to them. They sent them to one another, translated into every language, uncensored by any governing body.

Thanks to the neural processors, the predators of the old world had become the victims. Coalition executives were recognized on sight everywhere they went, even the men who'd paid good money for privacy over the years, who'd pulled strings only from behind the scenes.

No one would sell them anything; their money was worthless. No one would guard their houses. People boycotted giving them the aid and comfort and assistance that came from an entire society of human beings. Tom heard stories of paramedics leaving them on the streets when they bled and mechanics sabotaging their cars, fire-fighters allowing their buildings to burn.

They were exiles amid the society they'd tried to subjugate.

When Tom entered his mom's apartment, there was no power servicing it; someone must've seen that it was a residence of Dalton Prestwick, the CEO of Dominion Agra guilty of aiding and abetting the spread of the nanomachines. It was likely every electrician he'd called had refused to come and restore it. Maybe someone had even deliberately cut it off.

Tom's mother sat in the dark, facing toward the window. Far below her, the street crawled with cars, with human beings, with a world that had gone on, one that kept marching forward.

"Mom."

She looked back at him, that blankness in her eyes, nothing animating her but that neural processor regulating the chemical processes in her brain. "Hello," the machine in her head said to him, in perfect diction. "Thomas. My son. Why are you here?"

Tom drew a shaky breath, searching her for any sign of the woman from his memories. They were so distant to him, that pretty, laughing girl who'd become a parent too young, who'd had so little time left to her.

"I'm here to set you free."

She watched without interest as he drew the neural wire, and then he brushed aside her blond hair to click it into her brain stem access port. And then he clicked the other end into his own.

Her blue eyes stayed fixed on him, blinking every fifteen seconds, as Tom interfaced with her processor, connecting with her mind, searching for something human there. But no emotion registered. No reaction. Tom felt a great pang of regret, and with a flicker of his thoughts, he shut her processor off.

He caught her before she fell, and for a few heartbeats, there was no computer working in her head, and there was only whatever remained of his mother in there, her eyes clouded, staring into his as he carefully moved her back into her chair.

"I loved you, I remember," Tom told her, thinking of that girl again. "I think you loved me. I'm sorry I didn't realize that before. And I'm sorry I couldn't do this sooner. I was afraid."

For a moment more, she gazed at him, and then her eyes grew murky, the breath halting, whatever animating force that computer had forced into her neural tissue, finally releasing the last of its grip over a person who'd been destroyed long before.

He laid her out gently and closed her eyes.

A voice reached him from the depths of the apartment. "What have you done?"

Tom didn't turn to look at Dalton. "What I should have done a long time ago. She was a person once. She isn't yours."

He turned and watched Dalton sag onto the floor, his eyes swimming with tears. "But I loved her. I've never loved anyone but her."

Tom stared down at him, thinking of what Dalton had loved. A woman who said whatever he programmed her to say, who did whatever he programmed her to do. It wasn't love, not really. It was the same way Vengerov had regarded his creation, Vanya. It was a sense of possession. It was narcissism.

But Tom felt a curious emptiness where he'd once hated Dalton. "I know you think that."

Dalton rubbed his forehead. "I don't know what to do without her. I have nowhere to go. My wife left with the kids because the protesters wouldn't leave us be . . . People won't even give me the slightest courtesy on the streets. I had the neural processor before any of them. I had no choice!"

"Big shocker for you, wasn't it?" Tom said dryly. "You were every bit a disposable puppet to Joseph Vengerov as the rest of us."

"People hiss at me on the street. Someone threw a bottle at my head. There were cops just standing there, pretending they hadn't seen anything! I went to the hospital, but no one would treat me! The doctors and nurses walked past me like

I was invisible. I tried hiring security, but they charged me everything I had, and then they disappeared, and every time I try to call my lawyer, his receptionist drops my calls . . . Tom, you're not cruel. The public sees you and your friends as heroes . . . Please, Tom, I've taken care of your mother. I've loved her. Whatever you think of me, there has to be something I can do, somewhere I can go."

Tom considered him. "I know somewhere you can go." Dalton followed him from the apartment, simpering with gratitude, trying to figure out what Tom had in mind. Tom grabbed them a taxi. Dalton hid his face so the man wouldn't recognize him. He stopped thanking Tom when the taxi stopped at the address Tom had given—of a police station.

"What is this?"

"You want somewhere to go," Tom said. "This is somewhere to go."

Dalton goggled at him. He'd obviously expected Tom to get him on an airplane or do something to smuggle him out of the country. Like that would make a difference now.

"Turn yourself in," Tom said. "Confess to everything you did at Dominion Agra. Start with the nanomachines, maybe the way you robbed and exploited people with less power than you, and go into detail about all the bribery and corruption of public officials. Tell them all of it."

"I'm not going to prison!"

"Dalton," Tom said, leaning forward, "anywhere you go, people are going to recognize you. Some will abuse you, and most will let them. No one will help you. This isn't your world anymore."

"I know what they want," Dalton said hysterically. "Those people out there want to steal everything I have! They're jealous because I was successful and they weren't!"

"No," Tom said flatly. "They're not jealous. They never have been. Most of those people don't care about your wealth, and they don't want to steal it from you. If you'd earned it with some new idea or lots of hard work, not through stealing, bribery, and sucking up to powerful people, they'd actually admire you for your success. All they want is what they've always wanted, what they've been denied their whole lives—fairness."

"It's not that simple."

"Yes, it is. They want you to face the same consequences for your actions that they've faced for theirs. If you turn yourself in, you'll get a trial, you'll probably spend some time in prison, but you know what? People will be satisfied. You may even be able to come right out and live in society again afterward." Tom shrugged. "Or you can walk away and take your chances on the streets, but you're going to face justice in one form or another. It's really your choice about whether you agree to play by the same rules the rest of us do, or whether you run into an angry mob somewhere."

"But . . . but . . ." Dalton sputtered.

"We're done," Tom said. "Get out of the car or I'll tell the driver who you are. Whatever you do from here, it's not my problem."

And when Dalton stepped out, Tom yanked the door shut and left him to his fate. It wasn't his concern what happened to Dalton Prestwick.

Tom knew it was the last time he'd ever see him.

* * *

410

THE MILITARY WAS shocked to learn Tom had been alive since his disappearance over the Christmas vacation a year and a half before.

The public hearings were beginning, the world's attempt to make sense over what had happened with Joseph Vengerov, the nanomachines, the Pentagonal Spire. The investigators heard enough from Tom's friends to know he was connected with Joseph Vengerov's actions somehow, so he found himself at the center of a whirlwind he wasn't ready for. He couldn't talk about it, explain it, and certainly couldn't stand to expose all his memories with a census device.

He wasn't officially arrested, but Tom didn't know a better term for it. The first soldiers who came to debrief him were frustrated. The next were threatening. Tom descended into a silence that was first mulish and stubborn, and then suddenly a silence he couldn't break even if he tried as his sense of confinement set in.

For a short while, the sense of total detachment from the world threatened Tom again. Time began to stretch onward without end, days lost all coherence, all meaning. This time his father didn't come, nor did Blackburn. Because Blackburn was dead. It made Tom wince to think of it.

But then one day the door to his cell opened and it was Olivia Ossare who came in.

"Tom, I've secured an assignment as your caseworker." Her voice floated to him.

He stared at her dumbly, knowing her.

"I was so glad to find out you're okay," she said softly. "Do you feel like talking to me?"

He still couldn't manage a word.

She smiled. "That's okay. We'll just sit here, then."

It took several visits until Tom got his head on straight again, until he felt human enough to really give voice to the questions nagging at him. "Am I in trouble?"

"I think there are questions you'll need to answer. But later."

"Are my friends okay?"

"They're fine. They're very busy," Olivia said calmly. "There's been an onslaught of hearings."

"Am I going to have to do that?"

"Not until you're feeling better."

But he began to feel better quite rapidly, because the interrogators didn't return, and Olivia asked for his permission to share information selectively so they wouldn't have to. Tom agreed. He could talk to her. He kept talking to her.

Within a few months, he did end up testifying before the interim congress, filled with brand-new public representatives his neural processor didn't identify. They were all replacements; the people who formerly occupied their seats were rotting in prison now. He wasn't asked about his time with Vengerov. Somehow, Olivia Ossare and General Marsh had managed to get that classified as confidential medical history, off the record. Instead, he was a witness to testify in absentia against Joseph Vengerov.

Tom could do that.

His friends were all waiting for him when he was done, and they surrounded him like a phalanx as they stepped out of the Capitol together. Cameras flashed about them. For a moment, Tom felt utterly overwhelmed, moving down into the crunch

412

of the crowd, the scrutiny seeming to press in on all sides of him, people calling his name, shouting out questions—and then he spotted a familiar shock of orange hair in the crowd and jerked to a halt.

So did Vik. He bellowed a laugh.

"Beamer?" Vik shouted. "Stephen Beamer!"

"HEY!" Beamer yelled back, waving his arms.

Tom forgot all his unease, surprise and joy washing over him. He and Vik rushed over to their old friend from plebe year.

Beamer didn't remember a lot of his time at the Pentagonal Spire, because most of his memories of it had been removed with his Vigilant-grade processor. But he knew their faces, even if not their names. Beamer had left the Pentagonal Spire early on partly because he didn't like the idea of a computer in his head, partly because he missed his girlfriend.

He'd ended up with a computer in his head anyway.

"And my girlfriend dumped me two weeks after I got home," Beamer admitted later when they all sat in a restaurant, catching up.

None of them reacted for a long moment, uncertain how to take that. Only Vik's lips twitched. Then Beamer started chuckling, and it was okay. They busted up laughing until there were tears in their eyes.

Later when Beamer and his new girlfriend parted ways with them, the four of them lingered in the restaurant. There was no curfew now that the Intrasolar Combatant program was being decommissioned, and the Spire was a virtual ghost town as the new government debated how to use the resources previously dedicated to the war effort. Tom looked around and saw that they were alone, then admitted something to his friends.

"So I'm in . . ." Heat flushed his cheeks, but he felt like they should know. "I'm in therapy. The military's making me do it five times a week. Apparently if I don't do it, I don't get my stipend for these last few years for, uh, breach of contract or something."

Silence followed. Tom looked from face to face, feeling awkward.

Then, "Wait," Vik said, "are we not supposed to know this?"

Tom threw him a startled glance. "You already knew?"

"Thomas, you were being imprisoned for over a year," Yuri pointed out. "It is only reasonable you would face more extensive evaluation than most."

"Yeah," Wyatt spoke up. "What do you think I've been doing ever since I stopped talking for three months? It's standard procedure."

"But we were assigned to see Olivia right after Yuri's accident," Tom pointed out. "Then it ended."

"For you, not me," Wyatt exclaimed. "I never received orders to stop counseling."

"So it's not just me," Tom said wonderingly.

"Just you?" Vik laughed. "Please don't forget the brown-skinned guy who set off a nuke under Obsidian Corp." He jabbed a finger at his own chest. "There are some people very nervous about me who want to be very sure I'm completely sane."

They all looked at Yuri.

He blinked, then smiled. "I received a preliminary evaluation, along with everyone else."

He very tactfully omitted his real reply: he'd obviously been deemed the sanest of them, and not given mandatory therapy.

"So we're all crazy but Yuri," Tom concluded.

"Basically," Wyatt agreed.

Yuri rested a hand on his shoulder. "And if you think about it, Thomas, this is the way it always has been."

It was. Tom started laughing, a great weight sliding off his chest. In that moment, surrounded by his friends, the Senate hearings behind him, the future wide open ahead of him, he suddenly realized things were going to be okay.

CHAPTER THIRTY-TWO

IN THE MONTHS that followed, the world changed even more as people began trying their hands at programming their neural processors. Self-programming was no longer illegal, and in fact the ability to code and manipulate one's neural processor became a software requirement in the machines. Everyone learned with a download how to self-program.

Knowledge began to disseminate everywhere. It wasn't like the downloads Tom and his friends had received every day in the Spire, because these were all optional, all in public databases for people who were interested in learning new languages, new skills. The effect was incredible. People who'd never learned to read, who'd never been educated, could now make up for years of missed schooling with a few downloads.

New breakthroughs followed. Some inventions were minor things, like upgrades to the neural processors that closed the functionality gap between the Austere and the Vigilant grades, but others were major, like cold fusion, a working antigravity platform, a superior ionic engine that could propel a ship from Earth to Mars in four days.

People were beginning to call this age "the singularity," a time when infinite technological progress was finally possible. All the latent genius of humanity had been unlocked and was finally being used, with none of the old, entrenched power players in a position to halt it to preserve the status quo.

In the bright, shining new world, Tom finally grew ready to face something of the old one. He'd talked to Olivia Ossare about it; he felt ready.

At least, he had until a few minutes ago. Now he sat in the bar, words clogged in his throat. His father spoke first.

"You look familiar."

Tom glanced over at the man a few seats away from him, pretending he hadn't been working up to talking to him for a good hour now.

Neil peered at him, rubbing his chin. "Were you on the news?"

"Um, yeah, I was." Tom wasn't sure whether to feel disappointed or not.

Neil flashed a grin, and waved for the bartender to serve Tom a soda.

"I knew I recognized you." Neil moved over to the stool next to his. "You and a buncha other Intrasolar trainees, you all took down Obsidian Corp. together, huh?" He laughed and clinked his glass with Tom's as soon as the bartender set it down. "Way to go there."

Tom raised his glass, a lump in his throat. He'd been following Neil all day. His dad had a job now. He'd apparently programmed himself something that moderated his alcohol use as well. Tom had come here to give him his memory back, to undo what Vengerov had done, but something always stopped him. The memory of Dalton's words about how Tom'd ruined his dad's life . . . or maybe it was just the expression on Neil's face, the way he looked so young. Happy.

"What are you doing next?" Neil asked him. "I hear they're converting all you guys to some sort of international force . . ."

"A galactic legion," Tom said. "That's the plan."

First, he'd seen Elliot all over TV, helping to advocate for the idea: converting all the ships dedicated to the war effort into exploratory vehicles. Soon, the idea spread like fire, a great symbol of humanity stepping forward into the future, uniting across the bounds of country: a project funded and participated in by nations across the world, dedicated to exploring the solar system and beyond, and sending people into space again. Things happened faster now in the age of the singularity. The training facility had been set up in San Francisco. General Marsh had been chosen to head the venture. The first batch of astronauts had been drawn from many of the Intrasolar cadets, with no regard for country.

As a symbolic gesture, special priority was given to those cadets who'd participated in the effort to liberate the world from Joseph Vengerov. That's how Vik, Yaolan, Yuri, and even Tom joined up. For the first time, Tom lived not only in the same hemisphere as Medusa—as Yaolan—he lived a thirty-second walk down a hallway from her.

As for Wyatt . . .

She had the offer on the table, but she'd been elusive of late. Tom wasn't sure what Wyatt was up to, but whenever he saw her, she looked to be brimming with excitement, ready to burst with something she couldn't share with him. He knew she had a whole batch of new colleagues somewhere she'd been working with who were seriously brainy types like her. Aeronautical engineers, astrophysicists. She could only tell them she was working on something very important. Whatever it was, Tom was glad she'd found it. It was the first thing she'd really been excited about since Blackburn died.

Tom found it hard now to look at his dad's friendly, oblivious face. His gaze instead found the screen overhead, where an old clip of Joseph Vengerov was being discussed. The reporters were recounting his family history: divorced parents; a younger brother, Ivan, who was rumored to be profoundly disabled. It had hit Tom like a fist when he first learned of the existence of a real Ivan, an actual younger brother to Joseph who'd died years ago. He tried to avoid anything Vengerov related now.

But sometimes it was unavoidable. Today, the program discussed the way the tragic deaths of Ivan and their father, Alexei, resulted in young Joseph inheriting a majority share of LM Lymer Fleet and installing himself as CEO. Speculation now arose as to the suspicious nature of those deaths. Had those possible homicides been an early indication of what was to come? It was presented sensationally, like entertainment. Vengerov had morphed into a figure of morbid fascination for the rest of the world.

Tom looked away. He couldn't even stand to see him. He still felt such revulsion and loathing toward Vengerov, the emotions seemed to poison him.

"I knew that bastard years ago," Neil remarked, gazing up at the screen.

Tom cast him a startled glance, wondering what he still remembered about Vengerov.

"He hired me once," Neil said. "He couldn't win against any decent poker player because you could see his mind working it over, running probabilities and calculations . . . He always picked the most mathematically logical solution. Made him predictable. That's why he hired me, trying to figure out what he was doing so wrong. But that wasn't really his problem. He simply didn't know how to act like a human. He wasn't fooling anyone. It's my fault he learned to pass. I thought I was teaching the guy to bluff, not to act so stiff and calculating when playing the game, but really, I was teaching him to be a human being."

Tom stared up at Vengerov's face on the screen, a dark feeling inside him. Vengerov had disappeared after his defeat. No one had found him. He was the most wanted fugitive in the world now, but somehow, he'd totally evaded detection.

"I didn't know what was wrong with him then, but he makes sense to me now," Neil said. "As long as I think of him as a computer, not a person, a machine trying to act like the rest of us. That's why he did all this, that's my theory. He looked at the way our society works and saw who was in charge, who ran it all. If we'd been ruled by Gandhis, that computer in his head would've calculated the most efficient way to spread peace. But we were ruled by sociopaths—so that's what he learned to be. He became the best greedy, power-hungry sociopath of them all. That's why he wasn't content with all the power he had, all the wealth. He wanted the entire world and everyone in it."

Tom's gut churned. He didn't even want to think about

Vengerov, much less talk about him with his dad. He shoved up to his feet, realizing this had all been a bad idea. He couldn't do this. He simply could not.

Then Neil grabbed his arm, his brow furrowed. "Are you positive I don't know you, buddy?"

A great, crushing love swept over Tom. Neil had given up so much for him. He owed it to his dad to set him free, too.

"Yeah," Tom said thickly. "I'm sure."

He almost made it out of the bar that way. Almost. Because when he found Yaolan and whispered to her that he wanted to leave, she sighed, hopped down from her bar stool, and marched toward Neil. "You're being ridiculous, Tom."

Then she accessed the local server and deployed the program herself.

"Hey—" Tom objected.

"This is why you brought me along, isn't it? To make sure you followed through?"

"That wasn't my plan, no!"

"Then you're lucky you have me around." She rose to her tiptoes and kissed him. "Go sit with your father. I'll be outside waiting for you to realize I was right."

Tom knew so much about Yaolan now that he didn't before, like the way her entire school had collapsed during an earthquake when she was a child. The way she'd clawed out of the burning debris; the way she'd spent years in and out of hospitals, recovering from reconstructive surgeries, and the way she'd flatly refused to fight as a Combatant if the Chinese military insisted on subjecting her to another surgery to fix her scarred face. She'd been determined and fearless enough

421

to hold her ground for years. She was small, clever, and bossy. He found her unbelievably attractive, even if they annoyed each other sometimes.

And so now, Tom found himself with the choice out of his hands, standing there before his dad, a mixture of emotions inside him. He watched the program work its magic, the burden of years falling back over his dad's face, Neil's expression transforming from that light, carefree one to something more solemn. Then Neil found his feet, seizing Tom's shoulders, looking him over.

"You were just going to leave me like that?" Neil said.

Tom averted his gaze. "Yeah."

"Tommy, for God's sakes, why?"

"Because." Tom couldn't look at him. "I know the truth, Dad. I know everything."

"You know."

Tom met his eyes. "Yeah, I know about Mom. I know you never wanted this. Dalton told me everything."

His dad bowed his head. He sank down onto a chair, and Tom stood there, watching him numbly.

"You don't have to—" The words caught in his throat, and Tom realized suddenly he hadn't just been protecting his dad. It hurt him so much to see his worst suspicions confirmed, to realize how much of a burden he was on his only family.

But Neil caught his arm when he instinctively tried to pull away from him. He grabbed Tom's other arm, too, and pulled him closer.

"I made a terrible mistake once, Tom," Neil told him. "There are the right people and the wrong people to have kids, and your mom and I were the wrong people. I didn't realize how wrong we were until it was too late."

"When she started having problems."

"Before that, I thought I had the whole world in my palm. I could read *anyone*. But I didn't see it coming with her. She was like . . . like standing in the eye of a hurricane, Tommy. There was something mesmerizing about her when it was calm, but when she changed direction, God help you."

Tom stared at him. For the first time ever, his dad began to make sense to him.

"She left with you one day. There was no warning, nothing. You two disappeared one night while I was out." Neil searched his face. "I emptied my bank account trying to track her down, but it was the police who found her—when she set her father's house on fire, and half her neighborhood besides. You could've both been killed. She didn't even understand what she'd done afterward."

Tom found himself looking inward, suddenly breathless, remembering those memories Blackburn pulled out of his head with the census device. Remembering seeing his mother, giddy with excitement as they walked together down some dark street. The fire he'd seen in the moments before he'd shorted the census device out. Fire. It hadn't been from the census device. It had been something from his early memories.

"I couldn't take it anymore," Neil whispered. "Vengerov was right there on hand, this respectable business guy with a whole company in his control, and he said they could take her off my hands, fix her up. He said they had new procedures, the experimental ones that could . . . I believed him. I knew I couldn't take care of you myself, and he was going to find you a nice home, he said. For a short while I gave in to this idea I could turn back the clock, just reverse everything, get rid of all my responsibilities. That was my other mistake. I didn't know what he would do to her. To *you*. If I'd known . . . And the second I saw what his company had done to her, I went to get you back. I would've torn this whole world apart if they'd hurt you. You have to know that."

"You never told me any of this."

"After that surgery Vengerov had done to your brain, you didn't seem to remember her. Not anything. I couldn't change what happened. I thought it was better not to tell you right away. And the older you got, the harder it became to tell you. You didn't have your mother because of me. Because of what I did. I wasn't sure you'd forgive me, Tommy."

"You seemed happier without me," Tom muttered.

"Worrying about you has put some lines on my face, but I wouldn't trade you. Not for anything. If you hate me, I don't blame you, Tommy. I've hated myself for a long time."

"I don't hate you. It's just . . ."

"Just what?"

"Mom's dead."

Neil caught his breath.

"I turned off her neural processor." His voice was the barest whisper. "I'm sorry."

Neil stared at him for a long moment. "That wasn't your mother. If there'd been anything left of her, any trace, do you really think—" His voice broke. "If there'd been the slightest bit of your mother left in that shell, I wouldn't have let them keep her. If you turned off that machine in her head, you did the right thing for her. One of us did the right thing for her, thank God."

Then his father reached forward and drew him into his arms, and for a moment Tom stiffened, feeling a hand cup the back of his neck. Then he relaxed, the ghosts of the past receding.

"I'm sorry, Tommy. We'll go home, and then I'll do what I should've done years ago and tell you all about your mom. The person she really was on the best days. The woman I loved. And she loved you. She loved you so much . . . Also I've gotta meet your little girlfriend."

Tom pulled back, feeling a flash of pride at the reminder that he was with Yaolan now. Then he realized something.

"Wait," he blurted. "What do you mean, we'll go 'home'?"

```
1 0 0 1 1 1 1 1 1 1 1 0 0 1 1 1 0 1 0 1 1 0 0 0 0 0 0 0 1 0 0 1 1 1 1 0 0 0
0 1 1 0 1 1 0 1 1 1 0 0 1 1 1 0 0 0 0 0 0 0 1 0 1 1 0 1 0 0 1 0 0 1 1
1 0 0 0 0 1 1 1 1 0 0 1 0 0 1 0 1 1 1 0 0 1 1 1 0 1 1 0 0 1 0 1 0 1 1 0 1 1
1 0 1 0 0 0 1 1 0 1 1 0 0 0 0 1 1 0 1 0 0 1 1 0 0 0 1 0 1 1 1 1 0 0 0 0 1 1
1 0 0 1 1 0 0 1 0 0 0 0 0 1 0 1 1 1 0 1 1 0 1 0 0 0 0 0 0 0 1 0 1 1 0 1 1 1
0 0 1 1 0 0 0 0 0 1 1 1 0 1 1 0 1 0 1 0 1 0 0 0 0 0 1 0 0 1 1 1 0 0 0 0 0
1 1 0 0 1 0 1 0 1 1 1 0 1 1 1 0 1 0 1 0 1 1 1 1 0 1 0 1 1 0 1 1 0 0 0 0 0
0 1 1 1 1 1 1 0 1 1 0 0 0 0 1 1 1 0 1 1 0 1 1 1 0 1 1 1 0 0 0 1 0 1 0
1 0 1 1 0 0 1 0 1 0 0 1 0 0 0 1 0 0 1 0 1 0 0 1 0 1 0 0 0 0 1 0 0 1 0 1 0 1 0
0 0 1 0 0 1 0 1 1 0 0 1 0 0 1 1 0 1 0 1 0 1 1 0 0 0 0 1 0 1 1 0 1 0 1 0
0 0 0 0 0 1 1 1 1 0 1 1 0 0 1 0 0 1 1 0 1 1 0 0 0 0 0 1 0 0 0 0 1 0 0 0 1 0 0
1 0 1 0 0 1 0 0 1 0 0 0 1 1 1 0 1 1 0 0 1 0 0 1 1 0 0 1 1 0 0 0 0 1 0 0 0
0 0 1 1 1 1 0 1 1 0 1 0 0 0 1 0 0 1 1 1 0 0 0 0 1 0 1 1 1 1 0 0 0 0 1 0
1 0 1 1 1 1 0 0 0 0 0 1 0 1 1 0 1 0 0 0 0 0 0 0 1 0 0 0 1 1 1 1 0 0 1 1 1 0
1 1 1 0 0 0 1 1 1 0 0 1 1 1 0 0 0 0 1 1 0 0 1 0 0 1 0 1 0 1 1 1 1 1 0 0 1
0 0 0 1 1 1 1 0 0 1 0 1 1 1 1 0 0 1 0 1 1 0 1 1 0 1 1 1 1 1 0 0 1 0 0 1
0 0 1 0 1 0 0 0 1 0 0 0 1 1 1 0 1 0 1 0 1
0 0 1 1 0 1 1 1 1 1 1 1 1 0 0 1 1 1 1 0 0
1 1 1 1 1 1 0 0 1 1 0 0 1 0 0 0 0 1 1 1 1 0 0
1 0 0 1 1 0 0 0 1 1 1 1 1 0 1 0 0 0 0 0 0 1 0 0 1 0 0 1 0 0 1 0 1 1 0 1 0 0
```

CHAPTER THIRTY-THREE

NEIL'S NEW REGULAR job was supervising a local casino floor, watching for people using their new neural processors to cheat.

"So I was cutting back on drinking, and I landed this job, but I had this hole in my life I couldn't seem to fill," Neil remarked, showing Tom the two-bedroom condo he'd rented. "Something seemed to be missing. Now I know what it was."

"Your own place."

"No." Neil ruffled a hand through Tom's hair. "You know what I didn't have."

Later, Tom lay sprawled out in his own bed, in his own room, in his own family's apartment for the first time in his life, with his own girlfriend right next to him, her chin resting on his shoulder. "And your father has no issues with me sleeping here?"

"I told you, my dad's pretty laid-back about everything. Believe it or not"—Tom raised his eyebrows at her—"I was kind of more responsible than he was."

"You're right: that's very difficult to believe," Yaolan teased.

"When we visit my family, I assure you that you're going to be sleeping in the location most distant from me."

"As long as they're heavy sleepers, I can work with that," Tom said, grinning.

She drifted off curled up against him, and for a long time he just watched her. He'd realized he loved her that day in space, and even though she'd never said the words back to him, his feelings had never changed.

Not even, well, after . . . after getting away from Vengerov.

Tom tried to avoid thinking of Joseph Vengerov, because even now the memories were like a spear stabbing into him. He stared up into the darkness, thinking of the oligarch still at large somewhere out there, eluding the entire world and even the most advanced technology combing continents for him.

Unwittingly, his father's words drifted back into his mind: *I think of him as a computer, not a person, a machine trying to act like the rest of us.*

And then suddenly, Tom felt like he'd been struck.

It all came rushing back to him, those memories came back to him, the ones Vengerov gave him to create the other identity, to create Vanya.

All of the memories featured Vanya . . . *Ivan* by himself, excluded, an outcast unable to understand anything, unable to communicate anything, his only advocate his older brother, Joseph, who seemed some golden god in a world of chaos. Tom had taken for granted that Vanya's memories were fakes, manipulations, because they all featured Vanya's big brother, Joseph, a genuinely decent guy. He thought Vengerov made them just for him.

Even Olivia believed Vengerov invented Vanya's memories purely to manipulate Tom and cultivate a sense of "learned helplessness" that would fool Tom into thinking he'd always been inept, an outcast . . . and dependent on Joseph Vengerov.

But Ivan was real. Ivan had been real. Maybe those memories were really Ivan's genuine memories, too.

Cold sweat broke out over Tom's skin. No. Ivan may have been real, but Ivan was dead. How would Vengerov have gotten Ivan's memories to give to Tom?

Then it came to him.

Why would *Joseph* Vengerov, the perfect son, get the very first neural processor in his head? Why would Alexei Vengerov risk that with the son who had no need of it?

Tom's head spun with the answer.

Because he didn't. He didn't.

Ivan Vengerov really had been excluded, the shame of his father but unable to understand why, unable to grasp what he'd done wrong or what was so different about him in a world that made no sense to him.

Until a machine was installed in his head.

Ivan Vengerov got the first neural processor. Not Joseph. *Ivan.*

Tom imagined Vanya with a neural processor. He imagined the sort of a person Vanya had become after being given a superhuman intellect. Vanya must have understood the world for the first time, and he did so with the cold precision of a machine. He looked around at the way people treated him and saw the scorn and cruelty and ostracism in his life, all due to his disability. Vanya must have taken for granted that being human meant being pitiless to those weaker than him.

Neil had figured that out, too. Vengerov's neural processor

calculated exactly how he could become the best. And he hadn't started to become the best by aiming to be the world's most powerful CEO, he'd begun by becoming the perfect son in his family.

He'd become Joseph Vengerov.

Ivan hadn't died. *Joseph* had.

The person Tom knew as Joseph Vengerov was really Ivan, the actual, real-life Vanya with the computer in his head. That's where the memories came from. They were all real. All of them. Vengerov knew exactly what memories to give Tom to make him feel helpless because he'd lived through them himself.

And with that understanding, Tom grew certain to his very bones he knew exactly where Vengerov had hidden himself. He lay there paralyzed with the knowledge for a long moment, Yaolan sleeping against his chest, and one clear thought penetrated his mind.

He had to talk to Vik.

"TOM?" VIK SAID sleepily, peering at him in the conferencer, his dark hair tousled. He straightened instantly, growing more alert at something he saw on Tom's face. "Hey, Tom, what is it? What's wrong?"

Tom realized he was shaking all over. "Doctor. I know where he is. I know."

"You do?"

"I'm sure of it."

"What do you want to do?"

Tom scraped his hands through his hair. "I have to handle it. I have to do it myself."

429

"Then we'll go together." And Tom was so thankful that Vik didn't call it "glorious revenge." There was nothing glorious about it this time around. It simply had to be done.

VANYA'S FAMILY USED to stay at a dacha, a cottage in the Russian countryside far removed from civilization. It wasn't listed as an official family property or an Obsidian Corp. property. It was far out enough that there was no internet there, no technology to speak of.

It was one of the only ways Vengerov could have disappeared in the modern world.

And Tom remembered the fondness Vanya had for it. Ivan was given a pet rabbit there.

Certainly, Vengerov wasn't expecting him when he strode right through the front door. "Hi, Ivan."

Vengerov looked up from where he was flipping through old blueprints, staring at him like he was a ghost. Tom shifted subtly so Vengerov could see the stun gun in his hand. He had no intention of killing him. After all, Vengerov had no machines guarding him here, no lackeys, nothing even remotely accessible to a network. He was just one man.

And Tom and Vik were two.

Vengerov lurched to his feet and backed toward the rear door, but when it slid open, Vik was outside, smiling blandly.

"How's it going?" he said, blocking his escape. "I help Tom on all his vengeance crusades."

"He's a good friend that way," Tom said.

Vengerov considered the situation, then looked at Tom and raised his hands. No panic was on his face, just a cool sort of speculation. "Bravo, Mr. Raines. You located me. Are you here to kill me?"

"Actually, no," Tom said flatly. "I'm taking you into custody so you can stand trial. If you fight me, then I'll change my mind, Ivan."

Vengerov's gaze sharpened. "Why do you keep calling me that?"

"The same reason I knew where you'd be." Tom glanced around the cottage in a leisurely manner, trying to hide how disconcerting it was, recognizing it from Vanya's memories. The entire world had been combing the various inactive ships in space, searching for Vengerov's hidden spot in orbit. No one had considered the possibility he'd simply cut off all contact with technology or the internet and concealed himself on Earth.

"You didn't create Vanya's memories just to screw with my head," Tom said thoughtfully. "They already existed. They were yours. Your memories. You're Ivan. And because I had your memories, I knew about this great hideout. So I guess I wanted to say thanks, Ivan. You led me right to you. Now it's time to go."

Vengerov didn't fight. Tom had realized a long time ago that Vengerov had machines to do battle for him and thousands of underlings. He never did anything himself, not if the computer in his head calculated there was any possibility he could come to physical harm. Out here, in the middle of nowhere, away from the prying electronic eyes that could give him away to a world searching for him, Vengerov had no allies. His optimal course of action was to cooperate, and bide his time until he had a sure route of escape. Tom knew that.

So he cooperated. Vengerov's steps faltered at the sight of one of his own suborbitals, jury-rigged by Tom and Vik. They locked him in the back cabin, and then Vik launched them into space.

"You do realize, Mr. Raines," Vengerov's voice floated over the speaker, "if I am taken into custody, I'll have to show them my memories with a census device of all your time with me."

Tom tensed up. "So? I don't care."

"You seemed to care very much once upon a time," Vengerov said, sounding almost amused. "I seem to recall you begging me not to share your experience with your friends."

Vik slapped the intercom, muted it. "You don't need to listen to him."

"You don't need to do that," Tom said, staring at the console before him.

"Forget him. We got the bastard. That's what matters."

Tom looked at Vik, his best friend, his unconditional support. He finally told him the truth. "You know, he didn't reprogram me. I know I said that, but he didn't. Blackburn locked him out of my processor."

There was a long silence. Then Vik said, "I know."

Tom caught his breath. So Vik had realized it all along. Blackburn hadn't lied to them. His best friend had pretended not to know he'd been totally broken to make it easier on him. A hand seemed to catch his throat. Strange that Vengerov had broken him down by threatening to show his friends all those shameful weaknesses he'd tried to hide from them for so long . . . but it hadn't been necessary. He'd never needed to hide from them. Vik accepted even the worst of him.

And Tom realized suddenly that nothing Vengerov ever said again would hold any power over him.

At that moment, there was movement on the screen showing Vengerov. Vik pointed to it. Tom nodded. There were two camera feeds from the aft cabin. Vengerov had disabled the one he knew about. Tom and Vik exchanged a significant glance, knowing what was about to happen.

Vengerov was making his choice: whether or not he would undergo a fair trial. They watched him find the space suit, and secure it on his body. Vengerov flashed a look at the door separating him from their cockpit, and then with the space suit in place, he moved to the hatch. His hand began to twist it open.

Then as Tom and Vik watched, he shoved open the hatch and the current of air blew him into space. Naturally, Vengerov had to intend to use the space suit's propulsion system to seek shelter on one of his yet-undiscovered orbiting vessels.

He didn't know Tom and Vik had removed the propulsion unit.

Tom gave Vengerov just enough time to realize he wasn't in control of his momentum and enough time to try activating his transmitter—and find out it had also been removed from the suit. He couldn't even send a message with net-send on his neural processor: there was a jammer sewn right into his suit. If he tried to dig it out, the suit would rupture.

Tom flipped on the one-way speakers that he knew would pipe into Vengerov's helmet and said, "Hi, Ivan. I guess you'll have noticed by now that you have absolutely no control over your space suit and you're drifting aimlessly. I wanted to give

433

you a decision. Just like the decisions you gave me. You could go and face trial, or you could decide not to go to trial. You've obviously decided not to."

Vik wheeled them about so that directly in front of them their sensors could pick up the lone space-suited man drifting out against the dark tapestry of stars, Vengerov's momentum sending him floating away from Earth. His back was to the planet. That meant he would never see it again.

"It really is a waste," Tom told Vengerov. "You had the technology to change the world. The neural processors have allowed the singularity to begin. We all could've risen together, but that wasn't enough for you. The only way you felt powerful was to use that tech to stamp the rest of us down. If you'd tried to help humanity, you would've been the greatest person in history, the catalyst who changed the world for the better. People would've revered you. But here you are, just another megalomaniac about to die alone, and people will forget you. But you do have one last choice, Ivan—the same one you gave me. No one is coming to save you. You can float alone in space until your oxygen runs out, or you can take off your helmet."

And with that, Tom cut off the transmission.

Vik's hand was clenched in a fist. "Want to circle around so we can get a good glimpse of the look on his face?" he said darkly. "I'd like to get a nice long look at his expression right now."

Tom felt a surge of affection for his friend. He laid a hand on Vik's shoulder. "No, man. Let's go home."

He didn't need to see the shock, the disbelief, and then the fear on Vengerov's face when he ran calculation after calculation and still found no escape from his situation, when he understood there was no surviving this. That primal fear of death might be the first emotion Vengerov had truly felt since getting his neural processor, but Tom didn't care to relish it. He couldn't help thinking that the man who'd wreaked so much suffering on others had been a twisted outgrowth of the mistreated Vanya.

All he really wanted was for Vengerov to disappear. From his memory, from the world, from the universe. Tom and Vik soared away from that tiny space suit floating into the vast emptiness, drifting, drifting away—traveling a lonely path into the void until it vanished against the distant stars.

Sliding into view ahead of Tom and Vik, where Vengerov would never again see it, Earth stood bright and glorious. Lights glowed all across its surface, human civilization entering into its golden age, the final oligarch receding into oblivion.

1 0 0 1 1 1 1 1 1 1 0 0 1 1 1 0 1 0 1 1 0 0 0 0 0 0 0 1 0 0 1 1 1 1 0 0 0
0 1 1 0 1 1 0 1 1 1 0 0 1 1 1 0 0 0 0 0 0 0 1 0 1 1 0 1 0 0 1 0 0 1 1
1 0 0 0 0 0 1 1 1 1 0 0 1 0 0 1 0 1 1 1 0 0 1 1 1 0 1 1 0 0 1 0 1 1 0 1 1
0 1 0 0 0 1 1 0 1 1 0 0 0 0 1 1 0 1 0 0 1 1 0 0 0 1 0 1 1 1 1 0 0 0 0 1 1
1 0 0 1 1 0 1 0 0 0 0 0 1 0 1 1 1 0 1 1 0 0 0 0 0 0 0 1 0 1 1 0 0 1 1 1 1
0 0 1 1 0 0 0 0 0 1 1 1 0 1 1 0 1 1 1 0 1 0 1 0 0 1 0 0 1 1 1 0 0 0 0 0
1 1 0 0 1 0 1 0 1 1 1 0 1 1 1 0 1 0 1 0 1 1 1 1 0 1 0 1 1 0 1 1 0 0 0 0
0 1 1 1 1 1 1 1 0 1 1 0 0 0 0 1 1 1 0 1 1 0 1 1 1 0 1 1 1 0 0 0 1 0 1 0
1 0 1 1 0 0 1 1 0 1 0 0 1 0 0 0 1 0 1 0 1 0 0 1 0 0 0 0 1 0 0 1 0 1 0 1 0
0 0 1 0 0 1 0 1 1 0 0 1 0 0 1 1 0 1 0 1 0 1 1 1 0 0 0 0 1 0 1 1 0 1 0 1 0
0 0 0 0 0 1 1 1 1 0 1 1 0 0 1 1 0 1 1 0 0 0 0 0 0 1 0 0 0 0 1 0 0 0 1 0 0
1 0 1 0 0 1 1 1 1 0 0 1 1 1 0 1 1 0 0 1 1 0 0 1 1 1 0 0 1 0 0 0 0 1 0 0 0
0 0 1 1 1 1 1 0 1 1 0 1 0 0 0 1 0 0 1 1 1 0 0 0 0 1 0 1 1 1 0 0 0 0 0 0
0 1 1 1 1 0 0 0 0 0 1 0 1 1 0 1 0 0 0 0 0 0 0 1 0 0 0 1 1 1 0 0 1 1 1 0
1 1 1 0 0 0 1 1 1 0 0 1 1 1 0 0 0 0 1 1 0 0 1 0 0 1 0 1 0 1 1 1 1 0 1 1
0 0 0 1 1 1 1 0 0 1 0 1 0 1 1 1 1 0 0 1 0 1 1 0 1 1 0 1 1 1 1 1 0 0 1 0 0 1
0 1 0 1 0 1 0 1 0 0 1 0 0 0 1 0 0 0 0 1 0 0 0 0 1 1 1 0 1 0 1 0 1
0 0 1 1 0 0 1 0 0 0 1 0 1 1 1 1 1 1 1 1 1 1 1 0 0 1 1 1 1 0
1 1 1 1 0 1 1 0 1 0 1 1 0 0 0 1 1 1 0 1 0 0 1 0 0 0 0 0 1 1 1 1 1 0 0
1 0 0 1 1 0 0 0 1 1 1 1 1 1 0 1 1 0 0 0 0 0 0 1 0 0 1 0 0 1 0 1 1 0 1 0 0

EPILOGUE

"**S**ERIOUSLY, HOW ARE you feeling?"

"Vik, I don't care," Tom assured him. "You go first. We're cool."

It had been months since they'd jettisoned Vengerov in space. Today, Tom and Vik were on a ship again on a far more significant mission. Vik flashed Tom a crazy-eyed grin, and then he stepped first through the hatch of their lander, his boots crunching on the crimson sand of the planet Mars.

And in that way, Vikram Ashwan, an Indian astronaut with the Galactic Legion, became the first human being to step foot on another planet.

Vik and Tom had trained for the mission for months, ever since they'd been selected for the mission to become the first humans to walk on Mars. The newest technology made the trip quick, painless, and cheap, and it was only a precursor mission to the big one happening later this year—but the whole world was watching.

Vik went first, and then Tom followed him out of the ship, amazement spreading through him. Now the sky hung scarlet and vivid above them, the iron-red landscape stretching into the distance on all sides.

Vik stood in silent awe. Tom took his first steps and stared down at his boots now officially on Mars. It was the same location his avatar had conquered in that first training simulation for the Intrasolar Forces. Now he was here for real. In person. As some fourteen-year-old kid living out of VR parlors, Tom *never* would have thought it possible.

He started laughing, ecstatic with the realization. "Kapow!" he exclaimed. "I'm on Mars!"

"Argh, Tom, no!" Vik cried, his hands flying up to cup the globe of his helmet.

"What, man?"

Vik scuffled around, kicking up a sheen of red sand, exasperation on his face in the crimson light. "'One small step for a man, one giant leap for mankind.' Remember those words? First thing Neil Armstrong said when he stepped on the moon. First words matter. They are huge and historically significant. Momentous! And we are currently the first human beings on a planet that is not Earth. Our first words are . . ."

"'Kapow, I'm on Mars,'" Tom realized, aghast.

Vik nodded sadly.

"Can we take it back?" Tom whispered.

"This is being broadcast live all over Earth. I don't think we get take backs."

"Sorry," Tom told Vik. Then, suddenly aware of their invisible audience, he called, "Sorry, Earth! Over!"

"While we're being unprofessional," Vik said, turning toward the camera fixed to their rover and giving it a thumbs-up. "Love you, Sveta!"

Tom laughed, thinking of Vik's newest girlfriend and their

fellow Galactic Legion member, Svetlana Moriakova. She'd pretend to be embarrassed, but she'd be pleased by the gesture.

They set about their business, taking some soil samples. Vik planted a small Indian flag amid the hard red rocks. "I annex this planet for India."

Tom knew he was doing it to annoy him, but he still objected, "You can't do that. I'm American. My country gets a share."

"That's not how it works here in India, Tom."

"Fifty-fifty or we fight it out."

"Do we really want to start this brand-new chapter in India's history with Mars's first world war?"

Tom wanted to playfully nudge him, but they couldn't do that in space suits.

Vik flashed him a huge, crazy-eyed grin. "Hey, Doctor."

"What, Doctor?"

"We're on Mars."

"We *are* on Mars."

They couldn't stop grinning at each other.

THE CELEBRATIONS WERE in full swing when they returned to Earth, though the Mars mission had primarily been a test run for new landing technology before the major mission later this year. Wyatt's secret project had come to fruition: an interstellar engine that folded space in front of a ship and expanded it behind to allow faster-than-light travel. She'd been the team member to devise the final equation that led to the functional device. Finally, she was getting a chance to follow through on the goal she'd pledged right before Cruithne hit: she was helping to spread human life beyond Earth.

Naturally, the best of the young astronauts had been selected to fly the first mission, a trip to the Alpha Centauri star system, one believed to have habitable planets. The Mars mission had been Tom and Vik's; the interstellar mission would be Yaolan and Yuri's.

They all gathered together a few days before the interstellar mission, reading some of the news stories covering Tom and Vik's mission to Mars. Tom was a bit embarrassed by the scathing critique of his conduct titled "'Kapow, I'm on Mars': The Case Against Teenage Astronauts," but his friends all found it hilarious so it soon amused Tom, too.

"I had to promise General Marsh I'd come up with better first words than yours," Yaolan said, settling next to Tom, and he felt the usual flicker of surprise whenever he saw her lately. One of the post-singularity stem cell breakthroughs had enabled her skin to regenerate with just a misting spray, applied a few times a week. Yaolan had reluctantly sought the treatment, knowing a PR-friendly appearance would only strengthen her case for getting a spot on the interstellar mission.

Tom had admitted only to Olivia Ossare that he was worried she'd have nothing to do with him once the scarring was gone. He felt like a jerk even admitting that, but he'd been so sure once other guys started noticing Yaolan that she'd split and find someone better.

"That's not about Yaolan, it's about your view of yourself, Tom," Olivia had told him. "You need to give her the benefit of the doubt and trust in her feelings for you."

And she'd been right. Tom's fears had been unfounded. Nothing had changed, even if Yaolan now turned heads for a different reason than before.

439

"So, Yaolan," Vik said from across the table, raising a glass, "getting nervous yet?"

"Never," she vowed.

"I am feeling very apprehensive," Yuri assured Vik, not looking the least bit apprehensive at the knowledge his big mission was next.

Vik told Yaolan, "You've got to promise that if you meet some handsome alien out there, you're going to at least send Tom a message before running off with him."

"If I have time," Yaolan teased. "I'll obviously be busy figuring out how to make sweet love with this new alien lifeform."

"Maybe there will be something in the neural processor about this," Yuri suggested.

"You've updated your processor lately, haven't you?" Wyatt said abruptly, so intent, she was leaning half over the table. "Every time I talk to Tom, he's slacking off on his updates."

"I've got auto update for the software, but as soon as I update the hardware, it's obsolete again," Tom objected.

Wyatt shook her head. "It's called exponential technological progress for a reason. Get with the singularity, Tom."

Yaolan's eyes twinkled. "Wyatt, I wouldn't dream of leaving the solar system with obsolete hardware." She elbowed Tom lightly, because he'd do that. He smiled. "And Yuri would never do it, either."

"Of course Yuri wouldn't," Wyatt said, smiling at him.

Yuri chuckled, marveling at it. "Another solar system." His face was dazzled. "We will open our eyes and see all the stars from another point in the galaxy." He cast his gaze upward, and Tom found his heart fluttering as he looked up, thinking suddenly of how far away that was truly going to be.

He grew aware of the time in his neural processor, and said, "Hey, while we're all here, did you guys want to see the new memorial?"

Vik frowned a little, but Wyatt nodded readily, and Yuri gave a hesitant nod. Tom looked at Yaolan, and even though she'd never had any personal attachment herself, she knew he did. Her hand stole into his. "Let's go."

VIK WAS UNIMPRESSED. "He looks like a mad dictator."

All five of them stared up at the statue of James Blackburn, the ghost in the machine, planted amid the memorials to various late presidents in Washington, DC.

The title of "Ghost in the Machine" no longer belonged to Tom, the ghost who'd blown up the skyboards, nor to Joseph Vengerov, the ghost who'd used the agent of chaos to destroy any opposition to his nanomachines in the halls of power—but to the real one who'd struck the first substantial blows against the oligarchs who used to own the world, the real catalyst who'd changed history, changed the world.

"I do not believe he would approve," Yuri mused. "He would find this ostentatious."

"I like it," Wyatt said. She and Tom exchanged a significant glance.

"What do you think he'd say if we showed him the world now?" Tom wondered, glancing around, seeing the distant ships soaring through the air—actual ships with people inside, not merely drones surveilling them.

Now that the age of oligarchs was over, all the possibilities of the universe lay ahead of them. Sure, there'd be future villains, but the enemies of the singularity age were certain to be nothing like those from the world of old.

"I think he wouldn't believe it," Yaolan ventured. "I wouldn't have believed everything could change so much in so little time."

Tom looked up at the statue again. Blackburn had called himself a monster. He'd lost his family, and from then on, the only meaning he could see in his life was found in the destruction of his adversary.

But you were wrong, Tom thought to that person who would never answer on the other end of the neural link. *This all happened because of you.* Blackburn's existence had mattered more than he ever could've known. Not only to Tom and Wyatt but to all of humanity.

Tom just wished he could've realized it.

THE NIGHT BEFORE she was due to transfer to her interstellar ship, Tom and Yaolan took the new space elevator into orbit. There they boarded a starship and soared together around Earth, putting off the moment he dropped her off for her big launch. Soon she'd have new planets to see, a new solar system to explore, but for now they were content to watch as sunlight cast auroras across the vivid blue atmosphere of their planet.

"Tell me something," she said.

They'd turned off the gravity so they could drift together, gazing out the window. Her head rested on his chest, and his fingers splayed through her dark hair. "What is it?"

"Why did you let Vik step on Mars before you? You gamble over everything. I thought you'd have some contest to see who

442

won the first steps, but you simply gave them to him."

"He wanted it more," Tom said with a grin. "Hey, I can live with being Buzz Aldrin."

"But I know you were also in the running as the test pilot for the interstellar launch," she persisted. "You requested the Mars mission instead. You knew the interstellar launch would be the major project. You seemed as excited about it as I was."

"Maybe I was being realistic, taking myself out of the running. Long, isolated mission in space? They'd be crazier than I am to pick me for that."

"But you didn't even try. That's not like you." She raised her eyes to his. "You told me once you'd love to save the world. You'd brag about it forever. But you did save the world and you haven't been bragging."

He stroked her cheek. "Are you worried about me?"

"I'm going to be gone for a long time. I want to know you're okay, Tom."

"Yaolan, I'm not depressed." He gazed down at Earth, his heart full. "When I was younger, I'd have jumped all over the chance to make history and be the first to leave the solar system. I wanted to be somebody. To be important. But that was never really what I wanted. I guess in my mind, that was the thing I had to do to get a place in the world. I mean, I had nothing as a kid and I didn't belong anywhere. If I just did something spectacular, something nobody could ignore, that would all change and I'd finally belong. All along, what I was really aiming for was this."

"A chance to fly a starship?" Yaolan teased.

He laughed. "That's pretty awesome, I'll give you that. But, no. This. *You*. Vik. Wyatt. Yuri. People who belong to me. People I belong to. A chance to fit in somewhere, to be a part of something instead of an outcast. Don't you see? I *am* happy. I have so much now that some days I can't even believe it's all real." His eyes caught hers. "You know I love you, right? I mean that. I meant it the first time, I mean it now."

"I love you, too, Tom."

It was the first time she'd ever spoken the words to him, and Tom was thrilled.

Then she leaned forward and kissed him. Her black hair floated in a silky veil above them. A golden haze began to light up the curvature of Earth outside the window. Tom's heart pulsed with the sense that everything had fallen exactly into place.

Tom and his friends—no, his *family*—had forged their way through some of humanity's darkest hours. They'd been born into a world rolling downhill into an unprecedented age of technological tyranny.

Yet there'd been a reason for hope all along. Just down the road, there'd been another path, a difficult one, but it had always been there, waiting for those with the courage to stand against the last of the oligarchs. The darkness of their era had given them the opportunity to change history and usher in a new golden age.

Tom was at peace. That restless kid he'd once been had grown up into a man with a place of his own in the universe. People of his own. And a person he loved above all else.

"You know," he whispered in Yaolan's ear, "if you really do run off with some handsome alien, I'm going to follow you across the galaxy and start Earth's first intergalactic war just to win you back."

She laughed. "You better."

Tom drew Yaolan into his arms as their ship soared on through space, the sun rising out from behind their planet, an infinite number of possibilities just over the horizon.

ACKNOWLEDGMENTS

WHEN I WAS a kid, I took for granted that the future would be just like *Star Trek*. We'd explore space, meet aliens, and expand outward on a quest to learn more about this universe. As an adult, I've lived in an era of continuous cutbacks to NASA and of institutions too politically connected to fall. A vision of the future involving intergalactic humanity looks increasingly unlikely every day, but I have faith that can change.

I'm asked frequently what inspired *Insignia*. I could never give the true answer without revealing the entire direction of the series. Now I can finally tell the truth: I wanted to explore how a near future much like our present could be transformed into a future closer to *Star Trek*.

You can say it's naive or say it's foolish. But please never say it's impossible. My thanks to:

Mom, for your incredible drive and determination, your keen eye always catching what I don't, and your refusal to let me give up on myself. Your strength gives me strength.

Dad, for introducing me to science fiction as a kid, for giving me the ability to see beyond the limitations of our present reality, for discussing countless absurd hypothetical scenarios with me growing up (*"Would Stalin kill Al Capone or would Al Capone kill Stalin?"*), and for explaining so many concepts to me over the years when I needed more clarity.

Meredith, for all the guidance and wisdom about the publication world and life in general, for being a voice of reason when I doubt myself or overreact to anything, and for threatening bullies for me when we were kids.

Rob, the one this book is dedicated to, for helping me avoid any real-life pitfalls in a way no one else can and for always having a great sense of humor.

Jessica "Yaolan," for letting me use your Chinese name for a character *almost* as awesome as you and for introducing me to what a best friend was when I was four. I couldn't have written stories based on strong friendships without you in my life.

Jamie "Poosen," for all the silly jokes we shared, for writing that first story with me, and for being the other bestie who reminds me daily that the best thing in the world is someone who truly gets you.

The Todding.

Betsey, Stella, Madeleine, Grace, Aunt Jan, Aunt Maxine, Aunt Alice, and other wonderful relatives.

Judy and the Persoffs, the Hatten family, Barb Anticevich. Jackie, Lesley, Heidi, Stephen, Yae, Duncan, Alice and Tim, Christiane, and many other friends, relatives, and friends of relatives or relatives of friends who have supported me throughout this process and supported the book.

All the booksellers, teachers, and librarians who have shared this series with their kids.

David Dunton, my agent. Thank you for taking this journey with me and for connecting *Insignia* with editors. Thank you for reading every version of the book even when it was unnecessary, and always responding to my questions. I appreciate your patience and kindness, and thank you for everything. Also Sara Crowe at Harvey Klinger, for selling foreign rights.

My editors: first Molly O'Neill, the editor who acquired *Insignia* and read the first draft of *Catalyst*. Sorry we couldn't see this whole process together!

Sarah Shumway, for taking over and seeing me through the rest. I only worked with you for a short while, but your eye for pacing and your advice for humanizing elements of the manuscript truly strengthened it. Thanks for everything you did for the story even though it wasn't your acquisition. I really enjoyed the short time I worked with you.

Laurel Symonds, who was there from the first draft and became my third editor at KT Books. Thank you for taking over at short notice and being responsive to my queries and for being another set of eyes and advice.

There are more people to name at KT Books and Harper, from the amazing production team, to the people who have informed librarians and booksellers about this series—but I think you'd all appreciate it more if I stopped rambling and kept the page count down. Thanks to Fox for purchasing and renewing the rights and Kassie Evashevski for facilitating that. Thank you to the foreign publishers V&R Editoras, Hot Key Books, and others who have presented this story to your countries. If there is anyone I'm leaving out, please excuse me; I'm on a deadline.

To Michio Kaku, Ray Kurzweil, Neil deGrasse Tyson: thanks for helping people remember how to dream.

To John Roberts, Chief Justice of the United States: your tie-breaking vote on *Citizens United* put the multinational-dominated dystopia of *Insignia* in my head, so I owe the existence of this series to you.

And last of all, to the wonderful bloggers and readers who have made this process so worthwhile. Thank you for sharing in the *Insignia* experience with me.

S. J. KINCAID

US AUTHOR S. J. Kincaid originally wanted to be an astronaut, but she decided to become a full-time writer after spending a year studying in Edinburgh and living next to a haunted graveyard. However, after writing many novels and having had no success in finding a publisher for any of them, S. J. decided she would write one more, then give up for good. That last book turned out to be the phenomenally popular INSIGNIA, and she hasn't looked back since.

Follow S. J. Kincaid at www.sjkincaid.com or on Twitter: @SJKincaidBooks.

HOT
KEY
BOOKS

Thank you for choosing a Hot Key book.

If you want to know more about our authors
and what we publish, you can find us online.

You can start at our website

www.hotkeybooks.com

And you can also find us on:

We hope to see you soon!